CRITICAL PI

DONKEY SHOW

DONKEY SHOW

STEPHEN BAKER

atmosphere press

Chapter
ONE

The sun sank into the Juárez mountains, turning the desert sky bright red as Eddie Stevenson made his way down Kansas Street, from the parking lot to the newspaper building. The photographer had a nasty cut over his eye, matted blood in his black mustache, and dirt all over his shirt. He smelled like soiled diapers. Once in the newsroom, he wordlessly emptied broken cameras and flash gear from his black bag, leaving a pile on the assignment desk. Then he turned to no one in particular and said, "Rough shoot."

Ken Perry, the tall, tweedy editor with a desperate ambition to escape the sinking paper in El Paso, emerged from his corner office carrying the front-page layout. He recoiled at the sight of Stevenson, taking him at first for a vagrant. But when he recognized the photographer, he shepherded him into his office. Perry fumbled with papers on his desk, finally grabbing a 1993 Sun Bowl calendar. He placed it on a chair and gestured for Stevenson to sit down.

The editor perched on a corner of his desk. Before he could open his mouth, Stevenson said, "I got my ass kicked. They broke my cameras, too."

"Who's *they*?"

"Jiménez. You know. The drug lord."

Perry's face snapped to attention.

Two young thugs, Stevenson told him, had pulled him into their car, blindfolded him, and driven him to a place where they beat him, mock executed him with a pistol, and later stomped on his cameras. Then Jiménez himself came in, he said, and talked to him about American newspapers and the looming North American free trade agreement.

"Just a sec," Perry said. He opened the door of his office and shouted, "Hold the front page!" He called in the city editor, Duane Canfield, who was returning from the snack bar. And he told a reporter, Hank Klinger, to bring in a notebook and a pen.

"Did Jiménez say anything about our coverage, about Harley's story?" Perry asked Stevenson as Canfield and Klinger made their way into the office.

Stevenson's mind had wandered. "Huh?"

"Tom Harley. Your colleague. Who wrote the article he's so angry about. Did his name come up?"

"Oh yeah," Stevenson said. "He told me to tell Harley he was 'dead meat.'"

Chapter TWO

By the time Tom Harley walked into the office the next morning, a copy of the paper under his arm, he was a hero. Ken Perry, his tie already loosened a quarter of the way down his shirt, hurried out of his corner office to greet him. Harley had never seen the editor so giddy. Grabbing him by the arm, Perry led the lanky, death-threatened reporter into the corner office, followed by Canfield.

"I think there's been some kind of misunderstanding," Harley said, feeling dazed. He opened the paper as if to make sure he wasn't dreaming. "Photographer Abducted, Beaten in Juárez," the headline screamed. The subhead, nearly as big, read: "Drug Lord Jiménez Issues Death Threat to *Trib*'s Harley."

"I know you have some personal concerns here. And we're going to think about that first," Perry said. "Right, Duane?" Canfield nodded and sat down with a grunt, giving his walrus mustache a scratch. He patted the spot next to him on the couch. Harley shook his head and remained standing.

"None of this would have happened," he said, pointing at

Canfield, "if he hadn't rewritten my story."

"You left out all the good stuff, Harley," Canfield said.

"I told you it was hearsay!"

"You said no such thing, Harley. I know this is a tough time for you, but..."

"Hold on a minute," Perry said. "Let's rewind."

"On Friday I had this story about this company, Grupo Espejo," Harley said. "They got a lot of financing for assembly plants in Juárez. And Duane says..."

"Your story was a fucking bore, Harley," Canfield said.

"Right, that's what you said. So then," Harley said, turning back to Perry, "he starts talking about how with free trade, all those trucks will be crossing the border loaded with cocaine..."

"Of course they will!" Canfield said.

"So," Harley went on, "Duane wanted to turn a business story into a drug story. And then he asked me for color on Gustavo Jiménez. You know, I've been reporting that story on the underground economy in Juárez...sort of an ongoing project..."

"Ongoing," Canfield said, "as in never finishing the damn thing."

Perry ignored the sniping. "And so you told him about the palace he lives in, and his harem, and the pet tigers, and..."

"The glass eye," Canfield said. "He pops it out into people's drinks."

"It was hearsay!" Harley said. "And so naturally, when Jiménez sees the story, he gets pissed off, and here we are. Stevenson gets beat up and I'm...dead meat."

Canfield shook his head. "Harley, you were bragging about your reporting. You said you got it from the DEA."

Harley gnawed on his lower lip and said nothing. He wasn't about to confess that he'd overheard the bits about Jiménez's tigers and his glass eye at a Juárez lunch counter. This was right before he climbed back on his bike and pedaled across the bridge to the newsroom. Later, when Canfield grilled him about his underground economy reporting, he'd felt pressured to cough up something good. He should have guessed that Canfield would push the tigers into the lead.

Ken Perry reached into his jacket pocket for a lighter and worked on his pipe, surrounding his head with a cloud of smoke. "The long and short is that we have a hell of a story here, Tom," he said. "I know you're probably worried now. But you're going to look back on this as a career-maker."

The phone rang. Perry nodded at Harley, as if to punctuate the career message, and then walked to his desk to answer it. "Yeah, I'll take it in here." He shielded the phone from his mouth and whispered, "AP, Dallas."

"Let me tell you something," he said. "We're here on the border, and maybe we have a different way of looking at these things. But a gentleman named Jiménez just sent us a very clear, unequivocal message. He beat up our photographer and sent a death threat to our reporter, who incidentally, is reporting the hell out of this drug story... The message he sent us is that he can run around there in Juárez, selling drugs, poisoning our kids, raking in his millions, and then just thumb his nose across the river at us. We're taking that as a challenge... We're going to expose that *señor* and his whole rotten business, even if it takes us to the president of Mexico. And we're going to get him thrown in jail... No! Get the *drug lord* thrown in jail." Perry leaned back in his desk chair and puffed on his pipe.

He listened to a long question and rolled his eyes. "No, he is most definitely not hiding," he said. "He's sitting right here with me. Exactly. Harley, like the motorcycle. Our lead drug reporter. He's breaking this story wide open... Stevenson? He's...out of pocket right now. Recovering. How about we respect his privacy?"

As Perry talked, Harley recalled that he carried a flattened joint in his wallet. He'd found it a few weeks before by the curb at a Sun Bowl parking lot. His idea was to send it to his old college roommate, who still smoked pot, but he hadn't gotten around to it. Now that he was the drug reporter, he should probably flush it down the toilet.

"I'm on drugs now, for good?" he asked as Perry hung up.

"If we took you off drugs," Perry said, "Jiménez would think we were scared of him."

"Maybe *you* have no reason to be," Harley said.

"Listen," Perry said, "do you realize where this story could put you?"

"I'm trying not to dwell on it," Harley said.

"You're going to be on the front page of the *Dallas Morning News* tomorrow," Perry said. "The State Department's hot on this story. This is leverage, Tom. They can use this to make the Mexicans crack down on the drug business and all the corruption over there. But it's leverage for us too, and for you. You could work here another fifty years and never get another story like this."

"I think I'd trade this story for those fifty years," Harley said.

Canfield chuckled. Perry flashed a smile, but his thoughts had wandered. "I'm still trying to piece together this thing," he said. "We ran our story on Saturday, and then Stevenson was over there yesterday on assignment. What story was that for?"

"Our Saturday story went out on the wire," Canfield said. "The *Baltimore Sun* called yesterday morning, saying they wanted to run it. They asked for a picture of the new hotel Jiménez is bankrolling over there, the Zenith."

"The Xanadu," Harley said.

"Whatever. I sent Stevenson over there. He was shooting the hotel."

Perry looked perplexed. "The *Baltimore Sun*?"

"Why the hell not?" Canfield asked, sounding offended.

"Oh, I don't know. Harems don't seem like their thing."

"Maybe that's why they wanted a boring picture of a

hotel," Harley said.

"Okay," Perry said after a pause. "Let's think about tomorrow's paper." He pointed a finger at Harley. "You're going to go through your notebooks. Work your sources on the phone, and write a follow-up. We need more details on Jiménez's lifestyle. More about the orgies, his women, his business with the politicos over there. We're going to get inside that guy's skin."

Harley wondered how he'd ever come up with all this reporting. He looked to Canfield, who was leaning back on the sofa, his hands on his round belly. Harley smiled at him, signaling a truce. "I guess I'll have to trade in my bike for an armored car," he said.

Canfield laughed. "At least wear that helmet."

Harley played back Canfield's voice in his mind, repeating "hailmut" to himself a few times. Then he asked in a quiet voice, "Do you think Stevenson heard him right when he was talking about 'dead meat'? Does Stevenson understand Spanish?"

"He lives in the barrio with a Mexican girl," Canfield said.

"Do you know whether Jiménez was speaking Spanish?" Harley asked. He wondered about "dead meat." *Carne muerta?* No one ever said that.

Chapter
THREE

A couple miles away, across the border from the towering Asarco smelter, Gato pulled his '75 Duster up to the gate of the *Lavarama*. It was a car wash where he and his partner, Pascual, ran their drug business. Alfredito, the little car-washer, was sitting on the sidewalk outside the locked gate in the shade of the dumpster with his friend who worked a popsicle cart.

As Gato stepped out of the car to open the big sheet-metal gate to the car wash, he reached into his pocket and pulled out a five-dollar bill. He slouched more than usual as he reached down and handed it to Alfredito. "Go over to El Paso," he told him in Spanish, "and buy the newspapers."

"Over the bridge?" Alfredito asked.

"No, just down to the river, through the fence. You can cross on the stones."

Alfredo hurried away. When the popsicle boy saw the money, he tried to collect for back popsicles. Alfredito pulled away from him and jammed the bill into his pocket. The two boys ran toward the border.

Despite the fancy name, the *Lavarama* was just an empty dirt lot surrounded by cinder-block walls. The car wash sat right where the city of Juárez, with its paved streets, gave way to a shanty town called *Colonia 20 de Noviembre*. People there kept pigs and chickens in backyard pens. Dogs wandered the roads and nosed through garbage.

A water trough ran along one wall of the *Lavarama*. A pyramid of motor oil stood near it, and on a picnic table shaded by an umbrella was a selection of car waxes and detergents. A small brick building in one corner of the lot housed the office and bodega, or warehouse, where Gato and Pascual stored the cocaine, and sometimes marijuana.

Gato, gangly and bow-legged, with a Fu Manchu mustache, started to open the padlock on the office. Then he remembered to close the *Lavarama*'s gate and hang the hand-painted sign, *Cerrado*. He didn't want anyone coming for a car wash before Alfredito got back.

The office smelled like a bus-station bathroom and looked like the scene of a cockfight. There was a broken chair and a streak of blood along the wall, a cream-colored puddle of vomit under the desk, and even a few drops splattered across the oil-company poster of Miss Bardahl, a blonde in a bikini carrying a monkey wrench. Her oiled body seemed to glow. An inert pool of mineral water covered the desk and a section of the floor. That was Pascual's silly idea, to put soda water up the photographer's nose.

The toy pistol with the plastic ivory handle lay on the floor by a piece of the chair. Gato still marveled that the photographer took the plastic click of that pistol so seriously.

Gato turned on the radio to a *ranchera* station. Then he filled a bucket in the trough and began swabbing the floor. When the news came on, he stopped and listened. American politicians were making more noise against NAFTA, claiming Mexico was a country full of corruption. Well, that much was true, agreed Gato, thinking about the cops he knew, and about *don* Gustavo's connections in the political world.

Gato listened to the news, both hoping and afraid that they'd mention the beating of the photographer and the rest of the charade. The violence, he knew, had been a mistake. But Rubén, their American distributor, said the photographer was snooping around *don* Gustavo's businesses. It seemed at first like something the boss might be grateful for. News interdiction.

At the very beginning, before they knew what they'd do with the photographer, Pascual waved a real gun and introduced himself as Jiménez. The photographer shit in his pants, which wasn't funny, even though everyone pretended it was, and laughed. Then Rubén took over as Jiménez, and they replaced the real gun with the toy. The guy didn't even notice.

The radio news came to an end with no word about the photographer, leaving Gato a little disappointed.

Gato and Pascual had been working for Jiménez's organization for nearly three years. They started as drivers, picking up shipments in Chihuahua City and at airstrips around the state, and bringing them to Juárez.

Then the boss set them up at the *Lavarama*. They made more money there, running a small distribution center. *Don* Gustavo even gave them the chance to go into business for themselves. They set up their retail network for El Paso and paid Jiménez a cut.

In the middle of the summer, they hired Rubén to run El Paso for them. He was a U.S. citizen, born in an El Paso hospital. He spoke good English. He seemed much more interested, though, in learning about the drug economy, and less passionate about making money. He often referred to himself as a *"periodista,"* or journalist. But he never seemed to write anything and had nowhere to publish. Through long-empty afternoons at the *Lavarama*, Rubén talked to Pascual and Gato about their business, asking lots of questions. In time, he convinced them that they were getting screwed.

"You're peons," he said one hot afternoon.

"But if you work for us, you're even lower," Pascual argued.

"No," said Rubén, shaking his finger. "I let myself appear to be lower. But I have a different agenda than you."

◊

Gato was carrying the pieces of a broken chair out to the trashcan when he spotted Pascual slipping through the gate like a burglar. He always moved like that. Short and thin, with steel-rimmed glasses and close-cut hair, he wore a button-down shirt and carried a leather shoulder bag. Pascual appeared more scholarly than Rubén, who actually went to college in El Paso, or at least claimed to.

Pascual had a violent side. The day before, he'd wanted to hurt that photographer. Gato could tell. It was when Gato and Rubén told him to go easy that he exploded and pounded the flimsy chair in half with his fist. Lately, Pascual had been saying that violence was the only way up in the drug business. "No one promotes you for running a good warehouse," he said. "They don't even notice."

Gato glanced back from the trashcan to see his partner, shoulders squared and eager, heading toward the office. "Don't walk in there!" Gato shouted. "The floor's wet."

Pascual waved him off and tracked muddy footprints into the office. Gato heard him fiddling with the radio, turning from the *rancheras* to heavy metal. "Any news?" Pascual yelled.

"*Gringos* are saying there's corruption in Mexico," deadpanned Gato.

Pascual stuck his head out from the office, waiting for a serious answer.

"I sent Alfredito for the El Paso papers."

"Mmmmm." Pascual appeared to give the matter some thought as he walked out to where Gato was standing. "Do you think we went too far with it yesterday, using the *jefe*'s name?"

"Probably," Gato said.

They heard footsteps racing up the street and turned toward the gate. Moments later, Alfredito burst in with an armful of English-language newspapers. He dropped them on the ground, sending up a cloud of dust.

Gato rushed to the pile and picked up a *National Enquirer.* The front-page story was about Elvis, who, apparently, was alive on another planet. Gato found nothing new in the *El Paso Journal.* Then he saw the *Tribune*, with its banner headline about the drug lord Jiménez kidnapping the photographer in Juárez. A picture of Stevenson, looking dazed, stared up at him. Gato felt a wave of panic, followed by indignation. "How could they say it was Jiménez?" he said. "It wasn't him."

Pascual, standing beside him, answered, "Because we told him we were Jiménez."

"*You* told him you were Jiménez," Gato said. He was a good five inches taller than Pascual, but slouched to about the same level.

"Ah, don't start blaming. Look," Pascual said, pointing to Stevenson's picture, "you can see some of the *vomitón* on his shirt."

Gato raced through the article while Pascual, who didn't understand much English, picked up the *Enquirer.*

"*Hijole*," Gato said, reading. "They're asking the State Department to press for Jiménez's arrest."

Pascual shook his head, looking disgusted. "Why would an old woman with three *tetas* pose for a newspaper?"

Gato yanked the *Enquirer* from his partner's hands and flung it to the ground. "Listen," he said. "They might have to put Jiménez in jail to save NAFTA!"

Pascual smiled coldly and said, "*Don* Gustavo's arrest could work out nicely for us." He took the *Tribune* from Gato and studied Stevenson's picture. Then he turned the page and spent a few seconds gazing at Harley's face before dropping the paper to the ground and walking away. "I'm heading over there to take a look," he said over his shoulder.

"Where?"

"Across the border."

Chapter
FOUR

Harley, the *Tribune*'s new lead drug reporter, emerged from the dark lobby of the newspaper building into the blazing midday sunlight. He had no plan, but fear hadn't yet struck.

He had zero interest in tracking down Gustavo Jiménez, who evidently was stewing over the ridiculous article under Harley's byline. Harley wanted to keep as far as possible from the drug lord and his frightening world, but without losing his job.

To escape, he walked from the newspaper on Kansas Street to the biggest and grandest hotel in town, the renovated Paso del Norte, a century-old brick tower with a Tiffany dome atop its bar. It was an extravagant place to eat lunch. But Harley had things to think over, and he didn't want to run across any of his newspaper friends.

Passing the potted palms in the lobby, he peered into the restaurant and spotted a dark-haired woman he'd met a few weeks before at a party. She was sitting at a tiny cast-iron table, reading. He didn't remember her name, but could replay her voice in his mind. It was from New York, either from

Brooklyn, he figured, or Queens.

There was something tough about her, and moneyed. Her beige suit was linen, and she was nibbling on a $14 club sandwich. He saw that she was reading the paper, his paper, the front-page story about *him*. He studied her, waiting for her to notice him. It took about a minute, but when she raised her eyes and saw him, she smiled and invited him to sit down.

She said her name was Diana Clements and yes, she remembered him. She sat rigid in her chair, eyeballing him, her brown eyes speckled with gold. He fiddled with a saltshaker and started to say how weird it was to see his name as a headline instead of a byline...

She interrupted him, asking what he'd done to make a drug lord so angry. Her accent sounded exotic, even a little crooked, like one of the wives in *Goodfellas*.

"I'm not sure. This is new for me," Harley said slowly, searching for words. "Usually I write for the Style section, about bike trips in the Big Bend, balloon races... People get mad at me sometimes when I try to be funny, but..."

He wondered again if Gustavo Jiménez had actually called him "dead meat." He pictured himself hanging from a meat hook with a blue USDA stamp on his chest.

He looked at the woman across the table. She had her lips parted, and he could see a gap between her front teeth. She reached up to her neck and gave it a little rub where it met the shoulder, her thumb disappearing beneath the fabric of her blouse. He watched her fingers digging into the smooth skin and imagined himself leaning across the table and kissing her.

"Jesus," he said. It just came out.

"What is it?"

"Ah, just something disgusting I heard about Jiménez," he improvised.

She nodded, sensitive enough not to let it drop.

"Remember that radio reporter in Juárez who was killed a month ago?" he asked.

"Vaguely."

"Have you ever heard of anybody getting his lungs torn out?"

"On purpose?"

"As a way of getting killed."

She considered it for a second and shook her head. "No. Never. And I've heard about lots of different types of murders." She took a sip of coffee and put the cup down, leaving a red crescent of lipstick on the rim. "Your story must have made that guy really mad," she said

"That article was just a roundup of what people in Juárez say about him. But the paper played it up big."

"The tigers running loose in his house, and the harem?"

"Uh huh."

She shook her head. "I couldn't really figure out what he had to do with Grupo Espejo and the *maquiladora* industry. At my company, we do some financing for Onofre Crispín, who runs Espejo. Everybody was sort of blown away by the story."

"Those are examples of things they played up," Harley said. "I didn't exactly..." He groped for the right word. "I didn't authorize them to use it."

"You didn't write it?"

"I did, but not every word. They took some things I told them, and played it all up."

"You think all of this happened to Eddie?" She pointed to a color picture of Stevenson. His face was puffy, his shirt filthy.

"I guess so," he said, wondering why she called him Eddie, as if she knew him.

"But you think they're playing this up?" she asked.

"Of course, I mean, look at it. They love these stories."

"But do you believe it? Do you believe your paper?"

That was an uncomfortable question. He dodged it by asking her if she knew Stevenson.

"No." She fidgeted in her seat. "Not really. Not yet, anyway." She looked up at him. "I'll tell you something funny.

I was going to have lunch with him today. He stands me up. I buy the paper. No offense, but I don't usually read it. And it's about you and him, and then you show up for lunch. Funny, huh?"

"Weird," he said. He didn't like the idea of Stevenson moving in on this woman. "When did you set up this lunch with him?" he asked. "Yesterday?"

"No. Saturday. We met up with him..." Her voice trailed off. She rubbed her neck again and then rested her chin on her fist. "Are you worried?" she asked.

"I'm sure I will be once I collect my thoughts." He went on to tell her that he'd been out when they called to tell him about the death threat. He hadn't found out about it until the paper arrived. Yes, he agreed that he should buy an answering machine. But he hated them.

Harley talked on, telling her about Canfield and Perry, about his downstairs neighbor, Claudio, who mooched Harley's copy of the paper every morning. He told her how Claudio, a former copy editor, underlined mixed metaphors and split infinitives in his stories, wrote suggestions in the margins, and then left the paper at his door like a graded exam.

He was rambling. She was looking for the waiter, gesturing for the bill.

"So," he said, winding up, "Stevenson...Eddie came back, all beat up and telling them about this, um...threat against me. They were pretty upset that I don't have an answering machine."

"Tell them you unplugged it when you started getting too many calls from what's-his-name." She scanned the paper. "Jiménez."

"Good idea."

The two looked at each other across the table. "I'd better get to work," he said, getting up.

"No lunch?"

He didn't want to stay behind, eating alone. "Maybe later."

"Well," she said, "keep in touch."

"Right. What's your last name again?"

"Clements." She picked up the paper. "I won't have any trouble remembering yours."

◊

Harley lived in the historic part of El Paso, in a century-old building overlooking the Juárez Valley. During the Mexican Revolution, the building had harbored boys from rich families of Mexico's north. Even in exile, they could see their homeland. The building still looked like a fancy place, with its courtyard and fountain and a sturdy palm tree. But the apartments were affordable for a lowly newspaper salary. For Harley it was just a five-minute bike ride, all of it downhill, to the newsroom.

The first afternoon under death threat, he steered clear of the apartment. To keep him safe, Perry told him the paper would put him up at a hotel. So Harley rode straight uphill, toward the brown spur of Mt. Franklin that poked into the city. Near a Medical Center, right under Rim Road, he checked into the Cliff Inn.

As soon as he stepped into his room, he turned on the TV and began flipping channels with the remote control. Then he put it on mute and started making long-distance calls to friends around the country. He was eager to tell them about his new status, but only reached their answering machines. It wasn't until he called his ex-girlfriend, Cheryl, that a person answered.

Cheryl was low on Harley's list because her usual first response to any problems he had was to blame him. He attributed this to jealousy, and assumed that she was still upset about their breakup years earlier.

"This probably sounds stupid," Harley told her, after describing his situation, "but I finally feel like somebody recognizes my abilities."

"You mean the drug lord?"

"Not him. I just mean... Well, I told you it would sound stupid."

"You mean," Cheryl, said, "that when we went out to West Texas, you expected to be a star."

Harley had come to El Paso with Cheryl. They'd met playing volleyball in Austin. He was halfway through a master's in international relations, which he later abandoned, and Cheryl was finishing up her teaching degree. They became best friends and eventually ended up in bed. They lived together for the first few months in El Paso. Then Cheryl was offered a fifth-grade post in Katy, a Houston suburb. She'd hesitated, but when Harley didn't beg her to stay, she left.

"And now," Cheryl went on, "all these years later, you're finally getting some sort of notoriety. Even if it comes with the inconvenience of a death threat."

"Not really," he said.

"I mean, one minute you tell me this drug lord had a reporter's lungs ripped out. And next you're telling me that you're finally getting the respect you deserve. If you're getting respect for your death threat, that other reporter must be getting a Pulitzer for dying."

"No, no," he said. "That reporter was Mexican."

"So?"

"I feel like I called my friend and got the D.A."

Cheryl showed no pity. "Tell me why it matters that he was Mexican."

"It's an entirely different case..."

"Because he was Mexican? Isn't that what you like about El Paso, that the border doesn't mean anything? You ride your bike to Mexico to buy beer and hot sauce, right? And now you're counting on the border to save your life... I think you should just catch a plane."

"And go where?" Harley's parents had died in a car crash four years earlier—on the very day that the Berlin Wall came down. His only sister, June, was working as a lawyer in Tokyo.

"You could come stay here, if you wanted to," Cheryl said. "We have an extra bedroom."

"Thanks."

"No, really."

"I'm not going to run away, Cher," he said.

"You're going to become a real reporter now. Is that what you're saying?"

"I guess."

"You'll have to work a little harder. Cut back on bike riding, maybe. Stop studying Portuguese, or Urdu, or whatever language you're into now."

He was silent. He'd stopped flipping channels and was staring at a Roadrunner cartoon. Then he told her about his new beat. "Ken made me the new drug reporter today."

"Oh my God. What's Canfield think about that?"

"Probably thinks it's a riot. He spends most of his time reading the *Wall Street Journal*, calling up his broker."

Cheryl, who always asked him for at least one impersonation per phone call, requested some Canfield, one of her favorites.

He gladly launched into a loud drawl. "DAWGONE IT KLINGER, I WANT YOU TO GO OUT THERE TO FORT BLISS AND ASK SOME TOUGH QUESTIONS. YOU HEAR ME?"

Cheryl giggled.

"HARLEY, WHEN YOU FINISH YOUR AN-THRO-PO-LOGICAL PURSUITS, YOU MIGHT CONSIDER FINDING OUT WHAT THE HAY-L IS GOING ON IN OLD MEXICO. AND WHEN YOU WRITE THAT STORY, I WANT TO SEE THOSE TIGERS IN THE LEAD."

Doing voices lifted his spirits. He said good-bye to Cheryl and wandered into the hotel bathroom, shouting newsroom orders in Canfield's drill-sergeant voice. When the phone rang, he ran to it and, without thinking, answered with Canfield's "HELL-O."

"...Duane?" It was Hank Klinger, sounding very confused.

Harley harbored very few resentments, but everything about Klinger irked him. The young reporter was Canfield's favorite. He was astonishingly ignorant, but at the same time an excellent reporter, probably because he didn't mind asking stupid questions and was perfectly happy to bother people. His ambition was boundless. Harley even found himself objecting to Klinger's haircut, a mullet that crept down his neck in blond curls.

With the bewildered Klinger on the line, Harley decided to stick with Canfield's voice. "WHAT THE HAY-L YOU CALLING HERE FOR KLINGER, YOU DAWGONE WEASEL!"

"But... You told me to." He added a plaintive "Remember?"

"ALL RIGHT, ALL RIGHT. YOU WANT TO TALK TO HARLEY?"

"Yeah, please."

He paused, and then returned to his own voice. "Hi, Hank."

"Hi." Klinger had never sounded so meek.

"Don't tell me you're working this story with me," Harley said.

"Yeah. Canfield must have told you."

"Yeah... Now he's raiding my minibar. Hey!" he yelled away from the receiver. "Easy on those cashews, Duane. They're two-fifty a pop. And fattening."

He turned his attention to Klinger. "So you're working this story with me. But you don't know any Spanish, right?"

"I know some."

"Hmm."

"How about if I get started tonight looking up Stevenson?" Klinger proposed.

"Okay," Harley said.

"Can I talk to Duane again for a minute?" Klinger asked.

Harley didn't feel like bringing back the city editor's voice. Klinger might detect something on a second hearing. "He's taking a shit," he said.

"In your bathroom?"

"Where else?"

Klinger, sounding disgusted, signed off.

Chapter
FIVE

Pascual reached into his knapsack for his wallet and was surprised to touch the cold metal of his gun. He'd forgotten it was there. He was swiveling on a stool at a Dairy Queen on Paisano Drive, eating soft ice cream, and thinking about overthrowing *don* Gustavo Jiménez and replacing him. The idea, which came to him in a flash at the *Lavarama*, was to create more bad news in *don* Gustavo's name. With the NAFTA vote coming up, Pascual figured, the government would either throw Jiménez in jail or kill him.

Pascual had been reading a self-help book by a Mexican psychologist, Dr. Ernesto Rivapalacios. The doctor's idea was that by following some simple rules and setting clear goals, people could accomplish just about anything. Pascual carried the book everywhere. As he enjoyed the American ice cream and air-conditioning, he tried to plan his life with the focus and discipline of Dr. Rivapalacios. He wondered how to put his assets—$5 and a gun—to best use on this hot afternoon in El Paso.

He considered shooting bullet holes through the reporter's

window, or maybe scratching a message on his door. Walking near the Greyhound Station, he picked up a long nail on the street and considered using it to break into Harley's house. Or maybe draw the image of a skull, something frightening. He called an operator from a pay phone on the Plaza. He sweet-talked her in Spanish into giving him Harley's address.

Then he slung his knapsack over his shoulder, student-style, and walked toward the shady hill called Sunset Heights.

When Pascual reached the old yellow building on Prospect Street, it occurred to him that the reporter must be a very rich man from a rich family. A man with this much money, he thought, would probably be surrounded by armed body-guards—especially a day after receiving a public death threat.

But when Pascual peeked through the door's window, he saw a foyer with mailboxes and realized it was an apartment building.

A door opened. A thin man with a graying ponytail came out and asked him something in English.

Pascual said, "No, no, sorry." He retreated across the street and back toward the I-10 overpass. He ducked down behind a few bushes and reconsidered his plan.

Harley's downstairs neighbor, Claudio, stood outside the building, hands on his hips, looking Pascual's way.

Pascual pulled his gun out of his leather pouch and thought about throwing it down a drainage ditch. But after some rapid risk-reward calculations, he held onto it.

He waited behind the bushes until the man with the ponytail went back into his apartment. Then he stood up, dusted off his pants, and tossed the leather bag over his shoulder. He considered visiting Rubén, but decided not to chance it in El Paso much longer with his gun. He'd wait until dark and then walk back toward the Rio Grande.

◊

Eddie Stevenson lay on a motel bed in Truth or Consequences, New Mexico, watching MTV. He had the shades drawn and the air conditioner on. Stevenson had a hangover and a sore throat.

Worse, he felt guilty, though he didn't know exactly why— whether it was for leaving Estela, abandoning his job, or stretching the truth about what went on in Juárez. He thought about that woman he'd met after that party. Diana. He tried to conjure her face and then remembered that they had a lunch date. Was that for today or yesterday?

The TV played a video by R.E.M. called "Everybody Hurts." Stevenson moved to the edge of the bed and watched. It featured a bunch of desperate people in a traffic jam. At the end of the song, they abandoned their cars like zombies and started walking.

Stevenson could relate. After that incident in Juárez, he drove back in a fugue state with his busted camera gear, all of it except for his favorite Leica, which he'd apparently left behind. He could barely remember cruising aimlessly around El Paso, classic rock on the radio, wondering what to do.

Earlier, while those thugs were having their way with him, they kept his face wrapped in what smelled like someone's dirty T-shirt. At first, he believed his tormentor was in fact Jiménez. Then the figure started to sound like Estela's friend Rubén. But still, Stevenson was terrified. He dirtied his pants when one of them played around with the pistol, right by his ear. That cracked them up. Later, while they were putting the club soda up his nose, it occurred to him that even if the guy talking was Rubén, maybe Jiménez was there, too. Maybe they were working together somehow. At one point he vomited. They laughed some more and called him names like *cabrón*. They kicked around his camera equipment. Finally, they pushed him back into a car, still blindfolded, and let him out near his Dodge. He made his way to the bridge. As he inched forward in the slow customs line, sweating like a horse, his car

27

smelled more and more like used Pampers.

He had no desire to go home to Estela. Even if she and Rubén weren't involved, the barrio felt much too close to Mexico. He stopped by a Walmart near Fort Bliss, bought a pair of khakis, fresh underwear, and a three-pack of V-neck T-shirts. But he forgot to change before heading back to the office.

He walked into the paper that afternoon carrying the bag of broken gear. Aware that he still smelled awful, and embarrassed about the wrecked cameras, he planned to climb up the back steps and avoid the newsroom by cutting through the snack bar to the dark room. He'd fill out a lost equipment form and scoot. But the back stairs were closed. Next thing he knew, he was in Ken's corner office, explaining his story to Canfield and Ken Perry, both of them beside themselves with excitement, while Hank Klinger took notes.

Stevenson didn't alter the story much, but left out all personal connections, including his messy life in the barrio. It never came up. Canfield and Perry were too hungry for the Jiménez story to pry into Stevenson's affairs. From their perspective, every detail of his miserable afternoon was precious, a gift, especially Harley's death threat. They wanted that one verbatim, with the exact phrasing around 'dead meat.'

The only down note came when Stevenson—after some prodding—transmitted Jiménez's critique of Ken. "He said, 'Tell Ken Perry he's a horseshit editor,'" the photographer said.

Perry's smile dropped for an instant. "Since when does this dude get off as a media critic?" he asked, bothered, as Canfield hid a smile.

Stevenson hurried out of the building that afternoon, right to his car. After changing into the new pants, he drove north. He was eager to distance himself from Juárez and Rubén and Estela, and now, even more urgently, his own paper. If

Jiménez wasn't involved, he worried, how would the drug lord respond when the news broke?

Stevenson drove past Las Cruces and into the desert night. He stayed awake by sipping 49-ounce Big Gulps of Coke. Every twenty or thirty miles he stopped and wiped the dead bugs off his windshield with spit on a paper towel. Around midnight he finally pulled into a false-adobe motel. He was outside Truth or Consequences, but far too exhausted to note any irony in the name. The desk clerk, probably noticing the specks of vomit on his shirt, asked him to pay cash in advance.

The next morning, it took Stevenson a minute to remember where he was and to convince himself that the episode in Juárez hadn't been a bad dream. His fat lip was evidence, and the dirty shirt lying on the floor by the bed closed the case.

He decided to take a vacation. First he considered driving out to L.A., to swim in the Pacific. Then he decided instead to head down to Austin, to visit his brother. That would mean driving through El Paso, which bothered him a little. So he put it off and paid for another night in the hotel. He wished he'd brought along his bong, or at least a couple joints. He needed to relax and put all of this into context. By mid-afternoon, he settled on a six-pack of Guinness and a box of Marlboros as surrogate reefer.

While buying the beer, Stevenson saw a *Tribune* coin box. At first he tried to avoid it. He walked to the Dodge with the beer, climbed in, turned the ignition, and stole one more glance at the newspaper machine. That was when he saw the headline about the *Trib* photographer abducted in Juárez. It was bigger than he'd imagined. He got out of his car and walked over to the machine. At first he didn't recognize himself in the picture. Then he saw the shirt he'd worn the day before, with the filthy collar. His hair looked as if it had been rubbed in tar, and his expression was pure zombie.

Chapter
SIX

Hank Klinger looked up into the darkening sky and saw a woman leaning out the window, her long black hair waving in the breeze. "Are you going to throw down the key?" he yelled.

"Wha you say?"

Klinger saw the figure in the window wriggling, her head bobbing as if she were pulling on a tight pair of pants. "Are you going to throw the key?"

"Wha you name?"

"Hank Klinger." Estela, done with her wriggling, stared down impassively.

Klinger glanced up and down the sidewalk at the early evening shoppers prowling the pawnshops and discount shoe outlets. He wasn't used to the barrio, and it scared him a little. He could hear five or six songs playing at the same time. He noticed that a man working a candy stand on the corner was staring at him. He shouted up to Estela, "I'm from the paper? I just called a few minutes ago?"

"Wha you want?"

"Can I come inside and talk about it?"

Estela studied Klinger for a moment and then shook her head slowly. "Naa now. I don' think so. Sorry." She reached out a long brown arm and pulled the window shut.

Klinger tried the door again. Locked. He considered leaving. He didn't really know what he was going to ask this woman. And her English sounded problematic. But if she didn't want to talk to him, he figured, she probably knew something worth knowing. Her face appeared in the window. She had shadows around her eyes, almost like bruises. She waved him away.

Klinger stayed put. When sources want you to leave, you stay. He'd learned that from Canfield, and it paid dividends in the bail bond story. Time and again, bail bondsmen and cops and convicts told him to get lost. And when he stuck around they grew frustrated and often threw bits of information his way. "Listen," Canfield once said to him, "when you're investigating, your sources assume you're an asshole. The only question is whether you're a persistent one or a lazy one."

Klinger was persistent. This was a big story, one that could make national news. When Canfield assigned it to him, he mentioned the Pulitzer. That afternoon, the city editor sat him down and told him that he was giving him the chance of his career. Harley was lazy, an anthropologist, Canfield said.

Klinger's mission was to light a fire under the story and use Harley as a Mexico guide. "But if he tells you that something is wrapped in mystery, hidden behind Mexican masks, all that bullshit, fuck him," Canfield said, looking left and right to make sure no other reporters were within earshot. "Just go find it yourself and work it with me."

Remembering that conversation, Klinger wondered whether Canfield might be giving Harley a similar pep talk at the hotel and saying nasty things about him. The whole telephone episode bewildered him. Why would Canfield be wasting time up in Harley's hotel room, eating cashews? He must have been drunk, Klinger thought as he rang the bell again.

Just then, a skinny young man wearing a muscle shirt and dark glasses, carrying notebooks under his arm, walked to a spot below Estela's window and yelled up, "*Estelita! Abreme!*" Estela appeared again in the window and pointed to Klinger. Then she shook her head and disappeared. A moment later she opened the building door for Rubén, and Klinger followed him in. She led them up the dark, stifling staircase, giving both of them a good look at her hips swaying in the tight Guess jeans.

"*Y este?*" Rubén asked as they climbed.

"*Reportero,*" she said.

"Oh yeah?" Rubén said, looking over his shoulder. "What's your name, man?"

Klinger, surprised to hear English, said his name.

"Hey, I read your stuff," Rubén said as they reached the landing. "The bail-bond story. That was dynamite."

Klinger smiled. Estela opened the door with a key and said gruffly, "*Pasen de una vez.*" She stood sideways as Rubén walked past quickly, heading straight to a photo of himself hanging on the wall.

Klinger walked over to a sunken brown couch along the wall, clunking loudly in his new cowboy boots, and sat down. On the coffee table sat a glass water pipe, its sides caked with black resin. He reached to pick it up, looking first at Estela and her friend, who were arguing in Spanish by the kitchen. The pipe smelled like a swamp. A piece of debris flew up Klinger's nose and he sneezed.

"*Salud,*" Estela said instinctively. Then she continued talking to Rubén.

Klinger put down the pipe and wiped his eyes with his shirtsleeve. He watched the two of them in the corner and tried to listen. He heard Estela say "*cabrón.*" That was like calling somebody a bastard, he knew. He ogled at her profile, at her breasts as she waved her arms about and yelled at the guy. He wondered how Eddie Stevenson ever landed with this woman.

While Klinger stared at Estela, she and Rubén argued in Spanish about the incident with Stevenson in Juárez. Rubén assured her that her boyfriend was okay, that he and some friends just gave him a scare on the Mexican side of the river.

"What did you do to him?" Estela asked.

"Didn't you see the paper?"

"The paper? You did something to him that came out in the paper?"

"He's okay, he's okay," Rubén said, patting her arm. "He came back and exaggerated everything. And now they've made it into a big scandal."

As Rubén laid out the paper for her to see, Estela glanced at Klinger. He was staring at her.

"He doesn't understand anything," Rubén whispered. "Look at this." He pointed to the front page of the *Tribune*, with its lurid headline and front-page editorial, the photo of Eddie Stevenson in his filthy shirt.

Estela's dark eyes widened. "You... You did this?"

"It's nothing," Rubén said, glancing at Klinger, who was now sitting back on the couch, looking lost.

"But why? To protect me?" She touched the darkened skin under her eye.

Rubén lowered his eyes. "Sort of," he said. "But it's going to be useful for my career, my journalism."

Estela shook her head and called him the rarest mix of "*macho mexicano* and *maricón*" she'd ever met.

Klinger spoke up. "*Macho mexicano?*" he said with a cowboy accent. "Which one of you's a *macho mexicano?*"

Estela glared at him. "*Vete,*" she said. "Go. Go out. *Fuera!*" She pointed angrily toward the door.

"*Espérate,*" Rubén said. "Wait a minute. I want to talk to him about this story." He approached Klinger, holding out the newspaper in his hand. "What do you think really happened over there, Hank?" he asked. "Do you think the paper got it right?"

Klinger, still smarting from Estela's eviction order, took a second to focus on Rubén. "I guess so," he said, without much conviction.

"Did you consider the sourcing in this article?" Rubén said. "Whose word do they have except for our friend Eddie? Did you consider that?"

"Jeez, I'd like to talk about this," Klinger said, "but..." He looked past Rubén, at Estela, smoldering by the kitchen door. There was nothing to learn here, as far as he could tell. Just a woman who was nice to look at and this weird guy who acted like a journalism student on coke, asking these questions and bouncing on his toes.

"Do you know where our friend's at?" Rubén asked, smiling. "You know, Eddie?"

"He lives here, right?" Klinger said.

"Yeah. But I think he, like, split." Rubén paused for a second and added, quietly, "Where do you suppose he went to?" He stood before Klinger with his lips pursed and his eyebrows knitted, as if Eddie Stevenson might be in trouble and in need of help.

Chapter
SEVEN

Adam Pereira stood at Diana Clements' office door, trying to talk his way in. He was telling her about his visit to Onofre Crispín's Juárez mansion, and how the maquila magnate tried to get him to play racquetball.

Diana turned away from him, hoping he'd take the hint and leave. She gazed out her window at the mountain, about a mile from her perch at Dunwoody & Briggs, on the 16th floor of the Texas Commerce Building. Looking to her left, past the Asarco smelter, she could see the wind kicking up dust devils in Juárez. They seemed to peter out at the river.

Diana could see her colleague's reflection in the window: the starched white shirt and yellow tie, the hang-dog eyes looking at the back of her head, wanting so much for her to like him.

Adam was getting the message that she didn't want to hear about racquetball in Juárez. "So where'd you go for lunch?" he asked. "I was looking for you."

"Just...for a walk," Diana said.

She didn't mention that she'd walked south from downtown, through the sunbaked blocks of the barrio, looking for Eddie Stevenson. It was a crazy thing to do, but Diana had this image of Stevenson gagged and trussed to a chair, bleeding to death from a gunshot wound or a knifing, with no one to save him. She called the paper and told the woman who answered the phone that she was Eddie's sister and needed his address.

When she came to the old brick apartment building, the green steel door was ajar. She pushed it open. It smelled like boiled cabbage, and until her eyes adjusted from the blinding midday sun, she saw only black. After a few seconds she could make out a dark wooden staircase. She climbed it, knocked on the door, and then pushed it open. She found herself facing a beautiful Mexican woman ironing a big pile of shirts. Diana, embarrassed, fine-tuned her lie, saying this time that she was Eddie's cousin, and wanted to make sure he was okay. Estela, wearing an oversized Pearl Jam T-shirt and looking confused, didn't seem to understand. Diana took a little pad from her purse, wrote down her name and address, and gave her the piece of paper. "I'm sorry," she said, and retreated down the staircase and onto the street.

Diana couldn't understand why she felt anything for Eddie Stevenson. It had something to do with the way he talked to her that night, after the party, a directness that appealed to her, even though he was drunk and probably lying.

When she and her friend Elke walked out of the party Saturday night, they heard Stevenson's heavy footsteps following them down the walk. He joined them, talking only to Diana, treating Elke as though she didn't exist—which, for him, was a fact. He was drunk and rude, but Diana couldn't resist talking to him. He walked unsteadily on one side of Diana as Elke walked on the other. "You wanna go dancing somewhere?" he asked her. Diana shook her head but smiled. Then Stevenson stopped, and Diana stopped too, as Elke kept striding up the dark sidewalk.

Stevenson looked into her eyes, smiled crookedly, and

whispered, "Let's imagine we're in Paris, you and me." He pointed down toward the I-10 overpass. "Let's take a walk along the Seine."

"You mean along the Rio Grande?"

"Along the wild side."

"That's the corniest thing I ever heard." She glanced ahead. Elke was almost at the top of the hill. "Listen, I got to go," she said, and started to walk.

But Stevenson grabbed her hand and studied at her palm. "Lemme tell you something about your future," he said.

She started to pull her hand from him. But he gazed up at her, and suddenly appeared altered—not only sober, but serious. With his deep-set brown eyes, he seemed to look through her. Deep down, no matter how much she tried to repress it, Diana believed her life was mapped out, that every coincidence was a sign. With her hand still in Stevenson's, she braced herself for the future.

"You're going to make lots of money, or inherit it," he said, sounding impressed. She wondered for a moment if he'd learned somehow that she was a banker. But the message was so appealing that she found herself believing it. Then, still gazing at her, Stevenson said, "And there's one very important person in your future."

"I bet I can guess who that is," she said, smiling.

"That's right." He was looking earnest now, much more handsome than at the party. "It's me. But I'm not kidding. Dinner with me, tomorrow?"

Diana agreed to see him, but for lunch, on Tuesday, not dinner. That way, she could cut it off to go back to work.

The next morning, she regretted agreeing to the lunch. When it came to men, she made the worst decisions. She gave a thought to canceling it, but didn't. Then, when she showed up at the Paso del Norte and saw Eddie's picture on the front page, she immediately believed that he was right, that she and he were somehow linked. The newspaper was talking to her...

She noticed a red dot blinking on her phone. Sending Adam Pereira away with a flick of her eyes, she picked up the message. It was a raspy voice, Eddie Stevenson, apologizing for missing the lunch. He said he was in New Mexico, and had called around to get her work number. He'd be in touch when he returned to El Paso.

◊

Hank Klinger was flustered. Somebody was making eyes at him in the middle of the midday rush at Whataburger, the orange-roofed restaurant near UTEP. Klinger ran a hand through his blond mane and bit into his hamburger, trying not to look self-conscious. He looked down at his notebook, trying to ignore the small dark-haired guy. But he couldn't concentrate. Now the man seemed to be motioning to him. *It was the dude from Stevenson's apartment.*

"Do you mind?" Rubén said, sliding into his booth and depositing his cup of coffee on the table.

"Well, actually..." Klinger said, pointing at his notebook.

Rubén was already digging into a big manila envelope, pulling out newspaper clippings and a wad of three-by-five cards, bound with a fat rubber band. "I just thought I could help you," he said.

"With what?" Klinger asked.

"Your story." Rubén leaned forward and tapped his fingers on the table. "Listen, I got contacts over in Juárez you wouldn't believe."

Klinger didn't know what to make of this. Last thing he wanted was to work with this person. He didn't even want to tell him what he was up to. But the guy seemed to know. Klinger looked at the pile of dog-eared index cards. The top one had some meticulous writing in pencil, with red-lettered notes below it.

"Hey, I don't need help," Klinger said, closing his red notebook. He placed it on the table. Then, seeing DRUGS written on it in big letters, he quickly turned it over.

"I've done a shitload of work on this," Rubén said. "I want to help you."

Klinger took the last bite of his hamburger and glanced at his watch. "I gotta go," he said with his mouth full.

"Wait a minute, wait a minute," Rubén said. "Look. Go see one of my contacts in Juárez. If this person doesn't help you, then forget about it. I won't bother you no more."

"What's in it for you?" Klinger asked.

"You go see this contact," Rubén said, handing him a three-by-five card.

"There's the number right there. See the name. Pedro." He pronounced it in Spanish. "Call him Pete. He speaks English."

Klinger took the card. Maybe now, he thought, this maniac would leave him alone. "You don't expect me to pay you for this?" he said, folding the card and putting it into his shirt pocket.

"No, no, no, no," Rubén said. He stood up, waving empty hands at Klinger. "You go see Pete. He's expecting your call. Later you and I can chat about things."

Rubén drained his coffee, stuffed his cards and clippings into the manila envelope, and hurried away before Klinger could return the card with Pedro's number. He mouthed the words "good luck" to the reporter as he bolted out of the restaurant and into the heat.

As Klinger watched him hurrying down Mesa, the envelope under his arm, he realized he didn't even know the guy's name.

◊

The first thing that struck Harley as he walked into the apartment was Stevenson's festering water pipe. It was sitting on the coffee table, with its moldy debris floating on clouded water. He looked up at Estela and saw her eyes, big and black, set back above her cheekbones.

He yanked his reporter's notebook from his back pocket and sat on a sunken brown couch. He felt change tumbling out of his pocket and reached with a hand to catch it.

Estela hadn't wanted to let him in, but then seemed relieved to hear him speaking Spanish. Now she seemed friendly, even flirtatious.

She offered him a cup of coffee and he declined.

"*Agua mineral?*"

He shook his head. "*Tampoco, gracias.*"

An air conditioner behind him was making a grinding noise, but little in the way of cool air. He looked at the old hardwood floor and wondered what made it buckle. He imagined cockroaches coming up through the cracks at night. Estela sat in a folding chair, elbows on her knees, looking at him with those big eyes. Behind her was a framed photo on the wall. A skinny young man in a sleeveless T-shirt standing in front of a graffiti-covered wall, looking angry. One of Stevenson's pictures.

Harley had trouble figuring out exactly where to start. "This is a beautiful building," he finally said, speaking with the local Chihuahua accent. He pointed to the bay windows, which overlooked Overland Street. "They have windows like that in the old buildings in New York."

Estela shrugged. "The air conditioning doesn't work."

"A building like this in New York City would go for a million dollars."

"Maybe they don't need air conditioning there."

He looked down for a moment, feeling Estela's eyes on him. "Listen," he said. "What do you know about what went on in Juárez?"

"With Eddie?"

"Yes."

"I always told him not to carry all of those cameras over to Juárez. He doesn't even know his way around there. I told him that people would steal his equipment, and probably rough him up too. He paid no attention. He thinks I'm just some *campesina*. Now look."

"But you saw the paper..."

"About the drug lord? Hah. You don't believe that, do you?"

"Why not?"

Estela smiled at him and said something.

"What?" he asked.

"Come on. You're in the business."

He wondered if she knew something or was just playing the conspiracy game, blaming the Mexican president or the CIA for everything.

Estela stood up, walked to the couch slowly, and flopped down beside him.

Or maybe she was flirting, he thought.

She was close enough for him to see the long lashes, bending under the little globs of mascara. Her eyes were a little puffy, as though bruised. He wondered if Stevenson hit her.

"It's just a story," she said slowly, as if to a child. Her Spanish was from Mexico's north, but not the border. Maybe Chihuahua City, Harley thought.

"That's how newspapers make money," she said. "They tell stories."

"And how about the threat to me?"

"Which threat?"

"Jiménez sent back a message with Stev...Eddie, saying that I was dead meat."

"But," she said, building him back up. "You're not worried about that. You know the things they say in Mexico."

"You're right," he said, with more conviction than he felt. "I'm not that worried. But I'd like to figure it out. Why didn't

Eddie come back here?"

She waved her hand, dismissing the question, and said, "Bah!" He felt her breath on his face. "That's Eduardo," she said.

"What about him?"

"He's a child. He gets hurt, he runs away for a while."

Estela smiled at him. She was a large woman, built like a 1950s movie star, the kind they could cast with John Wayne or Burt Lancaster, but way too big for skinny guys like Sinatra and Fred Astaire. She seemed to treat men like little boys.

"So you don't know where Eddie is?"

She was gazing at him. "What's that?" Her voice had fallen to a whisper, and he had a feeling he was losing control of the interview.

"Where's Eddie?"

She shrugged and made a dismissive noise, "Ffff." He felt her breath again as she told him that someone from Eddie's family had been by, asking questions in English.

When she edged even closer to him, he stood up and asked: "Does Eddie hit you?"

"Hmmm?" She collected herself for a second, and then said, "Oh, you don't have to worry about that."

"I was just wondering..."

Estela smiled playfully and fanned herself. "What heat! Is your place air-conditioned?"

Harley's apartment had an even more primitive set-up, but he didn't know how to say "swamp-cooler" in Spanish. "Sort of," he said.

"Where do you live? North of I-10, no?"

"In Sunset Heights."

"Oh." She was disappointed. "That's an old neighborhood. There are much newer places, with big windows, over by Cielo Vista Mall."

She wanted to move away from the funk of the border, he saw, into a part of El Paso that felt like Dallas, or Kansas City.

He couldn't help her and didn't see how she could help him. They chatted for a few minutes, and then he retreated into the furnace of the barrio.

◊

Harley wandered north from Estela's apartment, on El Paso Street. When he got a whiff of tortillas, he ducked into Leon's Cafe, a little Mexican restaurant with checkered plastic tablecloths. Figuring he'd gather his thoughts over lunch, he took his skinny reporter's notebook from his back pocket and ordered *enchiladas con salsa verde*.

Jiménez, he wrote, and paused for a second, remembering the drug lord's first name. Gustavo. He tried to put Jiménez's business into the context of Mexican politics. Presumably, this man had a thriving drug business, and ran it with the support of the politicians and police in Mexico. But now the Mexican government wanted to sign this free trade agreement with the United States. And with Congressional pressure coming down on them from Washington, the Mexicans couldn't afford to let racy drug lords make a lot of noise and build luxury hotels on the border.

So what would he do in Jiménez's shoes? Harley thought about it, his pen poised over the notebook, his untouched bottle of mineral water bubbling by the basket of corn chips.

Try as he might, Harley couldn't come up with a plausible motive for Jiménez to beat up a photographer from El Paso.

But if Jiménez hadn't done it, who had? A steaming plate of enchiladas covered with a rich green sauce, topped with cream, and sprinkled with white cheese interrupted Harley's thoughts. He put down the pen and picked up a fork and knife.

As he finished lunch, mopping up the sauce with a corn tortilla, two Mexican men walked into the restaurant arguing loudly in Spanish about something they'd seen on the *Jerry*

Springer Show. One of them carried a newspaper under his arm. He sat down and laid the newspaper on the table, declaring that if his daughter were as fat as the one he saw on the show, he'd "chain her to a treadmill."

Harley glanced at the newspaper and saw the headline: "SE FUE EL TUERTO." He wondered who *El Tuerto* was, and why it was such big news that he'd departed. He marveled at the wealth of words in Spanish for body mutilation. A *manco* had one arm, a *cojo* one leg, a *tuerto* one eye. Cervantes was probably the most famous *manco*. He remembered the Spanish saying, "*En la tierra de los ciegos, el tuerto es rey,*" or, in the land of the blind, the one-eyed man is king. Then with a start, he recalled that Gustavo Jiménez was a *tuerto*. And now, according to the headline, he'd left town.

Chapter
EIGHT

Alfredito the car-washer was gone, probably off drinking a soda. Gato was off picking up a shipment at Villa Ahumada, an hour south of Juárez. A dusty blue Falcon sat baking in the *Lavarama* lot, waiting to be washed. For a moment, Pascual considered washing it himself, but then decided against it. He was wearing khakis and his usual button-down shirt, a white one. He didn't want to set any precedents.

He unlocked the office. It felt like an oven. He lifted the pistol from his leather bag and started to put it in the desk drawer. Then, impulsively, he aimed the gun out the window, above the Falcon, at the *Lavarama*'s wall. He pulled the trigger, just to see if it was working. The gun kicked and the explosion was deafening. The ringing in his ears sounded for a moment like a shriek.

Pascual put the pistol away as he added one more item to his mental to-do list: Find a quieter weapon. He reached into his bag for Dr. Rivapalacios' book. Then he went outside, where it was a bit cooler, and sat in the shade of the cinder-block wall to read. Pascual's favorite chapter, which he'd been reviewing for the past week, was called "*Triunfar! Claro Que Puedes!*" or, "Win! Of Course You Can!" The chapter seemed to be written just for him. The book didn't go into details about how to wrest power from drug lords like Jiménez. But clearly, if usurping power was a goal, and a series of logical steps led to it, Pascual could make it happen. *Claro que Sí!*, as Dr. Rivapalacios often wrote.

Pascual found the section on mentors perplexing. Dr. Rivapalacios suggested seeking out older people who have climbed the path you're on, to ask for their friendship, advice, and support. That didn't seem to fit with Pascual's plan. The less people knew about it, the better.

He thought about it a little, wondering if Rubén could be his mentor. He was a bit older, twenty-four to Pascual's twenty-two. He spoke good English and knew a lot about the United States, about politics and business. He'd also been to college—unlike Pascual, who'd dropped out of middle school when he was fourteen. Rubén, though, had his shortcomings. He was still learning the ABCs of the drug business. He didn't know how to use a gun. And he looked like a *maricón*. Pascual pondered homosexuality for a moment and then resumed reading.

A half-hour later, Pascual stood up, stretched, and wandered back into the office to turn on the radio. He switched from Gato's ranchera music and found a Metallica song on an El Paso station. Walking outside, he poured a bucket of water on the Ford and briefly considered washing it.

He was settling back with the book when he heard a pounding on the sheet metal gate. "Quién?" he yelled.

"Enrique." It was a child's voice.

"*Que?*"

"*Es que, es que...*" The boy started to explain something. But Pascual couldn't hear him over the music. He walked into the office and turned off the radio.

"*Es que... Se llevaron a Alfredito,*" the boy yelled, telling

Pascual that people took Alfredito away.

"Who?" Pascual asked.

"*La policia.*"

At first, Pascual wondered what Alfredito did to get arrested. Then he connected it to the beating of the photographer, and his throat went dry. He ran to the gate, looked out the peephole, and slid open the door for the skinny little boy to squeeze through.

Pascual recognized the kid as Alfredito's friend who operated the popsicle stand. He led him into the office and sat him down at Gato's gun-metal desk. The boy appeared tiny behind the big desk. He had a red popsicle ring around his mouth. He ran his fingers nervously through his short black hair, which stood straight up. "He wasn't doing anything," he told Pascual. "Just sitting with me on the sidewalk, eating a popsicle. He only had that one car to wash," he added, pointing at the Falcon. "He had just started."

"How many were there?" Pascual asked.

The boy looked at him blankly.

"How many cops? One?"

"Two."

"Are they people you know, that you've seen around here?"

The boy shook his head.

"Were they in a police car?"

He nodded.

"Did they say why they picked him up? Did they know his name?"

"They just asked him if he worked here. He said yes, and they took him." The boy looked down at the desk and started to fiddle with Gato's solar-powered calculator.

Pascual tried to think. He didn't know where the arrest orders came from, the government or Jiménez. He hoped it was the government. In that case, he could count on *don* Gustavo for protection, at least until the drug lord found out what Pascual and his friends had been up to with the photographer.

Pascual wracked his memory, trying to figure out who might have implicated the *Lavarama* in Stevenson's beating. He looked at the boy sitting across from him, looking less nervous now and working intently on the calculator. "What did Alfredo do?" Pascual asked him. "Did he tell you?"

"He was arrested for working here," the boy said simply.

This calm reasoning incensed Pascual, who jumped to his feet, took two steps around the desk, and grabbed the boy. He hoisted him up by his shirt and pinned him to the wall with a thump. "You ratted on him, didn't you! *Pinche guey!*" He banged the boy against the wall again, hard, just as he'd slammed the photographer. But this boy was much lighter, and Pascual was able to lift him higher and pound harder.

The boy started to cry. Pascual kept shaking him, ripping his shirt. He lifted his right hand onto the boy's neck. Then he heard a pounding at the metal gate. He lowered the boy, who was whimpering quietly, and pointed to the chair. "Sit there and stay there," he instructed him as he rushed to the gate.

Through the peephole, Pascual saw a small gray-haired man wearing a freshly ironed white *guayabera*, a type of pleated white shirt Pascual associated with barbers. "*Cerrado*," Pascual said, still breathing heavily.

The man looked at his watch. "I just came to pick up the Falcon. The boy said he'd be here until six."

Pascual whispered "*puta madre*" and opened the gate. "He didn't clean it well," he said. "You can just take it. No charge." Then he hurried back toward the office for the boy. But he saw him standing between the Falcon and the water trough, half crouched, his fuzzy hair on end and his eyes hooded, looking like a hunted animal.

"*Córrele chamaco*," Pascual said to him with a smile, telling him to run along. "We'll be seeing you later." The boy rushed out the gate with the Falcon, the car looking dirtier than ever. The gray-haired client gave Pascual a withering look.

Before Pascual could close the gate and collect his thoughts, Gato strode in, looking his usual sloppy self. He was wearing American short pants and a shirt with something in English written across the front. Gato waved and said "*Hola*," smiling broadly, as if he'd been sampling some of the product. He said that his Duster died, and he seemed happy that he got 1,000 pesos, or $300, from a junk dealer near the airport.

Pascual often wondered whether Gato had what it took to climb with him to the top. Pascual was always pushing Dr. Rivapalacios' book on his partner, telling him he could learn a lot from the chapter on clothes, especially the part about maintaining an erect and energetic posture. Dr. Rivapalacios was adamant about that. Maybe the book could also give Gato a sense of priorities. When they made their run against Jiménez, it would be suicide to be testing the product.

"*Oye, Gato*," he said. "We've got a problem, real serious."

Gato surveyed the carwash, still smiling, and walked with Pascual into the office.

"The police picked up Alfredito," Pascual told him.

"What did he do?" Gato asked innocently.

"*No mames!*" Pascual said. "What do you think he did? He worked here."

Gato's smile dropped. "Were they Jiménez's cops?"

Pascual shrugged. "All I know is what the popsicle kid told me."

"I saw that boy tearing out of here when I came," Gato said, questioning Pascual with his eyes.

Pascual looked down.

"As if someone was chasing him..." Gato continued.

"He was probably in a hurry," Pascual said.

Gato sat on the edge of the desk and picked up the same calculator the boy had been playing with. He bent over it, thinking. After a moment he looked up at Pascual and asked him, "Where are you going with this thing?"

"What thing?"

"What do you mean 'what thing?' The thing the police picked up Alfredito for. The thing you went to El Paso for. The thing... Whatever you did to that boy. What's your plan?"

Pascual stammered. "We're going to... We're going to..." He was about to say "overthrow *don* Gustavo." But he cut himself short. "We're going to keep making news in El Paso, applying political pressure and forcing some...changes in the...high command. And when that happens, we should be able to find something better for ourselves too. *A rio revuelto, ganancia de pescadores*," he said, repeating a Spanish proverb about good fishing in turbulent waters.

Gato rolled his eyes. "Is this a plan, or do you just like to hit people?"

"A plan," Pascual said, his voice coming out higher than usual.

"Did you take your gun to El Paso yesterday?"

"No."

Gato walked around the desk and opened the drawer. "It wasn't here after you left yesterday afternoon."

"Well, I took it," Pascual clarified. "But I didn't use it. In fact, I was thinking of throwing it away over there..."

"Because the police were after you?"

"Just to be prudent."

Gato shook his head. "This could get us killed."

"You have to be audacious to reach the top," said Pascual.

"Dr. Rivapalacios isn't going to get us through this," Gato said. "I want to know what your plans are. Because depending on what they are, I'll either leave or stay."

Pascual fought back a desire to grab Gato's know-it-all face and rip it apart. "Well, first," he said, affecting a carefree tone, "I'll stop by the police station and see what they have Alfredito charged with."

"And you call me a *pendejo*?" said Gato. "They'll just arrest you too."

"But *don* Gustavo won't let them touch us," Pascual said.

"He's probably the one who ordered the arrest. And even if he isn't, what power does he have now? We'll probably end up in the same cell with him, if we survive."

Pascual took off his steel-rimmed glasses, breathed on them, and polished them with his shirttail. "So how do we find out what they picked up Alfredito for?"

"Send his mother to the station," Gato said. He stood up and walked from the office, his baggy shorts flopping down to his knees. "I'm going to see Rubén," he said over his shoulder. "You'd better leave too. They might shoot us before they arrest us."

Chapter
NINE

When Harley stepped off the elevator by the newsroom, Canfield was standing by the door, expecting him.

"What have you got?" he asked.

Harley had the Juárez papers rolled up under his arm. "Were you waiting for me?"

"I looked out the window and saw you coming down Kansas."

"Oh."

"Talking to yourself."

Harley did that constantly, in one voice or another, and didn't try to defend himself.

"So what have you got?"

"Jiménez left town," Harley said.

"He just ran off?"

He nodded. "By the looks of it."

"Where'd you hear this?"

"Just around town. The Juárez papers have already picked it up."

They walked from the elevator toward the newsroom.

"Where would he be heading?" Canfield asked.

"That's what I've got to find out."

"They have an arrest warrant out on him?"

"Not as of this morning. But that might have changed. More likely he got wind of something coming, before it became official."

"Hmmm." Canfield looked down at his shoes, thinking. He pawed the linoleum tile with his foot. "You get a chance to talk over this whole thing with Stevenson yet?"

"I can't find him."

"Hmmm." More pawing. The silence made Harley feel edgy, and in a hurry to write his story.

"You don't think he's planning to sue us, do you?" Canfield asked.

Harley said he didn't know. He was eager to get away from Canfield, who seemed to be in a rambling and curious state of mind.

"Hey," Canfield said, brightening up. "Look at your cue. Klinger put together a nice background file on Jiménez." He headed back toward his terminal, adding: "Seems like he squeezed more out of one of those sources than you did."

Harley nodded dumbly at Canfield's insult, walked into the newsroom, and slumped down in his cubicle, surrounded by press releases, old newspapers, and a picture of himself smiling self-consciously atop Machu Picchu. He wasn't surprised that Klinger had already come up with a background file. It was just his style to copy the editors on it, letting everyone know he was racing ahead with the story. He called up Klinger's file and started to read.

To: Harley
From:Klinger
cc:Canfield, Perry
re: background on Jiménez
Date: 9-1

Tom,

I had a spare hour this a.m., so decided to call the DEA. Sorry if it's your source. Had to orient myself, and reading the clips didn't help much (No offense). Learned some interesting stuff on Jiménez.

From Timothy A. Giamotto, deputy district director, DEA: OFF THE RECORD (If this guy sees his name in the paper, he'll shit.)

Name: Gustavo Jiménez Pavon
Birthdate: 11-12-38, Chihuahua City
never married, lived with his mom (no name yet) in Juárez until a year ago, when he moved into a palace on the east side of Juárez, near the road to the airport.

Tall and skinny, about 6'4", he guesses, 180. His left eye is glass, from some barroom brawl in Chihuahua City when he was young.

Nickname: "El Tuerto", which I guess you know means one-eyed person in Spanish.

Hasn't got a hand in the growing heroin biz yet. Looks like Colombians out of Chihuahua City control that. He didn't have names to give me. Jiménez started making big money about three years ago, when he started taking payment in kind from the Colombians. In other words, they paid him for his distribution with cocaine, and he began marketing his own stuff. Much higher profits.

Now Jiménez is getting into the construction biz, as you mentioned in your story. Giamotto thinks it could be a career switch for him, if the Colombos get too powerful. To get big in those two businesses, drugs and construction, he must be well connected in the ruling PRI party. No names yet.

Giamotto says Jiménez started running a small cross-border retail business with an American base in Canutillo, just up the river. That was in the late '70s. Had a network of mules that carried small shipments across the river, and then a few dealers who sold nickel and dimes in El Paso. Nothing big. Local sheriffs tried to bust him. (No date yet; he was telling me this off the top of his head.)

He escaped. The story's awesome. He was sleeping in some barn in the Mexican neighborhood of Canutillo, called Chihuahuita. And most of the people there still have pigs and chickens in their yards. Anyway, Jiménez was sleeping in the barn, and the sheriffs knew that he had drugs there. So one dawn, about four of them went to bust him. They tried sneaking through the backyards of Chihuahuita. But all the animals started braying and barking and clucking, and that probably tipped Jiménez that something was up. He ran out of the barn, and through the next couple of yards, jumping fences. The sheriffs ran after him. Finally, when it looked like they had him cornered, he grabbed a piglet and held it up, squealing, as a sort of hostage. He put a knife to its neck. He said, hold it there, or I'll cut its throat. Giamotto says the sheriffs just stood there, not because they cared much about the piglet, but because cutting that pig's neck would have been so bloody. So they stood there a while in this kind of face-off. And then Jiménez suddenly jabbed the piglet in the ass with his knife and threw it right at them, bleeding and squealing, and he took off over the fence.

He kept on running, down to the river. And he swam across it, thinking he was crossing into Mexico. But at that point of the Rio Grande, he was only crossing into New Mexico. They just drove across the bridge and arrested him. But then he got bailed out and jumped.

Giamotto says to be careful with this story, to check it out a little, because he doesn't know how much is legend, and what's true. I bet we can use at least some of it at some point.

I asked Giamotto if Jiménez was known to be violent. He said no, more of a party animal. But he did mention one killing in Juárez a month or two ago, a radio journalist who ended up in the Rio Grande with his lungs ripped out (?!) You probably know about it. Giamotto says that a lot of people attributed it to Jiménez, since this reporter (name?) was hitting on him pretty hard. Anyway, he says he doesn't think Jiménez would have been dumb enough to kill that journalist, because it almost got him into trouble with the government, which is the last thing he wants. So why did Jiménez get himself involved with Stevenson??

Gotta run. Let's talk this p.m.

Harley glanced up from his terminal and saw Canfield talking on the phone. He was standing up and summoning him with his free arm. This had to be about Klinger. Harley walked toward Canfield's desk and heard the city editor saying, "...Yeah, we know he's left... But you say you got witnesses? A Porsche? Baby blue? Good detail, Klinger. Real good. You got these guys on the record?" Canfield arched his eyebrows at Harley. "Listen," he went on, "I got your partner here. What's that?... I'll ask the expert."

Canfield laughed and turned to him. "He wants to know what the word *pendejo* means."

"It's a cross between 'idiot' and 'asshole,' but tell him not to take it too hard," Harley said.

"I'll let you tell him that on a conference call," Canfield said, laughing. He sat down and began pushing buttons on the phone before appealing to Carmen, the office manager, for help. Then he yelled, "Shit!" as the line went dead.

Canfield swiveled around to Harley. "I can't see why their phone company's such a hot stock when the lines always go dead. IBM builds top-of-the-line computers, and their stock crashes, and goddamn Telefonos de Mexico can't pull off a five-minute call and everybody wants to own it..."

Harley cut in. "Klinger's got sources in Juárez?"

"He's over there, getting drunk from the sound of it," Canfield said. He leaned over to pick up his *Wall Street Journal*, which fell while he was trying to set up the conference call. "But he got details. Jiménez left Juárez alone, speeding south in a late model baby blue Porsche. At 8:30 a.m., Juárez time."

Harley leaned down toward Canfield's desk. "You say Klinger's drunk?"

Canfield laughed. "He's drinking with a bunch of cops in a pool hall. Probably taking shots of tequila with that red sauce. What's it called? Sangria?"

"*Sangrita.*"

"That's it. He could hardly talk, his tongue was so thick."

"Maybe I'd better go over there."

"Harley, you go over there, you'll get your neck slit."

"Oh, yeah." Harley thought about it for a second. "But if Jiménez left town, maybe it's not so dangerous now. I'm thinking that Klinger might not know who he's dealing with. If those cops belong to Jiménez, they might have been feeding him a line."

"It corroborates your reporting, right?" Canfield answered belligerently.

Harley was stumped for a moment, wondering what reporting Canfield was referring to.

"Well, yes," he said.

Carmen came up behind Canfield and tapped him on the shoulder. "Channel Eight's downstairs," she said, "with a camera. Should I let them come up?"

"Hold 'em off for a minute." Canfield stood up and grabbed him tight on the elbow. "Come with me for a second," he said, leading him into Ken Perry's empty office.

"Listen, Harley," he said, closing the door. "I don't know

much about Mexico. You know that. If I did, maybe I'd understand why everybody wants to buy that for-shit phone company." He had his face close to Harley, his breath smelling of tobacco. "But I do know a few things," he said. "I know about Cortes burning his boats in Veracruz. I know about Maximillian trying to run a European court in Mexico City, and getting executed for his trouble. But more important than that, or I should say, more relevant to our case..."

Canfield looked him in the eye and tightened the grip on his elbow. "I know something about the Mexico mystique. People think Mexico's some holy enigma wrapped in a tamale behind a mask. It's so mysterious, in fact, that only dummies even try to understand it."

He let go of Harley's elbow. In a calmer voice, he said, "Let's sit." As they settled on Perry's couch, Canfield started again. "There's a certain type of reporter that covers Mexico. I call 'em anthropologists. You've heard me. They're always telling you why, for one reason or another—the Mexican mystique or the many masks of Mexico... They're always telling you why they can't get information over there. They know so much about the country that they're convinced it's useless to ask questions. You can't ask a cop a question, because you don't know who owns him." He raised his voice. "And they make people like me feel like we're ignorant when we treat Juárez like any other place in the world and say 'go over there and find out what the fuck is going on!'

"But think about this, Harley," he went on. "You speak fluent Castilian Spanish and you know when you can say "tu" and when you should call somebody "usted," and when you can call someone a "*coño*" in polite society. And yet you're over here working your story on the phone, and Klinger, who doesn't know shit, is over there getting the story."

Harley nodded, surprised that Canfield knew the word "*coño*."

Canfield lowered his voice to a friendlier pitch. "What I'm

trying to say is, you've been writing anthro here for years. And now that you've got a hard-news story, it's tough for you to start collaring people and asking hard questions. I get this feeling you're tiptoeing around. You've been through a couple of tough days. But you've also got the chance of a lifetime." He paused, theatrically, and then whispered, "You could win the goddamn Pulitzer Prize! But you're not going to win it with anthropology. You're only going to win it if you go over there and get dirty. Ask questions. Even if you sound like an ignorant *gringo*. Even if you sound like me. Talk to people. You don't know the answers until you dig. Ask...the...fucking... questions."

"Fair enough," Harley said. "So let me ask you one question."

"Shoot."

Harley stood up so that he towered over the editor and then launched into Canfield-talk. "WHERE THE HAY-IL DID A GOOD OLE BOY LIKE YOU LEARN TO SAY *COÑO*?"

Canfield looked thunderstruck. "I'll be..."

"SOUNDS LIKE YOU BEEN DOING SOME AN-THRO-PO-LOGICAL RESEARCH OF YOUR OWN OVER IN THOSE DAMN JUAREZ CAT HOUSES!"

Canfield broke into a smile. "Dammit, Harley! You should find some way to put that voice to use."

Perry's phone rang. Canfield, still shaking his head, stepped to the desk and answered. "Yes, we'll pay for it," he said. He listened for a few seconds and muttered, "Jesus Christ. Okay, Klinger. Take a cab back here. We'll deal with it." He hung up shaking his head grimly. "Can you believe it?" he said. "They stole his goddam car while he was talking to the *cops*."

Chapter
TEN

Dawn in Colonia Club Campestre, the snootiest section of Ciudad Juárez. Onofre Crispín, wrapped in a kimono, took a glass of papaya juice from a maid and strolled through the atrium, past the quietly bubbling 17th-century fountain, and into the breakfast room.

Crispín sat at a massive table of worm-eaten oak that he'd bought at a convent in Michoacán years before. He flicked on the remote control and a wide-screen TV, built into the wall and surrounded by hand-painted tiles, flashed to life. It was a familiar El Paso commercial, an old man wearing shorts hawking Toyotas. Crispín took a sip of the papaya juice and grimaced. "Dolores!" he shouted.

"*Sí señor,*" she answered, hurrying through the atrium.

"You forgot to put lime in the papaya juice," he said in Spanish.

"*Ay perdóneme señor,*" she said to Crispín, who was intently touring the world of channels on his TV. He didn't answer. But as the maid walked away he yelled after her, "*Y Dolores!*"

"*Sí señor.*"

"*Un café también. Negro.*"

"*Sí señor, cómo no.*"

Only forty-one years old, Onofre Crispín considered himself the modernizer of northern Mexico, a private-sector peer of the president and his cabinet of American-educated economists.

The president and his team simply mapped out the future of Mexico, Crispín believed. But they relied on people like him—modernizers on the ground—to put up the factories, build the roads, link the cities with fiber-optic cable. In short, to make it happen.

In many ways, the job in Mexico City was easier. The government controlled the capital and dealt with the *gringos* in faraway Washington. Here in Juárez, though, two parties actually jockeyed for power, the ruling PRI and the conservative PAN. That made business much more complicated. And here, the *gringos* were right across the river, ready to raise a racket whenever anyone in Mexico offended their tender sensibilities.

The recent newspaper stories in El Paso, with their claims about *maquiladora* trucks carrying cocaine, made Crispín's life miserable. Investors were calling brokers in New York and Dallas, asking about rumors that drug money was driving up the Grupo Espejo stock. His American banker urged him to fly up to New York and soothe the analysts. "Even with the three-dollar drop, the stock's doubled in the last month," Crispín told him. "And you think the analysts need soothing?"

Instead, Crispín considered flying down to Mexico City and asking the commerce secretary for a show of high-level support. Maybe Crispín would have a sit-down with the president. It wouldn't be the first.

The maid brought in the demitasse of steaming coffee and the papaya juice, along with a small plate with half a lime. "*Gracias,*" Crispín said, squeezing the lime into the papaya juice. "You know, without lime it just doesn't taste like anything," he said with a smile, trying to make up for his gruff treatment.

"*Claro que no, señor,*" Dolores said.

But Crispín had shifted his attention from breakfast beverages to the TV, where a tall American with angular features and mussed-up brown hair was talking about danger. That had to be the death-threatened reporter.

"I found out about it reading my own paper, believe it or not," Onofre Crispín heard him say. The journalists' names popped up on the screen. Tom Harley, reporter, and Ken Perry, editor.

At that point, Perry jumped in. "Let's focus on what really matters here. There's a *señor* across the river from us who poisons our kids with drugs, lives like a prince, and when we write a story about him, well, he just beats the daylights out of our photographer and sends a death threat to our reporter. And where's the Mexican government while all this is happening? For them, it appears, this is just business as usual."

The TV reporter, off camera, asked Perry how the wounded photographer, Eddie Stevenson, was faring.

Perry ignored the question and pressed on. "Harley here likes to downplay it sometimes," he said. "He's a little uncomfortable in the spotlight. But the political question is whether we want to step up to the altar, economically speaking, with a government that coddles folks like Gustavo Jiménez."

Disgusted, Onofre Crispín put down his coffee and reached for his large cellular phone. He stood up and paced around the breakfast room, wondering who to call.

The reporter tried to ask Harley a question, but Perry kept talking. "This man Jiménez openly terrorizes the border, and for some reason, no one ever charges him with anything. Could it be political connections? I'd say yes. And I'd imagine he has pretty cozy ties with the *maquiladora* barons who really run Juárez's economy."

The television reporter finally turned to Harley. How would the reporter cover the story, he asked, with a death threat hanging over him?

"By phone," Harley said, smiling. "No, seriously. You know, Jiménez left town yesterday, heading south, apparently. So I don't think there should be a problem going over to Juárez."

The news broke for an ad.

Crispín extended the antenna of his cellular phone and punched in a number. Seconds later, he was talking to a groggy Juárez police chief, Roberto Muller.

"*Beto. Te habla Crispín.*"

"*Hombre...*"

Crispín cut short the pleasantries and told him about the television news. "I don't think you understand the damage this could inflict upon the country," he said, nervously scraping the sugar from the bottom of his coffee cup. "These irresponsible reports from El Paso could sink NAFTA—and all the work we've done to modernize Mexico."

"Uh huh," the chief said.

"It looks like the reporter, Tom Harley, might be coming to Juárez. I'm sure you have photos of him on record. Maybe if you just picked him up for a chat...I think he can be talked to. Much more than his boss."

"Mmm." Chief Muller thought it over. "Wouldn't they consider that some form of harassment? I just think..."

"Beto. Figure it out," Crispín ordered. "Take him out to lunch at Julio's. Feeding isn't harassing." He hung up and marched upstairs to get dressed, the kimono flapping at his shins.

Chapter
ELEVEN

Drunk and heartsick over his stolen car, Klinger still managed to write up the front-page story. And despite Harley's work, it was Klinger's well-known byline that ran under the Thursday headline: "Juárez Kingpin Scrams."

This put pressure on Harley to produce. He paced in his hotel room, drinking coffee, and putting together his plan. He would start at Jiménez's house. If no one answered, he'd look in windows, call on neighbors, maybe visit the *Xanadu* construction site. He went outside, determined to plunge into the reporting. While unlocking his bike, he had second thoughts. What would the drug lord's entourage think, he wondered, if he showed up at the door carrying his helmet, and with salt rings of dried sweat around his armpits? Deciding to take a more mainstream approach, he relocked the bike and climbed into his old Honda Civic.

Driving across the Bridge of the Americas, he imagined knocking on Jiménez's door and finding himself facing a beautiful woman, a member of the harem. She'd invite him inside to a party room with cocaine on the coffee table, in little vials with silver spoons, and a black velvet portrait of Elvis, or maybe Emmitt Smith, on the wall. He pictured a mountain lion padding through the room, looking at him with a bored expression, and then jumping softly onto an overstuffed couch, stretching and falling asleep. He wondered how he'd ask the woman the delicate question of whether she belonged to a harem...

In Juárez now, he noticed a car creeping up behind him. Looking in the rear-view mirror, he saw a policeman in a blue cruiser, lights on, motioning him toward the curb.

Harley watched the cop in the mirror. He climbed out of his cruiser and closed the door. Then he pulled up his belt, walking forward. Finally he stuck his head in the car window.

A fifty-year-old, Harley guessed, with a gray mustache and bright green eyes. He flashed a smile. His nametag read Pérez.

"*Buenos días, señor Pérez,*" Harley said.

"You ga two problems," the policeman said in English. "One, you go through a stop sign back there. Two, you were going nearly eighty kilometers per hour right here."

Harley didn't contest the charges. He sat quietly, waiting for the usual negotiations to begin. Pérez ordered him to park the car by the curb and turn off the ignition. This wasn't normal procedure. Then he ordered him out of the car, with his keys. Harley saw that he was facing arrest for business unrelated to stop signs or speeding.

Pérez asked for his identification and made a clicking sound with his tongue as he studied his license. "Six feet four inches. Is that two meters?"

"One ninety-four," Harley said, speaking English for the first time.

"And tell me, Mister..." He looked back at the license and asked Harley where he was going in such a hurry.

"I'm a journalist," Harley said. "I was driving to Gustavo Jiménez's house for an article I'm writing."

"He's not home, from what I hear," the policeman said. He

motioned the American toward the cruiser. After locking his own car, Harley jumped in the back seat.

"I wasn't expecting that you are so *amable* about this," Pérez said, looking at him in the rear-view mirror.

"I figure if someone wants to talk, we'll talk," Harley said. Pérez didn't respond. He pulled the car into a lot full of blue and white Ford cruisers.

The sergeant led Harley through the dingy waiting room of the State Judicial Police office. Harley had been there once before, waiting hours for an interview with the captain. They passed a pastry vendor he'd talked to, who spent his working days shooing flies and yellow jackets away from old éclairs and donuts. The vendor waved at Harley and gestured toward his glass stand, but lowered his arm when he saw the American was in custody.

Pérez led him to a desk, where a tired-looking clerk wearing a clip-on tie shuffled through a thick stack of papers.

Pérez leaned over and murmured to the man. He heard something about "an appointment with the *jefe*."

"*Claro*," the clerk said, nodding without looking up. He rapped on the desk three times with a brass paperweight, and another policeman stepped forward.

"*Regístralo*," the clerk said, ordering him to frisk the American.

"No, no," Pérez said, trying to stop his colleague. "He's here for an appointment. He's not under arrest."

Harley had stopped at a bank machine just before driving over and had $60 in his wallet. Worried they'd steal it, he plunged a fist into his pocket. But the policeman was able to push his fingers backwards, ever so gently, and pry his wallet free.

Harley flopped down in a folding chair, wondering what kind of form he'd have to fill out at the *Tribune* to get his money back.

Pérez came over to comfort him. "You don have to worry,"

he said. "They not going to steal nothing. They just look at your identification."

But his last words were drowned out by shouts at the desk. The cop who frisked him was shouting "*Mira, mira,*" and holding a flattened joint above his head. The clerk, looking up for the first time, let loose a loud whistle.

"Uh oh," Pérez said.

Chapter
TWELVE

Rubén's aunt Julita called his cluttered third-floor bedroom *"el gallinero,"* or "the hen house." Sometimes she asked her nephew what he spent so much time doing up there, with the temperature hotter than a Chihuahua hen house and all those newspapers cut to pieces on his table, overflowing onto the floor. He had clippings taped all over his wall. Didn't he want her to climb up there from time to time and tidy things?

No, Rubén said. Never. Those papers were necessary for a study he was doing.

Aunt Julita told him she'd never heard anything so foolish in her life. "Newspapers only teach you how to lie," she said more than once.

Rubén had been living with his aunt since his mother died. He was fourteen when he arrived at the bus station in Juárez. He didn't know a word of English. But he knew where he was going. He walked straight from the bus station to the river, asked another boy to watch his suitcase, and then waded in. Minutes later Julita opened the door of her tenement apartment on Fr. Rahm Street, two blocks north of the river, to a skinny, curly-haired boy, dripping wet. He never went back for his suitcase.

Rubén's mother, Esperanza, had waded across the river after her water broke, and she gave birth in Thomason General Hospital. That made Rubén a U.S. citizen, which meant he could have crossed the bridge and entered legally. But he didn't learn that until later.

He picked up English quickly from the TV and breezed through high school. He even went for a few months to the community college, where he studied journalism and wrote articles for the school newspaper. Julita told him that newspapers weren't for serious people. But quietly she was proud of him. His career in journalism ended, however, with an article that created problems for him. Julita figured the article must have been true, otherwise people wouldn't have been so upset. He never told her what it was about.

Julita didn't get out much anymore. For the last two years her knee had been swollen to the size of a grapefruit. The pharmacist sold her pills that at least made it easier to sleep. But the swelling didn't go down, and she couldn't afford a doctor. She often wondered how she'd get by if her brother ever stopped sending monthly checks from Chicago. She doubted she could count on Rubén as a provider. He was brilliant, but flighty.

For the last several days, Rubén had been all wound up, acting jumpy and excited. Julita's friend Ana, who brought groceries to the house twice a week, saw Rubén dash into the house one afternoon. He ran up to the *gallinero* and down three times while making himself a cup of hot tea. She asked Julita whether he was on any kind of medication. No, Julita said, "He's just excited by his work." When asked what kind of work Rubén did, she said she wasn't sure. Something to do with newspapers. It didn't seem to pay very well.

Thursday afternoon, Julita was scrubbing floors in the small living room and kitchen, a small pillow under her bad knee. She was anxious to make the house presentable for visitors. The night before, a tall, young Mexican man had knocked on the door. He had a friendly smile and slumping posture. He was Rubén's first visitor in years. She heard Rubén call him Gato, and the two of them had gone upstairs for fifteen or twenty minutes. When they came back down, Rubén had his arm on Gato's shoulder and was telling him how to get to Estela's apartment. "You can sleep on the couch," he said. "She'll appreciate the company."

The phone rang and Julita answered. A Mexican man asked for Rubén. She heard his thumping upstairs, and then he picked up his phone in the *gallinero*. "*Ya, Tía*," he yelled down to her, telling her to hang up.

Julita waited a moment. She heard Rubén speaking in Spanish. "What news do you have?" he asked.

"Very well, very well. All went very well." The man chuckled.

Julita moved the phone closer to her ear.

"Did he listen to you?" Rubén asked.

"*Si si si si si.*"

"Did he take notes?"

"You mean did he write in that little pad? Yes, plenty, at least for the first couple of rounds."

Julita laid the phone gently on the table and yelled up toward the *gallinero*. "Did you pick it up yet, *hijo*?"

"*Ya, Tía*," Rubén shouted down, sounding friendlier than usual. Julita hung up with only a vague idea of what her nephew was up to.

As his police contact talked, Rubén's mind wandered. He started to sketch out plans for further contacts with Klinger. Feeding stories to the El Paso paper, he thought, was much slicker and safer than Pascual's method of prowling El Paso with a gun. Later, Rubén would have to make the point to Pascual that the pen is mightier than the sword. He'd have to remember to take the next day's *Tribune* over to the

Lavarama.

"...So it was a misfortune," Rubén heard Pedro say.

"What misfortune?"

"I just told you."

Rubén asked him to repeat it.

"Well, as I said, towards the end of our session with him in the *cantina*, we'd all been drinking mezcal, and some of us weren't as alert as we might have been, and it turns out that one of the *camaradas* appears to have driven away in the *gringo's* car."

Rubén was stunned. "Who stole it?" He heard his aunt calling him from downstairs. "*Un momento!*" he yelled. Then he asked Pedro again, "Who stole it?"

"We'll get it back."

Rubén heard his aunt calling his name again, and then her heavy steps slowly climbing the stairs. "*Un momento,*" he said to Pedro. He put down the phone and stuck his head out the door. He could see the top of his aunt's head as she made her way up. "There's a nice-looking friend of yours downstairs, who says he must see you," she said. "Very well dressed."

Pascual, Rubén thought. The last visitor he wanted. "Tell him to wait a minute," he said, returning to the phone.

He picked it up. "Pedro?"

"*Sí?*"

"You say that one of yours stole his car?"

"You should have seen him," Pedro said, laughing. "He was drunk, as I've been telling you, and he ran up and down *Calle* Lerdo shouting '*Cabrón! Cabrón!*' and pulling at his hair. I know this is unwelcome news. But you would have laughed."

"What kind of car was it?" As Rubén asked the question, he saw Pascual, dressed in pressed khakis and an Oxford shirt, slip through his door and sit down carefully between the clippings on his bed. He laid his leather shoulder bag on the pillow and took out a paperback book. Pedro was talking, and Rubén had to interrupt him. "What kind? Did you say?"

"What kind of what?"

"Of car."

"Ah, a very beautiful red Pontiac. I can't say I blame them. The reporter was in no condition to drive anyway," Pedro added. "I mean we would have had to detain him."

Rubén wondered whether Pedro himself had stolen the car.

"We'll get the car back," Pedro said. "And you and I can discuss the bill later."

"Yes, later," Rubén said, hanging up.

Pascual closed his book, marking his place with a paper clip. "You're buying a car?" he asked in Spanish.

"No."

"I heard something about a red Pontiac."

"No, that's irrelevant..." Rubén paused and changed the subject. "What are you doing here?"

"There's...there's trouble in Juárez," Pascual said wearily.

He went on to tell Rubén about the police picking up Alfredito. Following Gato's advice, Pascual said he sent the boy's mother to the police station. But he never heard back from her. Instead, a whole delegation of men from the neighborhood pounded on the gate of the Lavarama and told him to leave. A few of them had guns.

Rubén wasn't surprised. "Did they know about the photographer?"

"Probably," Pascual said, lying back on the bed and looking deflated. "There was one other thing, too. They said that someone shot a gun from the Lavarama, and that the bullet hit some boy in the barrio. In the arm. Nothing serious. But they say they have evidence that the shot came from the Lavarama."

Rubén didn't need to ask if it was true. "What does this mean for us?"

"Changes," Pascual said in a low, determined voice. "Operations move to the north side of the river. You know," he added, "your greatest opportunities arrive at your lowest moments. It's merely a matter of recognizing and seizing them."

Rubén didn't bother teasing him about the lifted quote from Dr. Rivapalacios. He had his own bad news to report.

Chapter
THIRTEEN

Duane Canfield balled up the market section of the *Wall Street Journal* and threw it away. Hillary Clinton's health reform was murdering the drug stocks. He figured he'd lost $20,000 by betting on Merck over Telmex. And then he bought into this *maquiladora* stock that had doubled in two weeks, and it promptly dropped two points. Canfield scanned the newsroom, taking in his troops. Some reporters were reading newspapers. Others sat slumped in their chairs, the phone jammed between shoulder and ear, taking the usual information from the usual sources: the lists of drunk drivers and burglaries, the weather, details of the latest battles over bilingual education at the Ysleta School District.

Klinger, usually his most energetic reporter, was bent over his terminal, mourning his stolen Trans-Am. At one point, Canfield walked over to comfort him, saying that with pressure from the paper, the Mexicans were sure to return it. But Klinger shook his head slowly, saying, "They tear them apart, with blowtorches."

Canfield wondered how to keep the Mexican drug scandal

on page one without a story. He knew Perry would be no help. The editor had celebrated his TV performance and now reeked of Scotch and cigars. When Canfield told him he had no drug story for the front page, the editor in chief couldn't be bothered. "I'll write another editorial," he said. Then he tossed Canfield a fuzzy picture taken from the TV. It showed Perry gesturing expansively, his right hand in front of Harley's face. "Think we could clean that up for the front page?" he asked.

"I'd save it for your scrapbook," Canfield said, flipping the picture back.

Perry studied it for a moment. "It doesn't really do justice to Harley," he said. "He's kind of in the shadow there... You know," he added, trying to engage his city editor in a chat, "I've been thinking about Harley. Talented guy like that. Smart. All those languages. Damn good writer. No reason he couldn't take this story and run with it."

"I guess," Canfield said, looking bored.

"Where is Harley, anyway?" Perry asked. "I'd like to have a little talk with him."

"Damned if I know," Canfield said, standing up. "But I'd be a fool to count on him to fill page one."

Front-page relief finally arrived over the fax machine. The Border Patrol was announcing a new program to block illegal immigration and cut back on car thefts and purse snatching. "Operation Blockade," as it was called, would place a virtual wall of Border Patrol agents along twelve miles north of the river, from the Hacienda Cafe near the Asarco smelter all the way to the Zaragoza Bridge, by Ysleta. The idea was to discourage Mexicans from even dipping a toe into the Rio Grande.

Canfield loved it. He walked over to Klinger's desk and smacked him on the back. "Enough of your whimpering. You got a story to write," he said, dropping the release next to his keyboard. "Tie it to drugs."

The city editor saw Operation Blockade fitting into a

broad, front-page package. Klinger's story would detail how increased surveillance might put a crimp into border drug traffic. Ken would write an editorial commending the Border Patrol for responding so quickly to the *Tribune*'s call for government action against Gustavo Jiménez and other Juárez drug lords. Canfield would assign one of his reporters to write about Mexico's reaction to Operation Blockade, which was sure to be angry. And then maybe a business story about the effects this blockade would have on the *maquiladora* trucks going back and forth across the border.

As he pieced together the package of stories, Canfield gazed out the window at night falling on El Paso and wondered for a moment where Harley was.

Within two hours, the stories were almost ready. Klinger, short of other reporting, used some of the details those Juárez cops gave him before stealing his car. He stayed clear of names, but sketched the structure of the drug business, from the kingpins in Colombian cities like Cali and Medellin to their local envoys in Mexico, and underlings like Jiménez. He hinted at Jiménez's political connections and described his "stable of human mules, who carried drugs across the river, creating a convoy of narcotics." This convoy, Klinger wrote, would likely crash into Operation Blockade.

While Canfield was helping lay out the front page, Ken Perry emerged from his office reading the hard copy of the lead article. He looked concerned. He stationed himself behind the hunched figure of Canfield and coughed.

The city editor paid no attention. Perry coughed again, and then said, "Duane?"

Canfield looked up, and Perry gestured that he wanted a word with him. Perry led him into his office and shut the door. "Does this mean," he whispered, "that people who work in Juárez won't be able to cross the river unless they have a green card?"

"Yup," Canfield said, looking pleased.

"Even my maid?"

Canfield laughed. "And most likely your gardener too."

"It's not just me," Perry whispered angrily. "We're talking about real economic impact here. Think of all the work these people do on our side of the river."

Canfield didn't look impressed.

"I just think we should mention this in the coverage," Perry said. "It's not a win-win deal."

"You're right," Canfield agreed, placating his boss.

"We should come back with that angle tomorrow." Perry nodded, walked back to his office, and shut the door.

Then Klinger came over with more news. He'd found out, he said, that the new Border Patrol chief who was orchestrating this Operation Blockade was a Mexican-American whose grandfather had snuck across the border, from Juárez to El Paso, in the '30s.

Canfield beamed. This was too rich. He was about to order up a profile of the chief. But then he thought better of it. He'd hold that one as a second-day story, even at the risk of getting scooped by the *Journal*.

"Don't go with it tonight," he told Klinger. "I want you to follow that man tomorrow from the minute he drinks his first cup of coffee. I want you in his skin. You'll get your profile, and you might learn something about drugs while you're at it."

◊

The police escorted Harley into a small, windowless room with a blinking neon light and a linoleum floor worn down to the wood. Sit down, they told him. Then they shut the door.

Slumped on the lone chair in the room, he wondered just how much trouble he was in. Like most people, he'd gotten away with a lot in life. Some drunk driving in high school, coitus less than fully interruptus in a half dozen love affairs, raw oysters in Galveston. All kinds of mistakes in his reporting. And he got away with it all.

And now here he was in a Mexican police station for possession of a joint he had no intention of smoking.

Chapter
FOURTEEN

Stevenson would have been happy to jump in bed as soon as he walked in the door, without a word. But things were rarely that simple. He quickly saw that the way to the bedroom involved the usual string of rituals and talk. Women always felt this need to get acquainted.

The two of them sat in Diana's living room at sunset, music on, drinking margaritas. Stevenson yawned and then draped his right arm around Diana's shoulder with his hand dangling about three inches away from a breast. He felt her stiffen slightly and then relax.

"What's this music?" he asked.

"K.D. Lang. Like it?"

"Pretty nice," Stevenson said, wondering if Diana might be a lesbian. Diana grabbed his hand and pulled on the fingers affectionately, moving it away from her chest.

"So," she said, looking at him, "do you want to talk about what went on over there?"

Stevenson mixed a smile with a grimace. "Not...not now. Do you mind?"

"Oh no." She slipped out from under his arm, stood up, and poured some more margarita from a Mexican glass pitcher. "Want more salt on your glass?"

"Just ice," Stevenson said.

This was going to be complicated, Stevenson knew. He would have to negotiate the terms of his visit and decide how much to tell her, and then keep his lies straight.

There weren't many options. He was on the run, he felt, and he needed to sleep somewhere. Diana Clements' place on Memphis Avenue was the best option. Her duplex had French art prints on the wall and an old Bobby Kennedy poster in the foyer. A little porch faced the mountain.

Stevenson heard the refrigerator door shut and eyed Diana as she returned to the couch. She placed a glass bowl of guacamole with chips on the table. Then she smiled at him and plopped the ice into his margarita.

They sat quietly side by side, sipping and munching and listening to K.D. Lang. They hardly looked at each other, just glancing from time to time while reaching for the chips.

Then Diana piped up. "Tell me about your Mexican lover." She said it as if asking about his hometown, or favorite movies.

Stevenson had hoped to avoid the subject of Estela. He nibbled on his mustache, affecting a pained and sincere look. "We broke up," he said, raising his eyes to Diana.

"Just recently?"

"Uh huh. A couple days ago."

"I'm sorry about that. You've had a killer week, haven't you?"

Stevenson nodded. He studied her eyes. They were small and sharp, like gems, the brown sprinkled with golden specks. So much more chipper than Estela's black lagoons.

He knew he had to say more. Guessing from the Kennedy poster that Diana was liberal, he said, "It just didn't work out. There's a bourgeois side to her. Wants to spend all of her time at the mall."

"Did you move out?"

"Yeah. Pretty much."

"And now you want to stay here." It wasn't a question, but demanded a response.

"Oh," Stevenson said, waving his palm toward her. "Not really. Not at all. I mean..."

"Listen," she said. "You can stay here. We just have to figure out what kind of guest you're going to be, a refugee or..."

"I still have a lot of things to figure out," Stevenson said. "I don't think I'll even be staying in El Paso, not with what happened over in Juárez. It just makes me feel creepy." He told her he was thinking about driving out to L.A., because he felt like swimming in the ocean. Or maybe he'd visit his brother in Austin.

Diana interrupted him. "You're a bit of an escape artist wouldn't you say?"

Stevenson struggled to come up with an answer.

"You're taking a leave from the paper."

Another one of those statements of hers. Stevenson decided to slow down for a moment and figure out what he wanted from Diana Clements. He watched her as she sipped from her glass, her eyes studying him over the salt-coated rim.

He didn't want sex, he decided. She was already seeing through him now; sex would make it worse.

So if he didn't want sex, what was he doing? Stevenson picked up his margarita and took a slow sip. He tried imagine a sexless friendship with a woman. He hadn't had one of those since high school, and even then, it was only that way because the girls said no. He tried to imagine just sitting here with this woman, listening to music and drinking, without any of this tension.

What would they talk about? He didn't know. But he found the idea strangely appealing.

"Eddie," she asked. "Are you taking a leave from the

paper?"

"Yeah," he said, nodding.

"Did you tell Canfield? I think he was looking for you."

"How do you know about Canfield?"

"I called him."

"And asked about me?"

She shrugged. "What else? He's kind of friendly." Stevenson was shocked that this woman whose name he could barely remember had been calling his boss, asking about him. He remembered *Fatal Attraction*, where Glenn Close stalked Michael Douglas after a single fling, and he finally had to shoot her in the bathtub.

One more reason to have a sexless relationship, he thought.

"Who else have you been talking to?" he asked her.

"Well, since you asked, I went over to your apartment and talked to Estela. Or tried to."

"Jesus Christ!"

"It wasn't any big deal."

"So she's still staying there?"

"She was."

"What did she say?" he asked.

"Well, my Spanish isn't too good. But I'm guessing she'd sort of like to know where you are. Canfield would too. He says you're taking a leave from the paper."

Stevenson sat looking at his margarita, gnawing on the inside of his cheek.

Then, remembering something, he stretched back on the couch and reached into the tiny square pocket of his Levi's.

"Do you have a problem at the paper, Eddie?"

Stevenson didn't hear her. He was carefully extracting a skinny joint—a long-forgotten treasure—from his pocket. "Would you like to smoke this?" he asked. "With me?"

Diana shook her head. "You go ahead. I haven't smoked that stuff in years."

But after Stevenson lit the joint and inhaled deeply, she reached for it and took a small puff, as if to be sociable, and then a bigger one. Then she coughed. They smoked the rest of the joint together, Stevenson taking big puffs and Diana little ones, both of them dousing the burning in their throats with margaritas. Then they sat side by side on the couch, each in a trance.

At one point, Diana got up to change the music. She stood staring at her tape collection, apparently unable to make up her mind.

Stevenson gazed at her. The fact that she looked so appealing, he thought, would make this sexless relationship even more meaningful. He was intrigued by it. If Diana was just a friend, he could go back to Estela with nothing to hide, and be a father to their child—assuming she wasn't lying about being pregnant. He imagined playing with his little bilingual child in Ascarate Park, and taking pictures.

He thought about having Diana over to have dinner with him and Estela in the barrio. What language would they speak? He'd probably have to interpret, a job that would be easier once he really tackled Spanish. That was something he'd do soon, take a Spanish course at UTEP.

By the time Diana picked out the music and returned to the couch, Stevenson was visualizing his life as a border version of *The Cosby Show*. He now felt very close to Diana. By asking him these questions about his visit, she'd helped him come to terms with his own thinking. His return to Estela— and the baby—might not have happened if Diana hadn't pushed him.

"I'm really glad I came over here," he said to her.

She didn't respond for a second, and then said, "Huh?"

"I'm glad I came over."

"I don't think I should have smoked that pot," she said. "I feel...pretty weird."

She got up slowly and made her way back to the stereo.

She bent over and turned it down. Walking back to the sofa, she wobbled a little, and then plopped down, the outside of her thigh landing on his. Stevenson gaped at her face, about six inches from his.

He could see the faint black hairs on her upper lip. He could smell her. It wasn't a perfumed scent, like Estela's, but clean and human, maybe with a touch of soap. He studied her neck, the black hairs pulled up and clamped with a barrette. He blew lightly on the spot and saw goosebumps rising like little waves when a breeze blows across a lake. He considered the brown mole he'd been eyeing earlier. He wondered if this sexless friendship could survive just a little dry kiss on the mole. He leaned over, breathed in her fragrance, and brushed it with the outside of his lips.

Diana exhaled softly, as if releasing all the tension between them. She pivoted slowly, wrapped her arms around his neck, and fell back on the couch, pulling Stevenson on top of her, searching with her mouth for his.

Chapter
FIFTEEN

The police chief, barely visible behind a huge metal desk, was talking on the phone when they delivered Harley to the door of the dark office. Upon seeing Harley, the chief spoke a few words into the phone and hung up.

He flashed a smile and rose to his feet. Even upright, most of him remained hidden by the desk. "Roberto Muller, Mr. Harley. Please have a seat."

Harley wordlessly sat down on a folding chair and brushed his hand through his hair. Instinctively he reached into his back pocket for his reporter's notebook, but then decided to leave it there, since his status—as reporter or prisoner—was uncertain.

"I appreciate your coming by," Muller said in perfect English. He sat down behind his large desk and nearly dropped out of sight. "I understand we had you... How should I say...cooped up for a while. Sorry about that. Must have been a misunderstanding."

"That's okay," Harley said, barely whispering. He assumed the chief knew about the joint.

The small man shifted his chair and pulled his elbows up on the desk, bringing his face into view. He fiddled with his fingertips, linking them in the form of a church roof. He had a round, fleshy face and thinning brown hair combed across his head. He looked like a short German butcher, or maybe a well-fed accountant.

"Okay," Muller finally said, exhaling slowly. "Let's be frank. I had you brought in here. You know that. I'm sure you know why."

Harley nodded slightly. He found the little chief's precise English, so unusual along the border, a bit disorienting.

"How about this?" Muller said, standing up again. "We'll sit over on those easy chairs and have a talk, you and I. You tell me what you're looking for. I tell you the same. I bet we'll both come out of this meeting with a much clearer view of things."

He walked across the dingy linoleum floor to an even darker corner of the office, where a pair of Naugahyde easy chairs and a sofa were arranged around a coffee table. The only light came from two dim electric candles on the wood-paneled wall. Between them hung a photo of the Mexican president, with a green, red, and white sash over his shoulder.

"Since I initiated this meeting," Muller said as they sat down, "how about if I start by telling you what's on my mind?"

"Fine," Harley said.

"I'm sure you've heard all sorts of nasty things about the Judicial State Police. I'm sure you have because you've published some of them in your paper."

Harley made signs of protesting, but Chief Muller raised his small hands for a moment and continued. "I heard many of those things myself before I took this job. And many of them, I'm very sorry to say, are true. We have people here who are intimately—in-tim-ate-ly—associated with all sorts of criminal activity. You know that. I know that. Why should I hide it from you?"

He smiled for an instant and proceeded. "When I took this job, I told the governor—you know, he and I are both members of the opposition party, the PAN—I told him: 'Governor, I don't think I can straighten out the *Policia Estatal Judicial* all by myself. That would be like the task Hercules faced in cleaning the Augean stables.' You're familiar with the story?"

Harley smiled. "You'd have to reroute the Rio Grande through this building."

"Well, the governor—he's a very inspiring man—he told me to do the best I could. So here I am." He paused as if expecting a question. But Harley didn't know what to make of him.

"Now I hear that you were hoping to visit Gustavo Jiménez's house this afternoon..."

"Yes," Harley said. "You know that business with Eddie Stevenson, the photographer, and then the...the threat he brought back for me, it's raised a lot of questions."

"But you're aware that Jiménez left yesterday," the chief said.

"Where'd he go?"

The chief shrugged. "Who knows? South. I suppose I could find out if I wanted. But Gustavo Jiménez, he's not a man to be taken terribly seriously." He saw a look of astonishment on Harley's face. "I hope you didn't lose sleep over that death threat," the chief said. "Jiménez is just...a playboy. A rake. Do you use that word anymore? I very seriously doubt that he was involved with your photographer. And if he was, he was having a little fun, maybe drunk. He's never hurt a fly."

"How about the reporter who had his lungs..."

"Oh, that wasn't Jiménez's work," the chief said, with a dismissive wave of his hand.

"But people said..."

"Oh, yes. But he's just a..." For the first time, he struggled for an English word. "*Chivo expiatorio?*"

"Scapegoat," Harley said.

"Exactly. He's often used in that manner. He might face some problems resulting from this incident with your newspaper. He could even land in jail. I suppose that's why he left. But really, Mr. Harley, Gustavo Jiménez is quite an innocent, in fact, something of a simpleton. If I had only to worry about people like him, this would be a much simpler job."

The chief thought about it for a second, and conceded, "Well, I guess he does run a bit of the drug business..."

"Do you know him?" Harley asked.

"Gustavo? Of course. Everyone knows him."

At that point, Chief Muller jumped to his feet. "I've been extremely rude, Mr. Harley. Can I get you a cup of coffee, tea, *agua mineral?*"

Harley asked for a Coke.

The chief leaned out of his office and ordered a Coke and a coffee. Then he came back and pulled a box of Marlboros out of his shirt pocket and held out the box toward Harley. "It would be rude not to offer," he said, taking a cigarette for himself and tapping it on his thumbnail. "But I know Americans don't smoke anymore. At least Americans like you."

After the chief lit his cigarette, Harley asked him who, in his judgment, had beaten up Stevenson.

"Could be anybody," the chief said. "Probably not a very intelligent person. Might be a couple of my men. Who's to say?" He shrugged, pushing his chin up again. "If I had to guess, I'd say your friend Stevenson probably has relations that none of us knows much about, that he's compromised in some way. Could be money, maybe love. But I must say, I haven't delved into it. Despite the diplomatic stir and all the headlines, no charges have been filed. I can understand Mr. Stevenson's reluctance to come over here again to press charges. But until he does, we don't investigate."

"So," Harley said, "if Jiménez is an innocent dummy, which criminals around here cause the real problems?"

The chief sighed. "I'll be happy to tell you. But let's first order something to eat. If I'm going to tell you about crime here, we have to talk about politics and economics of the border. It's quite a long story."

Chapter
SIXTEEN

The lanky one with the short pants showed up at Estela's apartment at night, and by noon the next day, he'd already turned the living room into an extension of himself. First he scraped the tar and sludge from the sides of Eddie's glass pipe and then smoked it, stinking up the apartment. By breakfast time, his papers and clothes were piled on the coffee table, and he was busy scraping more tar out of the water pipe, followed by more smoking and coughing. Despite all this, Estela thought, Gato had a friendly smile.

But now that Gato's friend was moving in, things were getting more complicated. Estela had no idea where he'd sleep. This new arrival, Pascual, dressed better than Gato and seemed far neater. But Estela hadn't seen him smile yet. He sat on the edge of the sofa, reading a tattered book he carried, and then studying a map of El Paso. More than once, she heard him swearing under his breath.

Estela was drying dishes in the kitchen, eavesdropping, when she heard Pascual say something to Gato about a stolen car. Gato burst into a fit of laughter that was cut short by what sounded like a punch.

Estela glanced into the living room to see Gato struggling for breath and Pascual shaking his right hand as if he'd burned it.

"*Todo bien?*" she asked them. They both nodded, and she retreated to the kitchen.

If these were Rubén's friends, they were probably the ones who helped him beat up Eddie. It didn't matter much to Estela. Her life was full of men hitting women, the way Eddie hit her, and then men hitting men, usually while drinking. Estela's bruises were clearing up, and she imagined Eddie's were too. But Eddie was gone, and she had to find a new place to live.

Briefly, she held out hope that the tall *gringo* who spoke such nice Spanish, Tomás, might take her in. But when she got close to him, he ran away like a cat splashed by water. He was different from Eddie. He probably didn't hit women, if he had anything to do with them at all.

The sun was setting. Out the kitchen window, Estela could see the sky darkening from pink to red over Juárez, right over the mountain with big white letters on its side: *Lee la Biblia, Es la Verdad.*

When she first moved up from Villa Ahumada, she lived with some cousins in a tin-roofed shack at the foot of that mountain. It used to take her two hours in buses to get from her house to work at the *maquiladora*. She did that for a few months, spending four hours a day on the buses, and another eight threading little silver and copper wires into a piece of white rubber that looked like macaroni.

Then one afternoon she ran into Rubén, her childhood neighbor from Villa Ahumada. He was speaking English with an American on *Avenida Juárez* and was carrying a load of books under his arm. She didn't recognize him, but he remembered her. After she walked by him, he followed her, yelling, "Estelita!"

At first, she thought Rubén had a crush on her and was

shy. He couldn't look at her eyes and he fidgeted with his silver ring, taking it off his finger and spinning it around his baby fingernail, like those wheels that mice run around in pet-shop windows.

One day, he asked her out to dinner. Estela wore stockings and her best black dress, a tight one with a slit up the leg, and heels and a necklace made of little white shells that her aunt had brought back from Guaymas. Dressed like that, she waited for three-quarters of an hour in front of a juice bar on *Calle* Guanajuato, fighting off waves of men.

She expected Rubén to pick her up in a car and take her to a fancy restaurant in El Paso. This would be her first trip north of the border, and she was excited. But when Rubén showed up, he was on foot, wearing dirty blue jeans and a sleeveless T-shirt, which made him look scrawnier than ever. They ate at *La Nueva Central*, a Juárez café that felt like a bus station. Rubén ordered enchiladas and coffee for both of them, and then talked about politics and newspapers and the *maquiladoras*, drinking cup after cup of coffee. He talked about "*explotación.*" If that meant bad pay at the factory, Estela agreed. That night he still couldn't look at her eyes.

Estela carried a load of clean clothes from the bedroom of her apartment into the living room and dumped them on the floor. Gato was asleep on the couch, snoring gently. Pascual paged through a pile of newspapers from Juárez and El Paso. He still had the El Paso map spread open on his lap. He paid no attention to Estela as she set up the ironing board and stretched out one of Eddie's white button-down shirts.

She decided to try talking to him. "Looking for a job?" she asked in Spanish.

He raised his head, bothered. "No. I already have work."

"On this side?"

"No, in Juárez."

"Oh." She started ironing. "I saw you with the map and the newspapers, and I figured you must be looking for work."

Pascual nodded and returned to the map.

"You have any dirty clothes, I can handle them," Estela said to Pascual.

"Not yet," he said, without looking up.

Did this mean they were staying for a while?

She flicked a bit of spit on the iron. It sizzled. She liked ironing. It helped her think.

She remembered how angry Rubén grew as he told her about his disappointments in journalism. They were sitting in that same café, *La Nueva Central*, where they'd had their first dinner. He had been treated unfairly, he told her, and his work was lost. After he described the process—in far too much detail for Estela—he sat stewing. Estela remembered watching the muscle of his clenched jaw. It danced as if a horsefly was trapped inside. After that dinner, they walked across the Paso del Norte bridge to a bar in El Paso. That was where she met Eddie Stevenson.

Early on, Rubén seemed to appreciate Eddie, and even encouraged Estela to cozy up to him. Back then, Stevenson was working on a border project for the paper, and was planning to move into South El Paso. If Estela moved in with him, she could quit her $11-a-day job at the assembly plant. At the same time, the relationship offered Rubén a journalism connection, possibly a valuable one. As he saw it, Estela was like his sister, which made Stevenson practically an in-law, a *cuñado*. Rubén could drop in anytime. Maybe he and Stevenson would collaborate on projects. This gave him a foot in the door of the *El Paso Tribune*.

But it never developed into anything, mostly because Eddie Stevenson was lazy. "I already work at work," he would tell Rubén between hits on his bong. "Why would I ever work in my free time?" When Rubén asked him for an introduction to Duane Canfield, Stevenson brushed him off. "You don't have a college degree, right?"

"I've got seventeen credits," Rubén said.

"Yeah, well..." Stevenson performed a rueful shake of his head. "I don't think you're getting the picture," he said. "They're not *adding* jobs at the paper. They're *subtracting* them."

Estela didn't understand these conversations, but she could sense Rubén's growing frustration. That was what led him to start working across the river with these two guests of hers, Gato and Pascual.

It had been only a week earlier that Rubén asked her about the bruising on her face. When she told him that she was pregnant, and that Eddie hit her, he stormed around the apartment for a minute or two, even smashing a coffee cup on the kitchen counter. "That man is going to pay," he told her. But Estela didn't believe that he cared much. His face, she saw, was relaxed, his eyes bright. Any action he took, she suspected, would be for his journalism, not for her.

And that turned out to be the case. On the afternoon that Rubén showed her the newspaper with Eddie's picture on the front page, he assured her that it fit somehow into his career. This led Estela to wonder if she understood the word journalism—*periodismo*. She believed she did. But maybe on this side of the river, journalism was altogether different, a profession tied up with police work and punishment.

As she ironed, Estela saw that Pascual seemed puzzled about something in the newspaper. "Come here and take a look at this," he said, sounding a little friendlier. He opened up the *El Paso Tribune* editorial page and pointed to the words 'Editor in Chief: Ken Perry.' "This man here, is he the president of the paper?"

"Umm. I think so," Estela said.

"And where is the Thunderbird neighborhood?"

"Ahh, I think that's where rich people live. Come here." She led Pascual to the window, stepping over Gato's shoes and Pascual's knapsack. Estela leaned out and pointed north, to the darkening Franklin Mountains, now purple, with just a trace of pink at the top. "See those hills?"

Pascual gaped at her chest, where the blue fabric of the T-shirt was stretched tight. Then he glanced out the window.

"It's over there," she said. "On the west. It's called the Wessye."

Pascual nodded. "Listen," he said, fidgeting. "I have a bit of a problem with money. I have plenty back in Juárez, but I can't go over there until tomorrow, or maybe Saturday."

Estela nodded sympathetically. She understood financial problems.

"So," Pascual continued, "do you think I could have a little session on credit?"

"Session?" Estela asked, knowing what he meant, but playing for time.

Pascual grabbed her head with one hand, digging his fingers under her hair and pushing down towards his waist. With the other hand he unzipped his fly. "Just a little one," he whispered. "I won't even take off my pants."

Estela twisted free from him and swung a fist at his face. Pascual, still holding a handful of her hair, turned sideways. The punch caught him on the ear, sending his glasses flying. He tumbled, tripped over his knapsack, and fell backwards on the couch, landing on Gato's legs. Estela, pulled by her hair, fell on top of him.

Gato, his eyes still half-closed, surveyed the pile-up. "Hey Pascual," he said, "didn't your mama ever tell you not to pull girls' hair?"

Chapter
SEVENTEEN

The chief offered to send Harley back to the border in a cruiser, but the reporter wanted nothing to do with Mexican police cars. He said no, thanks, and the chief seemed to understand. He shook Harley's hand cordially, bowed slightly, and closed the door.

Harley made his way through the corridors back to the lobby. It was crowded, but the pastry vendor had gone. Outside it was dark and cool, and he smelled tortillas frying.

At first, he walked the wrong way down *Calle* Lerdo, eventually coming upon a strip bar called *La Lagunera*. A pink neon sign in the blackened window showed a garter-belted leg. He stood for a moment, looking at it. The detached limb reminded him of the little silver prayer charms the Mexicans offered to the Virgin—hearts, legs, arms, eyes, for whatever was afflicting them. He wondered which charm would do him the most good. A brain maybe?

A taxi driver came up behind him and whispered, "donkey show?"

"*Cómo?*"

"Donkey show, you wanna see?"

Harley heard *"Don Quichotte,"* and wondered for a moment why a Juárez taxi driver would be talking about *Don Quixote* in French.

"Girls," the driver said. "Pretty ones." He grimaced and pointed to *La Lagunera*. "But not here. Ugly! Fat!"

Usually a stickler for speaking Spanish in Mexico, Harley felt dreamy and found himself playing the *taxista*'s game. "What's a donkey show?" he asked in English.

The driver smiled and came close, gripping his arm.

Harley instinctively placed a hand on his wallet.

"You see a donkey? With a prick this long." The *taxista* put his hands a foot and a half apart. Harley could smell rum on his breath. "He does it with a very very beautiful woman," the man said, arching his eyebrows.

Harley wasn't feeling quite that quirky. "No, thanks," he said, striding off quickly towards brighter streetlights.

The driver ran alongside him. "It's worth the pain, my friend."

Harley eventually freed himself from the cab driver, but got lost in the process. Two women were calling to him. He walked away from them, toward a vacant lot. From there he could see the red lights on the radio towers atop the Franklin Mountains.

He directed his strides north. As he walked, he pulled out his wallet and checked to see if the cops had taken his money. He was gratified to see that they'd left him a $20 bill, along with a few receipts from bank machines.

It had been a bizarre meeting with the chief. Harley had quickly grown comfortable talking to him, even joking. But as they were finishing their liverwurst sandwiches, there was a knock on the door. The chief called out *"Pásale!"* and a man dressed in a waiter's black jacket entered carrying a white plastic tray. More food, Harley thought, as the man deposited the tray on the chief's desk, said *"Con permiso,"* and left.

Sitting on the tray was Harley's wallet. Next to it lay the flattened, curved joint. Harley felt a surge of panic.

The chief chuckled. He walked to the desk and tossed the wallet to Harley. "They told me about this," he said, holding the joint between his thumb and forefinger. "But I didn't pay any attention." He paused and then said, "It's quite surprising that they would plant something like this on you. Apparently they thought I needed more 'palanca.' How do you say that? Leverage. More leverage than I had." He smiled, holding the joint above a black waste-paper basket. "I suppose we should throw this away... Unless you want to smoke it?"

Harley shook his head violently. The chief chuckled again and let the joint fall into the basket. He didn't say another word about it.

But as Harley walked toward El Paso, he wondered if Chief Muller had quietly taken possession of him. How could he ever write critical articles about Muller, knowing that the chief could revive the drug case against him in the Mexican press?

Harley wondered what to do with all the history Muller gave him. It was more suited to a book than a daily newspaper. Muller outlined the power structure of Juárez. First, the chief said, there were the great landholders, like the Terrazas family, who owned pieces of Chihuahua that were bigger than states like Delaware and Rhode Island. Maybe even bigger than New Jersey. He wasn't sure.

This old money supported the ruling party, the PRI, and in exchange for that support, the government didn't expropriate their estates—or at least not too many of them—in the waves of land reform following the Mexican Revolution. The rural police served these landholders, breaking strikes at the sawmills and cotton plantations, scaring away rabble-rousers and revolutionary journalists, even killing a few. Muller smiled at Harley when he said that, and added, "But never Americans, as far as I can recall."

While the millionaires ran their *haciendas* in the

countryside, Juárez provided the nightlife for El Paso. There were all sorts of crimes and misdemeanors, and Juárez cops took bribes to look the other way. "They still do," Muller added matter-of-factly. The police also made money from Juárez's growing smuggling business, the chief said, "which is what brings you here." He smiled and Harley nodded.

Chief Muller took a sip of coffee and lit a cigarette. In the '60s, he said, lots of new players came to the Juárez area. America's drug appetite grew, which brought the *narcos*, who quickly established joint ventures with the local police. At the same time, industry came to the area. That brought American managers to the border, where they met tens of thousands of poor Mexican workers coming north from Durango, Michoacán, even Mexico City.

At first, the American companies set up sewing operations. But in the '80s, when the Japanese started taking away American markets, U.S. companies moved all sorts of manufacturing south of the border. "TVs, auto harnesses. You know what those are? The whole electrical system in your car?"

Harley nodded.

To build and run these new factories, the chief said, the Americans required Mexican partners. "They had no need for the sons of Chihuahua planters, or bartenders or corrupt policemen. They needed sophisticated, bilingual businessmen, people who were as comfortable in El Paso—or Dallas or Chicago for that matter—as in Juárez."

"People like you," Harley said, flattering the chief.

"Since you mention it, yes," the chief said as he exhaled. "But they were really looking for entrepreneurs with a vision for the region. Do you know, by chance, Onofre Crispín?"

Harley said he didn't. But the name was familiar.

"You wrote about him, I believe, in a recent article," the chief said. "Perhaps you didn't get a chance to interview him for that piece of work."

Harley recalled Crispín's name from the article about Jiménez and the tigers. Diana Clements had mentioned Crispín, too. He blushed. "Oh. Right," he said, nodding.

The chief described Onofre Crispín and other entrepreneurs like him as a great modernizing force along the border. They were men, he said, who owed nothing to the PRI. "These are the people who are bringing North American civilization south into Mexico. And I'm not talking only about foreign investment. They are also introducing new political ideas in Mexico. Many of them, you know, are members of PAN, the Party of *Acción Nacional.*"

"But it seems like the president is leading this revolution, and he's with the PRI," Harley said.

The chief nodded gravely. "But in his heart he's a *Panista.*"

Muller went on at length about Onofre Crispín. He was a graduate of Southern Methodist University, he said, fluent in English, a patron of the arts, a season-ticket holder of the Dallas Cowboys, perhaps a future governor of Chihuahua or—who could say?—President of Mexico. "If you want to learn about what's really happening here," he said, looking sternly at Harley, "you must talk to Crispín." He went to his intercom and ordered a secretary to bring Crispín's phone numbers for his guest.

Harley was still replaying the conversation with the chief that night as he paid a peso and walked across the bridge to El Paso. He was almost at the Paso del Norte Hotel, at the juncture between the barrio and downtown, when he remembered, with a start, that he'd left his car parked in Juárez. For a moment, he considered going back for it. But what would he do if he walked back there and didn't find it? Go to the police?

He walked into the Tiffany Dome Bar at the Paso del Norte and ordered a beer.

Chapter
EIGHTEEN

Diana Clements lay in bed listening to Eddie Stevenson's gentle snores, wondering if her superstitions had landed her with another loser. He wouldn't be the first. Outside that party, he had seemed so forward and direct. But while they drank margaritas, he was just feeding her a bunch of lines and waiting for sex.

Now, at three in the morning, with Eddie asleep beside her, Diana could feel a hangover coming. And her throat was scratchy from smoking that joint. She went into the bathroom for water and an Advil. Maybe she'd dump him in the morning. It wasn't as if they'd invested much in each other. Stevenson didn't know about her break-up with Raymond or her job at the bank. He didn't know where she was from.

She returned to bed and was surprised to find him awake.

"Cotton mouth?" he asked.

"Yeah."

"Me too."

"There's Advil in the bathroom, if you want."

"Thanks." He got up and made some noise in the

bathroom. Then he was back. Diana expected him to fall asleep. But instead, Stevenson propped himself on one elbow and considered her bedroom for the first time, studying the Matisse print she had over the desk and the bunch of red chile peppers that hung on the white wall between the windows. Then he pointed to a window and said, "Look at the moon framed by those cypress trees. Looks like Greece or Italy."

She nodded, remembering that he was a photographer.

"You can see the Juárez mountains in the moonlight," he said.

Diana twisted in the bed and looked. "Where?"

He pointed. "Out there."

"That's the hedge."

"No, no. Over there, see?"

"That's the roof of the Circle K."

"Oh. Yeah."

Then he rolled over and fell asleep.

Diana lay awake, wondering what she was getting into. Just two years before, in B-School, she seemed to have so many friends, and so many choices. But when she followed Raymond to El Paso, the whole world got narrow in a hurry. Raymond left her for another woman at his law firm, and Diana found herself alone on the border.

She was stranded halfway between Dallas and L.A., not rich enough to quit her job at the bank, and hating men. She began to hang out with Elke and her lesbian friends, who were fun and a little crazy. She went dancing with them a few times, but wasn't interested in sex. The night she met Eddie Stevenson, Elke had said that her friends didn't want her to bring Diana around anymore. They weren't interested in Elke's failed projects.

So later that night, when Eddie read her palm, Diana was in a receptive mood.

Looking at him curled up in bed, scratching his nose in his sleep and then rolling over, she felt disgusted with herself for following signs and superstitions. At some point she had to stop taking what was thrown her way. She'd known that for a long time.

She wondered if there was something wrong with her. She asked herself for the thousandth time why Raymond had left her. At first it was simple enough to explain: he wanted a woman who shared his passions—for law, cocaine, money, and golf. But now, lying beside this snoring photographer, she wondered if Raymond had spotted some defect in her. It was a question she'd buried for months.

She thought about it, watching a breeze ripple the white curtain. The wind picked up. She heard a plastic bottle rolling down the street. A garbage can lid blew off and clanged on the sidewalk. Clouds covered the moon, and she heard the first thick drops of rain ping on the metal awning over her porch.

By morning, the rain was gone, leaving behind just a slow dripping from the gutter. Through the open window, she could smell the charcoal odor of desert creosote, which followed every rain.

She opened her eyes, expecting to see Eddie Stevenson. But he was gone. He'd snuck out to avoid the morning after, she thought, hating him, and hating herself for inviting him in, especially when she knew he was lying about Estela. She felt abused and angry.

She took a shower, practicing what she'd say to Eddie when she saw him again. She dried herself and wrapped the towel around her hair. When she walked out of the bathroom, wearing only the turban, she saw Eddie standing at the doorway, carrying a bunch of red carnations and a bag of bagels. "Jesus!" she said, covering herself with her arms.

"Come here," he said tenderly.

"No, wait a minute." She felt confused. "Let me get dressed first." She pointed at a window. "The neighbors..."

Dropping this guy wasn't going to be quite as easy as she'd thought. By the time she came out of the bedroom, wearing a dark blue dress with black buttons up the front, he had set up breakfast, with cappuccinos and bagels, the carnations in a vase. He'd even cleaned up the margaritas and chips from the night before.

Stevenson appeared startled to see her in business clothes. "I forgot you had a fancy job," he said. "It's not a law firm, is it?" he asked.

"Finance."

"Oh. I was going to say that if you were a lawyer, maybe you could handle the case if I decide to sue the paper."

Diana sat down and reached for a bagel. "I could help you invest the money if you win," she said.

"I don't know. It probably won't turn into anything..." He took a bite of a bagel, and cream cheese spilled out the sides of his mouth.

"At some point," Diana said, averting her eyes while he wiped his face, "we're going to have to talk about what we're doing here."

Stevenson, his mouth full, nodded. After swallowing, he said, "But not today..."

"When?"

He shrugged.

"I don't think you're being straight with me about Estela."

"We broke up," he said.

"Hmm."

"I can't believe you went over there," he said, shaking his head. "We hardly knew each other."

"We do now."

Anxious to change the subject, Stevenson sipped his cappuccino and grimaced. "I still have this cut in my mouth. It's a little sensitive."

"So I was saying," Diana continued, "I don't think she knows you've broken up."

"I thought you didn't understand her Spanish."

"Not much... She was ironing a big pile of your shirts. I'm

guessing they were yours."

Stevenson smiled. "She's a nut about ironing."

Diana looked straight at him, waiting for a serious answer.
He took another drink of coffee and put down the paper
cup. "Listen," he said, "there's some things I guess I should tell
you. This whole thing isn't probably as simple as it looks." He
went on to describe Estela's friendship with Rubén, and
Rubén's ties to the drug world as he understood them. He
didn't mention that Estela was pregnant, or that he'd hit her.

"And you think this guy, Rubén, set up this whole beating
in Mexico because of something related to Estela?" she asked.

"I don't know why he did it. But I'm pretty sure he was
involved. I think I even heard his voice once. And Estela knows
about it. She has to. So I'm staying away from her..."

Diana leaned back in her chair, twirling a bit of hair by her
ear with one finger and waiting for Stevenson to say more.
She enjoyed conversations like this. They gave her a sense of
power.

"She and I weren't right for each other, anyway," Eddie
said. "Nothing like you and me."

Diana let that one pass.

"But the story you told the paper..." she said.

"I wasn't going to spill out my whole private life! Anyway,
I told them the truth. Just left out a few details."

"A few crucial details."

Stevenson shrugged.

Diana pressed on. "Did you tell Tom Harley about those
details?"

"Ahhhh. Yeah. For the most part. He knows what's going
on."

"What, you called him from Truth or Consequences?"

"No. Before I left."

She cleared her throat.

"He wasn't there," Stevenson said, as if recalling. "But I
left a message on his machine. Told him not to get all bent out

of shape. But I didn't think it was going to turn into such a big stink..."

"He doesn't have a machine."

"Yeah he does."

She shook her head. "He hates them."

Stevenson started to protest. But Diana glanced at her watch and stood up. "I'm late," she said. She rushed around the apartment, gathering her purse and car keys. "Just one more thing," she said as she opened the door. "Why did you follow me out that night, after the party?"

Stevenson, relieved by the change of subject, smiled. "It was either you or that friend of yours," he said. "It was a no-brainer."

Chapter
NINETEEN

"It's open, *Está abierto*," Claudio shouted.

Rubén, holding a manila envelope, opened the door. He peered in to see his former professor in a black silk bathrobe, vacuuming the living room floor.

"Look who's here," Claudio said, surprised. He hurried to unplug the machine. "Lemme just put this stuff away and..." He disappeared with the vacuum cleaner into the bedroom.

Rubén sat on the couch, holding the large envelope on his knees. He stared at a large Aztec statue in the corner. It had a blue face and huge round eyes, and wore a jagged crown on its head.

"Want a cup of tea?" Claudio shouted from the bedroom.

"Yeah, sure," Rubén said.

Claudio emerged still in bare feet, wearing khakis and a grey T-shirt, his greying hair gathered in a ponytail, horn-rimmed glasses sliding down his nose. "Two for tea," he said.

"Who's that?" Rubén asked, pointing his chin toward the statue.

"Oh, that's Tlaloc, the rain god," Claudio said. "My father

picked it up somewhere in Morelos, I think in Tlayacapan, or maybe it was Tepoztlán..."

"He looks incredibly pissed off," Rubén said.

"Maybe rain gods aren't happy in the desert," Claudio said, chuckling at his little joke.

Rubén, no longer interested in the statue, had picked up the newspaper from the coffee table, with its headline about Operation Blockade. "This won't last," he said, shaking his head. "The Latinos are too strong here to put up with it."

"Latinos are some of the ones who want to keep the Mexicans out," Claudio said. "You should have seen all the letters to the editor we got at the paper. 'This is an American city, you should cover American news, signed, Juan Torres, El Paso.' And the paper's playing right into it," he said, "tying everything in Mexico to drugs."

"That's sort of what I came to talk to you about," Rubén said.

Claudio had moved to the kitchen, where he was pouring drinking water from a big glass jug into a teapot. He put the teapot on the stove, lit it, took down teabags and a jar of sugar, and then dried off two delicate Chinese teacups and saucers. Walking back into the living room, he said, "You come here to talk about the *Tribune*?"

"About the journalism in it," said Rubén. He opened the manila envelope and dumped dozens of newspaper clippings, marked with blue ink and yellow highlighter, onto the coffee table.

"This is a case in point about everything I've been telling you," he said earnestly. "It's so fucked up, man." He paused and tried to clean up his language. "Excuse me. I mean what they did with this story." He started to arrange the clippings into small piles. "It's all lies and make-believe. *Es una farsa.*"

"You came here to tell me that?"

"I want to go through this story with you and show you how wrong everything is."

"And then what?" Claudio asked.

Rubén shrugged. "Then I'll leave."

"No, I mean, what do you accomplish by showing me that the *Tribune* does sloppy work? I don't work there anymore."

"First I'll show you how they're doing the story wrong. Then I'll do it right," Rubén said. He looked up at Claudio, who was standing by the coffee table, scanning the piles of clippings.

"I don't see where I fit in," Claudio said.

"You'll be my editor."

The teapot started to whistle. "So now you think you need an editor," Claudio said, disappearing into the kitchen. "That's quite a concession, coming from you, Rubencito."

Claudio and Rubén had worked closely together on the community college newspaper, *Semana*, the previous school year. Claudio was faculty adviser. Rubén, his most talented student, edited the paper and reported all the big stories. He wasn't much of a writer at that point. He still thought in Spanish, Claudio believed, and struggled with English grammar.

But in twenty years in journalism, Claudio had never seen a more tenacious reporter. By the end of his first semester, Rubén was out-reporting the *Journal* and the *Tribune* at City Hall and on drugs.

His biggest splash came at the community college itself. In the course of his drug reporting, he found out that a director was funneling most of the college construction projects to his cousin's company. At first, Rubén didn't quite see the story. Claudio had to define conflict of interest for him. The notion was foreign to Rubén, who assumed that the whole point of any business was to make connections, and then to cash in on them.

Even when they published the story, and the director was fired, Rubén was far from satisfied. He was convinced that the self-dealing at the community college was only a thread of a much bigger story, one involving drug money and politics and both sides of the border. He would write a blockbuster on drug trafficking, he told Claudio. It would rock the power elite in El Paso. He already had reporting on it, he said.

One afternoon, Claudio sat down with Rubén to review the developing story. Rubén had a box full of five-by-seven cards, with the confirmed facts in red ink and conjecture in pencil. He spread them across Claudio's desk, and then unfolded a map of El Paso and Juárez. It was covered with little boxes connected by arrows. This was the drug network, he said, with its tentacles reaching from the border assembly industry into city hall.

Claudio had a hard time focusing on all the boxes and arrows, but the cards were clear enough. The confirmed facts in red ink pointed to what appeared to be a run-of-the-mill drug story. They included tonnage figures for exports and imports, the number of addicts in El Paso and elsewhere, and a Who's Who of *narcos* in the north of Mexico. In the red ink, Claudio didn't see any high-impact stories.

But the penciled conjecture was incendiary. It pointed to business connections between members of the City Council and the *maquiladora* magnate of Juárez, Onofre Crispín. It drew lines between Mexico's ruling Institutional Revolutionary Party, Colombian drug lords, and the local Republican committee in El Paso. NAFTA fit in too, though Claudio couldn't understand how. On one card, Rubén, apparently in a burst of excitement, had written: "If proven, this could destroy both the Bush family and General Motors Corp."

Claudio told Rubén to narrow the focus of the story. "To prove it all," he said, "would be like trying to win ten Pulitzers at the same time."

"But they're all little pieces of the same big story," Rubén said.

In the end, Claudio ordered him off the drug story. To his surprise, Rubén didn't fuss too much about it. He cheerfully shifted his focus from scandal to cuisine, writing a story about growing vegetarianism in Tex-Mex food. For the last issue of the year, he splashed the Tex-Mex story across the front page. It was a strange choice, Claudio thought at the time. But instead of looking into it further, he simply fixed a slew of spelling and grammar mistakes on the page, okayed it, and left for a weekend of water skiing in Elephant Butte.

When Claudio returned to the college the following Monday, he was shocked to see the new *Semana* in the racks. Gone was the vegetarian story. In its place was a screaming misspelled headline about money "lawndering." Beneath it was a familiar map of El Paso and Juárez, with arrows connecting little boxes on both sides of the Rio Grande.

Claudio managed to reclaim 1,493 copies of the paper. He kept one for himself, locking it in his bottom desk drawer as a memento, and destroyed the others. That meant that only six were circulating. And those six, it appeared, never made it to the newspapers or TV. *Semana* escaped the incident without facing a single libel suit, which Claudio considered a small miracle.

Still, he had to discipline Rubén. After much soul-searching, he suspended him from the newspaper for a year. Rubén seemed unfazed. He dropped out of school and continued investigating the drug market in Juárez. Claudio often wondered if he was investigating from the inside, dealing drugs—making money from his sources: The kid still wouldn't recognize a conflict of interest if it bit him.

Claudio walked into the living room carrying two cups of steaming tea. He wants me to be his editor, he thought sadly, looking at the skinny young man hunched over the clippings, and he doesn't have anywhere to publish.

Claudio pushed aside a few of the clippings and set down the teacups.

"Here's what's wrong," Rubén said. "First, this Stevenson goes over to Juárez. He's stoned out of his brain. He drives over there and eats lunch at Julio's—you know Julio's, on *16 de Septiembre?*—He drinks margaritas there, and then he goes over to the hotel, the *Xanadu*, and starts taking pictures. Now in that condition, how the hell does he know who he was talking to?"

"How do you know all this?" Claudio asked.

"There," Rubén said, pointing at him. "You're a good journalist. You ask me about my sources. You ask me how I know and I'll tell you. But the editors at the *Tribune*, that *huevón* Canfield... Stevenson comes back from Juárez probably still smelling of tequila and pot, and he says he's been beaten up by a drug lord, and they put it across the front page. No further questions!"

"I was wondering about that myself," Claudio said, sipping his tea. "It's as if they..."

"As if they would print anything about Mexico and drugs!" Rubén said.

"But I'm sure Stevenson must have known who he was dealing with," Claudio said. "They just forgot to write that part into the story."

"He didn't know!" Rubén shouted.

"How do you know?"

"I have my sources," Rubén said, pursing his lips to suppress a smile.

"Get out of here."

"I'm not kidding."

"And your sources tell you he was stoned and drunk?"

"Exactly."

"And how about the rest of it? Were you watching him drink margaritas at Julio's too?"

"No. That I got from my sources."

"And you won't tell me who they are."

"With time, with time," Rubén said, holding back another smile.

Claudio stood up. "You're just playing stupid games with

me, Rubén. You want to tell me something, but you want me to beg you for it. I'm not going to do it." He carried his teacup into the kitchen and shouted back. "You want me to be your editor, and you don't even have anywhere to publish." Then he stuck his head out from the kitchen and barked at Rubén. "I don't care about your conspiracy theories."

"Okay, okay," Rubén said, jumping to his feet. "Sorry, sorry. Do you have any idea what kind of a prick this Stevenson is? He punches Estela in the face."

Claudio stared at him, startled by his change in tack. "What's that have to do with the story?"

"Nothing. I just thought you should know."

"That's a big problem, and it's not just in Mexico."

"Stevenson's not Mexican," Rubén said.

"So what?"

"You said it was a problem in Mexico. He's not Mexican."

"What in the world are you getting at?"

"Forget about it." Rubén sat down again and picked up the clippings. "Let me just tell you what I think about this story, and then I'll leave you to your vacuuming. Here's what I think: The papers here will print anything sensational they hear about Mexico, with no questions asked. I want to prove that. I want to show exactly how bad they are. I want to expose them."

Claudio took a deep breath. "Everybody already knows these papers are...not so great, Rubén," he said. "It's not an exposé if you show that a bad paper is bad. Now if you did it with the *New York Times*..."

"But I'm going to show everything, step by step," Rubén said, "how they take lies in Mexico and turn them into headlines here. Don't you see how important it is?" He waved his clipped copy of the Stevenson kidnapping story. "This is a lie, and they print it as truth. And so people here think that Mexicans are animals. *Unas bestias.*"

"I think your time would be better spent discovering the

truth yourself, and worrying less about other people's lies," Claudio said, piling the clippings back into the manila envelope and stealing a sip from Rubén's tea, which was untouched. "And anyway, you haven't proven to me that the story's based on lies. I think those *narcos* are after him. There was this guy the other day who came in looking for..."

"For who?" Rubén asked.

"Harley," Claudio said, pointing upstairs. "You know, the reporter who lives above me."

"He does?" Rubén lifted the teacup to his mouth and put it down, apparently remembering that Claudio had drunk from it. "What makes you think the guy was after him?"

"He was looking at the mailboxes, and when I came out he ran away and hid in the bushes by the overpass."

"What'd he look like?"

"Sort of a preppy."

"You report it to the police?"

"No. For all I know, he might have been a student at UTEP. Still, I was a little suspicious."

"You tell Tom Harley about it?"

"I haven't seen him," Claudio said. "He's staying some-where else... And as I say, I can't blame him. I think some nasty people are after him, for some reason or another. It sure isn't for breaking great stories."

"You don't think he's much of a reporter?"

"I don't know if he wants to be."

"How about Hank Klinger?" Rubén asked. "Is he hot?"

"Rubén," Claudio said, "when you use the word "hot" like that, it means 'sexy.'"

Rubén flushed. "I meant is he..."

"He's Canfield's favorite," Claudio said, relaxing on the couch as he settled into shoptalk. "He's ignorant as hell, but a pretty good reporter."

"You think he'll do pretty well with this drug reporting?"

"I don't know," Claudio said. "I know he doesn't speak

Spanish. I can see him swallowing a lot of different lines over there. He's very eager."

Rubén coughed and suppressed a smile. "How about Ken Perry?" he said. "You think he'll stick with this story?"

"All the guys he plays golf with are going to start getting on his case for trashing free trade," Claudio said. "I can't see him sticking with it too long unless there's a real upside for him, like a big award. I know he wants a Pulitzer. But the idea that he could win one at that paper, with that reporting, is a joke."

"But he still believes it, right?"

"He's delusional, I guess," Claudio said, standing up.

Rubén gathered his paper and envelope from the table and stepped toward the door. "I'm going to keep on this. I know you think it's crazy, but you'll see," he said. "Next time I'll come with documentation."

"I'll look at it, I guess," Claudio said. "But don't get all catty with me about your sources."

Chapter
TWENTY

Duane Canfield called Harley "a goddamn pussy," and pulled him by the elbow into Ken Perry's corner office.

Perry, talking on the phone, gestured for two of them to sit down. Canfield immediately sank back in the couch while Harley sat erect on the edge.

"...We may have to pay more," Perry was saying. "Well, someplace in this city, there must be an American who'll clean a house... Okay, I'll ask around." He signed off and took in his two visitors.

"I told you that goddamn blockade was going to make life miserable," he complained to Canfield. "My kid won't eat breakfast. He's crying for María, María, María..."

Canfield nodded. "We should probably go ahead and do a disruption story today, don't you think?"

"Just send a reporter and photographer to Thunderbird. It's a slam dunk."

"That seems too pat," Canfield said. "The poor people up by the country club without their maids and gardeners. How about if we look for some middle-class folks that are hurting from the blockade. People you wouldn't expect."

"Thunderbird *is* middle class," Perry answered, stiffening in his chair. "That's where the problem is. I know."

"Okay, okay." Canfield waved both hands in surrender.

"So," Perry said, putting the unlit pipe in his mouth and leaning back in his chair, "why were you calling Tom a pussy? My wife even heard that one."

"Harley here got arrested and locked down in a Mexican jail yesterday, and he doesn't want to go with the story. Says it'll burn his sources," Canfield said.

"I didn't say it would burn them," Harley said. "But we'll get more mileage out of them if we don't blow this thing out of proportion."

"You know what a euphemism is, Harley?" Canfield said. "You probably know how to say it in six languages. Getting more mileage out of sources by not blowing things out of proportion is a eu-phem-i-sm for not burning 'em."

Harley weighed the semantics. "I think a euphemism has to be one word..." he started to say, but Perry interrupted him, asking if he'd really been thrown into a Mexican jail.

"It wasn't exactly jail," Harley said. "Just a room. They had me there for a couple hours. But I think it was all just a misunderstanding."

"But you were arrested?"

"Picked up. A cruiser stopped me when I was heading east, to Jiménez's house."

"And the cop knew who you were?"

"Of course he knew who he was!" Canfield said. "He took him to the station, where they booked him. And then they locked him up for four hours. And Harley doesn't think it's worth writing about."

Canfield heaved forward on the couch. "I'm going to call in Klinger," he said. "He's going to interview you," he said to Harley. "And he's going to write a story based on your account. Meanwhile, you're going to write a sidebar, something about

My Goddamn Day in the Black Hole of Calcutta."

Harley nodded solemnly.

"I don't get it," Perry said. "Did they tell you when they arrested you that your reporting was anti-Mexican or something?"

"No," Harley said. "First the guy stops me and tells me I was speeding, which wasn't exactly true. Then, instead of waiting around for a few pesos, like they usually do, he pushes me into the cruiser and takes me to the station. And that's where they shut me up in the room."

"Harley," Canfield lectured, "you've been writing for years about Indian mating rituals, and what have you. Now you got a real story, and you have to put that anthropology behind you. If you weren't so busy looking for excuses for the Mexicans, you'd recognize official harassment when you see it. That's going to be the point of our coverage."

"But the chief just wanted to talk to me," Harley said. "That's why I was brought in. He was waiting the whole time I was in that room."

"Waiting to harass you," Canfield said.

"No. Just to talk."

"You're going to take his word for that? This jerk has you arrested and held, and you excuse it because he just wants to *talk*?"

"What'd he say?" Perry asked.

"We talked for about two hours."

"And became fast friends," Canfield said. He held up two fingers together. "Like this."

Harley didn't respond, but then remembered that he'd left his car over there. "I'd better go pick it up," he said.

"Jesus!" Perry said, throwing up his arms.

"It's probably gone by now," Canfield said. "Talk to Klinger and write your first-person piece. Then you two can both go car-hunting in Juárez."

◊

Klinger wasn't around to interview Harley; he was tracking down the new Border Patrol chief, whose grandfather long ago snuck across the border. So Harley sat down at his terminal and began to outline a first-person account of his day in Juárez. His problem was the joint. Writing the truth—that he unwittingly carried drugs into Mexico—would get him fired.

The choice boiled down to omitting the joint altogether and praying that the Mexicans wouldn't bring it up, or charging the Mexicans with planting it on him. The planting gave him a much better story, but of course it was a lie. And if he even mentioned cops planting a joint, Canfield would splash it across the front page, provoking the Mexicans to respond.

Harley was still tinkering with the lead when Canfield stopped by. Maybe, Harley thought, as the city editor approached, he could refocus his story on the interview with the police chief, and steer clear of his detention. "You know, I didn't get to tell you much about the talk I had with the police chief," he said.

"No, you didn't," Canfield said, resting a buttock on the corner of Harley's desk.

"He knows Jiménez. Says he's a small-timer, a scapegoat."

"That's 'cause he's in bed with him, right?"

"I don't think so," Harley said. "This police chief..."

"Is a model of civic virtue."

"I wasn't going to say that."

"Well, let me ask you," Canfield said. "Do you think Jiménez is a small-timer?"

"I don't know, yet."

"But you think we should tell our readers that maybe, just maybe, this vicious drug lord we've been screaming about is just a pussy cat?"

"Probably something between a pussy cat and one of those tigers prowling around his house."

"Well that's for you and Klinger to figure out," Canfield said, speaking like a teacher to a slow learner. He tapped the terminal screen. "In the meantime, write up your first-person story in a hurry. And put in lots of color."

Harley began to type:

Whoops. Something I forgot about when I made my television debut on a Thursday morning news show: The people who sent me a death threat might be tuning in.

It wasn't until later in the afternoon, when I found myself cloistered in a dingy cell at Juárez police headquarters, that I considered my potentially hostile viewers south of the border.

The adventure began around lunchtime on Thursday, four hours after appearing on El Paso Sunrise with my boss, Ken Perry. I'd answered a few questions about Gustavo Jiménez, the reputed drug lord who reportedly had referred to me on Monday as "dead meat." Since Jiménez had left Juárez on Wednesday, heading south, I felt a bit safer—safe enough, in fact, to venture into Juárez. My mistake was to announce my plan on TV.

A minute after I crossed the Free Bridge, a blue police cruiser was behind me, lights a-swirling.

The policeman, a Sgt. Pérez, seemed friendly and courteous, as he told me that I was speeding. But instead of extorting the usual dollar or two for a soft drink, he pushed me into his cruiser and hauled me off to the headquarters of the State Judicial Police.

As we worked our way through Juárez's congested traffic, I tried to remember exactly what I'd said on TV, knowing that it could be used against me. I didn't come up with much, since—truth be told—Ken Perry did virtually all of the talking.

I prepared to charge the police with harassment. But

then it occurred to me that if I was locked up in a cell, deep in the bowels of the Judicial Police Building, I could charge them with all sorts of crimes—and no one would hear me. I remembered that I was in a foreign country, one with no First Amendment protections and only a hazy recognition of legal concepts such as habeas corpus. This was enormously depressing.

Worst-case scenarios popped into my mind. If some child had been run over within the previous day or two, they could charge me with hit-and-run. Or maybe they could plant a marijuana cigarette or a packet of cocaine in my wallet. I gazed out the back window, at the bank towers of El Paso, and the gentle slopes of the Franklin Mountains, and I wondered when I would see them again up close.

One of my worst cases almost came true. As police officers inspected my documents, I heard one of them suggesting planting marijuana into my wallet. Clearly, he didn't know I understood Spanish. And I didn't let on. For a minute or two, several of them debated the idea. They might have implemented this strategy if one of them had had a joint handy. Luckily for me, none did.

Nevertheless, they called an armed guard, who escorted me down a seemingly endless corridor and finally shut me in a small room. For hours, the guard waited there while I pondered my grim future as an inmate.

But then I heard a voice outside my door. "Señor Harley," he said in Spanish. "The chief wants to talk with you." So I proceeded to the office of the Chief, Roberto Muller. He said that he merely wanted to talk with me. That was the reason for my arrest. And the delay? He said it was just an administrative mix-up.

Hours later, I emerged from the State Judicial Police Building. It was dark. I rushed north to El Paso on foot. So great was my hurry, in fact, that I forgot to pick up my car. I guess I'll go now to see if it's still there. Nah... On second thought, I'll wait a while.

Chapter
TWENTY-ONE

Pascual and Gato had never seen so much green in their lives. They marveled as they made their way past the country club. Its carpeted fairways stretched up the side of the desert mountain. They gawked at all the sprinklers in the residential neighborhood of Thunderbird, some of them sending the water in long waves back and forth, others whirling in circles. Passing in front of one lawn, where the water splashed onto the street, Gato stood still, spread his arms, and let the water rain down on his head and chest. "*Ay qué delicia!*" he said.

"Stop that," Pascual hissed, dancing away from the water. "You're making a spectacle of yourself."

Pascual had a vague plan for this excursion to Thunderbird. He and Gato would shoot holes in the windows of Ken Perry's house. Afterward, he'd call the paper, or maybe one of the Spanish-language radio stations, and claim responsibility in the name of Gustavo Jiménez.

Pascual hadn't discussed these plans with Gato. After Estela kicked them out, he merely told Gato that a contact in Thunderbird owed Rubén money, and that they could pick it up. Since they were running out of money and had nowhere to sleep, it seemed like a reasonable approach.

"Where's this contact going to be?" Gato asked.

"Cherry Hill," Pascual said. *"Veinticinco sesenta y cuatro Cherry Hill Lane."*

"How much does he owe?"

"Rubén doesn't remember. About $500, I think."

"Let's hurry," Gato said. "Once it gets dark, they start arresting people like us in neighborhoods like this."

◊

"It's just something I heard from a couple of the women at golf today." Ken Perry's wife, Karen, set the patio table for dinner as she delivered the rumors to her husband.

"An advertising boycott?"

"Something like that." Karen lit an orange candle and placed a platter of corn on the table. "They weren't that comfortable talking about it. But I thought I should tell you."

"For attacking NAFTA?"

"Uh huh." Karen disappeared into the kitchen and called Timmy to supper. She told him to turn off the TV. Then she returned with the butter and salt.

"Wait a minute, Honey. Slow down." Ken was pacing on the patio with a computer printout rolled up in his fist. "They said that if we didn't stop attacking the free trade agreement, their husbands might call an advertising boycott? That's what they said?"

"They said they were talking about it."

"And did they say anything about the drug lord beating the crap out of our photographer?"

"No."

"To hell with 'em," Ken muttered. He sat down and moved his place setting, and then spread the printout of his latest editorial on the glass-top table. When his wife and four-year-old son were seated, he began reading aloud. "'There comes a time, in the life of a community, when it has to unite together...' Ooooh. Unite together," he said under his breath, pulling out a pen and making a note. "That's superfluous, isn't it? I'll have to call in a fix on that one."

Karen, who was buttering an ear of corn for Timmy, looked up. "I think that beginning, 'There comes a time'? It sounds very familiar... Timmy! Not to Bessie. It's bad for her!"

Timmy had given the corn to a fat collie, and was giggling as the dog made off with it.

Ken put aside the editorial, bothered, and picked up a chicken drumstick. "You say everything sounds familiar. If I listened to you, I'd never write anything." He took a big bite and chewed vigorously.

"I think it's from Roosevelt's war declaration," Karen said, buttering another ear of corn. "Or maybe something Martin Luther King said."

"Yeah, sure. Or maybe Gandhi."

Karen ignored him. "I want you to eat at least four green beans, Timmy. Here. I'll put a little butter on them."

"And salt!" shouted the boy.

"Okay, just a little salt."

For eight months of the year, the Perrys dined on this shaded patio of their ranch-style house. As they ate, they could hear the next-door neighbor, Gladys Cummings, struggling to give pruning orders to her gardener in Spanish. "*Cortar muerto*," she said. "*Vivo bueno, muerto malo.*"

Ken watched the scene in the Cummings' garden for a few seconds. "How'd her gardener get across the river?" he asked his wife.

"He probably lives in the barrio," she said.

Ken reached for an ear of corn and spread on a dollop of butter. "Well, maybe he knows someone down there who could clean our house."

"Maybe," Karen said, wiping her black bangs from her forehead.

◊

"*Puta madre*, that dog's coming right toward us," Gato whispered to Pascual. The two men were lying in the bushes behind the mesquite tree, halfway between the Perry and Cummings houses. "Let's leave, now!" Gato said.

"Can't," Pascual said. "If we do, they'll see us." The woman with black hair was facing their hiding place. The man, who had to be the editor, had a sideways view. But he seemed too busy eating to notice them. Pascual heard a child's voice, but the barbecue blocked his view.

The dog seemed to be slowing down, sniffing, with the ear of corn still in its mouth. "*Vamos*," Gato whispered. "*Ya!*" But Pascual didn't budge.

The dog took a few more steps toward them and then lay down. She put the corn between her front paws and began to lick it.

"What are we doing here?" Gato whispered. "You said you just wanted a look." He rolled over and tried to pull some prickles out of his arm. This neighborhood might look soft and green like the jungle, he thought. But down on the ground, under these bushes, it was still desert. He felt dirt caking the inside of his nostrils.

Pascual still hadn't told Gato about the gun. He quietly unclipped the shoulder bag and reached inside. If that dog comes any closer, he thought, it dies. He fingered the gun, but didn't pull it out.

"I'm out of here," Gato said, pushing up with his elbows.

"Keep still," Pascual said. He pressed down on Gato's back with his right hand. With his left he pulled out the pistol.

"*Ay Dios!*" Gato said. "You didn't say..."

"*Silencio!*"

Pascual aimed the pistol at the dog. The collie stopped licking the corn. She looked up with her head tilted and ears cocked, a puzzled look on her white face.

"I'm going to kill it," Pascual said through clenched teeth.

Then they saw the little boy running toward the dog. He was wearing a green *Ninja Turtles* tee shirt. "Come back here, Bessie," he said, laughing. "Come back here with that corn." He stopped and turned back toward the table. "Mommy, I think she's going to bury it, like a bone!"

"Don't take it away from her, Timmy," Karen yelled back. "Remember, she snaps!"

Ken Perry paid no attention to the boy or the dog. He had a big red *Bartlett's* book of famous quotations on the table and was paging through the Roosevelt section.

Pascual saw the woman stand up and walk toward the little boy. "Timmy, didn't you hear me?" she said. "I told you not to pat the dog while she's eating..."

Pascual had the pistol trained on the dog. Then he aimed it at the woman as she approached them. He gnawed on the inside of his lip. She was leaning over the little boy, pulling him back from the dog, who was still licking the corn.

Gato was trembling beside him. "*Por Dios,*" he whispered. "Don't shoot."

The dog looked up, right at them, and began to walk toward them, wagging her tail in small, low arcs.

Pascual aimed at her.

Gato saw the flesh of Pascual's finger flatten against the trigger.

"No!" he yelled. He reached for the gun, but Pascual held firm.

The woman saw the gun and threw her arms around the boy. She tackled him, rolling on top of him. She put her hands to his face, and then twisted her head to look back toward the bushes.

Gato backed out from under the bushes and began

running up the driveway, leaving a cloud of dust behind him. The dog barked and ran after him, stopping at the hedge.

Pascual saw the editor hurrying down with a piece of paper in his hand. Scrambling back from under the bush, just a few feet from the barking dog, Pascual stood up and pointed his pistol toward the picture window at the house next door. He pulled the trigger. The explosion jerked his arm into the air. He heard shattered glass falling and a scream as he ran up the driveway toward the shade trees of Cherry Hill Lane.

A few minutes later, Pascual came upon a gray Lexus with the doors unlocked and the keys in the ignition. He combed the neighborhood in the Lexus until he found Gato hiding behind a bush. He coaxed him into the car, and the two took off down the mountain and toward the barrio.

Chapter
TWENTY-TWO

One tiresome problem with Mexico, thought Onofre Crispín: Not enough racquetball players. In the sports corner of his pink Juárez mansion, Crispín had installed an air-conditioned court, just across from the pool. It had a TV embedded in the wall. But he had no one to play with.

Wearing a sleek white sweatsuit with red bands around the collar and wrists, Crispín rallied by himself, rocketing backhands against the wall, about a foot off the ground. On TV, some lightweight from the *Colegio de Mexico* was raving about NAFTA.

The telephone rang. Crispín put down the racquet, walked to the back of the court, and picked up the phone. "*Bueno.*"

"*Está el jefe de policia para verlo, señor.*"

Crispín told the guard, Oscar Olmos, to let the police chief in. He'd forgotten that Muller was coming to lunch. He didn't feel like eating yet and wondered if it would be rude to summon the chief to the racquetball court. Maybe they could talk while he hit the ball. Or maybe Muller knew how to play...

A minute later, Olmos poked his head into the court. An

enormous Oaxacan with his black hair greased back and a nose with a big bump halfway down, he always kept his body off the court, as if the black ball were a bullet. "I have him sitting out on the patio," he said, flinching when the ball came his way. "I had the girl serve him a glass of papaya juice."

Crispín reluctantly put down his racquet and went to greet his visitor.

He found him sitting at the heavy oak table, wearing a black suit and a tie that dug deeply into his neck. He mopped his forehead with a napkin.

Crispín sat down and asked him for the latest news on Jiménez.

"Gustavo's laying low," Muller said, taking a sip of papaya juice. "He doesn't have a clue. Turns out the ones who beat up the photographer run a warehouse for him at a car wash, on the westside, by the river."

"How do you know this?" Crispín asked.

"We heard about it from the neighbors, and one of the kids who washes cars."

"They actually wash cars there?"

"As a side business," the chief said. He told the *maquiladora* magnate that a few off-duty cops had further screwed things up with the *Tribune* by stealing a reporter's car.

"That's the reporter who brought the joint into Mexico, right?" Crispín laughed. "Sounds like a *pendejo*."

"No. You're talking about the guy who got the death threat," the chief said. "The one they stole the car from is young, with a strange haircut."

"Maybe I should talk to the first one. What's his name again?"

"Tom Harley."

"Right. The *pendejo* who wrote that *pendejada* about *maquiladoras* and drugs... Harley Davidson," Crispín murmured. "I was thinking of getting one of those."

Chapter
TWENTY-THREE

Eddie Stevenson lay back on Diana Clements' bed, trying to focus on the Saturday *Tribune.* He was feeling edgy, hungover. Gazing at the paper, with its front-page immigration story by Klinger, Stevenson found himself worrying about his job. Maybe he was screwing things up by taking this leave, and by talking to lawyers about a lawsuit. He thought about burned bridges, which led him to wonder what Estela was up to. He heard Diana singing in the shower and felt like yelling for her to shut up.

The phone rang.

Stevenson answered. "Hello."

A man asked if it was Diana Clements' house.

"Uh huh."

"Is she there?"

"She's uh, busy now. You want to leave a message?"

"Is that you, Stevenson?" the caller asked.

"Yeah, who's this?"

"Tom Harley."

"Harley!"

They were both silent for a moment, until Stevenson said, "Did you want to talk to Diana?"

"I did. Didn't expect you to answer her phone."

"Yeah, I'm just sort of camping out here for a while."

"I see."

"Hey," Stevenson said brightly. "I talked to a lawyer yesterday. It sounds like I can get a lot of money from the paper if I sue. And you probably can too. I was thinking..."

Harley interrupted. "Did that guy really call me 'dead meat'?"

Stevenson stammered.

Harley continued. "I mean, was it 'dead meat' or '*carne muerta*'? Was he speaking Spanish or English?"

"Ah, English," Stevenson said. "But I..."

"Listen, we got to talk," Harley said. He asked Stevenson if he'd heard that a couple of armed men had attacked Ken Perry's house.

"Ho-ly shit." Stevenson was awed. "Did they shoot anybody?"

"Just a window."

"They get caught?"

"No."

"I don't see anything about it in the paper. Just this story by Klinger..."

"Listen," Harley said, all business. "How about if I come over? Where is it, near the zoo...?"

"Not far..." Stevenson, sitting on the side of the bed, looked up as Diana walked in from the bathroom, wearing a red bathrobe cinched tightly with a sash. "How about a little later in the day?" he said into the phone.

"I'll be over in about an hour," Harley said, and hung up.

"Did I hear you say Harley?" Diana asked.

Stevenson nodded.

"He knew you were here?"

He pretended not to hear the question.

She turned away from him, opened her robe, and began fishing through her top bureau drawer.

Stevenson watched her step into her panties, still covered by the robe. Then she dropped the robe to the floor and, in one quick motion, pulled on a turquoise T-shirt, pushing both arms out at the same time. She pulled out a pair of white shorts from her second drawer. She positioned herself sideways in the mirror and ran a hand down her stomach, as if making sure it was still flat.

"He's coming over in an hour," Stevenson said.

Her eyes widened. "You invited him to my place?"

"He invited himself and then hung up."

"Hmmm." She sat down next to him on the bed and began putting on white socks. She pointed her toes as she did it, softly flexing the muscles in her calves. "How'd he know you were here?"

"He didn't. But he recognized my voice."

"You mean he was calling for me?"

He nodded. "At first."

"That's interesting."

◊

Reawakened to dangers, Harley locked his bike to a telephone pole a few houses down Prospect Street from his apartment. He looked up and down the street before hurrying up the steps to his building, his battered white helmet still strapped around his chin.

When Harley was nervous, he did voices under his breath, the way some people hum or whistle. Now, as he emptied his overflowing mailbox into his brown backpack, he was doing a raspy Eddie Stevenson, talking about legal suits and *carne muerta*.

He heard Claudio's door open.

"So they finally let you out of jail in Juárez."

Harley zipped shut the backpack and turned around. "You read the story?"

"Pretty strange stuff, Tom."

"It wasn't exactly jail," he said. "They just sort of lassoed me in there for a talk."

"And what if you didn't want to talk?"

"Well, I guess I didn't have to... You know where it all started?" Harley asked, changing the subject. "I was on my bike at the Sun Bowl a couple weeks ago, and I saw this joint in the parking lot. And then it turned out..."

"They caught you with a joint over there?"

"Sort of. I forgot I had it. I don't even smoke the stuff. I was going to send it to a friend..."

"So they held you on drug charges?"

"I don't think they charged me with anything. It was all murky. They kept me in a room for a while. Then I talked to the police chief for hours."

"Did he offer you some sort of quid pro quo for letting you loose?"

"No. In fact, he was the one who mentioned that they probably framed me."

"But that wasn't what he believed!" Claudio said. "He was giving you a look at his side of the bargain, letting you see what he'd say if you kept your side up. Don't you see?"

"I see it okay," Harley said, feeling defensive. "But he never told me what my side of the bargain was. He just gave me this long talk about Mexican politics."

Claudio shook his head. "Two things I don't understand," he said. "One, why the cops let you go, and two, even more bizarre, why you came back and wrote about it."

"Canfield made me."

"You're getting batted around, Tom," Claudio said. "You've got the police chief and Canfield and Ken Perry, and they're all using you. You have to take control of the story."

"I never had a story like this."

Harley went on to tell Claudio about the attack at Perry's house the night before, about the two guys under the bushes, one of them with steel-rimmed glasses and a gun. Perry had called him in a panic at about nine, he said, telling him to write the story. But by the time he reached Thunderbird, the editor, concerned about his family, told him to sit on the story at least over the weekend, until he had evidence to tie the shooters to Gustavo Jiménez.

"You say one of the men wore wire-rimmed glasses?" Claudio asked.

"The one who shot out the window."

Then Claudio told Harley about the intruder a few days earlier, who looked at first like a UTEP student, but ran off to the I-10 overpass when Claudio opened the door.

"I should probably write some of this down," Harley said, pulling his reporter's notebook from his back pocket.

"This is really too much," Claudio said.

"What?"

"You. Covering an ongoing crime story in the first person."

"Yeah," Harley said. "I've been thinking about that myself."

Chapter
TWENTY-FOUR

Hank Klinger sat at his kitchen table, carefully cutting out his immigration story from the *Tribune* and pasting it into his clip book. This was one of his best stories in weeks. In fact, he was considering sending it to the editors at the *Dallas Morning News*, which he viewed as his next career step.

Klinger didn't like to admit it, but Rubén had helped him pull the immigration story together. First, Rubén called to express his sympathies about the stolen Grand-Am. Klinger would get it back, he said. His friends in the police were busy working on that. Then he told Klinger about the Border Patrol chief's border-hopping Mexican grandfather. That was a scoop.

Later, Rubén came up with a photo of the old man for Klinger. He said he was just making up for the stolen car. But it was clear to Klinger that Rubén was angling for a job at the paper. He didn't look the part of a reporter and his English grammar was borderline. The poor guy didn't realize that he'd have to get a job offer from Canfield, which was almost unthinkable.

The phone rang. Klinger answered, half expecting Rubén to be calling with another tip. But instead, a man introduced himself as Byron Biggs of the *New York Times*. Klinger's heart galloped. Biggs was saying something about coming to El Paso.

Coming to see him?! Klinger wondered if he'd have time to rework his resume and buy a decent suit. Maybe get a haircut. But as he listened to Biggs, he realized that this wasn't an editor on a recruiting mission: He was the Houston bureau chief, already in El Paso on a reporting trip, and was after Klinger's sources.

"I was wondering if we could have lunch someplace," Biggs said, "and talk about a couple of these stories."

"Sure, sure," Klinger said. He was disappointed. But still, if he got to know Byron Biggs, and helped him out, maybe he could string for the *Times* from El Paso.

Klinger suggested meeting at Luby's, a downtown cafeteria a couple blocks from the paper. Biggs balked for a moment, but Klinger assured him the food was good.

"Okay," Biggs said. "How'll I recognize you?"

"I'll be carrying a red notebook with some clips," Klinger said. "And," he added, wishing it weren't true, "I have pretty long blond hair in the back."

◊

Pascual had borrowed a pair of Gato's baggy blue shorts and Estela had loaned him a big paint-splattered T-shirt from Eddie Stevenson's wardrobe. It pained him to dress like this. But he suspected that once the police found the stolen Lexus, they'd be combing the barrio for a Mexican prepster.

Gato, who'd unearthed Stevenson's stash behind the coffee cups in the kitchen, exhaled a cloud of smoke. "You look better this way," he said. "More relaxed."

Pascual paid no attention. He sat on the couch in his sloppy clothes and pouted. Things weren't working out for him. Even though Estela finally let them in the night before, after a lot of banging on the door, she made Pascual feel like an outcast. She went out of her way to avoid looking at him. At breakfast, when she was eating oatmeal and he asked for some, she practically flung the pot at him and said, "Scrape it."

Worse, she seemed to be cozying up to Gato, probably just to make Pascual jealous. After eating, Pascual tried to convince Gato to go out for the newspapers. Gato wasn't interested. So Pascual had to venture outside in shorts and a T-shirt. He sensed people were laughing at him. Then he bought the papers and saw nothing about the attack at the editor's house the night before. Not a word!

How could Pascual stir up trouble for his boss if the newspapers didn't cover his attacks? He wished he could call the papers and claim responsibility for the attacks in *don* Gustavo's name. But his English was shit. Grumpier than ever, he climbed the steps back to Estela's apartment and plotted his next move.

Maybe, Pascual thought, he could track down Jiménez in Guadalajara—or wherever he was—and then offer himself as an ally, one arriving at the boss's time of greatest need. The idea intrigued him.

But what could Pascual offer Jiménez, other than friendship? He didn't have money or political contacts. In the end, *don* Gustavo would probably just use him as a soldier. Cannon fodder... No, it wasn't the right time to drop the current plan. A good idea would come.

Pascual picked up the *El Paso Journal*, the paper that hadn't written anything about the attack on the photographer in Juárez. He studied the bylines. Rick Jarvis, Anna Symonds, Ignacio Torres... That name gave him an idea.

He would call this Ignacio Torres and speak with him in *Spanish*. Flipping through the paper, Pascual found a telephone number on the editorial page. He picked up a couple of quarters from the coffee table and dashed out of the apartment with the paper in hand.

Standing at a phone booth on Stanton Street, Pascual flipped through the paper and found another Spanish name, Lucinda Rodríguez, for backup. Then he dialed the *Journal*'s number.

A woman answered. "*El Paso Journal.*"

Pascual paused a second, and said, "Ignacio Torres, please."

Next thing he knew, another voice said, "City desk."

"Ignacio Torres, please."

"Uh, I'm not sure he's here. Lemme check." Pascual heard the man asking, "Anybody seen Nacho around?" He came back to the phone. "He's not here. Want to leave a message?"

Pascual switched to plan B. "Lucinda Rodríguez, please."

"Uh, she's on the sports desk. I'll transfer you."

Another voice answered, "Sports."

"Lucinda Rodríguez, please."

"Just a minute."

A woman's voice. "Hello."

"Lucinda Rodríguez?"

"This is Lucy."

Pascual launched into his message. "*Llamo de parte de don Gustavo Jiménez para reivindicar el...*"

"Wait a minute, wait a minute," she said. "I don't speak much Spanish."

Pascual slowed down. "*El... ataque... contra... la... casa... de...*"

"Hold on a minute," she said. "Let me get somebody who speaks Spanish."

She put down the phone, and Pascual could hear her asking for help.

Looking around, Pascual saw that his phone booth was next to a bus stop. Shoppers carrying plastic shopping bags were lining up next to him. They were laughing and talking in

Spanish. Pascual could hear every word, which probably meant they could hear him. He considered hanging up and trying later.

Then he heard an American voice on the phone, a man asking how he could help. "*Habla Rick Jarvis. En qué puedo servirle?*"

Pascual, with one eye on the shoppers, whispered, "*Hola.*"

"*Hola. En qué puedo servirle?*"

Pascual cleared his throat. He cupped his mouth and whispered into the phone, claiming credit for the attack in *don* Gustavo's name: "*Llamo de parte de don Gustavo Jiménez para reivindicar el ataque...*"

"*Usted es Gustavo Jiménez?*" the American asked.

"No," Pascual explained in slow, clear Spanish, "I'm calling in his name."

"You represent him?"

"Exactly. And last night he ordered an attack against the home of *señor* Ken Perry, which was carried out at approximately 20 hours."

"Holy shit," Rick Jarvis said in English. Then he switched back to his laborious Spanish. "You attacked Ken Perry's home in the name of Gustavo Jiménez at 8 o'clock last night."

"Precisely," Pascual said, feeling pleased.

"What's your name?" Jarvis asked.

"My code name," Pascual said, improvising, "is *Comandante* Enrique."

"*Comandante* Enrique?"

"At your command." Now he was having fun.

"How can I..." Jarvis's Spanish gave way for a moment. He started again: "How can you prove that what you are saying is true?"

"Call Ken Perry. Or go ask the police," Pascual said. The women lined up for the bus now seemed to be listening to him. The *gringo* was asking another question. But Pascual abruptly said "*adiós*" and hung up.

Chapter
TWENTY-FIVE

Looking over Eddie Stevenson's shoulder into the bedroom, Harley could see Diana Clements, eyes down and jaw clenched, snapping the blanket on the bed and pounding the pillows. Then she began to jam clothing into a bureau and slam shut the drawers. She was seething about something, which told him to leave her alone.

Stevenson, leaning back in an easy chair, didn't seem to notice. He was telling Harley about the two nights he'd spent in Truth or Consequences, coming to terms with life as a marked man. "I don't know why," he said, "but I had this real strong urge to go swimming in the Pacific Ocean. Even though I freak out a little about sharks."

"How about we go out for a cup of coffee?" Harley suggested.

"We can probably have one here," Stevenson said, gesturing toward the kitchen with his face. "Probably have to make it ourselves though. She's not really the waitress type." He yelled back towards the bedroom. "Okay if we make some coffee, Diana?"

"Go ahead."

"You want some?"

"Not now. Thanks." She slammed shut another bureau drawer.

Stevenson mouthed some words to Harley and smiled.

"What?" Harley asked.

Stevenson, still smiling, whispered, "On the rag."

"Oh." Harley wondered for the hundredth time why Diana Clements had let this guy into her life.

Stevenson groaned as he climbed out of the easy chair. "I'm still feeling that beating I took," he said, making his way into the kitchen. "I'm worried my kidneys might be damaged." He began opening cabinets in search of coffee utensils. He located a coffee pot and a black plastic funnel. "We just need one of those drip filters," he said. "Lemme see if she knows..."

"Wait a minute," Harley said, grabbing Stevenson by the arm. He found the filters and put water on the stove.

Looking the photographer in the eye, he asked, "The guys who beat you up, what did they look like?"

Stevenson sighed at the change of subject. "They had my eyes bound most of the time."

"But you must have seen somebody before they covered your eyes. How did they get you into that place?"

"Well, I was taking pictures of that hotel, the *Xanadu*. And a couple guys who worked for Jiménez picked me up in a car and said the boss wanted to talk to me before I took more pictures. These were young guys, go-fers I figured. Then, as soon as they had me in the car, one of them pulled out a gun and told me to put my head down. They covered my eyes. I really didn't see them again. Then they took me to this place, about a fifteen-minute ride. Bumpy."

"But what did these go-fers look like?"

"Mexican kids. You know. Black hair. I never got to see Jiménez. He was behind me the whole time."

"How did you know it was him?"

"Well... He introduced himself. And the kids seemed to pay him respect. You know, calling him '*señor*' and '*don* Gustavo.'"

"And the kids? Did one of them wear glasses?"

"Oh. You think Jiménez might have sent them over to shoot at Ken's house?" Stevenson frowned, coming to terms with a new idea.

"Could be," Harley said.

"He wouldn't have sent them on a mission like that, into Texas," Stevenson said, pulling the boiling water off the stove. He poured it too fast into the funnel, and water with coffee grounds bubbled over onto the counter. "Shit," he said.

He ripped five or six paper towels from a rack and mopped off the counter and a little puddle on the floor. "He'd send over more sophisticated guys for an attack in El Paso," he said. "Those kids barely knew how to speak English."

"But Jiménez knows English?"

"Oh, yeah. You could tell he'd been around El Paso a lot."

"Did he say 'dead meat' in English, or '*carne muerta*'?"

"Dead meat. Definitely dead meat. That I remember," Stevenson said, nodding.

"So. Did one of these guys wear glasses?"

"You know what kills me," Stevenson said, ignoring the question. "I lost my Leica over there. Thing's worth fifteen hundred bucks. I brought back all the other worthless stuff that belonged to the paper. And I left my own camera over there. I could kick myself."

Harley tried again. "You must have noticed if one of those guys wore glasses."

Stevenson looked for a place to throw out the wet paper towels. Giving up, he laid them on the counter. "I think they both wore glasses," he finally said. "One of them was like a hippie, with a Frank Zappa mustache. And the other one, with a gun. He was sort of...neater. More clean cut."

"Metal rims? Did either of them wear glasses with steel frames?"

"Maybe... No, I think they were plastic... No. Shit, I can't remember."

Stevenson poured the coffee into two brown, earthenware mugs. He took a sip and hunted for sugar.

"So you haven't been back to your apartment since this thing in Juárez?"

"Nope... Hey," Stevenson said, brightening up. "Maybe you could stop by and pick up my clothes."

Harley ignored the request. "I know it's none of my business," he said, "but what happened between you and Estela?"

"Oh, it was happening for a long time, a couple of weeks maybe. I just decided to break it when I was up there in Truth or Consequences. You know, I had a chance to think about things."

Harley took another sip of the bitter coffee and blew into the cup, saying nothing.

"I'll tell you what happened," Stevenson said, lowering his voice to a whisper. "She wanted to get married to me, and move to some condos near Cielo Vista. So she got herself pregnant."

"Got herself pregnant?"

"Trapped me," Stevenson whispered. "Or tried to. Then when I called her on it, she really got pissed off. Like offended. Her and her friends."

They stopped talking as Diana walked into the kitchen. Appearing calmer now, she looked up and smiled at Harley.

She reached up for another mug and poured herself some coffee. "I smelled it and changed my mind," she said. She leaned up against the dishwasher, between the two men, and took a sip. Stevenson edged away from her.

"So Eddie thinks he can make a lot of money suing the paper," Diana said. "I tell him he'd better be ready to handle some pretty intense cross-examination. Those plaintiffs' attorneys make it all sound so easy when they're looking for work."

Harley nodded, though he knew next to nothing about attorneys or cross-examinations.

"Who's your lawyer?" he asked Stevenson.

"I don't have one yet; I've talked to a few."

"Oh."

More silence, broken only by the sound of sipping and Stevenson drumming his fingers on the counter.

"I haven't seen you since that day at lunch," Diana said to Harley. She asked him how he was making out.

"Some ups and downs." Harley didn't want to bring up his detention at the Juárez police station. "Did Eddie tell you about the attack on our editor's house last night?"

"Yeah. It made me wonder how smart I was to have him hanging around here." She said it matter-of-factly, as though Stevenson were far away. "Or you either, for that matter." With that she smiled at Harley, showing him that little gap between her teeth. She opened the refrigerator door, pulled out a quart of milk, and poured some into her cup. "That's bitter coffee you make, Eddie," she said.

"Harley made it," Stevenson said dully.

Chapter
TWENTY-SIX

As he pushed his tray along the rail, Hank Klinger informed his guest, *New York Times* reporter Byron Biggs, that the meatloaf at Luby's was "awesome."

Biggs, a small, wiry man with a fringe of black hair around a big bald head, looked skeptically at the dish. "I usually try to eat Mexican food when I'm down on the border," he said.

"Then try the chili," suggested Klinger, who was already supervising the pouring of gravy onto his mashed potatoes.

As they sat down in the nearly deserted cafeteria, just two blocks down Kansas Street from the paper, Biggs asked Klinger if it was a Luby's in Waco, or maybe Temple, where a gunman shot a dozen customers a few years before.

"Probably was." Klinger nodded as he loaded a forkful of meatloaf into his mouth. He chewed for a moment and added, "Luby's are real popular."

Biggs looked blankly at Klinger and then tried a small forkful of chili.

"What I mean," Klinger explained, "is that a guy with a gun could probably find a dozen people to shoot at a Luby's, because they're so popular."

Biggs surveyed the empty cafeteria, where only one man sat at the counter. "We must be early," he said.

"Weekend," Klinger said. "That's when whites—I mean Anglos—head out to the malls and leave downtown to the Mexicans."

"But the Mexicans can't cross now, with Operation Blockade, right?" asked Biggs, perking up as he hit upon the subject of his upcoming story.

"Some still cross," Klinger said. "But I guess they don't come to Luby's. How's the chili?"

"It's okay."

As Klinger finished his lunch, he moved his tray to one side and placed his red *Drugs* notebook and an envelope full of newspaper clippings on the table. Then he laid out the Operation Blockade story for Biggs. He gave the *Timesman* phone numbers for all of the relevant sources, from the Border Patrol chief to academics at UTEP who could discuss immigration trends. Biggs took out his own notebook and scribbled down the numbers.

"Is this your beat, immigration?" Biggs asked. "Or do you cover everything that has to do with Mexico?"

"I just cover the big stories, wherever they are," Klinger boasted. "I'm sort of a cherry picker." He opened his drug notebook and asked Biggs if he planned to write anything about the Jiménez story.

"I...don't know," Biggs said. "It's kind of a crazy story. I see the other paper hasn't even picked it up."

"That's the way they operate," Klinger said. "When we get way ahead of them on a story, they pretend it doesn't exist."

"In any case," Biggs said, "I usually leave stories like that to our Mexico City bureau. I only had one year of college Spanish, and my professor was from Madrid. You know, he spoke pure Castilian, with the *TH* sounds on all the Zs. So I have trouble with Mexican Spanish. I really admire you guys," he went on, "who can cross the border and report in Spanish. You must be fluent, right?"

Klinger blushed. "I'm pretty good," he said. "But even I sometimes have some trouble understanding this border lingo. Some of my sources on this drug story—undercover cops, people like that—have probably never opened a grammar book in their lives."

He flipped through the notebook, eager to share his reporting with Byron Biggs. "See this, Jesus Silva?" He pointed to the name in his book. "This guy works for the cops, but has friends who run drugs. See, he gave me the name of a town south of Juárez that's run entirely by the *narcos*. I'm going to be following that up as soon as I get my car back." He looked at Biggs, who was nodding, his pen poised over his notebook.

"The trouble is," Klinger explained, "is that they know who we are now. Just last week, they stole my car while I was reporting over there. And the cops over there arrested another reporter, and held him for a few hours."

"The photographer? They arrested him?"

"No. The other reporter. Harley. Tom Harley."

"Oh, I didn't see that."

"We didn't give it much play," Klinger said. "I think our editors are a little bit worried. You know, for our lives."

Biggs asked Klinger how he saw the drug story fitting into the ongoing debate over North American free trade.

"It's definitely an issue," Klinger said, combing his hair with his fingers. "I mean, the Mexicans need NAFTA. And they're willing to...pay any price, as it were. That gives us a certain amount of leverage...at this juncture..."

Biggs looked at his watch and closed his notebook. He thanked Klinger and gave him his number at the Paso del Norte Hotel. "Oh, one more thing," he said, standing up. "Do you know anyone who could work a couple days as an interpreter?"

Klinger thought about it for a couple seconds. "I'm going

to be too busy to do it myself," he said. "But I do know one guy. A Mexican-American who's really interested in journalism."

◊

Standing outside Diana's house with Eddie Stevenson, Harley was having trouble getting answers from the photographer. "Did you get the feeling that these guys were serious about hunting me down?" he asked.

"I can't tell you, Harley." Stevenson opened the door to his Dodge.

"Come on."

"I felt they were crazy," Stevenson said. "Which I guess means they're capable of anything."

"Think they were on drugs?"

"Maybe one of them. The guy who cracked the table with his fist. But Jiménez was under control. He talked in this whisper, right behind me. Talked about all sorts of things. He even had comments about the paper. He said your article was full of shit. That's when he sent the message to you. And he also—and this is what I thought was funny...I *would have* thought it was funny," he corrected himself, "if I hadn't been getting the shit kicked out of me. He said to tell Ken Perry that he was a 'horseshit editor.'"

"He used those words?"

"Yup."

"That part didn't make it into the paper..."

"What do you expect?" Stevenson swung into the car. "Want to get some breakfast?"

"I already ate," Harley said, moving towards his bike. "Anyway, I've got to get working on this story about the attack at Perry's house. He wants it in the paper Monday."

Stevenson started his car. It sputtered and sent out a cloud of black smoke.

"Hey," Harley shouted. "Where will you be if I need to find you in the next few days?" He pointed to Diana's duplex. "You staying there?"

"Sure," Stevenson said. "Wouldn't you?" As he drove off he waved his left arm blindly out the window.

◊

Oscar Olmos, Crispín's imposing bodyguard, parked the Jeep at a dusty corner in west Juárez, right next to a little store. He stepped over the dog sleeping in the doorway and grabbed a Squirt from the refrigerator. He opened it and pulled down a bag of *Sabritas* potato chips from a shelf. "*Cuánto me cobra?*" he asked the old woman behind the counter, wanting to know how much she charged.

"*Buenas tardes,*" she said.

"*Qué me cobra, señora?*"

"*Cómo?*" She turned down the radio.

Olmos placed a couple of coins on the counter.

She dropped them into a box below the counter and began to fish around for change. Olmos told her not to worry about it. He poured half the bag of chips into a massive hand and pushed the load into his mouth. Then he took a swig of Squirt and swished it around like mouthwash.

"Any place I can get this Jeep washed around here?" he asked her in Spanish.

"I wouldn't know, *señor,*" she said.

"I tried that car wash around the corner. But it was closed."

"Closed. Yes."

A little boy wearing no shirt and striped pants that looked like old pajamas came into the store. He reached into a pocket, put a coin on the counter, and began pulling penny candies out of a big jar.

"You think they're just taking a lunch break?" Olmos asked the woman. "The car's very dirty, with all this dust in the air." "I wouldn't know to tell you, *señor*," she said.

The little boy looked up at Olmos. "You want your car washed?" he asked. "My friend and I can do it." Before Olmos could answer, the boy hopped over the dog and out the door, shouting, "Alfredito, Alfredito!"

Chapter
TWENTY-SEVEN

Downtown was dead, with so little traffic that Harley was free to fishtail on his bike as he passed the paper. He straightened out when a taxi passed him. That was when he saw Klinger coming out of Luby's Cafeteria with a short, bald man. Harley waved and yelled "Hey!" as he whizzed by. But Klinger didn't see him. The other guy looked too mature to be hanging around with him.

As Harley locked his bike to a chain-link fence by the Police Headquarters, he wondered why anyone would eat lunch downtown on a Saturday, and at Luby's, of all places.

Behind the dispatcher's desk, he saw the big cop who'd given him a hard time the night before, at Ken Perry's place, for trampling footprints. The cop was flipping through papers on his gray steel desk, but looked up when he approached. His nametag read Sgt. Raymond Buendía.

"I told you to stay put last night, and you moved," he growled with the trace of a smile. "I saw you."

"I jumped to the grass," Harley said.

"Yeah, with those long legs you probably did. Well, we

have some clues to go on. I don't know if I should tell you about them, though."

"Come on." Harley sat on the corner of Buendía's desk. "More witnesses?"

Buendía looked at him for a moment. "You going to take your goddamn helmet off?"

"Oh, yeah." He unbuckled it and jammed it into his knapsack.

"Witnesses aren't clues, first of all," Buendía said. "But there was a stolen car near that house last night, at about the same time. We found it over on Paisano and Stanton. It has prints all over it, and a little blood on the passenger seat."

"Blood?"

"Probably just from a scratch. But it could come in handy. What these guys really liked were the power windows. There are prints all over the buttons."

Buendía looked up at Harley, looming over his desk. "Wanna sit down?" he asked.

Harley sat. "So you think these two guys left the car in the barrio and then crossed into Juárez on foot?" he asked.

Buendía shrugged. "They might still be here. There's still more money on this side of the border, if that's what they were after."

"Did the prints match up to anything?"

"They're putting them into the computer now. We'll see."

"And the blood?"

"That won't get tested until we catch somebody."

"You think maybe these guys were just crackheads?"

"I don't know what I think," Buendía said. He was getting a little snappy.

Harley paused, waiting for the sergeant to say more. But instead of talking, the policeman began organizing his desk. He placed the papers into neat piles.

"Listen," Buendía finally said, looking around to see if anyone was within listening range. "Can I go off the record with you?"

Harley nodded.

"I'm telling you this, because I know you're sort of involved in this case, not just as a reporter, okay?"

Harley kept nodding.

"If we believe these guys were tied to a foreign drug lord, we have to handle it as a terrorism case. We do that, we have to call in the FBI. We do a DNA test on that blood. We put those prints through the whole...the whole Interpol network. The chief doesn't want to call in the FBI if it just turns out to be a couple of crackheads. Know what I mean?"

"Uh huh," Harley said. The word "terrorism" knocked him back a bit.

"But if it is terrorism, we probably *do* want the FBI. The trouble is, we don't know. That's why I'm working on a Saturday."

"Are you talking to the Juárez police about it?"

Buendía dismissed the question with a flick of his hand. "No comment. That's what you say, right?"

"Come on. We're off the record."

The sergeant looked around again. The office was practically empty. "Listen," he said. "For all we know, those two guys *were* Juárez cops. *You* know that."

The sergeant's phone rang and he picked it up. "Yeah... Uh huh. Just what I was talking about." He arched his eyes at Harley, asking him to leave.

But Harley stood above him with his thumb and forefinger in a nearly closed circle, asking for one more question.

"Wait a minute," the cop said, putting one hand on the receiver.

"What kind of car was it?" Harley asked.

"Gray 93 Lexus, New Mexico plates. It's all in the report."

Harley skipped down the stairs and out into the heat and unlocked his bike. He pedaled back to the *Tribune* to call Chief Muller from the newsroom.

The office was emptier than the police station, since the *Trib* didn't publish a Sunday edition. He sat at his desk and dialed Muller's number. A secretary told him the chief was out. Was there someone else who could take the call? "No," Harley said in his Chihuahua Spanish, "I need to speak to the chief."

"Then call Monday," the secretary said, hanging up.

Harley figured he'd call back and talk tougher, in English, maybe set her back on her heels. But he had to wait a few minutes for it to work. He walked down the dark hallway to the snack bar, mulling his strategy, and bought a Hawaiian Punch.

Harley saw Rick Jarvis of the *Journal*, whose offices were on the other side of the same building. He was sitting at one of the tables with one of his editors. They were looking at Harley, apparently waiting for him to leave. He decided to make their life difficult. He opened his Hawaiian Punch and waved at them. Then he sat down and picked up a *Journal* sitting on the table. He paged through it, waiting for Jarvis and the editor to start talking again. They didn't.

Harley pretended to ignore them, reading an article about a dog that followed its master across the river to Juárez when the man began working as a *maquiladora* manager.

"Hey," he yelled over to Jarvis' table. "Did this dog make it back past Operation Blockade?"

The two men smiled without answering. Then they made off to their offices. Harley finished his drink and returned to the empty newsroom.

When Muller's secretary answered this time, saying, "*Bueno, Jefatura*," Harley put her on the defensive by bulling ahead with rapid-fire English. "Put me on the line with Chief Muller please."

"Ah. The chief, he is not here," she said in slow English.

"Can you patch me through to his house or cell phone?"

"Sorry?"

"Damn it. Connect me to his house."

"One moment."

Next thing he knew, the phone was ringing, and Chief Muller answered. "*Bueno?*"

"Chief. Tom Harley here, from the *Tribune*."

"Mr. Harley."

Before the chief could ask him about his silly first-person article, Harley rushed to tell him about the attack at Ken Perry's house.

"Oh my," the chief said. "I didn't see it in your paper this morning. You say it was two young men wearing glasses?"

"At least one of them wore glasses," Harley said. "With metal rims."

"And you know they were Mexicans?"

Harley thought for a moment. He'd never doubted they were, but had no evidence. "No," he conceded. "I guess we don't know that. But it looks like they stole a car and took it back to the border."

"Ah, hum."

"Have you heard anything about Jiménez? Or do you know how I could find out whether he's got anything to do with this?"

"Tom, we already discussed this."

"I know, I know. But you were just surmising that he wasn't behind it. I need facts. I need...I guess I need to find him and ask him."

"Well, I can't help you much there... Though I did hear he was staying somewhere near Copper Canyon."

"Who told you that?"

"Ah...I don't remember."

"At a private home near Copper Canyon?"

"I couldn't say. But... Have you called Onofre Crispín? Remember I told you..."

"Not yet," Harley said. "I haven't had time."

"He is anxious to get to know you. Wait a minute here."

Harley heard the chief moving around and talking. Then his

voice returned. "Tom, I have Onofre Crispín on the other line here."

Harley listened as the chief explained in Spanish that he had the "*joven americano*" on the line. Then he told him about the attack at Perry's house.

When he returned to Harley's line, he said, "Onofre Crispín wants to know if you're a football fan."

"Well," Harley said, surprised by the question, "sort of."

"He wants to know if you'll go with him tomorrow to the Cowboys game."

"The Dallas Cowboys?"

"Dallas, yes."

"That's like 600 miles!"

"He has a jet."

"Maybe I should talk to him."

"He's in his car, on his cellular now, and I'm beginning to lose him." He switched to Spanish. "*Onofre... De acuerdo. Se lo digo.*"

"Tom, he'll have you picked up at 11. Where do you live?"

Harley didn't want to say.

"Where do you live, Tom? I'm losing him."

Harley sighed. "Cliff Inn, up near Providence Hospital," he said.

Chapter
TWENTY-EIGHT

Claudio, sitting on his couch with a cup of tea in his lap, couldn't see exactly where Onofre Crispín fit into the story. "The police chief set you up with this rich guy?" he asked.

Harley had his feet up on the coffee table, next to his bike helmet, and was sipping a Corona. "Exactly."

"This is the Juárez police chief who furnished you with the alibi for the drugs they caught you with in Mexico?"

"I guess you could say that."

"Tom. Are you getting the feeling that you're not really in control of this story?"

"I'd say that's a bit of an understatement."

"You mean you're getting jerked around."

Harley took the last swig of his beer and put the empty bottle on the table. "More or less."

"You know why that is, Tom? Because everybody's got an agenda, except for you."

Harley covered his eyes with a hand and groaned. "Oh, not now."

Harley and Claudio had been friends and neighbors for

Stephen Baker

four years, and Claudio never let a month go by without zeroing in on what he viewed as Harley's chief character defect: a lack of focus. As Claudio saw it, Harley kept his ambitions to himself as a hedge against failure. He dabbled in a hundred things—the bike racing, the languages, the impersonations—so he wouldn't have to put himself on the line in any one area, especially his career. This way, when he came up short as a reporter, he had a built-in excuse.

Claudio had stood up and was pacing between the statue of the rain god and the window. "You can't just flirt with this story the way you do with everything else," he said. "You have this way of gliding along, talking to the police chief and watching the Cowboys game with this *maquiladora* magnate, writing whatever Canfield tells you to write, as if it's all just an interesting life experience. A movie."

"But it is..."

"Right. But you should be directing it, not leaving it to everybody else. You need to take action."

"Hold that thought," Harley said, standing up. He walked into the kitchen and opened another beer. Peering into the refrigerator for something to eat, he settled on a half-full can of chopped liver. "You got any crackers in here?" he shouted.

"Next to the blender."

Harley came out with a small brown pile on a plastic plate, surrounded by Ritz crackers. "So what's everybody's agenda?" he asked, returning to the sofa.

"You know as well as I do," Claudio said. "Perry wants to move to a bigger paper, Canfield wants to get rich, Klinger wants to get famous..."

"And how about Eddie Stevenson?"

Claudio shrugged. "Sex and drugs, from what I can tell."

Harley considered that for a second and sipped his beer. "And how about me?"

"You tell me."

He looked up at the ceiling. "I'm going to have to chew on

158

that one a while."

"Everybody has a very clear agenda except for you. It's as if you think it's beneath you. That's your problem with women, too," Claudio went on. "You want them to love you, but you spend half your waking hours with that stupid helmet on, just trying to scare them away, from what I can see."

"It doesn't help that they see me hanging out with the likes of you."

"True enough," Claudio said, looking a little hurt.

Harley piled a cracker high with chopped liver and guided it into his mouth. He heard the *tamale* man who passed by every Saturday with his cart. He sounded a long steam whistle that cried like a dying train.

He looked around the apartment, at the statue of Tlaloc standing in the corner and the red and blue Navajo rug hanging above the couch. Claudio was hunched over his tea, running a hand through his long hair, free now of its ponytail.

Claudio stood and walked to a small desk by the wall, where he picked up a yellow legal pad and a couple of pens. "Why don't we sketch out just what you know about this story, and who your sources are. Maybe if we put our heads together, we can get ahead of it a little."

"Okay."

Harley started by describing how Canfield tied the *maquiladora* investment to the underreported drug story, and insisted on leading with the tigers.

"I can see where *don* Onofre Crispín might have been a little pissed about that," Claudio said, making a note. "You might not have a fabulous time at that football game tomorrow."

"Right."

Then Harley related Stevenson's version of the beating in Juárez. He told Claudio about Klinger's car getting stolen, and outlined his talk with Juárez Police Chief Roberto Muller, who maintained that Gustavo Jiménez was a "pussy cat." Finally, he detailed the attack at Ken Perry's house, including the information about the stolen Lexus with bloodstains on the passenger seat.

"And you say the cops are holding back on this story because they don't want to bring in the FBI?" Claudio asked.

"I wouldn't say they're holding back. They just want a clearer idea of things."

"Kind of like us," Claudio said with a smile. He took a sip of tea. "Where did you see Eddie Stevenson? Over at that apartment in the barrio?"

"No. He hasn't gone back there. He's staying with a woman on Memphis, near Copia. Diana Clements."

"Elke's friend?"

"Could be."

"So," Claudio said, "he gets beaten up in Juárez, and then never goes back home?"

The room was getting darker. Harley stood up and reached for the light switch. "Okay if I turn this on?" he asked.

"Let's wait a bit and catch the sunset," Claudio said. He crossed the living room to raise the blinds, exposing a bruised sky over Juárez. "So," he continued, "Stevenson gets beaten up and never goes home again? That's what I'd call fishy."

"Estela's pregnant," Harley said. "And he thinks she let herself get pregnant to trap him."

"So he's not going back to her unless she gets an abortion?"

"Now that he's with this other woman, I can't see him going back at all. In fact, he asked me to pick up his clothes. He's talking with lawyers about suing the paper."

"That gives him a vested interest in Jiménez and the beating. If there's a hole in the story, he's going to want to cover it up." Claudio sounded disgusted. "Are you going to go over there to pick up his clothes?"

"Would you?" Harley asked.

"Certainly not as a friend. But I might as a reporter. I think it might be worth snooping around there a little."

"I was thinking the same thing," Harley said. "Stevenson told me this morning that Estela was angry at him. Then she mentioned something about her friends being angry too."

Claudio nodded gravely, and then whispered, "Jesus!" He stood up and strode back into the kitchen. "Another beer?" he yelled.

"Not yet," Harley said, wondering why Claudio jumped up so suddenly.

He heard Claudio singing to himself in the kitchen over the sound of running water. The singing sounded forced and atonal.

Harley stood up and wandered into the kitchen. "What did I say in there to startle you so much?" he asked.

Claudio rinsed his cup, reached metal tongs into a big ceramic tea jar, and took a pinch. "I realized that I know one of Estela's friends," he said in a low voice. "And for all I know, he's probably involved. In fact, I'm pretty sure he is." He turned toward Harley. "I don't want to get him in the headlines—though that's probably what he's after."

"This is a friend of yours?" Harley asked.

"A former student of mine."

"Who works for Jiménez?"

"I don't think so. But... How about if I talk to him? I bet I'll be able to get you the story about what really went on in Juárez."

"How about if I talk to him?" Harley asked. "You were just saying I needed to take control of the story."

"The trouble is, this guy wants attribution. So much that he could get himself into a big mess," Claudio said. "You just go ahead and report the story. If I find out anything, I'll let you know."

"You think you might know something by tomorrow night?"

"Good chance. But if you're in such a hurry, I think you're

wasting precious time taking a plane ride with the *maquiladora* king."

"You still talk like an editor."

Claudio patted him on the shoulder as he headed toward the door. "I never stopped being one," he said. Then his eyes widened and he shouted, "Down! Down!"

He tackled Harley and both men sprawled on the hardwood floor. Claudio scrambled toward the kitchen, shouting, "He's got a gun!" Harley lay back and wrapped his arms around his head.

In the window, he saw the shadow of a figure wearing a black ski mask. He was hunched over, tinkering with a pistol. Harley simply stared at him while Claudio shrieked from the kitchen, "Get in here, hurry, get in here!"

Harley didn't move. He heard Claudio crawling behind him. Then he felt Claudio's hands under his armpits, tugging at him, dragging him toward the kitchen. Then he saw the man in the ski mask point the gun and fire. POCK. Harley heard glass shatter and felt nothing. Claudio was still pulling him, groaning. POCK. Another shot, then the sound of the footsteps racing down Prospect Street.

Claudio and Harley lay for a moment on the kitchen floor. "You okay?" Claudio asked.

"Yeah."

Harley climbed to his feet. "I'll see if I can find him," he said, hurrying toward the door.

Claudio tackled him a second time. "*Imbécil*," he said in Spanish as they crashed to the floor. "You don't chase a man with a gun!"

Harley looked up and saw the statue of Tlaloc staring strangely, as if it recognized the shooter. Then he noticed that the statue had a splintered bullet hole through the eye. "Tlaloc's a *tuerto* now," he thought, wondering if that might link the shooting to Gustavo Jiménez.

Then he ran out to his bike.

Chapter
TWENTY-NINE

Rubén's Aunt Julita watched the visitor shifting his weight uneasily. He studied the portrait of President Kennedy, and then the picture of a younger Rubén, his hair long and frizzy, accepting the journalism award at Bowie High School.

"Can I get you more lemonade?" she asked him in Spanish, trying not to stare at the large bump on his nose.

Oscar Olmos placed a hand on top of his glass. "*No gracias, señora,*" he said, twisting his broad face into a smile.

"If you'll just relax, Rubencito should turn up before long," Julita said. She suspected that this man, who said he worked for one of the captains of industry, was bringing Rubén a job offer. She didn't want him to leave. "I might be able to find a beer in the refrigerator," she said, standing up.

Oscar Olmos cocked his head to one side and cracked a downward smile, as if to say that a beer might taste good.

Julita hobbled from the small living room into the kitchen. Olmos looked at his watch. 7:35 Juárez time, an hour earlier in El Paso. Things were going slowly. He hadn't found the two men at the carwash, but the boy who worked there told him about Rubén, *el americano*. The boy had keys. He took him into the Lavarama and up to the office, where he showed him a white block pad. Rubén's El Paso address was written neatly on the first page. With the address in hand, Olmos hurried back to his truck and set off for El Paso.

His assignment was to find the carwash people and deliver a simple message: Leave town right away, or die. That was essentially what *don* Onofre had told him, though not exactly those words.

The aunt didn't seem to know where Rubén was. Olmos, who never felt entirely comfortable north of the border, wondered how to proceed. He couldn't write down the message and leave it with her. Put things like that in writing, he knew, and you got in trouble, especially north of the border. Plus, he couldn't see himself handing this woman a death threat for her nephew. He could hear her moving around bottles and cans in the refrigerator, looking for a beer.

He leaned back in the easy chair and was surprised when it suddenly reclined and a footstool popped up to lift his legs. He thrashed about for a couple seconds, trying to get back to earth, but managed only to push the seat back further. Now he was lying flat, with his feet as high as his head, maybe higher. There had to be some button to push, he figured, running his hands along the arms of the chair.

"That's more like it," Julita said as she returned. "Nice and easy." She poured a Coors Silver Bullet into a tall glass and placed it on a coaster next to Olmos, who looked like a man about to get a tooth pulled.

"Rubén adores that chair," Julita said. "Sometimes I think about moving it up into his room. That's where he spends most of his time. Studying. Doing his journalism. He could relax in the chair and read his newspapers. It might be good for his stress."

She paused for a moment and looked at Olmos, who was trying to pour beer into his mouth without spilling it. "He's a bit tense, you know," she went on. "But so are many of the young people you meet these days. Especially the ambitious ones. And Rubén is certainly ambitious. What industry did you say you were representing?"

"*La maquiladora, señora*," Olmos said. He managed to swallow some beer and then caught himself grimacing. American beer was such piss.

"*La maquiladora?*" Julita was distressed. Surely they weren't recruiting Rubén to work at one of those long tables, putting together toasters or car parts! Her nephew was a man of letters, not a worker in a blue smock.

"Rubén," she said, "is a nervous boy. High strung. It's probably because he's so intelligent. You know he's been to the university, and was director of the newspaper there?"

Olmos nodded, wondering why she was telling him this.

"So," Julita said sternly. "Let's be clear."

"Of course," Olmos said. He saw a wooden lever sticking out of the armchair. Did he dare push it down?

"If you are looking for *maquiladora* workers, my nephew is not the appropriate person. Now...perhaps a managerial position inside one of the factories might be..."

Olmos reached down, pushed the lever, and plopped back to the ground. The chair shook the table next to it, nearly tipping over the glass of beer. He reached over and steadied it.

The woman was going on about her nephew.

Olmos made some positive noises and tried another sip of the watery American brew.

"Would you like to see his bedroom?" the woman asked.

"What!?"

"No, you must understand," she said, blushing, "his bedroom is his office. I thought that if you had a look there, you would see what a serious young man you're dealing with."

"Let's have a look," Olmos said agreeably. He stood up from the chair and drained his beer. Maybe he could leave some sort of message up there.

He followed the woman as she climbed up the narrow staircase. "I call it the '*gallinero*,'" she yelled back. "I think he sweats down to his bones up here. You'll see."

The heat in the room almost took Olmos' breath away. He saw piles of newspapers next to the bed and desk, and newspaper articles taped to the wall. He wondered what sort of fanatic he was dealing with. "I tell him he needs a fan up here," Julita said, flattening the sheets on Rubén's narrow bed. "But with all these papers, well, you can imagine... It would be like a real hen house, with the feathers flying."

From down the stairway they heard the sound of a door opening, followed by Rubén's voice, shouting, "*Tía!*"

Julita and Olmos hushed.

"This is my aunt's place," they heard Rubén say in English. "You can just sit in that chair while I run up for the file. But watch it when you lean back."

A softer voice answered.

"Oh, sure," Rubén said. "You want to come up. No problem. It's a little messy, but..."

Olmos and Julita stood frozen in Rubén's stifling bedroom. "Come," she whispered. She pushed open the door and began walking down the steps, Olmos right behind her. "Rubencito?" she called down sweetly.

"*Tía?*" Rubén was climbing the steep stairs. A short bald man came up behind him.

After some confusion in the narrow stairway, Rubén and his companion, *New York Times* reporter Byron Biggs, retreated down the steps to make room for Aunt Julita and her large visitor. Rubén, looking confused, politely shook hands with Olmos, and then introduced him in Spanish to the *Timesman*. Biggs, who didn't understand a word, appeared mesmerized.

"Señor Olmos represents an industry in Juárez, Rubén," Julita said. "I told him that perhaps you would consider a managerial position, but that you were not one of those people who would put on a blue smock."

Rubén nodded blankly.

"I work for *don* Onofre Crispín," Olmos said. "Perhaps you know of him?"

Rubén perked up at the mention of Crispín's name. "Of course," he said, nodding.

"He wants to send along his warm regards, to you and your two companions, Pascual and Gato, and to extend best wishes for your journey. You were leaving tomorrow, did he hear? Or was it tonight?"

"Leaving?" Julita asked.

"Yes, yes," Rubén said affably. "Those plans are still to be ironed out. Señor Olmos, maybe you could take back a message to *don* Onofre Crispín." He placed a hand on the shoulder of the disoriented Byron Biggs and said, "This reporter from the *New York Times*—you're familiar with El *Times* de Nueva York? The most important newspaper in the world? He's writing a front-page article about certain scandals that have occurred in Juárez, and I've told him that an interview with *don* Onofre was absolutely indispensable. That is, to put everything into perspective. So maybe you would be kind enough to tell *don* Onofre that this señor Biggs and I will be coming by Monday, at an hour of his convenience?"

Chapter
THIRTY

As Claudio shouted at him to stop, Harley unlocked his bike and pulled the chain loose from the wrought-iron fence. Then he hopped on the Raleigh and raced down Prospect, strapping on his helmet with one hand.

It was dark. As he approached the overpass, he slowed down and peered into the bushes. No one there. As he rode over I-10 he saw a black spot on one of the westbound lanes. He stopped and looked. The ski mask. A truck ran over it and deposited it fifty yards down the road, toward the Asarco smelter.

Harley rode on toward downtown, feeling a rush of adrenaline. He wasn't too worried about the gunman. The man had a chance to shoot him and had aimed instead at the Aztec statue. Harley leaned left and turned onto Franklin. A few homeless men were slumped against the mulberry trees outside the library. The gunman could be sitting among them. But Harley figured that unless the man was very cool, he'd be hurrying back to his home base.

He continued east on Franklin, past the Santa Cruz bar and

the boarding hotels. Drinkers milled about on the sidewalks, a couple of them wearing stocking caps, ridiculous in eighty-five-degree heat. They looked too drunk to be suspects. He zipped through an empty parking lot to Kansas. By this point, he was probably past the shooter. He turned right on Mills and rode back towards Pioneer Plaza.

Mills Street was more crowded, with swarms outside the *casa de cambio*, the Arby's, and McDonald's. Finding him now would be tough. Harley dismounted and walked his bike along the sidewalk, gazing at the Saturday-evening crowd. He scanned the faces, some of them oval Mayas, with receding foreheads and long Roman noses, looking like drawings of the Indians who met Cortes at Veracruz. Others had round faces, like Fernando Valenzuela's.

Then he saw the glint of a pair of steel-rimmed glasses. A young man with short brown hair was looking at him. He abruptly turned and hurried away. Harley followed him, pushing and prodding through the crowd with his bike. The man wore chinos and a blue golf shirt. He carried a leather bag over his shoulder. Harley saw him duck to his left into Kress's, an ancient five-and-dime dressed with minarets that made it look like a mosque. Harley tried to catch up, but had to stop for a mother and father leading a toddler by the hands.

He gazed into Kress's for a while. But it wasn't worth waiting there: the store had doors on two streets.

His only chance, he decided, was to circle the area on bike, looking to get ahead of the shooter. Figuring he would head into the barrio, or even Mexico, Harley pedaled south, past the used clothing stores and pawnshops, and then he began weaving back and forth on cross-streets, just hoping to run into something. This was Stevenson's neighborhood, virtually shadeless, probably ten degrees hotter than Sunset Heights. The street corners smelled of sunbaked piss.

As Harley rode past Overland, he looked up at Stevenson's apartment. He could see Estela's form behind the window. It looked like she was talking on the phone. He pulled on the brakes and scooted up the curb. Claudio had suggested snooping around Stevenson's place, he thought, pressing the bell. Why not now?

Estela yelled out the window, *"Quién?"* Harley saw her leaning out the window, black hair falling in front of her eyes. She brushed it out of the way and saw him. "Ah!" she said, looking pleased. *"El famoso Tomás Harley."*

Chapter
THIRTY-ONE

Estela hurried down to the front door wearing tight blue jeans and an untucked pink T-shirt embroidered with flowers. Her face looked much better than last time. No sign of bruising around the eyes. As Harley navigated the bike up the narrow stairway, she warned him in Spanish that the apartment was a total mess—*"un desmadre."* She'd been packing her things, getting ready to leave, she explained, when a couple of guests arrived.

"You're leaving El Paso?" he asked.

"I'm still not sure," Estela said, pushing open the door and stepping over a box. "Here, sit here, on the sofa." She said she might stay with some *"amigas"* in El Paso, or else go back to Mexico. It depended on a few things.

Harley settled back on the couch and put his white helmet on the coffee table. He heard a man's voice humming. "Is that someone in the bathroom?" he asked.

"One of my guests." Estela rolled her eyes. "When you have a place on this side of the river, people are always dropping by."

"A friend from your hometown?" Harley asked, trying to remember which town she came from.

"Sort of. A friend of a friend. And then there's another friend I don't like too well. But he's not here now."

Harley smelled marijuana, probably from the guy in the bathroom. Estela looked far too clear-eyed for smoking. She stared at his face, appreciatively, and then flashed a brilliant smile. He smiled back and then looked down at the water pipe on the coffee table. He wondered whether to tell her he'd seen Stevenson. When he looked up, she was still gazing at him, her head cocked.

"What is it?" he asked, feeling uneasy.

"You're very beautiful," Estela said. "You'd look like an Italian movie star if you just dressed better. You'd look very sexy—'*muy sexy*'—with a cigarette in your hand, and a jacket over one shoulder."

Harley blushed. "You should see me in my bicycle helmet," he said.

That one left her puzzled. Yet she was smiling fondly, as if they were old friends.

"I saw Eddie this morning. And he's..."

"He's with that woman, isn't he?" Estela said contemptuously.

"Which woman?" Harley asked.

"You tell me."

"Diana?"

"*Eso, Dee-ana.*"

"Did he tell you he was going there?"

"He didn't need to," she said with a dismissive wave. "When she came over here asking about him, I knew where he was headed. Maybe he was already there..."

"She came here?"

"Uh huh."

"So... Do you know what really happened in Juárez?"

"I don't know...and it doesn't cost me any sleep." She was

hurt by the news about Stevenson, and working not to show it.

"No idea?"

Estela shrugged. "He was abusive, and people like that, they get abused. Go and see that woman, *Deeana*, in a few days. See if she has bruises... He's not gentle," she continued. "Not like you."

Harley ignored the compliment. "You're saying the beating in Juárez was payback for...his mistreatment of you?"

"Oh, you *gringos* take everything by the letter! Who knows why it was done? Maybe nothing happened at all. Maybe it was the government." She sat still for a moment, looking stern. "Yes, it was probably the government."

He heard the shower running. Looking at one of Estela's boxes, he saw a framed photograph of a skinny man in a white undershirt, looking angry. "Who's that?" he asked, pointing at the photo.

Estela looked over. "Rubén," she said, as though Harley already knew him. "Eddie took that photo. Part of his border project."

"Maybe you can go stay with him," he suggested.

She shook her head. "He lives with his aunt... Maybe," she said, widening her eyes, "maybe I could stay with you. Just for a couple of days."

"Oh, I don't know." He was taken aback by the suggestion. "I mean... I'm not staying at my apartment now. I'm at a hotel."

"You're sweet to offer," Estela said, standing up. "But I wouldn't want to stay in your place all by myself."

The bathroom door opened and Gato walked out, slouched and bleary-eyed. He smiled at the pair on the couch. Then he walked into the bedroom and shut the door.

Chapter
THIRTY-TWO

Eddie Stevenson sat at the bar drinking Cutty Sarks on the rocks and watching the San Francisco Giants maul the expansion team from Miami. He'd had a rough morning with two lawyers. They'd asked him questions that weren't any of their business. He'd walked out on them and taken refuge at Paxson's, a spacious bar up Mesa that had fishnets on the walls and wooden rakes and plows hanging from the ceiling. Stevenson ate bowls of free popcorn and washed down the salt with sips of cold whisky. Suing the paper might not be as easy as he'd hoped.

He wouldn't go back to Diana's duplex for a while. Give her time to get over whatever was bothering her. Maybe he'd stop by his old apartment, deal with Estela if need be, and pick up his pot and some clothes. Then he'd swing by Diana's place with a joint or two. He wouldn't carry his clothes in there right away. He could tell she was sensitive about those things.

He'd leave the clothes in the trunk. But then they'd smoke a joint and build up some rapport. Gently, he'd steer the conversation toward cohabitation. He could hear Diana saying, with that raspy voice she had after smoking, "Well, you know, if you want to stay here for a few days, it's okay." And then he'd say, as if the idea came out of the blue, "Well, I don't want to impose or anything. I mean, we still have to learn a lot about each other and all. But I do have some clothes out in the car..."

Stevenson paid his bill, left a dollar tip on the bar, and stumbled off the barstool. He made his way out of the restaurant, struggling to keep his balance. When he pushed open the door and walked outside, the sunlight blinded him and the late-afternoon heat almost buckled his knees. He was sober enough to know he was too drunk to drive. So he turned on the tape deck in his old Dodge and listened to *The Police* for a few songs until the heat made him feel light-headed. He moved the car to a parking space in the shade. Then he reclined, with the tape still playing, and fell asleep.

When Stevenson woke up, it was dark, and the sweat on his shirt and the back of his head was beginning to chill him. He started the car and pulled into the southbound Saturday evening traffic on Mesa. He didn't feel all that drunk. He worked his way all the way down Mesa past UTEP, screeching as he turned left onto Schuster. From there he drove east, practically on autopilot, past the mountain and Harley's hotel, to Diana Clements' duplex off Copia. Pulling in, he remembered that he planned to stop by Estela's place first. He'd do it later.

He walked up to Diana's door and tried to open it with his car key. After he scratched at it for a while, he pounded a fist on the door, and Diana answered. She was wearing red rubber gloves and a paisley headband. "I'm cleaning the toilet," she said, without inviting him in.

Stevenson murmured something, brushed by her into the living room, and flopped down on the couch. Following him, she bent low and looked into his eyes. "You're drunk!" she said.

"So what?" He tried to smile.

"It's criminal to drive in that condition. You could have killed somebody."

Stevenson opened his arms wide. "Come here," he said.

"The hell I will. You smell like a brewery." She puzzled for a second. "Or a distillery."

"Come here," he coaxed.

"No."

"Baby." He tried to say the word affectionately, but it came out more like a taunt.

Diana's eyes fired. "Don't you ever call me that again."

Stevenson buried his chin in his chest, trying to win her pity.

"I have some news to give you before you go," Diana said, her gloved hands on her hips. "Somebody shot at Tom Harley this afternoon."

"Where'd you hear that?" Stevenson asked, perking up.

"A friend."

"The one you were at the party with?"

"Uh huh."

"And where'd she hear it?"

"From Claudio. Tom was over at his apartment when the man shot at him."

"God." Stevenson sounded shocked. "Is Harley gay?"

"I wouldn't know."

"Jesus." Stevenson shook his head. "He didn't get hit, did he?"

"No."

"So who did it?"

"You tell me."

Stevenson looked glumly at the floor, trying to focus his mind. He lay back on the couch, hoping that Diana, pitying him, would climb on top of him.

"I also learned something else about you," she said.

"What?"

"Is Estela pregnant?"

"No."

"No?"

"What's happening is, she's probably going around saying she's pregnant to make people think that I've, like, ditched her."

"So she never told you she was pregnant?"

"Oh, she mentioned it a couple of times. You know, her period was late. But I didn't believe it. She just got herself pregnant to try to... I mean, she *might* have got herself pregnant to..."

"To what?"

"To trap me!"

Stevenson was fast losing hope that Diana would lie on top of him. She paced behind the coffee table, looking like a prosecuting attorney.

"Listen," she said, making a tent with her gloved fingertips, "I think it's time we cut our losses on this. I know it's partly my fault. I invited you over here. But I don't think it's working, and so..." She looked from her fingers to Stevenson, who now had his eyes closed and was pretending to sleep.

"Get up!" she said.

He grunted and rolled to one side.

She leaned down and yelled in his ear. "Get up!"

He grunted again.

She reached down and grabbed his head to shake it. But Stevenson extended his arms and yanked her on top of him.

Diana tried to pull herself loose. But he'd locked onto her tight. She kicked and tried to hammer with her fists. It was hard though, because he had her arms pinned to her side, and he softened the kicks by rolling on top of her. She tried to scream. He muffled it by planting a big whiskey kiss on her mouth.

She bit his lower lip with her canines, hard, cutting him.

Stevenson grunted and punched her in the ribs. Then he pressed harder upon her and lay his scratchy face against hers. He still held his eyes closed, as if this were all happening in his sleep. His blood trickled across her cheek and onto the sofa.

They both breathed heavily, resting. Diana's ribs ached with each breath. She wondered if she could coax him off her, or if she'd need to use force. If he ever let go of her arm, there was a brass vase within her reach on the coffee table. She could crack him on the head with it. But what if she tried and didn't knock him out? Then he might kill her. He didn't seem like a killer. But he didn't seem like a rapist either. And that's what he was doing, in this cadaverous mode. Raping her. Or maybe it was just a very strange fight... She wondered how she'd wash the blood off the sofa.

Then she heard him snore lightly. This was her chance. She pushed one leg against the back of the sofa and managed to shift her weight underneath him, putting herself closer to the coffee table. Then she wriggled an arm free. He was snoring louder now and his head, no longer against hers, was sideways on the pillow. His lip looked white where she'd bitten it.

Stretching her left arm, she reached the brass vase and pulled the pansies out. She lifted it. Square on the bottom and round on top, it probably weighed a pound. To swing the vase, she needed to get out from under him. She put the vase back on the table and gently pushed his shoulder up. He grunted and rolled back on top of her.

Diana lost all patience. She screamed and pushed with all her might, lifting him from her and then jumping from the couch. She reached for the vase and held it in her right hand as Stevenson opened his eyes.

"What's going on?" he mumbled.

"Out!" She lifted the vase above her head, spilling water on the carpet. She was primed to dent his forehead with it.

"Okay, okay, okay." Stevenson climbed to his feet and tried

to say something to her.

"Out!"

"Okay!" He hurried out the door and slammed it behind him.

Diana, her heart pounding, spun around, the adrenaline making her feel like a warrior. She saw Stevenson's keys on the couch, near the blood spot on the white cushion. She put down the vase, picked up the keys and walked to the door. When she opened it, Stevenson was standing there, looking penitent. Using the same hurling motion that she'd prepared for the vase, she threw the keys at him and shut the door.

Chapter
THIRTY-THREE

Estela and Harley sat on her unmade bed—just a mattress on the floor—looking at Eddie Stevenson's photos. Harley wasn't much interested in them. Estela nestled close to him, and when she liked a photo, she would touch his arm and say, "*Bonito, no?*"

They were about halfway through the thick pile when he heard someone open the front door. A voice yelled, "*Aló?*"

Estela shouted in Spanish. "Get in the bedroom and shut the door! I want privacy."

Harley heard a man muttering. Then footsteps and the bedroom door shutting, and muffled men's voices behind it.

Harley stood up and walked back toward the living room. "You don't have to lock up your guests for me," he said.

"I don't want to see them," she said, following him. She had the photos in her arms. They sat on the couch and kept looking at them. Harley didn't want to be there, but wasn't sure how to get away without being rude.

Then there was a banging on the stairway and the door rattled open. In walked Eddie Stevenson, looking like an immigrant who'd crashed head-on into Operation Blockade. He had scratch marks on his face and a swollen lower lip, and his clothes looked dirty and slept in.

Harley stood up.

"Harleyman!" Stevenson yelled. "I shoulda known I'd find you here."

He was drunk.

The photographer weaved across the room, toward Estela. She sat on the couch looking grim, her posture rigid, chin jutting angrily, head tilted back.

"Estelita," he said soothingly, sitting beside her.

She wouldn't look at him.

He took her hand. "Look at me, baby," he said.

She pulled back her hand.

"Harleyman," he said. "Translate for me, will you? My Spanish is shit sometimes. Tell her I'm uh..." Then he switched to Spanish. "*Cómo estás, baby? Qué pasó?*"

Harley heard giggling from the bedroom. He saw a leather knapsack on the coffee table, next to his bike helmet, and noticed the water pipe was missing. The guests were smoking, he figured, and listening to this soap opera in the living room. He picked up his helmet and strapped it on.

"Look at my lip, Estelita," Stevenson was saying. "I got punched." He looked up at Harley. "How do you say 'lip,' anyway? Lipio?"

"Labio."

"Oh yeah. Reminds me of other lips..." He flashed a grin. "Don' worry," he said. "She doesn't understand shit."

"Jes I do," Estela said angrily in English. "Leave, Eduardo. And take the....stuff."

Stevenson swung around, focusing for the first time on the apartment. He looked at the boxes of his things piled neatly in the corner, next to Harley's bike. And then at Harley. He wasn't processing information quickly.

The phone rang.

Estela rushed to answer it. "*Bueno?*" She listened, said, "One *momento*, please," and handed it to Stevenson.

He took the phone and settled on the couch as if he'd never left. It was a freelancing assignment, and he sounded almost sober as he talked about shipping schedules and rendezvous points in Juárez.

Harley grabbed his bike and started to point it toward the door. But Estela placed a hand on his arm. "Stay," she whispered in Spanish. "I don't want to be here alone with him."

"You have your friends in the bedroom," he said, opening the door.

Estela glanced toward the bedroom and then looked back at him blankly.

Harley made it down the steps and was maneuvering his bike onto the sidewalk when he heard Stevenson stumbling down the stairs behind him. "Hey, wait up! Harley!"

The photographer nearly tripped over the ledge at the door and dropped two of the three boxes he was carrying, making a loud clatter. As he gathered them, he looked up and smiled, stretching his puffy lower lip. "Hey Harley," he said, "N.Y.T!"

"What's that?" Harley just wanted to get on his bike and leave.

"*New York Times.* I'm shooting for them Monday."

"You're kidding. Which story?"

"Jiménez, I guess," Stevenson said, looking puzzled. "I didn't even ask."

"Do you think they know that you're, sort of, involved?"

"Probably... Doesn't matter." Stevenson sounded defensive. "You're involved, and you're writing about it... I got to make a living."

"You're not going back to the paper?"

Stevenson shrugged and started to pick up the boxes and carry them to his Dodge. "Depends..."

"Depends on what?"

"On, you know, the suit. I went to lawyers... Ahh, I don't want to talk about it."

Harley climbed on his bike and turned it north.

"Hey, wait a minute," Stevenson said. "Who shot at you today?"

"Where'd you hear that?"

"Fuckin' ahhh, whatshisname. Claudio."

"Huh?"

"Yeah, I went over there to give him his Saturday rubdown, and he said you'd already been there, and somebody took a shot at you." Stevenson cackled.

Harley wondered how Stevenson had heard about it. But he wasn't going to give him the satisfaction of asking again.

"Who did it?" Stevenson wasn't kidding now.

"Probably the same people who beat you up."

Stevenson climbed into his car and reached for his keys. "They have empty rooms at that hotel of yours?" he asked. "Or are you staying at Claudio's now?"

"They probably have rooms at the hotel. But if you're suing the paper, I doubt they'll pay your bill... You're not staying at Diana's?"

"Fuck no." Stevenson fired the ignition. The engine roared, and he revved it up before letting it settle into a rough idle. He pointed to his lip. "See that? She fucking bit me. The animal."

Harley swung onto his bike and waved, pedaling ahead of Stevenson on Stanton Street. Then he continued north and east, toward Memphis Avenue.

Chapter
THIRTY-FOUR

Diana hesitated before unfastening the chain. As Harley walked in, the first thing he noticed was the sofa pillow stained red. "I bit him," she said.

"He told me."

"He wouldn't let me go, and so I just bit him."

"He told me you bit him," Harley said. "I figured he must have done something to you. That's why I came over, to see..."

Diana interrupted. "You want a cup of coffee?" He nodded, and as she boiled the water and poured the grounds into a paper funnel, he settled in at the kitchen table.

They drank coffee and talked like old friends who had lost their way, and then found it. Diana told him about her relationship with Raymond, and the move to El Paso, and how he'd left her for another woman at her office. She told him how lonely she'd been, and how she met her friend Elke. "I was a lesbian project of hers," Diana said matter-of-factly. "It didn't happen. But I'd like to think we're still friends."

Harley wanted to ask her what in the world she saw in Stevenson, and how she got into the fight. But that could wait.

He told her about himself, his bike riding and impersonating. Then he told her about his afternoon with Claudio, and the masked man at the window with a gun. He expected her to be surprised, even impressed. But she just looked at him with her head cocked, gnawing her lip. Thinking.

He went on to describe his misadventures with the Mexican police. He played up the humor, even joking about the joint. When he saw her eyelids were getting heavy, he glanced at his watch and said he had to go, mentioning the trip the next morning with Onofre Crispín.

Diana perked up. "You're *traveling* with him?"

He nodded.

"Just the two of you, flying to the Cowboys game?"

"I think."

She smiled and shook her head as if Harley was the luckiest guy in the world. She talked for a while about the Grupo Espejo stock, how the prospect of North American free trade was driving it up. Harley didn't understand much about stocks and wasn't much interested in them. He didn't see why investors would be bidding up Crispín's company just because of NAFTA.

Diana explained that it was a "speculative bubble." Investors, she said, were dumping money into any new Mexican stocks, hoping that each one would be the next Mexican miracle, the next TelMex.

Now it was Harley's eyelids getting heavy.

"Hey!" Diana grabbed his shoulder and shook him. She was wide-eyed and flushed. "When you're with Crispín tomorrow," she said, "ask him who his investors are. There are lots of rumors."

"Right," he said. A few minutes later he rode back along the dark streets to the Cliff Inn.

◊

Onofre Crispín's invitation, it turned out, was not to fly to Dallas, but simply to watch the Cowboys game on his rear-projection TV at his pink stucco Juárez estate. Trouble was, Crispín had the TV schedule wrong: the Cowboys were playing a Sunday-night game in Phoenix. That gave the *maquiladora* magnate an open afternoon with Harley. "It's a good thing you wore tennis shoes," Crispín said, eyeing Harley's large feet. "I don't think mine would fit you."

Harley had played some squash in college, and racquetball was about the same: quick wrist strokes and dance out of the way of the ball. It was easy for him, and he could see right away that he was better at it than his host. Crispín, though, was highly competitive. He grunted on every ball, and swore under his breath when he lost points. Harley couldn't wait for it to end. After he won the first game, Crispín said, "Let's do best of three." When Harley won the second, his host changed it to best of five.

The men didn't get to talk much until afterwards. Crispín was lying facedown on a massage table, a white towel draped over his midsection. His enormous chauffeur, who had picked up Harley at the hotel, was giving him a vigorous rubdown. The racquetball clearly had put Crispín into a dark mood.

Speaking English, he asked Harley how the newspaper was proceeding with the Jiménez story.

"We're just following the news as it happens," Harley said.

"What news? What do you mean, 'as it happens?' There was one incident, a regrettable incident. What else is there?"

Harley realized to his horror that he'd forgotten to call the editors after the shooting at Claudio's house. He'd played detective and forgotten about his job. Burying a story like that could get him fired, especially if the *Journal* got it first. As Crispín talked, Harley tried to come up with a strategy, or at least an excuse he could give Canfield and Perry.

"WHAT ELSE IS THERE?" Crispín asked.

Maybe he could call Perry from Crispín's place, Harley

thought, and explain...what? That he'd been hunting down the shooter for the last eighteen hours? "Do you have a phone?" he asked Crispín.

"Of course I do," Crispín snapped. "Now tell me how you see this story developing."

"Oh, I don't know," Harley said. "I guess we'll follow the diplomatic news. How the Mexican government responds to things. What they do with Jiménez. That sort of thing."

"And did it ever occur to you—I'm sure it has—that this incident was organized... How do you say, *mise en scene*...?"

"Staged," Harley said.

"Precisely. That this incident was staged by people with a political agenda? And that you are being manipulated?"

"Which people would that be?"

"Anyone who is opposed to the economic modernization of Mexico."

"And who would that be?"

"Use your head!" Crispín shouted, startling him. "Trade unionists. Students. Communists. You're a journalist. Dig. Find out!"

"But not Jiménez?"

Crispín, his head sideways on the massage table, reached back with this arm, showing Olmos a spot that needed attention. "Make it crack," he said in Spanish. Then he switched to English. Based on what he'd read, he said, this Jiménez ran a prosperous drug business. "Now why in the world would he be interested in blocking NAFTA?"

"You mean that NAFTA will benefit drug lords?"

"I do NOT! You are twisting my words."

"More commerce, more traffic," Harley went on. "Isn't that what you're implying? That drug lords are interested in tearing down trade barriers?"

"I say nothing of the kind."

"Do you know Jiménez?" Harley asked.

Crispín shook his head. "Never met him."

Chapter
THIRTY-FIVE

The gray-haired woman in a blue polyester dress invited Claudio into a hot apartment smelling of Pine-Sol and shouted upstairs: "*Rubencitooo, está el profesor Claudiooo.*" Then she led Claudio into a living room arranged around a shrine to the Virgin of Guadalupe and asked him if he wanted a glass of limeade.

Claudio said he would, and sat down on the corner of a sofa.

Rubén thumped down the stairs and hurried into the living room. "Hey man," he said to Claudio. He was wearing a sleeveless undershirt, tufts of hair flaring from his underarms. Looking somewhere over Claudio's right shoulder, he reached out and offered an awkward handshake. Then he climbed into a big easy chair and reclined so that his knees blocked the view of his face.

"Good news, man," he said before Claudio had a chance to talk. "I'm doing some work for the *New York Times*."

"You're kidding."

"No. The reporter's down here, and I'm going to be like,

his guide in Juárez."

"His *Lazarillo*, huh?" Claudio said, using the Spanish word for a blind man's boy.

Rubén thought about that one for a second as his aunt brought in a tray with three glasses of limeade. "You mean I'm like, rising from the dead or something, like Lázaro?"

"No, I don't think you fell that far," Claudio said. Then, for the woman's benefit, he switched to the formal Spanish he'd learned from his father, a Mexico City professor. "I came by to see if you've made any progress on that story you were working on."

"Which story?"

"The one that's been in the paper."

"Oh." Rubén leaned forward to take a sip of limeade, then reclined again. "Mmmmm. Not much," he said.

"He's been doing a lot of work on it, though," said Aunt Julita. "Right, Rubén?"

Rubén didn't answer.

"I ask," Claudio said, "because I had, let's say, an intrusive visitor last night, and I thought you might be able..."

"Rubén has visitors," Julita said. "Every day more of them. I tell him, 'Rubén, you must treat them with respect. Invite them in, introduce them to me, offer them something to drink.' The simple things, you know, *Profesor* Claudio."

"Exactly, *Tía*," Rubén said. "So was this visitor especially rude or something?" he asked, smiling past his knee.

"I thought he might be someone you know."

"I doubt that."

Julita piped up. "Maybe..."

"*Tía*," Rubén said. "Why don't you bring us some of those cookies you have."

"*Con mucho gusto*," Julita said. She took Claudio's empty glass and hobbled off into the kitchen.

"A man shot through my window last night," Claudio said, returning to English. "Tom Harley was there."

"Jesus," Rubén muttered.

"I figured it was one of the guys who beat up Stevenson. Now you've had five days to work on that story. You're too good of a reporter," Claudio said, appealing to Rubén's pride, "not to know who did it."

"You see the guy?"

"He was wearing a mask."

"They didn't catch him?"

"No."

Rubén was quiet, thinking. They could hear Julita in the kitchen cracking ice from trays.

"Anybody get hurt?" he asked.

"Tlaloc was left half blind."

"Huh?"

"It's not important," Claudio said. "Come on. Tell me who these guys are."

"Okay," Rubén said, sighing. "I came up with a few things. People in Juárez are saying it's a couple of guys who work for Jiménez. They run some sort of operation in Franja del Rio. You know, just across the border from the Sun Bowl."

"So is Jiménez behind it?"

"I'm not sure."

"What are they after?"

"I don't know. You get a lot of different stories over there. But some people think they're trying to get Jiménez arrested, so they can move up in the organization."

"What are their names?"

"Ah... All I hear are their aliases."

"And?"

"And what?"

"The aliases, what are they?"

"Gato and Perro, or something like that... I've been pretty busy with this *New York Times* deal, and I haven't really been able to follow this up... Did you call the cops about that guy last night?"

"Of course I did. The guy shot a gun, Rubén."

"And what'd they say? The cops?"

"Not much. They dusted the window ledge for fingerprints and pried a slug out of a statue I have. They'll be doing forensics, I guess."

"They asked a lot of questions, I guess."

"Some."

"Did you tell them about me?"

"What about you?"

"I don't know. I just thought that since we talked about the case and I'm following it pretty close and have a file on it and all, I don't know... And that reporter Farley..."

"Harley."

"Whatever. Is he going to write a story on it?"

"Maybe. I don't know. He took off after the guy, and I haven't seen him since."

"Took off after him?" Rubén sounded surprised.

Julita returned with a fresh glass of limeade for Claudio and a plate of Fig Newtons.

"*Gracias,*" Claudio said, taking two cookies.

"*No hay de qué.*"

As Rubén reached for cookies, Claudio took a wild stab. "Is Gato the one with the wire-rimmed glasses?"

"No, that's Pa... No, I think that's the other one, according to what I've heard."

"You started to say his name."

"Well, I've heard his name is...Paz. But that's just talk."

Claudio considered it. He looked at Julita, who was gazing out the window, ignoring the English conversation. "Don't be absurd," he said without raising his voice. "Paz is a girls' name. You know these two guys, and you're a lot more involved than you're telling me."

"Hey, come on," Rubén said, not protesting too much.

"You think they're staying on this side of the border?"

"Probably not."

"But it's hard to cross, with this blockade."

"Maybe they have green cards..."

Claudio thought about that, sipping his limeade. He considered asking Rubén's aunt about the two men. But Aunt Julia, seeing that the conversation was continuing in English, stood up, excused herself, and made her way back toward the kitchen.

Claudio again appealed to Rubén's pride. "You know," he said, "I still keep a copy of that big story you did, on the whole drug network. It's still a wonderful piece, if you can just nail down some of the reporting."

"Yeah," Rubén said, perking up. "That's what we're going to do this week."

"We?"

"Byron Biggs and me. The *Times* guy."

"He's doing the big drug story?"

"I think he's doing Operation Blockade..."

"But you're going to lead the blind man to the drug story."

"Yeah. We got an interview tomorrow with Onofre Crispín."

Claudio looked puzzled. "How's he fit into it?"

"The money laundering. Don't you remember?"

"Oh, right." Claudio recalled Rubén's drug chart on the front page of *Semana*, with all the arrows going from one box to another. Crispín must have been one of the links between drug traffickers and American banks or corporations. "And are you going to brief the *Times* reporter on this?"

"A little."

"You've got to watch it, Rubén, or he might think you and your theory are...nuts," Claudio said, wondering just how sane Rubén was. "Those *Times* reporters aren't big on conspiracy theories."

"Right," Rubén said.

"I mean, I doubt this reporter's going to appreciate getting manipulated into your story."

"He will when he sees he could win the Pulitzer!"

Claudio nibbled on a cookie and listened to the Tejana music coming up through the floor from the boutique downstairs. He wondered about Rubén's mysterious love life, which was probably just as feverish and fantastic as his drug reporting. He sucked on a piece of ice from his empty glass. It was hot in this apartment. He figured it had to be broiling upstairs in Rubén's garret. "How about if we take a look at some of your reporting?" he asked.

"Okay," Rubén said, without budging from the easy chair. Then his smile flashed from behind his knee. "And guess who's shooting the pictures for the *Times*?"

"Not Eddie Stevenson."

"Yup." Rubén was leaning sideways on the easy chair, smiling ear to ear.

"You're shitting me."

"The guy needs work."

"Since when do you care about him? You said he hit Estela in the face, that he was a drunk and a drug addict."

"Yeah. But he's a damn good photographer..."

"The *Times* reporter will fire you both when he finds out," Claudio predicted. "They can't hire a photographer who's involved in the story. Remember what conflicts of interest are, Rubén?"

"Yeah, I remember," Rubén said, pushing down the wooden lever and climbing out of the chair. "They're hiring him for Operation Blockade. If they don't want Stevenson for the drug story, that's okay."

Chapter
THIRTY-SIX

"Mexican caviar," pronounced Onofre Crispín.

Harley moved his head closer to the plate of what looked like short-grain rice and sniffed. "Smells like garlic. And olive oil," he said.

"*Escamole.*" Crispín enunciated the word slowly. "Would you like to try some, before I tell you what it is?"

"Go ahead and tell me. I've eaten roasted grasshoppers before, and iguana." Harley sniffed it again. "Garlic and olive oil make just about anything taste good."

The two men sat at a stone table in Crispín's garden, in the shade of a trellised roof woven with grape ivy. A couple of exotic water birds huddled under a small willow tree.

Crispín poured tequila from a jar into shot glasses. "This is sipping tequila, 100-percent agave," he said. "No lemons, no salt. None of that nonsense. You drink this like a fine Scotch whiskey or cognac. Take a sip and then try the *escamole.*" He called the servant. "Teresa. *Las tortillas blancas, para el escamole!*"

Harley focused on Crispín's Spanish. The man wasn't from

Chihuahua. That much was clear. He had a high voice, a little cloying, with just the hint of a defect in the R's, almost as if Tom Brokaw were speaking Spanish. He recalled that when he'd lost a couple of tough points in racquetball, Crispín shouted, "*Me cago en la puta madre.*" Spaniards talked about shitting on whore mothers. Mexicans, as a rule, didn't. The man probably had spent some time in Spain. Or maybe it was just a conceit.

Harley took a sip of the tequila. Rich and warming, it practically slid down his throat. "Uuuu, that is special," he said.

Crispín grinned and took a long pull of his own, draining most of the glass. "Now try this," he said, pointing to the *escamole.*

Harley reached with a small spoon for three or four of the grains. He rolled them around in his mouth, tasting the garlic and that other spice, one he'd smelled in Estella's apartment. *Epazote?* He chewed gently. The grains seemed to flex between his teeth.

"Ants eggs," Crispín said.

"Really?" Harley swallowed them, then quickly took another sip of tequila. "I figured it was some sort of egg when you called it Mexican caviar."

"Of course, we have real caviar, if you'd prefer..."

"No, no," Harley said, dipping with the spoon for more *escamole.* "This is just the ticket."

He mentioned that he'd enjoyed the racquetball, but soon regretted bringing it up. Crispín, his pride wounded, complained of an aching Achilles tendon and a loose string in his racquet. Then he said that Americans focused far too much on winning and losing.

"I would have been perfectly happy," Harley said, "if you hadn't even taught me how to keep score."

"Tall men like you," Crispín said, looking at him knowingly, "they can act unconcerned, devil-may-care, even dress a bit sloppy. It's an affectation we short men cannot afford. But," he said, "deep down you are intensely competitive. When you saw I was favoring my left foot, you immediately sent all shots to that side. Do not deny it," he said sternly, shaking his head. "Winning is nothing to be ashamed of... Though you won't really know you can beat me until I play with a good racquet and a healthy foot."

They went on to chat about the Dallas Cowboys. Emptying his tequila glass and refilling it, Crispín said he'd been a fan since the '70s when he went to college at S.M.U.

That led Harley to ask him about his family background, his studies, and how he came to be the *maquiladora* king of Juárez. Crispín, sipping at his tequila, answered each question at length, as if being interviewed for a major magazine profile.

Harley listened politely, nodding, picking at the ant eggs occasionally, but taking no notes.

Looking to the left of the willow tree, beyond the spiked cast-iron gate, Harley could see Mt. Franklin, looking blue in the distance, slanting down into El Paso. Scenic Drive was a faint gray line along the skirt of the mountain, with an American flag at its highest point. It looked like a dot. Just a ten-minute bike ride east from that flag was Diana Clements' duplex on Memphis.

He looked at Crispín, who was telling him about going on a "road show" with his investment bankers, and how they'd enjoyed a $13,000 bottle of Bordeaux in Paris. "Tasted like Welsh's, with just a little vinegar," he said with a practiced chuckle. It was probably the hundredth time, Harley figured, that Crispín had repeated the same line.

Crispín explained to him that the Espejo stock "hiccupped" after an anti-NAFTA protest in Detroit. "We're going to be bigger than Grupo Carso," he said.

Harley had no idea what he was talking about. But he did recall Diana urging him to ask Crispín something about his partners.

Crispín, though, was waxing on about his childhood in Monterrey and his relations with the president's family. He kept licking his lips as if they were chapped. "His father worked in the government. But we got together when they came back to Monterrey."

Harley nodded, doubting it was true.

Crispín emptied another glass of tequila and refilled it. "You don't want any more?" he asked, waving the jar in the direction of Harley's glass.

"Thanks. In a minute." He could hear the liquor starting to tangle up Crispín's tongue. This always happened earlier when speaking foreign languages. Harley knew from experience.

"Are you married?" he asked Crispín.

"Divorced," the Mexican said, smiling. "There are too many lovely women in the world for a man to be tied down to one."

The usual bragging. Harley switched into his Chihuahua Spanish and asked Crispín who the president was going to pick to replace himself, a decision that was due in a month or two.

Crispín, who had the tequila glass at his lips, held it motionless and stared at Harley. "Was that you talking?" he asked in Spanish, licking his lips again.

"Of course it was me," Harley said, sticking with the same accent.

Crispín studied Harley, and then glanced to both sides, as if he expected to see another Mexican talking. "But you have the voice of a...a *campesino*!"

"It's my *Chihuahuense* accent."

"But Americans shouldn't speak like that." Crispín still talked as if dealing with a ghost.

"It's something I picked up."

"Well, I'd drop it," Crispín said, snapping out of his reverie, "unless you want to join the circus—or make a living picking onions."

"So who's going to be the next president?" Harley asked, imitating the voice of Chief Muller.

Crispín looked at him, stunned. "So you do voices," he said softly.

"It's just a pastime," Harley said, returning to his own voice in Spanish, a little embarrassed to be showing off so much. "Who's it going to be? Colosio?"

"Probably," Crispín said, "though he's not a good choice."

"Why?"

Crispín drank half a glass of tequila, savoring it for a moment. "He's too romantic. He thinks he can be everything to everybody, a little like President Clinton. What we need is a hard man with clear ideas—a pragmatist who's not afraid to make enemies."

"But people like that don't win elections..."

"They don't have to here!" He pushed the jar toward Harley. "You're hardly drinking at all."

Harley poured a few drops into his glass. "You sound as though you don't believe in elections," he said.

"I don't." Crispín looked at him defiantly. "Not here." He licked his lips, then blotted them with a napkin.

"But the police chief said you were Panista. And I thought the whole platform of the PAN was honest elections."

"Chief Muller is a Panista, and he tends to think all reasonable people agree with him. That's naive. If we are going to turn Mexico into a modern country, we first modernize the economy. Then we can worry about elections." Crispín grabbed a white tortilla and piled some *escamole* on it. Then he wrapped it into a tube and jammed half of it into his mouth. "Power determines politics," he said, chewing. "It's not the other way around."

"The drug dealers have power..." Harley said.

"Yes, they do."

"So how do you deal with them?"

"I knew you'd get to this line of questions, sooner or later."
Harley smiled.

"Well, I don't have to worry about them," Crispín said,
"because I'm not in politics."

"But you've got power. And you say that power precedes
politics."

Crispín finished his *escamole* burrito and wiped his
mouth. "Teresa," he shouted. "*Más tequila!*"

Harley had finished only one shot of tequila. Crispín, by
his reckoning, had consumed nearly a pint. If he was going to
grill him, now was the time.

Crispín, however, started talking on his own. "The *narcos*
are capitalists. They're simply responding to an immense
market over there." He waved toward El Paso. "Now as a
society, we can turn them into devils, the way you do, at your
paper, and go to war with them. That becomes very bloody
very fast. Or we can be pragmatists."

"In other words, do business with them?"

"I do not mean that!"

"But deal with them pragmatically…"

"Exactly. Come to certain agreements, modus vivendi, you
know. Avoid fatal collisions. Train wrecks."

"So how do you come to these agreements with someone
like Gustavo Jiménez? Do you sit here in this garden, with
tequila and *escamole*, and work things out?"

"I told you I don't know him."

The servant arrived with a fresh jar of the golden tequila,
covered with a white cotton cloth. Harley began to wonder
how he'd get home if his host passed out. He'd probably have
to find the man with the bump on his nose, Olmos, and beg a
ride, at least to the bridge.

"So you deal with Jiménez through intermediaries? Your
investment partners? Or people like the police chief?"

Crispín shrugged and wet his lips, as if the question was
too foolish to answer. He poured more tequila into his glass,

spilling some on the table.

Harley persisted. "So how do you avoid these...train wrecks?"

"Listen," Crispín said, slurring more. "You've got a garden. Your neighbor has a garden. You don't trample all over his garden, and he won't trample all over yours. Live and let live. And you might even let him build a path through your garden, if it's in his way—and to keep him from stepping all over your Belgian endives, or whatever you happen to be growing. You know," he added, "with the modernization of agriculture, we actually have some Mexicans growing Belgian endives? It's a very promising export market. Labor intensive. They're going to make a killing with NAFTA."

"You were saying, you might let them build a path through your garden?"

"Oh yes, yes. This tequila is very good, isn't it? Like an excellent single malt Scotch whiskey. Or even better."

"And if you let them cut a path through your turf, what do they do for you?"

"They don't shoot me!" Crispín laughed loudly. "Or take me to some absurd car wash and beat the piss out of me."

"So you're hostage to them."

"No, no, no," Crispín said, still smiling. "I was just joking."

"But you have a business relationship."

"Relax, relax, for the love of God. You're young, you're ambitious, a magician with your voices, for God's sake," Crispín said, looking at him fondly. "I was just trying to tell you a few things about power in Mexico, to educate you. And all of a sudden you're trying to get me to say that I'm in bed with these drug dealers. That's not what I meant. And if I see that even implied again in your paper, I'll..."

"What do you call these eggs?" Harley asked. "*Escamole*? I like squeezing them one at a time between my canines, and feeling that tiny pop."

"Exactly, exactly," Crispín said, cheering up. "But if you eat them one by one, you'll take all day. Here," he said, tossing him a tortilla. "Wrap a pile of it in that."

Harley rolled a heaping spoonful of *escamole* into a burrito. "So how do you deal with them?" he asked.

"With whom?"

"People like Jiménez."

"Holy God! Listen. I'm not saying I do. But I don't pursue them. I don't take part in hostile, unproductive political rhetoric."

"You mentioned something about beating you up in a car wash? Is that where they beat up Stevenson?"

"Yes," Crispín said flatly.

"Yes?"

"Yes, yes, yes, yes, yes," Crispín said, looking now like a sad old man. It was as if the tequila, which had him so excited a few minutes before, had vacated his head and settled in his stomach.

"In a car wash?" Harley said it in English, just to make sure.

"Yes, this side of Anapra." Crispín stuck with Spanish.

"Who were they?"

"Boys, boys," said Crispín, pronouncing "*muchachos*" wistfully, as if he ached. "Young men who want to turn back the modernization of Mexico, God knows why."

"Do they work for Jiménez?"

Crispín shrugged. "Maybe, maybe not. It's not of importance... It's like the man who tried to kill President Reagan. I remember reading once that he worked in a record store. Or was that the one who killed the Beatle? No matter. Let's say he worked in a record store. Is the record store connected to the shooting? No. His work is how he makes money. The shooting is what he does to satisfy his...his passion. His madness. But he must be stopped."

It sounded to Harley as though these *muchachos* worked for Jiménez. He wanted to ask Crispín about them. He wanted their names, the name of the car wash. He wanted to know how Crispín learned about this. But he worried that irritating questions would derail the interview. He recalled that he hadn't told Crispín about the shootings in El Paso, at Perry's house, and at Claudio's. Maybe if he provided him with more details, Crispín would offer more of his own.

"You know," Harley said, "a couple of nights ago, two men with guns attacked the home of my editor."

"*Ay, noooo.* Is it going to be in the paper?"

"Eventually."

"*Puta madre,*" Crispín said in a soft voice. "They're killing Mexico."

"And then last night, a man shot at me through a window. But missed."

Crispín looked at him soberly. Then, trying to smile, he reached for the jar of tequila. "Come!" he said. "Fill your glass."

Chapter
THIRTY-SEVEN

The vacuum cleaner stopped and popped open. A red light announced the bag was full. Diana Clements, wearing the faded blue silk bathrobe she'd had on all day, looked in the closet for a refill, but found only an empty box. She swore quietly. She'd worked her way through the bedroom, which still smelled of Eddie Stevenson and his pot. But right before she reached the spot where Eddie had spilled the ashtray, the machine quit.

Diana pulled the bag out of the vacuum cleaner and carried it to the kitchen wastebasket. Then she reached in with her fingers, past the rubber opening, which reminded her of a diaphragm, into the dirt. She pulled out a gob with her finger and thumb. It felt like peat moss.

Dinnertime. And instead of eating, she was unloading soot—and still wearing a bathrobe. Diana felt more alone than she'd ever been in El Paso, which was saying a lot. Her three days with Eddie Stevenson left her shaken and alone. She needed to talk to someone, but had nobody. Elke was off in New Mexico with her latest "project." And even when Elke was around, she wasn't much interested in talking about men.

Pulling more dirt out of the vacuum bag and dropping clumps of it into the scrap basket, Diana wondered if she was getting herself into trouble with Harley, if he was a liar. She knew right off that Eddie was, but found it charming, for some strange reason. Part of his shtick. Diana enjoyed it for about a day, playing with him. She shuddered, remembering that death grip on the couch. Her ribs still ached. If she got involved with Harley, there would be no talking about Eddie Stevenson, she vowed. None.

She put the bag back into the machine and turned it on. It sounded okay. But when she ran it over the gray spot on the carpet, it didn't work. The machine smelled of burning rubber. She turned it off and put it away, not even bothering to open it and inspect the damage.

She turned on the TV and saw the Cowboys in their silver and blue uniforms. Funny, she had heard from Harley that it was an afternoon game... Then an announcer mentioned some-thing about the weather in Phoenix, not Dallas. Could Tom Harley have been lying about something as meaningless as a football game? Maybe he hadn't gone to the game at all.

Diana picked up the phone and called Harley's room at the Cliff Inn. He answered on the second ring.

"You said you were going to the Cowboys game," she said, without even saying 'Hi.'

"We played racquetball instead, and ate some weird caviar."

"I just turned on the TV," Diana said, "and I saw the Cowboys playing in Phoenix."

"Who's winning?"

"Have you been drinking?" she asked.

"Golden single-malt tequila with ants eggs."

With time, Diana got the story from him, about the *escamole* and Onofre Crispín's racquetball court, and his hulking servant, Olmos. After the meeting, Olmos had driven

Harley to downtown Juárez, where he was surprised to find his car in place and intact. Bridge traffic was backed up, probably due to Operation Blockade. On bike, he could have jumped the line, saving almost an hour.

Diana told him about sitting at home all morning reading financial prospectuses, and about the meltdown in her vacuum cleaner.

"I was sitting there with him, eating those ants eggs and talking about the drug business," Harley said to her. "I could make out Scenic Drive in the distance. I figured your place was a ten-minute ride from there, all downhill."

"And what would you have done when you got here?"

"You tell me."

"Not watch the football game."

"And not fix your vacuum cleaner," he said.

"So what would you want to do over here?" she asked.

"Hmmm. I don't know. Maybe do my Ronald Reagan imitation for a minute or two... You're not a Republican, are you?"

"Independent. Let's hear your Ronald Reagan imitation."

"You want me to come over?"

Diana paused and nibbled her fingernail, tasting the dirt from the vacuum bag. "I don't think so. Not tonight."

"You try to avoid evening encounters, don't you?" he asked.

"Usually."

"Me too. Takes some of the tension out of things. Remember the first time we talked, at lunch?"

"Uh huh."

"I had this very strong desire to invite you upstairs for a nooner."

"Oh God, what a word."

"You want to have breakfast tomorrow? At the Paso del Norte?" he asked.

"Okay. Eight?"

"How about 7:30? I think I'll be running around on this drug story. Actually," he added, "maybe you can help me out."

◊

Broke and unarmed, Gato and Pascual wandered through South Paso. Estela had kicked them out of the apartment, and came close to smashing Pascual in the head with Eddie Stevenson's bong. After they scurried outside, Pascual discovered that she'd taken his gun. It wasn't worth going back for, Gato told him. Instead he steered his angry partner to Rubén's house. His aunt welcomed them and called up the stairs for "Rubencito." He hopped down the stairs looking distracted. He seemed to focus only when Gato handed him the keys to the *Lavarama*.

"I don't need these," Rubén said, the keys lying in his open hand.

Gato whispered to him that he could go over there, scrape a few grams of cocaine from the bodega shelves. There should be enough there, he said, to give them some walk-around money.

"Okay," Rubén said, "but I'm really busy."

"But you'll do it," Gato said.

When Rubén didn't answer right away, Pascual grabbed him high on his shoulder and squeezed hard, digging his thumb into his neck. "You're going over there, right?" he said.

Rubén took a step back, freeing himself. "Okay, okay," he said, rubbing his neck.

They agreed to meet at El Paso's Pioneer Plaza. Gato and Pascual made their way to the square, where a group of homeless men gave them cover. They settled in for a long wait, the two of them taking turns napping on concrete benches and keeping watch.

The clock radio on the Perrys' bedside table read 12:31 a.m. when the phone rang. Ken grumbled, figuring it must be a problem with the newspaper presses. Delays, which cost money, riled the corporate bosses in St. Louis much more than botched stories and misspelled headlines.

As the phone rang again, Karen Perry pushed her husband's shoulder. "Answer it!"

"Hello."

"Mr. Perry?"

"Yeah."

"Sorry to bother you so late. This is Rick Jarvis from the *Journal*. I'm working a story on that attack at your house the other night. Wondering if you see any connections to the Stevenson beating..."

"Jesus Christ," Perry said. "You wait 'til we go to press. Is that the idea?"

"Uh huh. More or less."

Perry wasn't inclined to help the *Journal* scoop his paper on the attack at his own house. If ever there was a story he owned, this was it. "Listen, Rick. No comment, okay?"

"Okay. How about just verifying some facts for me?"

"No, I don't think so." Perry lay back on the pillow and sighed. He looked over at his wife, who was up on one elbow, mouthing the words: "*The Journal*?" He nodded.

"Listen, I know this is a little awkward for you," Jarvis went on. "But it's not in your interest for our article to be inaccurate. So if you could just help..."

"Forget it!" Ken said.

"The Chamber of Commerce President says there's no evidence tying drugs to *maquiladoras* or Jiménez to the attack on Stevenson."

"Which industry's he defending, *maquiladoras* or drugs?" Perry asked.

"What's that?"

"Forget it."

"How about the shooting Saturday night at the Olivares apartment on Prospect Street?"

"The what?"

"I have here the police record, saying that a masked man fired two shots into the apartment of Claudio Olivares on Saturday at..."

"Hey, come on, Rick. You know that Claudio's a former employee of ours. But I think it's a stretch to connect his...misfortunes with all of the other events."

Jarvis waited for more.

"Claudio didn't get hurt, did he?" Perry felt dumb asking the question, and admitting he didn't know.

"No," Jarvis said.

Perry then set out to undermine the *Journal* story. "Sounds like you're on a little bit of a wild goose chase," he said. "It's a fact there was a shooting in my neighborhood the other night. But it was at my neighbor's house. The shot went through Gladys Cummings' window. That must be in the police report. Now it's a wild stretch for you to connect that to the Stevenson beating."

"But according to the police record, you made that connection yourself."

"I just asked them to look into it. But I don't really believe it."

"Uh huh," Jarvis said.

"And the shooting at Claudio's house," Perry went on. "Claudio hasn't worked at our paper for what? Two years? It would be the height of irresponsibility to try to tie that to any of this other business."

"When you say 'other business,' you mean the attack on your photographer and the one at your house."

"No, I don't mean the attack at my house. There was no attack at my house."

"Oh, excuse me," Jarvis said. "It's just that you said 'other business,' as if it was all connected."

"It isn't. But given what you have in the police record, I can see how you might tie..." Perry cut himself off, depriving Jarvis of a quote.

"You might tie..." Jarvis said, eager to get the rest of the sentence.

"Forget it." Perry looked at his wife, who was lying on her back, looking straight up at the ceiling. "But to connect something with Claudio to this is just absurd, flat out absurd."

"Had you heard about the shooting at Olivares' house?"

"No comment."

"But you knew that Tom Harley was there?"

Ken swore silently. "No comment."

"But the fact that he was there makes the connection a little less far-fetched, wouldn't you say?"

"No comment," Perry said. Then he slammed down the phone and shouted, "JESUS H. CHRIST!"

The noise woke up Timmy, who started crying. Karen dragged herself out of bed to comfort the four-year-old, while Ken telephoned the Cliff Inn.

A minute later, he was threatening to fire Harley.

"I took off after the guy," Harley explained, "and spent all day yesterday in Juárez, trying to track him down."

"You find him?"

"It's two guys, connected to the Jiménez empire, who run their own business across the river from the Sun Bowl."

"You have their names?"

"Not yet."

"What kind of business are they in?"

Harley thought about it for a second. "Drugs."

"So you can't exactly look 'em up in the Yellow Pages," Perry said, heavy with sarcasm.

"They have a front business," Harley said, recalling Crispín's words. "It's a car wash. I'll find them."

"You'd goddamn better, Harley. We're getting shut out on our own story today, thanks to you. You better hit a home run tomorrow."

"Right," Harley said.

◊

Breakfast at Paso del Norte was awkward at first. Neither person knew where to start. Harley didn't want to ask Diana about Stevenson right away, thinking it would be rude. So they both took a long time studying the menu, and then ordered the same thing: buttermilk pancakes with cappuccinos. "If you want orange juice or anything, this is all on the paper," Harley said.

"You mean I'm a source?"

"Sort of."

She didn't look too happy about that. She twirled a finger in her hair nervously, and looked at all the businessmen at other tables, reading their *Wall Street Journals* and *USA Todays*. This gave him a chance to look at her, the brown eyes with little specks of gold in them. He remembered noticing them that first day. It looked like she used a little makeup to accent her high cheekbones, which were a nice feature. Her lipstick was a little too red, he thought. Her nose was long and thin, with a Mediterranean slope to it.

The waitress came and they ordered. Harley focused on Diana's accent.

"Are you from Brooklyn?" he asked. "Or Queens?"

"Both," she said, laughing. "My family moved from Flushing to Carroll Gardens when I was eight."

"And you stuck around New York until you came here?"

With that, Diana launched into the story of her unhappy life with Raymond. She told him how they'd met at NYU, and argued all the time. About the noises he made when he ate his cereal, his slurps when he drank orange juice, and the way he undressed women with his eyes. Through it all, she stayed with him, and moved in with him when they went to B-School together at Stony Brook.

The pancakes arrived. Harley began eating as Diana talked. He looked at her, careful to chew quietly, and listened to the story of this woman who apparently left dozens of close friends and all of her family to follow a complete jerk to El Paso. He kept nodding, frowning with concern.

She shook her head, as if flushing out the bad memories, and asked Harley if he'd ever been married.

No, he told her. But he'd come out to El Paso with his girlfriend, who promptly dumped him for a job near Houston. "She's married now, with kids, in Corpus Christi," he said.

"Oh. I'm sorry."

"That's okay," he said, smiling. "Now I won't feel like such a jerk asking you about Eddie Stevenson."

She looked like a child facing a heaping plate of Brussels sprouts. "I vowed I wasn't going to talk to you about him."

"I don't care about you and him. I just want to know what he told you about what went on in Juárez."

"But that's not why we're having breakfast, right? That's not why you invited me?"

He put up both palms and assured her it wasn't.

"You know," Diana said. "I don't think we should sleep together for a while—I mean, if you were thinking about…us, that way. There's just too much going on right now."

Harley was shocked that she'd brought it up. "I know what you mean," he said, his heart racing.

Chapter
THIRTY-EIGHT

"So it turns out I was getting to know the wrong reporter." Onofre Crispín, dressed in his kimono, was speaking Spanish on the cellular phone. He had the *El Paso Journal* opened on the massive oak table in his breakfast room, and was scanning the drug story. "Do you know this Rick Jarvis?" he asked.

Chief Muller said he didn't, adding that details such as bylines didn't make much difference.

"In Mexico," Crispín said, referring to the nation's capital, "they're sweating every detail. I told you, I've already had two calls this morning, one from *Gobernación*, one from Commerce. They say the president is ready to get involved himself. He thinks this could kill NAFTA."

"Did you tell them to arrest Jiménez?" Muller asked.

"Are you kidding! He's in my summer house."

"That probably wasn't the best idea."

"Maybe not. But still, arresting him still wouldn't do any good!"

"It might appease the Americans..."

"But the *cabrón* has a big mouth," Crispín said. He lifted

an empty demitasse to his lip, trying to coax one more drop of espresso from it.

"He'll keep quiet if you make it clear that it's just temporary—and in the best interests of Mexico."

"He's no patriot."

"Well then, in his own best interests."

Crispín mulled it over for a second. "What am I listening to you for?" he asked. "You set me up with the wrong reporter. His car was never stolen."

"Hmmm," Muller said.

"If this goes on, we'll have politicians from Washington down here by the week's end, looking into human rights."

"Is that what the story says?"

"I'll read it to you," Crispín said, turning back to the front page. "The headline says, 'El Paso Journalists Under Siege.'"

He began reading in English:

"Gunmen with possible links to reputed Juárez drug lord Gustavo Jiménez launched weekend attacks on an editor and a reporter of the El Paso Tribune, *a newspaper that has been calling for Jiménez's arrest. No one was injured in either attack, and the gunmen remain at large.*

"The first attack came Friday evening, as two assailants charged out from under a bush, firing at least one gun in the direction of Tribune *Editor Kenneth Perry, his wife and four-year-old son. A bullet shattered the window of a neighboring house, belonging to Gladys Cummings, of Cherry Hill Lane, in Thunderbird.*

"The following day, a man identifying himself only as 'Comandante Enrique' called the Journal *and claimed credit for the attack. Speaking Spanish, he said that Jiménez, reputed to be a leading drug trafficker in Juárez, 'ordered an attack against the home of Ken Perry, which was carried out at approximately 8 p.m.'*

"The same day as that phone call, a single gunman

Stephen Baker

wearing a black mask fired two shots into the Sunset Heights apartment of Claudio Olivares, a former Tribune assistant city editor.

"*The apparent target of the shooting was Olivares' guest,* Tribune *reporter Tom Harley. Last week, the* Tribune *charged that Jiménez had abducted and beaten staff photographer Edward Stevenson, and had sent back a death threat to Harley, the paper's lead drug reporter, calling him 'dead meat.'*

"*The assailant fled the scene on foot, heading south on Prospect Street, pursued by Harley on bicycle, according to El Paso police. Olivares refused to comment on the attack. Harley was unavailable for comment.* Tribune *Editor Perry said it was 'a wild stretch ... to connect this to the Stevenson beating.'*

"*However, according to the police, the* Tribune *editor urged El Paso Police detectives to investigate links between the gunmen and Gustavo Jiménez. "He told us, 'You're blind if you can't see that Jiménez is behind this,'" said Police Sgt. Raymond Buendía, who rushed to the Perry home following the Friday shooting.*

"*According to Buendía, the two assailants, men in their twenties, ran away from the Perry home and quickly stole a silver Lexus, which they drove downtown, abandoning it at the corner of Mesa Street and Paisano Drive, near the Varuta Casa de Cambio.*

"*We found blood on one of the seats," said Buendía, who speculates that one of the assailants suffered a small cut while hiding under the bushes near the Perry house. He said police have no records of any 'Comandante Enrique.'*

"*The motives for the attacks remain unclear. Jiménez, 55, known as a flamboyant figure around Juárez, has long denied reports of connections to the fast-growing border drug business.*

"*In an interview with* La Jornada Juarense *last June,*

214

he said that his investments were limited to a cellular phone concession and a new hotel, El Xanadu, on Avenida Insurgentes.

"But in a front-page story last week, the Tribune, *citing unnamed sources, named Jiménez as the lead figure in a Juárez drug cartel.*

"Further, it speculated that Jiménez stood to profit from a $1 billion maquiladora development, Vision 2000, to be built by Juárez maquiladora magnate Onofre Crispín.

"Three days following the article, Tribune *photographer Stevenson claimed that he was abducted by a group of men, including Gustavo Jiménez.*

"In lurid coverage since then, the Tribune *has pushed for Jiménez's arrest. Signed front-page editorials have charged Mexican government officials with complicity in the drug trade.*

"Wednesday morning, Jiménez fled Juárez, heading south in a blue Porsche, according to Juárez news accounts.

"Appearing on local news last Thursday, Perry predicted that Mexican government inaction in the face of charges against Jiménez would feed opposition to the North American Free Trade Agreement, which is scheduled for a vote in Congress in six weeks.

"Lawyers in El Paso say privately that Stevenson has been making inquiries about a possible lawsuit against the Tribune. *Perry had no comment, and Stevenson has not responded to phone calls.*

"Already, American anti-NAFTA forces, in Congress and at the leading trade unions, have charged that corruption and human rights abuses in Mexico undermine continental free trade.

"A spokesman for the AFL-CIO said Friday that the incidents in Juárez are 'worrisome' and 'merit our close attention.'

"But NAFTA supporters are skeptical of the entire story. 'There's not one shred of evidence tying the Mexican government to Jiménez, drugs to maquiladoras, or Jiménez to the beating in Juárez,' said El Paso Chamber of Commerce President David Bayard.

"'Unfortunately,' he added, 'the Tribune *is just out trying to make a name for itself—and is willing to sacrifice NAFTA to that end.'*

*"*Tribune *editor Perry questioned whether Bayard was 'defending the drug traffickers.'*

"That's it," Crispín said grimly. "Now, I want you to set up a dragnet, if need be, and arrest those two hoodlums."

"But they're in El Paso..."

"Don't you have relations with the police over there?"

"Bad ones."

"Figure out some way to arrest them," Crispín ordered. "Or I'll do it myself."

Chapter
THIRTY-NINE

Pulling Rubén along to translate, Byron Biggs had already interviewed four or five cops and about fifteen or twenty everyday people along Avenida Malecón. And it was only 8:30 in the morning. Stevenson had shot three rolls of Tri-X. He had pages of names written down in his pocket notebook, along with descriptions of subjects. But most of them were the same. Mustache, eyes squinting in the sun, medallion around neck, T-shirt.

"How about a little breakfast?" Stevenson suggested as they passed a café smelling of chorizo.

Biggs looked at his watch.

"Get a taco to go," Rubén said, interpreting the gesture. "We got El Paso interviews starting in an hour. And then we're back here at two for Crispín."

Stevenson stopped at the café, which had a stainless steel counter to serve the street traffic, and ordered three tacos *al pastor*.

As he ate, he watched Rubén and the reporter. The two of them stood on the corner of *Avenida 16 de Septiembre*, the smoky rush hour traffic roaring past them. Rubén, looking like a scarecrow in khakis and a blue blazer that hung nearly to his knees, didn't stop talking. He cupped his hands to shout in the guy's ear. Biggs nodded, wrote down a word or two in his notebook, and nodded some more. Stevenson wondered if the reporter realized he was listening to a madman.

Stevenson hadn't had a chance to talk with Rubén about the attack in Juárez. He wanted to tell him that it was okay, no big deal. He still didn't know exactly why Rubén and his friends had done it, but it could end up making him a lot of money. Even if the suit didn't get to court, he might still win a decent settlement—as long as the connections between himself and Rubén and Estela never came to light.

He had to talk to Rubén. But the guy never stopped moving. The few times they'd exchanged words, Rubén avoided eye contact. He flitted around. Maybe Biggs would eventually take him aside and tell him to calm down. To shut the fuck up.

They went on with more interviews, more pictures, and all the Mexicans repeated similar lines: "It's an insult to our country. We do the work nobody over there wants to do. Texas was stolen from us."

Rubén translated and the *Times* reporter scribbled madly, as if fascinated by the insights.

One Mexican—"black mustache, silver chain, missing front tooth," Stevenson noted, along with his name—mentioned that since the border was so tough to cross, he'd just have to move away from it, maybe to Chicago or Houston. Biggs thought that was terrific, and he told Stevenson to shoot the guy from numerous angles. "Maybe we'll use some of this for a magazine piece," he said.

Later, they piled into Biggs' rented Taurus, Rubén in the jump seat, Stevenson and his gear in back, and crawled back toward El Paso on the Santa Fe Bridge. The line was slow. Biggs looked at his watch every fifteen or twenty seconds.

"So, like I was telling you," Rubén said, "you got all these connections between the drug industry and the...the legal industry here. The drug lords got money, and they launder that money in the hotels, the racetracks, the *maquiladora* parks. That's what you're beginning to see over here." He gestured back toward Juárez. "Now, when they want to clean up and throw the drug people in jail, they're not going to be able to, because the drug lords, they're all like, joint venture partners with big business. You know what I mean?"

Biggs nodded absently. He was looking at a tiny boy with a clown's smile painted on his face, knocking on windows to sell tiny four-packs of green Chiclets. "Shouldn't that kid be in school?" he asked.

"Just keep your window shut," Stevenson said. "He won't bother you."

"You understand what I'm telling you about the drug business?" Rubén asked.

"Yeah," Biggs said. "But that's not the story I'm here to do."

"But you saw the *Journal*'s story today? About those attacks?"

"I read it. But I don't know what to make of it." Biggs thought for a second. "You know, I subscribe to these papers in Houston, get them a couple days late. You never really know whether to take their stories seriously, because they're so damn inconsistent. It's impossible to tell what's real and what's hype."

"That's a fact," Rubén said, shaking his head, one journalist to another. "But you can ask some of these people about it. Like Crispín. The guy we're going to be talking with this afternoon? Ask him."

"Okay, okay." Biggs sounded weary. He lowered the rearview mirror to look at Stevenson, who was lounging in the back seat, framing a shot of the two flags at the apex of the bridge and the river below, its cement channel looking like a sewage canal. The line of green Border Patrol vans, deployed every two hundred yards, stretched east, toward Socorro and San Elizario.

Biggs asked Stevenson what he thought of Rubén's theories.

"Huh?" Stevenson put down the camera.

"Do you think those men who beat you up had ties to General Motors?"

"Ah, I don't know."

"But what do you think?"

Stevenson looked at Biggs, who was eyeing him in the rearview mirror. He looked at the back of Rubén's curly head, which was uncharacteristically still. "I'll tell you what I think," he said. "First and foremost, I'd say they were incredible assholes."

Rubén's head didn't move.

"That's a safe bet," said Biggs as he inched the car forward. "But do you think they're connected to the leaders of global finance and industry?"

"I wouldn't know."

"What about Gustavo Jiménez? What was he like?"

"A jerk. A phony. I could tell he spoke English as well as you or me, or Rubén, at least. But he used this phony accent, sort of effeminate. The thing that I remember most about the guy was a real strong odor. A real bad case of B.O., I'd say."

Rubén shifted his weight in his seat and moved his nose an inch or two toward his right armpit.

"Of course, I didn't have that much chance to get to know him that well," Stevenson added, "since I was getting beat up and mock-executed most of the time."

"How did you know it was Jiménez?" Biggs asked.

"You're not going to write any of this, are you? I mean, I'm not giving interviews."

"Why not?"

"Personal reasons."

"Okay, off the record. Why do you think he had you beaten up?"

"Ahhh, I don't know. Probably wanted to get his name in the newspaper."

◊

Rubén had skipped the rendez-vous. In the morning, Gato and Pascual returned to his place and banged on the door. The aunt, earlier so friendly, eyed them warily. She said he was gone, busy with his journalism.

So after scrounging for food in the garbage outside Leon's Cafe and stealing a mango from a sidewalk vendor, they headed back to Juárez.

It was while they were crossing the bridge that they saw Rubén headed the other way. He was sitting in the front seat of a Ford Taurus, stuck in the lanes of U.S.-bound traffic. A bald guy was driving, and the photographer they'd beaten up was fiddling around with a camera in the back seat.

Was Rubén betraying them? The bald man had to be some sort of American cop, they figured. And the three of them were on their way back from the *Lavarama*, probably carrying the cocaine Pascual and Gato were counting on. Good chance the police now had fingerprints to link the Lavarama to the raids in El Paso, and the stolen Lexus.

As they walked along the pedestrian passage, separated from the cars by a tunnel of cyclone fencing, Pascual reached a hand up to Gato's head and grabbed a handful of curly hair. He pulled hard, without saying a word.

"*Ay guey!*" Gato said, pushing back.

"I told you not to give Rubén the key," Pascual said quietly. He let go of Gato's hair.

"You did not."

Pascual didn't answer.

Deep in thought, the two men passed the twin flags at the

top of the bridge and began the descent into Mexico. They passed the customs booth and crossed *Avenida Malecon.*

"Where now?" Gato asked.

"Home. When tested by the outside world," Pascual recited mystically, "one finds that the home is the source of one's strength."

Gato rolled his eyes.

"But first," Pascual said, "we need to find some wheels."

◊

Canfield's voice thundered through the newsroom. "Of course it's a story!" he said to Rudi Torres, his assistant. "Maybe the way you see it, if somebody gets shot at, it's probably not a story. No, we just sit on shootings, especially if they involve one of us. Let the other paper deal with that..."

As he spoke, the city editor glanced at Harley. The reporter sat hunched over his desk, talking on the phone, a finger in his other ear as he tried to ignore a steady stream of abuse.

Harley had gleaned a few details on the case from Diana Clements over breakfast and was discussing it with Claudio. "Stevenson told Diana it was more complicated than it looked," he said. "He mentioned something about problems with Estela and her friends."

"Their aliases are Gato and Perro," Claudio said.

"And they work at a car wash?"

"Yes."

"And how about your guy?" Harley asked. "Where does he fit in?"

"My former student? I think we can leave him out of it, for the time being."

"But what's he say?"

Harley looked up at Canfield, who was now clowning in the next cubicle, his big belly jiggling, pretending to shoot the reporter. "Hey, if it doesn't hurt real bad, it's probably not worth writing about," he announced to everyone else in the newsroom.

A few people chuckled.

Harley pointed to his phone, asking Canfield to be quiet.

"...with the power politics of the drug family," Claudio was saying.

"What's that? I was interrupted."

"That these kids, Gato and Perro, are apparently trying to get Jiménez arrested, so they can move up in the organization," Claudio said.

Harley looked over at Canfield, who was still mocking him. Now he had a phone pressed to his cheek and a finger in his other ear, and a terrified look in his eyes. The city editor dropped the stunt and shuffled back to his terminal when he saw Ken Perry stalk in, a copy of the *Journal* in hand.

"So Jiménez isn't even behind this thing?" Harley asked Claudio.

"Probably not, though I can't really be sure," Claudio said. "This source of mine isn't exactly disinterested in the case."

"You'd be helping me a lot if you told me who this guy is. I'm under a little pressure here to come up with something, pretty soon."

"All right, all right."

They agreed to meet in ten minutes to search out the car wash together.

Chapter
FORTY

The boy with the popsicle cart told Harley and Claudio that they'd missed the owners of the *Lavarama* by about twenty minutes. Harley felt a bit relieved. He had mixed feelings about confronting drug runners, especially in a dusty slum like this one. He bought a couple of *tamarindo* popsicles and gave one to Claudio. "So did they leave on foot?" he asked in his Chihuahua Spanish.

"In a car, a big car." The little boy with fuzzy hair that stood straight up pointed down the same dirt road that had brought Claudio and Harley to the gate of the *Lavarama*.

Harley looked at the door, a big panel of steel, closed with a padlock and chain. The wall around the car wash was about nine feet up, he figured, with a row of broken bottles poking along the top. He didn't feel like sacrificing his hands to climb over it.

"Think it's worth it to chase after them?" he asked Claudio in English.

Claudio shrugged. He looked like a GQ version of a foreign correspondent, wearing wrap-around sunglasses, a white linen shirt with pleats down the front, and faded blue jeans. Leaning against his Jeep, he surveyed the wall around the *Lavarama*. "It probably makes more sense to do some reporting around here," he said.

Claudio began to interrogate the popsicle vendor in his academic Spanish. "So one of them fired a gun out of the car wash," he asked, "and hit someone?"

The boy nodded gravely.

"Would that have been Gato or Perro?"

The boy smiled, showing a row of tiny teeth brown with decay. "There's no 'perro,'" he said. "It's Gato and Pascual!"

"And which one fired the gun?"

"That would be Pascual," the boy said. "Gato never hurts anyone." He said that after the gunshot, angry neighbors banged on the door of the car wash and told Gato and Pascual to leave.

Claudio tried to nail down the chronology. "Did the men come and pound on the door on Tuesday?" he asked.

The boy rolled his eyes up, thinking, and said, "Yes. Tuesday."

"Are you sure it wasn't Wednesday?" Claudio asked.

"It very well might have been Wednesday," the boy conceded. "It was several days ago."

"And what were the police asking Alfredito about?"

The boy shrugged. He was listening to a woman's voice, calling, "Santiaaaaaago!"

"Did you hear about a beating that occurred here?"

He shook his head.

"*Santiago, donde andas!*"

"*Aqui, mama.*"

A young pregnant woman rushed around the corner with a baby in her arms.

"*Santiago, no molestes a esos señores!*"

"*Mamá, son clientes.*"

"*Ven aquí, m'hijo.*" She swooped in and gathered her son by the shoulders. Saying "*con permiso*" to Claudio and Harley, she hurried away, dragging the popsicle cart behind her.

◊

With Pascual at the wheel of the stolen Impala and Gato fooling with the radio, the two partners crossed Juárez, from the slums by the river to the avenue of junkyards, or *Yunques*, near the airport.

They'd struck out on drugs. As soon as they had opened the door to the Lavarama, and before they had a chance to scour the bodega for cocaine, one of their few steady customers, a barber named Luis, pulled his dirt-caked white Valiant up to the entrance. He said he'd been waiting a week for a car wash. Pascual started to say they were still closed, but Gato motioned the car in. "We need the money," he said. He told Pascual to scour the bodega while he washed the car.

While Gato began to pour buckets of water on the Valiant, the barber followed Pascual into the office and sat on the corner of the metal desk. He glanced at the camera hanging from a nail in the wall, and then back at Pascual.

"You need a haircut," he told him.

"Not today," Pascual said, standing by the door to the bodega.

"You have to be more careful with that pistol of yours," the barber said. "People around here are talking about shooting you."

Pascual opened his knapsack and pulled out a pair of chinos "Hey, listen," he said, unbuttoning his shorts, "clear out. I need some privacy."

The barber paid no attention. He stood up, grabbed Stevenson's Leica, and inspected it. "A rangefinder," he said, using the English word. "What a relic!"

"You think it's worth anything?" Pascual asked, awakening to the camera as an asset. He zipped up his pants and began pulling on a belt.

"Maybe the lens. But not the machine. I didn't even know the Germans made cameras."

"Well, put it back there and clear out. I've got to mop the floor."

At that moment, Gato poked his head in. "That will be twenty pesos," he said.

"Twenty! That's four haircuts."

"I waxed it."

"Come on. You haven't been working more than two minutes," the barber said, reaching to hang the camera on the wall.

"It's quick-drying wax."

Gato looked at Pascual, who was pointing at the bodega. He still hadn't had a chance to open the door.

The barber peeled a bill from his pocket and handed it reluctantly to Gato. "No tip for you," he grumbled.

Just then, a blue police cruiser pulled into the *Lavarama*, blocking the Impala. Gato ran toward the gate, yelling, "Move out, move out!"

The policeman flashed a metallic smile. "Where have you boys been?" he asked. "People have been looking all over for you."

"Pull out," Gato said. "We've got to get this Valiant out. We're closed."

Pascual climbed into the Impala and gunned the engine. But the cop didn't budge. "There's an order out for your apprehension, connected to a shooting in the neighborhood," he said, still smiling.

Gato reached into his pocket and pulled out the twenty pesos. "Here, take this," he said.

The policeman dangled the bill between his thumb and

forefinger, as if holding a dead mouse by the tail. "It's very small," he said.

"It's all I've got."

Pascual revved up the Impala.

"New car?" the policeman asked, pushing the bill into his shirt pocket.

"Listen. We have to move," Gato said.

"I'll consider it a down payment."

The cop backed out, followed by the Valiant, still wet and streaked with dirt. Pascual pulled out in the Impala. Gato ran along behind him. He locked the gate and jumped in.

An hour later, hungry and broke, they were looking to unload the car. They stopped at two used car lots and asked. No one wanted a '76 Impala without keys. They moved on to junkyards. Gato convinced a dealer to take a look at the spare tire, which was probably worth a few pesos. But they couldn't open the trunk.

"How about the radio?" Gato asked.

The dealer leaned in and took one look at the AM unit. "Forget it," he said. "I'll take the battery, though."

"But if you take the battery, we'll have to leave the car."

"That's a fact," the dealer admitted.

As they approached the airport, Pascual saw a police cruiser parked sideways across the avenue. He hit the brakes. "We're fried," he said.

But the policeman didn't pay attention to him, looking instead toward the airport. As honking cars piled up behind them, Pascual and Gato realized the blockade wasn't targeted at them. Gato climbed out of the Impala and walked up to the cruiser. "What's going on?" he asked.

"They're flying in a prisoner, and taking him to the prison," the cop said, gesturing toward the state pen across the street, the *Centro de Rehabilitación Social,* or *CeReSo.*

Gato barely needed to ask who the prisoner was as a

convoy of police cars began to wind out the drive of the airport and onto the highway.

"Gustavo Jiménez?" he asked.

"*Claro*," the cop said. "Who else?"

Chapter
FORTY-ONE

While maneuvering the Taurus from I-10 access road onto the Mexico-bound lanes of the Cordova Bridge, Byron Biggs lectured Rubén on what he called "the elements" of his immigration story. He had quotes from the Border Patrol chief and a political quote from Washington. Those were key elements. He had a Mexican government response and plenty of quotes from would-be Mexican immigrants. He had the El Paso Chamber of Commerce on the record and an angry quote from *La Raza*. He had immigration statistics. That was pretty much all he needed.

Rubén argued that insights from a leading Mexican businessman could fit into the story. Biggs conceded as much. But as elements went, he said, it was pretty small. So why travel all the way to an exclusive neighborhood in Juárez, with a photographer, just to interview this Oscar Crispín?

"Onofre," Ruben said.

"Whatever. I could be back at the hotel filing this story by now."

"True," Rubén said, "you could be writing a story with lots

of these elements in it, and then catch a 6 p.m. to Houston. But I've been reading your stuff, Byron," he said, trying out Biggs' first name, "and—no offense—you could use an impact story or two, for sure."

"Just what I need," Biggs snapped, "a heavy hitter like you to help turn my career around. Make yourself useful, why don't you?" He handed him the tape recorder. "Make sure there's a blank tape in there, and the batteries are okay."

Rubén stripped the cellophane off a new cassette. "If I see the interview's not getting anywhere," he asked, "okay if I jump in?"

"That's out of the question," Biggs said.

"All right, all right."

Stevenson sat in the back, enjoying Rubén's show. He and Rubén actually had some fun over lunch, joking around about Biggs, what a hard-ass he was. Without getting into specifics, they'd also reached an agreement about the beating in Juárez. Rubén said he was sorry about it, indirectly admitting that he had a hand in it. And Stevenson let him know that the beating, while painful, had a financial upside for him. The result was that neither of them would be undercutting each other's story, since they each had a stake in it—though Stevenson still couldn't figure out exactly how Rubén was planning to cash in.

"The one thing that bugs me," Stevenson said as Rubén waved to the waiter for a second Coke, "is that I left my camera over there. A Leica. You know the German cameras? My brother gave it to me."

Rubén fished into his pocket. "Here," he said, throwing a ring with two keys on the table. "If you want to go over there, you can pick it up. I'd go myself, but I'm going to be too busy the next couple of days."

Stevenson shook his head. "I wouldn't want to run into those guys again."

"Oh no, they're on the U.S. side now. Don't worry about

them." Rubén went on to give Stevenson directions to the *Lavarama*, drawing a little map on a napkin. "If you find something in the bodega, right next to the office, I'd say 'help yourself,'" he said. "Those freaks owe it to you."

◊

"So it appears they sent the army to arrest him," Chief Muller said.

"Jesus!" Crispín filled a tiny shot glass with golden tequila and downed a shot. "Any news reports on it yet?"

The chief shook his head. "They're calling a press conference in Mexico City"—he glanced at his watch—"in an hour. The attorney general."

Crispín poured a couple of drops into the shot glass and raised it to his nose, then returned it to the oak table. "You think they'll ask whose house he was in, in the mountains?"

"Sure they'll ask," Muller said. "The question is whether the government will say."

Crispín's head glistened with sweat. He licked his chapped lips and then rubbed them together. He'd spoken with two undersecretaries early in the morning—friends of his. At that point, pressure to arrest Jiménez appeared to be cooling down. After all, the drug lord would be more likely to talk loudly from jail than in hiding. He might say things that could embarrass the government and derail NAFTA. But later they got word about the latest front-page story in the *Journal*. That's when the President sent the army to the mountain chalet, near Copper Canyon.

"In the capital," Crispín said, "I don't think they fully appreciate the delicate balance here, the alliances we must construct, in order to achieve modernization."

"Come off it!" Chief Muller said. "They have plenty of those alliances in Mexico City. You sound like you're on the witness stand, for God's sake. It's the *gringos*," he added, "who don't understand that delicate balance you're talking about."

Crispín nodded dumbly and looked at his watch. The *New York Times* reporter was coming in a half-hour, apparently in the company of one of the hell-raisers from the car wash, if Olmos was to be believed. Crispín hadn't told the police chief about his bodyguard's information-gathering foray to the carwash and Rubén's El Paso garret.

"You think Jiménez will talk?" Crispín asked.

"Not if he's well looked after, and knows that he'll be released as soon as it's politically feasible."

"Do what you can to communicate that to him."

"Fine," the police chief said, standing up. "But there's one other problem. I would imagine that in the capital, and in Washington, they expect these attacks on American journalists to end now that Jiménez is under arrest. But what happens if the attacks continue?"

"It's up to us," Crispín said grimly, "to make sure they don't."

◊

"See that restaurant?" Harley pointed to a little café with checkered tablecloths. "That's where I had lunch and heard all those stories about Jiménez."

"A journalistic landmark," Claudio said. "Let's get something to eat."

Harley and Claudio were returning from police headquarters. They hadn't found Chief Muller there. But to their surprise, they'd come across a lieutenant who supplied them with information about Pascual and Gato (whose real name, apparently, was Félix). There were no charges against them, but the police wanted to question them about a shooting in the *Colonia 20 de Noviembre*.

"Any connections to Gustavo Jiménez?" Harley asked.

"None that we know of," the lieutenant said. "But—not for publication, eh?—we should be learning a lot about Jiménez in the next day or two."

Harley had no idea why they'd be learning so much in the next day or two. But from a morning of reporting, he had quotes, anecdotes, and history—enough material about two maniacs named Gato and Pascual for a good twenty-inch news story.

They both ordered fried bass. Claudio asked for a *Dos Equis*; Harley had mineral water, with lime.

"*Les traigo pan o tortillas?*" the waiter asked.

"*Tortillas.*"

"So..." Claudio said, dipping a chip in a bowl of green sauce. "Tell me about Estela."

"Estela?"

"Stevenson's girlfriend."

Harley told him what he knew, and how she seemed interested in him. "I think she's just looking for a place to stay. She probably can't afford the rent in that apartment in the barrio, and she wants to move north of I-10."

"Well, I'd watch it with her," Claudio said. "I think she could be a link between Eddie Stevenson and our new friends Gato and Pascual."

Harley thought about that for a moment, but then began working on a lead for his story. Based on his interviews, he had a connection between Jiménez and the boys from the *Lavarama*. He wished they'd been able to find Alfredito, the car wash employee. He might have been able to link Jiménez to the beating, or the shootings in El Paso. But he wasn't around.

"You think Jiménez plays much of a part in this story?" he asked.

Claudio pursed his lips. "He's sort of like the donkey in the donkey show. Have you ever been to one?"

Harley shook his head. "Just a few days ago, I heard a

taxista say 'donkey show.' I thought he was talking about Don Quixote in French."

The waiter brought their drinks, along with a sliced lime on a butter plate.

"You know how it works?" Claudio asked after the waiter departed. "They start out by telling people about this sex show with a donkey. Then they take people to the regular strip clubs, where they overcharge them for the drinks and give the *taxista* a piece of the take. The *gringos* say, 'Where's the donkey?' and the *taxista* takes them to another club, saying '*Más tarde, más tarde.* It doesn't start until later.' By four or five in the morning, the *gringos* are so drunk that they wouldn't even recognize the donkey if it showed up. I'm not sure it ever does."

The waiter deposited the two fish on the table.

Harley spun the saltshaker between his fingers. "Well, if Gustavo Jiménez is the donkey," he said, "I'll have to find some way to keep him in the show. Canfield will fire me if I turn away from it now."

"I don't imagine you'll have any problem writing him into the story," Claudio said. "Wouldn't be the first time."

Chapter
FORTY-TWO

Pascual turned the Impala off the blacktop and down the dirt driveway leading to the penitentiary. In the parking lot, a Mexican TV reporter was doing his stand-up, the big cinder-block prison behind him. Technicians were busy pulling TV equipment out of a van while two dozen other reporters and photographers lined up at the door.

"Let's go in with the reporters," Pascual said, reaching behind the steering column to disconnect the ignition.

"Dressed like this?" Gato pointed to his bare legs.

"Since when do you worry about clothes?"

"But they'll only be letting in the journalists."

Pascual was already out of the car, hurrying to get in line.

Gato watched Pascual hustle up to the building. He had his T-shirt tucked into his khakis, which made him look neater than most of the other journalists. Digging through Pascual's clothes, looking for another pair of long pants, Gato came upon the book by Dr. Rivapalacios and pulled it out.

He opened it to a chapter called "Mentors: Friends You Need." On the margin of the first page, Gato saw three names in Pascual's neat block writing: Gato, Rubén, *don* Gustavo. A thick line ran through his own name, which hurt his feelings a little, and another through Rubén's. Gato looked over to the line of journalists and saw that Pascual had butted to the front of the line. He clearly was eager to talk to his mentor.

◊

Eddie Stevenson had never seen anyone mug so shamelessly for the camera. They were sitting in the garden under a lattice woven with ivy, Biggs and Rubén in small cast-iron chairs and Crispín in a bigger one, the tape recorder on the table. While he talked with Biggs and ignored Rubén, Crispín kept a steady eye on Stevenson's camera and maintained his face at a three-quarter angle. He had some white powder on his head, probably to keep it from shining.

The interview was worthless, as far as Stevenson could tell. Biggs asked the usual questions about immigration, whether it was a political safety valve for Mexico, whether differences over Operation Blockade could derail NAFTA. And Crispín, steadily looking at the photographer, said that yes, it was important, but that no, NAFTA was simply too big and too important to be sunk. "NAFTA's a win-win proposition," he said a number of times. Biggs nodded and Rubén sat looking frustrated, an interpreter with no interpreting to do.

After about twenty minutes, Crispín offered the journalists some iced tea along with Ritz crackers and a bowl of what looked like day-old oatmeal. He called it "Mexican caviar," and asked them to guess what it was.

Rubén, sensing that the business side of the interview was drawing to a close, piped up in English. "What do you say about reports that Gustavo Jiménez has ties to the *maquiladora* industry?"

Biggs rolled his eyes and put a spoonful of *escamole* on a

cracker. He took a small bite.

"Those are pernicious rumors," Crispín said sternly, keeping his nose at a forty-five-degree angle from the camera. "They are initiated by opportunistic and irresponsible media in El Paso, and have no grounding in the truth."

Biggs coughed and lifted a napkin to his mouth. Then he took a long drink of iced tea. "What is that?" he asked, pointing to the *escamole.*

"You don't like it?" Crispín forgot for a moment about the camera. "It's just something that we call *escamole.* We don't need to go into it..."

"It's ants eggs," Stevenson said. "I had it one time at a restaurant over here. It's kind of squishy..."

Biggs jumped to his feet, bumping into the table, and asked about the bathroom. A maid led him into the house.

Stevenson kept taking pictures as Rubén leaned over the table and spoke with Crispín in Spanish. Stevenson couldn't hear what they were saying, but was surprised to see the *maquiladora* magnate listening so closely to Rubén, of all people. Crispín nodded grimly. Maybe he took Rubén for a second *Times* reporter, Stevenson thought as he snapped more photos. Hearing the click of the camera, Crispín looked up again, nodded one more time, and then hurried into the pink mansion, apparently to see how Byron Biggs was getting on.

◊

Diana heard a noise at the front door and looked out the peephole. She saw Estela carrying a box from the curb. She opened the door and saw three other boxes piled on her stoop. "Hola!" Estela said as if they were old friends.

Diana didn't know what to make of this visit. It was as if Eddie Stevenson's troubled life, with all of its drama and dangers, was merging with her own. But she didn't see how she could turn Estela away. So she told her to pile the boxes right inside the doorway, just so they'd be safe while she visited.

Estela, wearing a black San Jose Sharks T-shirt, nodded and said, "*Claro que si.*"

Diana didn't understand Spanish that well, but she could make out that Estela was looking for Eddie. Or maybe she was saying the boxes belonged to Eddie...

She asked Estela if she wanted some coffee.

"*Cómo?*" Estela asked, already making herself comfortable on the couch.

"Do you want *café?*"

"*Claro que sí, gracias.*"

"You take it with sugar?"

"*Con azucar? Si. Dos, por favor.*" Estela looked back and flashed a brilliant smile, and then furrowed her brow and appeared to add something serious. "*Me botaron hoy del departamento.*"

Diana was stumped. Something about a department. She wondered how Estela got the idea that she understood so much Spanish. They'd hardly spoken when she went looking for Eddie Stevenson. But Diana noticed that Mexicans often assumed she spoke Spanish, maybe because of her Mediterranean looks, or because unlike many Anglos in El Paso, she didn't wave her hands frantically and shake her head when spoken to in Spanish.

Diana had an Italian grandmother and a Portuguese grandfather, who spoke to each other in their native languages for fifty years of marriage. She listened to them at family meals, her grandmother's waltzing Italian and her grandfather answering in what sounded at times like Russian. She got to the point where she could understand a bit. Spanish wasn't so different.

Now, she thought, carrying a cup of coffee to Estela, it was time to ask some questions.

But how to begin? "You speak English, don't you?" she asked Estela as she sat down.

"Jes," Estela nodded and put her thumb and forefinger a half-inch apart. "*Pero muy poco.*"

"But you understand it."

"*Claro.*"

"Why did you come here?"

Estela pulled a slip of paper out of her back pocket. It was the address and phone number Diana had left with her when she was looking for Stevenson. "I haf no otter..." She gave up. "*No tenía donde dormir.*" She made a gesture of throwing some-thing out a window. "*Me botaron del departamento.*"

"You want to sleep here?"

Estela shrugged. "*Si.*"

"No, no, no."

Estela slumped on the couch, disconsolate.

"I'm sorry. Maybe I can help you find Eddie."

"I don like Eduardo. *Es abusivo.*"

Diana felt a surge of sympathy for this refugee with her boxes and hockey T-shirt, this fellow victim of the *abusivo* Eddie Stevenson. "Okay," she said. "You can stay one night. *Una noche.* But tomorrow you'll have to find someplace else. Do you understand?"

Estela nodded eagerly. "*Mañana busco a Tomás. Sabes donde está?*"

Diana shook her head. She hardly knew any Mexicans, none named *Tomás.*

She looked at Estela, who appeared happy now, holding her coffee mug with two hands. Estela smiled, showing a row of the straightest, whitest teeth Diana had ever seen. "You can sleep here on the sofa," she said. "You want some dinner?"

"*Tal vez más tarde,*" Estela said. "*Es temprano.*"

She wanted to eat later. Diana wondered what they'd talk about all evening. She didn't want to discuss Eddie Stevenson or the Juárez drug lords.

Estela rose and walked to the doorway, where she picked up one of the boxes and brought it back to the living room. "*Me siento desnuda sin los aretes,*" she said, opening the box.

"*Aretes?*"

Estela pointed to her ear and said, "Yewelry for here."

"Oh, earrings."

"*Si. Aretes.*" She dug through the box with one hand, pushing aside T-shirts and a pink nightgown, a bra, underwear. She began to unload her things onto the coffee table. Two Cosmopolitan magazines in Spanish, more clothes, a pair of white Reeboks. "Uuuuy!" she said, pulling out Stevenson's sooty water pipe. "*Esto lo voy a tirar.*"

Diana wasn't listening. She was looking at a Phillies cigar box, with the lid pulled back, showing a gray metal tube. "What's this?" she asked, reaching for it.

"*Ah, eso,*" Estela said. She casually opened the cigar box and pulled out a pistol, saying something about friends leaving it with her. Squinting one eye, she pointed it out the window.

"Put it down!" shouted Diana.

"*No pasa nada. No está cargada,*" Estela said.

Diana didn't care if it was loaded or not. She wanted the gun out of her house. "Put it down!" she commanded, knowing better than to wrestle for it.

"*Mira,*" Estela said. She pulled the trigger and it produced an empty click. "*Ves?*" She pulled it again and BAM! The shot echoed loudly as a shower of white ceiling dust fell to the carpet.

Chapter
FORTY-THREE

When struggling to write a lead, it seemed Harley could hear every conversation in the newsroom. Rosie, the receptionist, told someone on the phone that Ken Perry was meeting with Chamber of Commerce directors. Two cubicles over, he heard Klinger bragging on the phone about his immigration exposé, calling it "a sweet hit."

Harley tried to tune out the noise and typed a new lead: "From a car wash in the dusty *colonia* of Franja del Rio to the verdant gardens of Thunderbird, two modern-day Mexican desperados are trying to shoot holes in NAFTA—with a pistol..." No, he thought. Too corny, and Canfield will want Jiménez in the lead.

He heard Canfield grumbling about an IBM story on the wire. "No wonder their stock's in the goddamn toilet!"

Harley tried not to listen and wrote another lead: "When gunshots coming from a Juárez car wash found a human target a week ago, angry neighbors said 'enough.' Little did they know that they were merely chasing the shooters across the river, to El Paso, where drug-related..." No, no, no. Way too long.

He tried another: "Eleven-year-old Jose Luis Gordillo knew something fishy was going on when police came to the car wash and dragged away his friend Alfredito..." Too indirect.

He stood up and headed to the snack bar for a quick soda, maybe something with caffeine.

Canfield yelled his way. "Harley! When are you going to have that drug story written?"

"In an hour," he answered.

Canfield looked at his watch. "Seven twelve," he said, writing the numbers on a yellow Post-it note and sticking it on his monitor. "It's in my cue by 7:12, written to twenty-one inches and no goddamn holes in it."

"Right," Harley said.

He bought a JOLT! Cola, returned to his cubicle, and wrote the story.

Two low-level drug dealers with ties to reputed Juárez cocaine king Gustavo Jiménez are carrying out a wave of terror against this newspaper's employees, a Tribune *investigation has revealed.*

Working from a car wash in the dusty slums of Franja del Rio, just across from the Sun Bowl, the two men in their twenties, known as Gato and Pascual, have targeted the Tribune *as part of a bizarre strategy to climb to power in the drug world, according to sources close to the men.*

Emboldened by the upcoming U.S. Senate vote on NAFTA, they apparently hope that the wave of embarrassing news, generated by the Juárez beating of a Tribune *photographer and two subsequent shootings in El Paso, will force the Mexican government to make valuable concessions to them—that the Mexicans, in effect, will pay them to stop the violence.*

A State Judicial Police source in Juárez confirmed that

the two alleged traffickers "could very well be attempting to hold NAFTA hostage," with their barrage of violence, which began last Monday with the beating of Tribune *photographer Ed Stevenson, and continued with errant gunfire attacks in El Paso on a* Tribune *editor and reporter.*

It is still not clear how much influence reputed drug lord Gustavo Jiménez exerts on his two presumed lieutenants. Following the beating of Stevenson and the subsequent rash of publicity—including numerous calls by this paper for his arrest—Jiménez fled Juárez heading south, and hasn't been heard from since. Well-connected sources in Juárez speculate that he's residing near the Copper Canyon, in Chihuahua's Tarahumara Mountains.

According to neighbors in the sprawling slum of Franja del Rio, young men known simply as Gato and Pascual ran until last week a cocaine and marijuana distribution business for Jiménez from a car wash called La Lavarama.

It was presumably at the Lavarama *that* Tribune *photographer Stevenson was abducted and beaten a week ago. Municipal Police picked up a twelve-year-old car-washer, Alfredo Ortega Paez, last Wednesday for questioning about the beating. Later that afternoon, following angry threats from neighbors, both Gato and Pascual abandoned the car wash, presumably crossing the river— armed—into El Paso.*

El Paso Police did not locate them. But following a Friday night shooting near the Thunderbird home of Tribune *Editor Ken Perry, a silver Lexus stolen in the neighborhood was abandoned at the corner of Mesa Street and Paisano Drive in South El Paso.*

"We think they probably holed up for a day or two in the barrio," said Police Sgt. Raymond Buendía. He speculated that the ongoing Operation Blockade prevented them from crossing the border at will. "If I had to guess," he added, "they probably went back to Juárez for money."

El Paso Police have blood samples from one of the men

and numerous fingerprints from the interior of the Lexus. The investigation, said Buendía, "is ongoing."

The two suspects did not return to the Lavarama until yesterday morning, appearing briefly in a blue Chevrolet Impala. Neighbors said they spent fifteen minutes at the car wash, apparently to pick up something. They washed one car, for which they collected twenty pesos.

Later, they talked briefly with a State Judicial Police-man—whose name is unknown to the neighbors—and took off in the Chevrolet, heading west. Police officials in Juárez confirmed that a search for the two men is underway, for "questioning concerning a number of matters."

Of the two men, neighbors said that Pascual was the more violent. A neatly dressed man of about 24, he often shot a pistol into the cinder-block wall of the Lavarama. And he was known to beat the young car-washers. A day after the Stevenson beating, one of his shots apparently went over the wall and hit the forearm of a teen-aged boy two blocks away.

Following that incident, an armed contingent of neighbors complained to the police. Some of them banged on the door of the Lavarama, calling on the two men to leave.

Neighbors, who did not reveal names for fear of retaliation, said that the car wash business was a flimsy front, and that dirty cars were routinely turned away. "The only cars that got decent washes," said one neighbor, a woman who lives a block away, "were the police cruisers."

She said that locals assumed the police were providing protection for the drug activities. State Judicial Police officials admit that such cozy deals are a problem, but add that they're cracking down on them.

Police in Juárez say they have no evidence linking the car wash to drugs or the empire of Gustavo Jiménez. Yet a source who knows both Gato and Pascual confirmed yesterday that the Lavarama was a drug distribution *outlet, with a storeroom next to the office serving as a cocaine and marijuana warehouse.*

He also said that Stevenson was beaten there, and that one of his cameras still hangs on the office wall.

He speculated that the two men were eager to "muddy the waters" of the drug business by launching high-profile attacks on the Tribune's *employees. "This would create a climate," he said, "in which they could rise in the drug business."*

Harley sent the story to Canfield's cue at 7:09. Then he pretended to relax and read the newspaper. But he kept an eye on Canfield, expecting the city editor to explode any second with a torrent of angry questions.

But Canfield lumbered over to his desk with a smile. "Not bad, Harley. You did some reporting," he said. "Good to see." He lowered his voice and added, "You got to tell me who that source is at the end, the one who knows 'em."

Harley could have kicked himself for adding those paragraphs from Claudio's source. "I can't tell you," he said.

"Sure you can. You got to."

"One of my sources talked to him. But he wouldn't tell me who he was or what his name was."

"So that's all hearsay," Canfield said, shaking his head. "We can't use it."

Strange, Harley thought, how Canfield raised his standards for stronger stories. "How about this," he said. "We could change the one source to plural, and take out the direct quote. Because more than one person told me about that camera hanging on the office wall."

"Okay," Canfield said, nodding. "Rework those last three grafs and send 'em back to me. In a hurry."

Chapter
FORTY-FOUR

Eddie Stevenson shipped the six rolls of film to New York and then drove back to the Cliff Inn and raided the minibar. He drank the two little Absolut vodkas mixed with Squirt before he noticed the red message light blinking on his phone. He called and heard a message from yet another lawyer who didn't want his case.

Probably because the victim's Anglo, Stevenson thought. He heard a caller on the radio talking about how white Anglos were the only powerless minority. It was starting to make sense to him. If he were Mexican, those ambulance-chasing lawyers would be crawling over each other for his case. He opened the minibar, picked out a Gilbey's gin, and mixed it with the last drops of Squirt and melted ice. If he were Mexican, Stevenson thought as he polished off the drink, Estela would never have dropped him in the first place.

He opened a bottle of Johnny Walker Black, then thought better of it. He screwed on the top, grabbed another Scotch and a Don Pedro brandy, and jammed the three bottles into his jeans pocket. He hurried out the door and down the hotel corridor, the bottles jingling against his keys.

The sun hung low in the sky over Juárez, but the temperature was still in the nineties. The old Dodge felt like a furnace. Stevenson lowered both front windows and took off. He climbed up Schuster and turned east, thinking about stopping at Diana Clements' house. Then he remembered their tiff on the couch. He pulled south onto Piedras and headed downhill towards the barrio.

Going home. Stevenson cheered up. Why hadn't he considered this before? He thought about curling up with Estela, and then drinking some white wine and smoking a couple bowls. Listen to some music with her. Stevenson raced under I-10 and turned right on Paisano, tires squealing. He thought about translating a Grateful Dead line for her: "What a long, strange trip it's been." He worked at it. *Largo raro viaje.* No, noun first. *Viaje largo raro.* Of course, he'd have to explain the double meaning of "trip" for her. Lots of things she didn't understand.

He turned onto El Paso Street and parked in front of *El Encanto,* a little clothing store where they always had salsa playing. Climbing out of the car, Stevenson felt something wet running down his leg. He reached into his pocket and pulled out the emptied bottle of Johnny Walker Black. Cursing, he threw it toward a trash can. It missed and skittered along the pavement without breaking.

He crossed the street, smelling the whiskey and feeling it trickle down to his sock. He'd have to wash up, he thought, climbing the stairs of the apartment building. Estela wouldn't want him smelling like some of the bums on the street.

He opened the door to a deserted apartment, with nothing but a pile of refuse, old hangers, and cracked Tupperware dishes sitting on the buckled living room floor. Looking for his pot, Stevenson checked the unplugged refrigerator. It was empty, except for ice trays and an old box of Arm & Hammer. He found a rag under the kitchen sink and wiped the trail of liquor off his leg. Then, disconsolate, he walked back to his Dodge and, for lack of anything better to do, drove across the Stanton Street Bridge to Mexico.

◊

"I was about an inch away from telling him all about you," Claudio said. "Because I suspect you're behind a big part of the story."

Rubén smiled. "No way, man. I'm working this one as a journalist."

"A journalist who still doesn't have a clue about conflicts of interest."

"I'm conflict-free, man." Rubén drained his can of Mountain Dew and sucked out the last few drops. "Conflict averse."

They were sitting in the courtyard garden outside Claudio's apartment, next to a dry fountain. Rubén had shown up still wearing his oversized blazer, a reminder of his day working for the *New York Times.* He'd brought along a six-pack of Dew and a day's worth of stories to tell.

"So anyway," he told Claudio, punching open a fresh soda, "I get this feeling, this strong feeling, that our friend Crispín is calling a hit on Pascual and Gato."

"Based on what?"

"He thinks they're getting in the way of NAFTA, and his projects."

"No, no," Claudio said. "Your feeling. What's that based on? Something Crispín said?"

"No, more the way he acted, the way he looked around."

Claudio looked dubious. He took a sip of Mountain Dew and grimaced. "This stuff's like syrup, Rubén!" he said.

"If you don't like it, leave it for me," said Rubén, sounding offended.

Claudio ignored him and took another sip. "Listen," he said. "You get into problems because sometimes you base things on certain 'feelings' you have, intuitions. And a lot of them have to do with conspiracies. There was a time, back in the '70s, when lots of people believed in conspiracies. You know, the Kennedy assassination, the big business interests in the Vietnam war, business manipulating the networks, the news, the elections..."

Rubén nodded. "Ex-act-ly," he said.

"But for journalism, you need hard evidence."

"That's right," Rubén said, still nodding.

"And all you have is feelings."

"Oh, no, man. He wants to kill those guys. He sent a hitman to my aunt's house a few days ago, looking for them."

"A hitman?"

"Well, a thug, for sure."

"How do you know he came from Crispín?"

"He told me so. Big guy with a bump on his nose."

Claudio took a deep breath. "Rubén, I think it's interesting that Crispín sent a man to El Paso to ask questions. That would be a good story all by itself, if you could prove the guy really was coming from Crispín—and if you weren't directly involved in the whole thing."

"I'm not!" Rubén protested.

"Okay. But you still don't have anything close to a murder tip."

"Oh yes I do." Rubén smiled knowingly.

"Now you're getting catty with me again about your sourcing," Claudio said, putting his soda down on the edge of the fountain. "But let's assume that you do have hard evidence. You've got a moral obligation to warn those kids about it. Sometimes, Rubén, I get the feeling you'd let somebody get hurt if it would make a better story."

"Hey, man," Rubén said, still smiling. "What were you saying about feelings? You can't trust them."

Chapter
FORTY-FIVE

When Diana opened the front door, Harley saw chunks of plaster and white dust on the floor, and Estela's boxes piled along the wall. Had Eddie Stevenson come back with a gun?

Then he heard the toilet flush.

"I've got a guest," she said with an embarrassed smile, pointing to the boxes.

"Stevenson?"

"No, it's not..."

The bathroom door opened and Estela walked out. "*Hola Tomás*," she said. She waved at him with the tips of her fingers and sat down on the couch.

"So you're Tomás!" Diana said.

"I guess that's what she calls me."

"She said she wanted to stay with Tomás. I didn't know she was talking about you."

Harley looked at Estela, who was trying to follow the conversation from her perch on the couch. He smiled at her, still wondering what she was up to, and then asked Diana what had happened to the ceiling.

"*Un pequeño accidente*," Estela said.

"Yes, *un accidente*," Diana said, with what sounded to Harley like a touch of Portuguese. Without moving from the doorway, she described the incident with the gun, telling Harley how it made her feel almost ill to see the gun, and how she had this feeling that it would go off. Then it exploded and her ears were still ringing. She put the pistol in the back of the toilet, she said, in the water, where that pink floater thing was. Seemed like the safest place for it. "Can you believe what one little bullet did to the ceiling?" she asked.

Diana stopped talking and the women were quiet for a moment, waiting for him to weigh in.

Harley walked toward Estela and asked her in Spanish what was new. She told him how she was kicked out of her apartment, and the only address she had was Diana's. She was hoping, she said quietly, that she would find him through Diana, and stay with him for maybe a couple of days. But she didn't want to impose.

He struggled for something to say. "Those friends who were staying with you, you couldn't stay with them?"

Estela dismissed them with a wave of her hand. "They don't have any place to stay at all," she said.

Harley remembered the giggles from the bedroom and the bong disappearing from the coffee table, replaced by a leather knapsack. *That leather knapsack*—like the one he'd seen on the guy he was chasing through Kress's. He wondered if Estela could possibly have been harboring Gato and Pascual. Unlikely, he thought. But possible.

Now, as Estela sat patiently waiting for him to offer her a place to stay, Harley struggled to piece together the puzzle. Stevenson had said that Estela's friends were mad at him. But why would Gato and Pascual be angry? Was one of them Claudio's secret source? If so, why would Claudio go through the motions of reporting in Juárez?

Diana was crouched by the stereo, putting on a tape of

ranchera music, no doubt for Estela's benefit. Standing up, she grabbed a broom and started to sweep up the debris from the floor. She seemed cheerful. She knew nothing about Pascual or Gato, Harley thought, and appeared pleased that he'd shown up. The bullet in the ceiling and the gun in the toilet probably just made the evening more memorable.

The gun. Harley wondered if it was the same one. What was Estela doing with it? Was she working for Pascual and Gato? Did they send her over? He looked at her, leaning back on the sofa with a long brown arm stretched out along the top of the cushions, beating a hand in time to the music.

"*Es triste, la música, verdad?*" she asked Diana.

Diana nodded. "Why don't you sit down?" she said again to Harley, gesturing toward a canvas director's chair.

Harley sat on a corner of the coffee table. He was thinking he should call the police. "Did you say you put the gun in the toilet?" he asked her.

She nodded. "In the back, behind the floater."

"Okay if I take a look?"

"Okay."

"Would you come with me?"

"To the bathroom?"

"To look at the gun," he said, telling her with his eyes that there was more to it than that.

"All right," Diana said, looking flustered. She asked Estela if she wanted a beer, and Estela said, "*No, muy amable, pero otro cafecito, si.*"

"*Un momentito,*" Diana said, following him into the bathroom.

"Listen," Harley whispered. "I'm thinking that the gun she has might be the same one that they used to shoot at me. And at my editor's house."

"Huh?"

"And those two guys who were doing all this? I think they might have been staying with her!"

"That's ridiculous!"

"Shhhh!" he put a finger to his mouth. "I'm not kidding."

She stepped over to the toilet. "Well, do you want to see the gun?"

"No. It doesn't matter."

"So you're saying she's a part of this? That it's some kind of plot?"

"Maybe."

"And she came over here because..."

"I don't know." He reached over and flushed the toilet, to make noise, before realizing how strange it might sound to Estela.

"I think you're more than a little bit paranoid," Diana said, raising her voice to be heard.

The water stopped running into the toilet and it was quiet again. Harley turned on the tap and began to wash his hands.

"I was wondering if I should call the police," he said.

"Come off it. This is just a theory of yours, right?"

"Yes. But everything sort of fits." He rinsed his hands and reached for a towel.

"And if the police pick her up," Diana said, "what do you think she's going to say about you? Aren't you a little tired of being in the news?"

"Geez, I hadn't thought of that."

They walked out together and saw that Estela had disappeared from the couch. Then her voice came from the kitchen, asking where Diana kept the coffee filters.

◊

The call came at half-time of *Monday Night Football*. Onofre Crispín muted the TV and picked up the phone.

"Onofre." It was Chief Muller. "Jiménez is cooperating."

"Good," Crispín said. "That means he's not as stupid as I

feared."

"He said the two men will be at the car wash tomorrow morning. He's sent them there."

"Both of them?"

"I think so... In any case, I'll send out forces to apprehend them," the chief said.

"Don't do that."

"Don't?"

"Don't send them until noon."

"But they might miss them!"

"Are you thick?" Crispín shouted into the phone. "Send them at noon. Not before."

"Oh," Muller said. "I see."

"Very good," Crispín said, softening. "And that's good news, about Jiménez cooperating."

"As you say, he's no idiot."

◊

The Juárez cab driver tilted his watch toward the lighted stage so he could see it. "They bring the donkey in about fifteen minutes," he said. "Half hour at the most late."

"You're full of shit," said Eddie Stevenson, looking at yet another stripper writhing around a brass pole.

The cab driver ordered two more shots of tequila. "These ones on me," he said.

"Yeah, with my money." Stevenson had trouble focusing on the dancer. He'd seen so many, they were all starting to look alike. Most of them spent a lot of time showing their butts and kept their tops on until the very end. There was one, a couple clubs back, a blond with a nice little body, who smiled at Stevenson and he smiled back. The cab driver brought her to the table for a drink, and she sat in Stevenson's lap, letting him reach under her shirt and play around with her breasts for a while. That was enjoyable, though Stevenson didn't like the cab driver watching. She invited him back to her place. But at that point Stevenson was still looking forward to a donkey show, and he turned her down.

He lifted his wrist to look at the time and saw that his watch was gone. He didn't care much. He patted his pocket. The wallet was still there, and his keys. He thought about his car. It was parked in a lot. Better just to leave it there. He felt something else jingling. He reached into the pocket and pulled out the two keys Rubén gave him. He'd forgotten about them. Maybe he'd have this cab driver take him over to the carwash, pick up the Leica. Do something useful.

"What time you got?" he shouted across the table.

"*Cómo?*" The cab driver was staring at the dancer, a heavy girl with round hips.

Stevenson pointed to his bare wrist. "Time!"

The dancer must have heard him, because she came to the edge of the stage, leaned over, and wiggled her butt in the cab driver's face, nearly touching his gray mustache. She reached back and lifted the G-string a few inches, giving him a look. He smiled, enjoying himself. When she made her way back to the brass pole, he looked at Stevenson. "You wanna invite her for a drink?"

"What time you got!" Stevenson shouted.

"Oh." He looked at his watch. "Four twenty-five. Donkey should be here in ten, fifteen minutes more."

"Fuck you." Stevenson downed a shot of tequila and immediately regretted it. He stood up, wavering, and rushed to the bathroom, knocking down a couple of chairs on his way.

Chapter
FORTY-SIX

DRUG LORD ARRESTED, the *Tribune* headline read, with the subhead, *Trib Coverage Prods Real Reform in Mexico.*

Standing at his cubicle, Harley raced through the first paragraphs of Klinger's story, and then read the self-congratulatory front-page editorial. The Mexican government, Ken Perry wrote, deserved credit for heeding the sound advice of its sternest critics, including the *Tribune*. Indeed, the arrest of Gustavo Jiménez marked the triumph of an effective journalistic campaign for truth and justice, values all too often forgotten amid breathless tabloid coverage of celebrities' love lives and diseases. Now that Mexico had taken firm action, Perry said, it was clear that the southern neighbor was a serious and worthy partner for North American free trade.

Harley turned to the jump, where he saw a chopped-down version of his own article.

Canfield yelled to him, "You missed the story, Harley."

He nodded. "Looks like I did."

"It came across A.P. We had Klinger add to it. We called your hotel, your apartment. We even called your friend

Claudio." He paused for a second to let that one sink in. "Couldn't find you."

"Sorry about that," Harley said.

But Canfield wouldn't let go. "They send the goddamn army to arrest the guy. They took him from the airport to the prison in a convoy. Might as well have been the Macy's parade. The AP's there, the *Dallas Morning News* is there. And you're over in Juárez, snooping around with your good friend Claudio, and you miss it. Maybe you can explain that to me."

The entire newsroom hushed, waiting for Harley's answer.

"I don't think Jiménez has anything to do with the story we were covering," Harley said in a low voice.

"BULLSHIT!"

"He wasn't even there when they beat up Stevenson."

"THAT'S A LIE!"

"I'm going to prove it to you."

"It better be good, Harley," Canfield said in a low growl. "You got a shitload of catching up to do."

◊

Gato said he wasn't going back to the *Lavarama*, no matter how much money *don* Gustavo offered. "Drop me off at my sister's place," he told Pascual.

"You didn't talk to him. You don't know how sincere he was."

Gato had waited for hours in the Impala and ended up sleeping the whole night on the front seat. At daybreak, Pascual pounded on the window, waking him up. He'd spent the entire evening with *don* Gustavo, in his compound, and the drug lord had been nice enough to let him sleep on a sofa there. Pascual had emerged from the prison energized from the time with his mentor, and with a mouthwatering offer.

"I don't care how sincere he seemed," Gato said, rubbing the back of his neck with both hands. "We can't trust him... You know where my sister lives? Behind *El Gigante*? Drop me off there."

Pascual sat up on the edge of the back seat and looked down at Gato. "Twenty thousand dollars," he said, stressing each syllable. "Do you know what that is?"

"I know exactly what it is," Gato said. "It's three magic words that *don* Gustavo said to you. And those three words are so powerful that you're willing to get yourself killed for them, even if there's no connection between those words and a pile of money."

Jiménez was already making himself at home, setting up shop, according to Pascual. The jail keepers called him "*don* Gustavo," and he gave them big tips, in dollars.

Pascual witnessed this. It was after the press left that Jiménez invited Pascual into his quarters for a talk. He showed him his new cellular phone, a black Motorola with a long antenna. "I like to stay in touch," he said. Then he dispatched a jail keeper for a tub of shrimp cocktail, two bottles of white Spanish wine, and a box of Swiss chocolates. Sitting on the edge of his bed, *don* Gustavo predicted the president would have him released a week or two after NAFTA passed. But he might hold him until the end of the presidential term, at the end of '94. "You have to learn to accept these inconveniences," he said philosophically. "It's part of the business."

That was when he offered Pascual $20,000 to pick up some documents at the *Lavarama*. The deed, he said, had the name of his brother-in-law on it. He worried that the police might find it—and his brother-in-law could wind up in jail too. "And we don't want that," Jiménez said to Pascual. "He's got children, and a good wife."

"So all we have to do is pick up the papers," Pascual told Gato. "It's a test, as he sees it. Once we pass that test, he'll give us more responsibilities and more money. He says that now more than ever he needs friends like us."

"Did you talk to him about me?" Gato asked, uneasy at the idea.

"Not exactly. Not in detail."

"Excellent."

"I mean, I didn't tell him you used the product or anything."

"Terrific. Just drop me off at my sister's."

"But this is what we've been working for!"

Gato moved his head back and forth, cracking his neck, and then sat up. He raked his hand through his thick black hair and looked out the window at the junkyard by the prison, where they had parked the night before. A rooster poked its head into a rusty old oven. Gato heard ranchera music. "Pascual," he said, "did you notice how much *don* Gustavo paid the jail keeper to go for the wine and shrimp cocktail? And the chocolate?"

"A hundred dollars," said Pascual, nodding. "I saw it."

"Then why doesn't he pay the same person two hundred dollars, or three hundred dollars, to go pick up the deed at the *Lavarama*? Why pay us twenty thousand?"

"Don't you understand anything?" Pascual said. "He's asking us to be partners!"

Gato shook his head. "If you drop me off at my sister's, you can get some breakfast there. She makes good *menudo*."

Chapter
FORTY-SEVEN

It was foolish to take the Jeep Cherokee, Olmos had argued. People around the car wash had seen him in it before, when he was first trying to track down those lunatics.

"Then park far away and walk!" Onofre Crispín had said without looking away from the TV. "Some exercise would do you good... Say what you will," he added. "You're not taking the El Dorado."

Olmos now maneuvered the Jeep through downtown Juárez, past the cathedral and the outdoor market, and then onto the bumpy dirt roads of the *colonias*. He shifted into four-wheel drive. The two men in the back seat kept quiet. Olmos looked at them in the rear-view mirror, the older one with the blue GM baseball cap, looking out the window; the younger one, his nephew, with his black hair slicked back like a young Pedro Infante, calmly picking his nose. Olmos didn't even remember their names. It was better that way.

He pulled the Jeep into an ally a few blocks uphill from the car wash. Radios blared, dogs barked. Olmos could smell pig shit.

He turned around. Both men were looking right at him, but at his nose instead of his eyes. "It's just down this hill, on the left," Olmos said.

They nodded.

"Any questions?"

They both shook their heads. The nephew reached up and picked his nose again, this time with his thumb. "You going to be here?" he asked.

"No. I'm leaving."

"Then how do we get out of here?"

"Take a bus. Or walk."

Both men nodded again as if they expected nothing more. Then they climbed out of the Jeep. The old one waved at Olmos as he turned around and headed back.

◊

Rubén looked through the viewfinder at the sheet-steel door of the *Lavarama* and pushed the red button. But the throwaway camera he'd bought at Kress's didn't seem to work. The button went down halfway and then tilted, as if something was holding it up on one side.

He looked at his watch. 8:35. There might be time to go downtown, buy another camera, and get back. He'd come on a little van—*un pesero*—that worked these slums. If it was turning around at *colonia* Sara Lugo, he might catch it a block up the road.

He saw two men walking toward the *Lavarama*, one with a baseball cap, the younger one with his hair greased back. "You guys know if the *pesero* back to town comes by that road up there?" he asked in Spanish, pointing up the hill.

They both shrugged.

"I bought this camera," Rubén explained, "and this little red button seems jammed."

The older man didn't seem at all interested. But the young one reached for the camera. "Let me see that thing," he said. Rubén handed the black and yellow camera to him and the man grabbed it with two hands. With the lens pointing up, he pressed the red button hard. It didn't budge. "This is disposable?" he asked.

"Uh huh," Rubén said.

"There's no way to buy more film and reload it?"

"Watch you don't get your thumb on the lens," Rubén said. "See?"

"Let's go!" the older man said, tugging at his companion's shirt.

The young man leaned over the machine and moved his thumb and the camera clicked. "There!" he said triumphantly, and handed it back.

"Thanks," Rubén said. "Hey, if you come out in the picture, I'll send you a copy."

"Don't worry about it," the young man said as his companion pulled him away by the arm.

◊

The map Rubén drew on the napkin had a few landmarks on it—an elementary school, a Baptist church, a general store—but no street names. "The streets don't have names, man," he told Stevenson while he drew it up. "Fact is, they aren't really streets. More like paths."

Now Stevenson held that napkin in his hand, and he could swear the taxi was taking him past the same school for the third time. Feeling nauseous, he asked the cab driver to turn around. Even his Leica wasn't worth this much hassle.

"If I take you back, that's another twenty dollars," the cabby said. "You already owe me fourtee."

"Fourteen?"

"*Cuarenta.* Four-oh."

"What for?"

"The mess you make in my cab!" the driver said, turning around and pointing to a wet spot on the back seat. The old man looked in even worse shape than Stevenson. His skin was yellow, the bags under his eyes almost black. Stevenson felt sorry for him for a couple seconds, and then remembered that the cabbie had already stiffed him for $120 and a watch.

He looked out the window and glimpsed a white brick building with a tin roof and a sign: *Iglesia Bautista.* "There!" he said, recognizing the Baptist Church. "Now turn right!"

The cabbie turned and almost ran into a metal door with the word '*Lavarama*' painted in red. Stevenson told the cabbie not to stop there. He didn't want to attract attention. Instead, he had him drive a couple blocks down the same dirt road. They argued for a minute about money. But when Stevenson pulled out his wallet and showed him he was flat broke, the cab driver showed some compassion.

"You don't want me to wait here?"

"No, go ahead."

"This *barrio* is trouble.. *Es bien peligroso.*"

"Get lost."

The cab driver put the car in reverse and tried to kid with Stevenson. "*Esa güera,*" he said, referring to the blond stripper. "*Quería tu cuerpo.* She really wanted your body, fren."

"Well," Stevenson said, getting out and slamming the door, "at least she got my watch."

The cab took off, leaving behind a long tunnel of dust, and Stevenson walked toward the *Lavarama.* He was hot and nervous, and his shirt smelled like vinegar. The sun bothered his hangover eyes. He reached into his shirt pocket and was surprised to find his Raybans in their case, undisturbed by a night trailing the donkey show. He put them on and felt better.

The *Lavarama* was a block ahead. He saw a kid there with a popsicle stand, and a couple of men standing by the corner, licking red popsicles. An innocent enough scene, Stevenson thought, trying to relax. He wished the cab driver hadn't told him the neighborhood was so dangerous. Now he worried about *cholos* with switchblades behind every building he passed.

He pictured himself walking into the *Lavarama* and running right into the same guys who beat him up. Or maybe cops who would charge him with drug dealing. He wondered how the paper would cover the story if it happened a second time. Probably ignore it. He could hear Canfield saying: "If it happens once, Stevenson, you're a victim. If it happens again, you're an asshole."

As Stevenson approached the *Lavarama*, he noticed the two men licking popsicles were looking at him. He walked right past the door, pretending to be heading somewhere else. His heart was racing. He nodded at the group by the popsicle stand but kept his mouth shut. He was safer if they didn't know he was a *gringo*. Estela always said that he looked like a Mexican, with his dark hair and mustache, until he opened his mouth. On this return trip to the *Lavarama*, Stevenson would keep his mouth shut.

Judging from the sun in his face, he was walking due east. The border was probably only a few hundred yards away. He'd feel safer once he reached it, even if there was no border crossing. He imagined some sort of bazaar along the border, with women selling tacos and strings of chorizo.

He looked to his left and saw the Cristo Rey mountain, with the statue of Jesus on top. That was where Chihuahua, New Mexico, and Texas met. If it was north of him, the border couldn't be far. Stevenson had taken hundreds of pictures of Mexicans crawling through holes in the fence nearby. As he walked east, the blue Franklin Mountains rose ahead of him, calling him home after an endless night in Juárez. He resolved to forget about the camera and cross the border.

Yet, few minutes later, Stevenson began to feel foolish. This wasn't such a dangerous neighborhood. He waved to a couple of old ladies in white dresses who were talking and sprinkling water on the dirt road, trying to keep the dust down. They smiled and waved back, and one of them said something in Spanish.

They can't even tell I'm a *gringo*, Stevenson thought, feeling more confident with each step. Now things were getting more congested. The buildings were closer together and more single men hung around on the corners. Then, after passing an abandoned warehouse with faded political posters on its walls, he saw the border: the Rio Grande, looking more like a creek, with a long, desolate stretch of cyclone fencing behind it. On the other side he saw a deployment of green Border Patrol vans, one every hundred yards, their snouts pointing at Mexico.

Operation Blockade, Stevenson thought. He patted his pocket. The wallet was still there, with his driver's license. But he couldn't very well duck through a hole in the fence waving his ID. They'd probably arrest him. Plus, he couldn't see any holes in the fence. Just a lot of Mexicans milling around, looking angry, and those vans waiting to catch them.

A couple of them came up to him smiling. "*Te vas?*" one of them asked.

"Huh?"

"*Cruzas?*"

They thought he was Mexican, and wanted to know if he was crossing. Stevenson didn't want to open his mouth, for fear of exposing himself as a *gringo*.

"No, no," he said, pointing to the ground. He wanted to say, "*Me quedo*," to let them know he was staying. But he knew his accent would betray him. Estela said he spoke like an American, even when he said "*Sí*" and "*No*."

And these guys heard it. They started laughing, showing their bad teeth, saying things about *gringo* and *lana*—slang for money. Stevenson turned away from them and walked fast toward the *Lavarama*, saying "shit, shit, shit" with each step.

Chapter
FORTY-EIGHT

The nephew's finger was bleeding. He'd grabbed one of those broken bottles while climbing over the wall and sliced the index finger on his right hand, just below the first knuckle. The two men sat in the dark bodega, hidden behind a couple of oil drums. The uncle ripped a strip of cloth from his shirt and wrapped it around the cut. "There," he said. "I told you to wear gloves."

"It smells like a pharmacy in here," said the nephew, paying no attention to his wound. He stood up and ran a finger on his uncut hand along a metal shelf. Then he smelled the finger and touched his tongue to it. "*Cocaína*," he said.

"*Claro*," whispered his uncle. "You knew the people we're…meeting here are in that business."

Energized, the young man explored the shelves with both hands. "Look!" he said. "Here's a bag, with lots of it!"

"Shhhh!"

He reached inside the baggie with the forefinger of his good hand. He pulled it out and snorted from his fingertip, then dug down for more.

"Stay away from that!" his uncle whispered.

The young man ignored him. "This stuff is pure," he marveled.

"Shhhh!"

◊

By the time Stevenson reached the *Lavarama*, the popsicle stand was gone, the dirt road deserted. He looked left and right before pulling Rubén's two keys out of his pocket. He tried to push one of them into the padlock, but his hand shook so badly he had to lift his leg and steady his hand against his thigh. Stevenson figured his nerves were jangled from the all-nighter in Juárez and the hangover. He pushed the key in. It didn't work. He looked up and down the street again. Was it normal for a street like this to be so empty? Stevenson worried for a moment that this was some sort of trap. He inserted the second key and the padlock jumped open.

Relieved, he pushed open the creaking metal door and walked into the *Lavarama*. He took in the empty lot and saw nothing but a cement trough, now dry, and a table in the sun with a pyramid of motor oil cans on it. He remembered none of this from his ordeal a week ago. Strange that anybody would run a car wash in a neighborhood of nothing but dirt. Stranger yet, he was taking refuge, of sorts, in a place where he was abducted and tortured. He reached back and closed the door and bolted it with an iron rod. He saw the walls were covered at the top with the broken bottles embedded in cement. Now he felt safe. Maybe he could call a cab from here. Just wait here in the little cement office until he heard the horn honk, then have the cab take him all the way to El Paso.

Stevenson walked toward the office, where Rubén said the Leica was hanging. When he saw footprints in the dirt, and a couple drops of blood, he froze. Then he figured the blood had to be his own. Strange, though, that it still looked so red after a week. But maybe the same dry desert air that kept mummies from disintegrating also preserved blood. No, that didn't make sense: Desert air preserved mummy skin, but not blood. He opened the door to the office.

◊

They could see better now that their eyes were used to the dark. They heard the door open, and the nephew ducked behind one of the barrels. He'd taken seven or eight snorts and was feeling confident that he could shoot with his left hand. He was going to have to; he couldn't expect his uncle to take on both of them.

They listened. One man seemed to be standing in the doorway, mumbling to himself. The wooden door between the bodega and the office was cracked open, and through the crack they could see a man's shadow. The uncle tapped him on the wrist and mouthed the question: "One or two?"

He shrugged. Then he listened. The shadow wasn't moving. The mumbling continued, almost like an old lady with the rosary. The young man nervously dug into the baggie again and then tried to sniff the powder without making noise.

◊

Coming with a camera was a silly idea, Rubén thought. He couldn't linger for long outside the *Lavarama* door. It would look suspicious. And he might get picked up by the police, who were on the lookout for Gato and Pascual. So he strolled around the neighborhood, the throwaway camera hanging from his wrist.

Rubén suspected that Gato and Pascual would be coming by, and that Crispín sent people to kill them. Claudio would call this a conspiracy theory, but some conspiracies were real.

People died from them every day. The outcome, he knew, was impossible to predict. But Rubén was ready to record what happened with his camera. Later he would write the story.

So far, nothing. One more turn around the neighborhood, Rubén thought as he approached the *Lavarama*, and he'd head back to El Paso. But then he saw the padlock was off, and the door was bolted from the inside. Maybe Pascual and Gato were already there.

◊

The office smelled of Pine-Sol. On the wall was a giant Bardahl poster of a half-naked woman covered with engine lubricant. She looked like Estela. The same heavy breasts, the hip bones that stood out wide, almost like handles. This one had blue eyes though, and a little pug nose, nothing like Estela's long sloping nose, one of Stevenson's favorite features.

He'd have to get back together with Estela, Stevenson thought, still looking at the Bardahl woman. What was he doing fondling strippers in Juárez when a woman like that was waiting for him in El Paso?

He looked at the rest of the office wall. The Leica wasn't there. He muttered a curse and walked to the metal desk. Maybe it was in one of the drawers.

◊

They heard him pulling open drawers, still talking to himself, or humming. It was only one man. That much was pretty clear.

With the gun in his left hand, his finger on the trigger, the young man pointed toward the door and looked at his uncle. He mouthed the word "Now?"

The uncle brought his finger and his thumb together, as if to say, "*momentito.*"

◊

Stevenson found the camera in the bottom desk drawer. It looked good as new. Now, if he could just find a phone to call for a cab... Looking around, he noticed dusty footprints leading to a wooden door. He remembered Rubén telling him something about picking up some drugs. Maybe that's where they kept them. Of course, Stevenson wasn't dumb enough to walk through a Mexican *barrio* carrying drugs. But still, he might find something to enjoy while at the car wash.

He took two steps toward the door and started to pull it open when he connected the footsteps with the fresh blood outside. He gasped and turned around, reaching for the office door just as a man bolted out of the dark bodega and fired two shots in his back. Eddie Stevenson lunged one step and crumpled to the floor, right under the poster of the Bardahl woman.

◊

Rubén heard the shots. He had to fight back an impulse to bang on the *Lavarama* door. He saw the popsicle boy wheeling his cart away from the car wash, fast, getting away from trouble. And a woman who was washing a window up the street ducked inside her house.

Rubén snapped a picture of the door, for lack of any other subjects. Then he looked around for a place to hide. He walked around the corner.

◊

The uncle sat down at the metal desk and carefully wiped the pistol with his frayed shirt. Then, still holding it by his shirttail, he carried it outside and laid it in the dry trough. He reached into his pocket for a knife and used it to open one of the cans of motor oil sitting on the table. Then he poured the golden oil on the gun and tossed the empty can over the *Lavarama* wall.

He walked back toward the office, scuffing at the footprints in the dirt. Inside, he bent over Stevenson's body. He untied the dead man's black Reeboks and pulled them off. He put one next to his own black leather shoe. Too small. "Enrique!" he whispered.

Enrique stuck his head out of the bodega, his nose white with powder. "What?"

"Put these on." His uncle tossed him the Reeboks.

"Wait a minute." The nephew reached into Stevenson's pocket and pulled out the wallet.

"Put that back!" his uncle snapped."

Enrique ignored him and looked for money. He frowned. It was empty. Then he paused and looked at Stevenson's Texas driver's license. "What are their names supposed to be?" he asked his uncle.

"Pascual and Gato."

"But Pérez or González, something Mexican, no?"

"Put that back in his pocket and put on the shoes. Hurry!"

Enrique closed the wallet and returned it to Stevenson's pants. "This one has an American name," he said.

"Probably stole it from a Gringo," his uncle said. "Put on those shoes."

"Why?"

"Tracks."

Enrique leaned over and picked up the Reeboks. "They stink!" he said.

"Put them on."

As the young man laced up the shoes, his uncle fetched the cocaine from the bodega. He dug a finger into it and pulled out some powder. Then he leaned over Stevenson and shoved the powder up the dead man's nose. He repeated the operation with the other nostril. Then he took Stevenson's right hand

and put his forefinger in the bag, covering it with cocaine. He closed the baggie, rolling it into the shape of a burrito, and jammed it into the photographer's pants pocket.

"Hey!" Enrique protested.

"Quiet. We're leaving."

"What do I do with my shoes?"

"Shhh. We'll carry them out and get rid of them somewhere."

"But these Reeboks are too small."

"Scrunch your toes."

◊

Rubén walked up the block, away from the *Lavarama*. He saw a blue police cruiser drive by. He waited a minute or two and ventured back. Looking down the road, toward the border, he saw two men walking, already a block away. They were the ones who helped with his camera. He wondered if they could be the gunmen. Probably not, but he snapped a picture of them anyway. Funny for the flash to go off in this blinding desert light, he thought. He inspected the gadget, looking for some way to deactivate the flash. He didn't want his pictures to be overexposed.

He saw another police cruiser coming toward him. Or maybe it was the same one. He walked up the block to get out of harm's way, the camera dangling from his wrist.

Chapter
FORTY-NINE

Harley had driven his Honda Civic across the Stanton Street bridge and worked his way west, to the dirt roads across from the Sun Bowl. He was looking for the *Lavarama* when he glanced in the rear-view mirror and saw a police cruiser, lights flashing, racing toward him. He touched the brakes, expecting the worst, but the cruiser rocketed by at about seventy, throwing a blanket of dirt and pebbles onto his windshield. He put on the wipers just as a second cruiser zipped by, honking, and dumped more dirt on his car. He looked back and saw more cruisers coming.

Traffic was knotted outside the *Lavarama*. A half dozen cruisers were lined up along the car wash wall, blocking one lane. And at the intersection of two dirt roads, soldiers were climbing out of a dark green army truck with a camouflaged tent on top. Other cops still looking for parking places honked and yelled out their windows to clear the road.

Since Harley was last in line, he was able to back up and find a parking place a few blocks uphill from the car wash. He walked down towards the honking, shading his eyes with a hand. At the car-wash gate, a stern-faced soldier carrying a machine gun stopped him. "*No hay paso,*" he said.

Harley dropped into his Chihuahua accent and asked what was going on.

The soldier looked at him, confused. "*Perdón, señor,* are you with the DIF?" he asked in Spanish.

That had to be some branch of the police. Harley toyed with the idea of saying yes, but decided against it. "I'm with the press," he said.

"Keep out, then," the soldier snapped. He had a long nose and sloped chin, like the Maya bas-reliefs at Palenque.

"What's going on?" Harley asked.

The soldier looked straight ahead and didn't answer.

"Come on. I could have told you I was with the DIF, and you'd be saluting me."

The soldier looked right and left to make sure no one was watching him. "There's been a murder," he said.

"Who's dead?"

"A *narco.*"

"And did they catch the killer?"

A group of officers walked out the door, joking about something. The soldier saluted. Then he looked at Harley and nodded. "They have them both inside."

"Two killers?"

"The killer and the dead man."

Harley could see police peering into a small brick building. He wondered which one was dead, Gato or Pascual. Maybe one murdered the other. Or maybe they both killed Claudio's source. But if that had been the case, they'd probably have arrested two killers.

Harley heard a siren. An ambulance came tearing around the corner, throwing up a cloud of dust. It triple parked, and a couple of medics rushed past him carrying a rolled-up stretcher.

It must have been a setup, Harley thought, for all these

cops to be here just in time for a killing. Most likely, Jiménez ratted on his underlings to get out of jail.

Harley was wondering how to tie all the pieces together when a small, wiry man carrying a throwaway camera approached the soldier and asked what was going on. He called the soldier "*tu*," and the soldier, stone-faced, didn't respond.

"They have a dead *narco* and a killer in there," Harley said in his Chihuahua Spanish.

The small man looked up at him with wide eyes.

"Which *narco*?" he asked in Spanish.

Harley shrugged. "They won't say."

"Are you with the press?"

"*El Paso Tribune.*"

"So you speak English?"

"Uh huh."

"Me too," the man said. "I'm with the *New York Times.*"

More foot traffic poured past, and a crowd of policemen and soldiers gathered at the doorway to the *Lavarama* office. The men with the stretcher were having trouble getting through. The soldier told the crowd to back away from the gate.

Harley looked at this fellow reporter. With his black T-shirt, dirty brown pants, and sneakers, he hardly looked like a *Timesman*. But he recognized his face from somewhere... It took him a minute before he connected him to Stevenson's photo in Estela's apartment.

"So you're with the *Times*?" he asked.

"Photographer," Rubén said, lifting his camera toward Harley's face.

"With that thing?"

"They smash so many cameras over here, it's the only choice."

Harley was about to ask him if he was friends with Estela when he saw a black Grand Marquis rolling toward them, flanked by a couple of cops on motorcycles. Right behind them came a caravan of trucks and vans, stirring up more dirt.

The Grand Marquis pulled to a stop, and Chief Muller stepped out, his pink German face squinting in the sun. He saw Harley and waved nervously, and then looked back at the entire Juárez press corps. People were pulling video cameras from vans and hurrying toward the car wash gate.

Muller worked his way through the mass of reporters gathered at the gate and called for their attention. Harley wondered why the chief didn't take off his black jacket, or at least loosen his tie. It seemed to dig an inch into his neck.

A few photographers, including Rubén, clicked cameras in Muller's face. The TV cameramen yelled for them to clear away.

An aide whispered into Muller's ear. The chief nodded. Then he said in his ornate Spanish, "Ladies and gentlemen of the press. We're here to announce both bad news and good. The bad news is that the scourge of violence continues to afflict Ciudad Juárez, and has claimed yet another life." He wiped his brow. Harley felt like reaching over and loosening his tie for him. "The good news," Muller went on, "is that the victim appears to be one of the leading drug *traficantes* in our city, and his murderer is in our custody."

"Who are they?" Rubén yelled.

Muller raised his palm.

"We're not going to release the name of the victim until we have positive identification," he said.

"Who's the murderer?" Rubén asked.

"If you'll just have the goodness to wait a moment," Muller said. "As you are well aware, the State Judicial Police have been subject to considerable criticism, most of it coming from outside our country. But with the arrest yesterday of suspected..."

An aide hurried up to Muller and whispered something into his ear. Muller's face turned from red to white, and he mopped his forehead again.

He looked back toward the bodega. Three or four policemen were pulling a young man out the door. His mouth was bleeding and one lens of his steel-rimmed glasses was shattered. His hands were cuffed behind him, and the policemen were tugging at his arms and kicking at his legs, calling him "*guey.*"

"That's Pascual Garza!" Rubén yelled. "Are you charging him with murder?"

"If you'll just permit me a minute," Chief Muller said.

The police dragged Pascual past Harley and the other reporters. A couple of them yelled questions to him, asking if he'd killed anyone, or if he was connected to Gustavo Jiménez.

Pascual shook his head and forced a smile, showing a row of broken teeth, just as the cops threw him into a police van and slammed shut the door.

Harley turned and looked at Muller. An aide whispered to him. Rubén was perched about two feet away from them, aiming his throwaway camera at their faces. Cameras like that, Harley knew, didn't work well at such close range. He wondered who this person was, and whether he knew anything about photography.

As the police van carried away Pascual, the Juárez reporters murmured that if Pascual was the killer, the victim must be the man known as Gato. They were confirming this to each other when Rubén yelled: "THEY'RE SAYING THE DEAD MAN'S AN AMERICAN!" He rushed past the gate and across the *Lavarama* lot. The rest of the press corps followed, including Harley.

Soldiers blocked them at the office door. But Harley stood a good head taller than everyone else and could see inside. He saw a poster of a half-naked woman smeared with motor oil. Below her, policemen were hunched over a body. He could see only the dead man's blue jeans and bare feet.

The Mexican reporters asked him what he could see.

"Nothing yet," he said. "Just his shoeless feet."

Then one of the policemen stood up and Harley got a glimpse of Eddie Stevenson's face. "Oh my God," he said in English.

The reporters asked him what he'd seen. But he just shook his head.

Behind them, Chief Muller asked for the crowd's attention. The press corps turned around, focusing its cameras on the police chief.

Rubén then broke past the soldiers in the door, rushed to the corpse, and snapped a flash photo.

"*Alto!*" a policeman shouted. Two soldiers grabbed him by the arms and lifted him out of the bodega. One of them reached for the throwaway camera.

"Leave him alone!" shouted Muller, and they released him.

"The dead man," Muller said, "is Edward Stevenson, an American citizen with apparent ties to the drug industry in Juárez. He was found with cocaine both in his body and in his possession."

The reporters murmured.

Harley felt lightheaded. He walked slowly away from the press corps, towards the wall of the car lot. He sat down on the edge of a dry trough and put his head in his hands. He tried to pray for Eddie Stevenson. It had been years since he had prayed, and he didn't know exactly how to start. "Dear God," he said to himself. Then what? "Please let Stevenson..."

But he couldn't stop wondering what Stevenson had been doing at the *Lavarama*, and why he got killed. He tried to remember the last time he'd seen him. It was right after that awkward episode with Estela, when Stevenson came in drunk. Later he got that photo assignment. Harley played the scene in his memory, with Stevenson hurrying after him, and saying "NYT Harleyman!"

The *New York Times*. But if Stevenson was shooting for the *Times*... He looked up and saw Rubén hurrying out of the car wash, the throwaway camera hanging from his wrist.

The rest of the press contingent was walking toward Harley, en masse, to ask questions. Perhaps the tall *gringo* could tell them something about the dead *gringo*.

They gathered around him, training their cameras on him, and asked about Stevenson. Before he could answer, one young woman pointed into the trough and yelled, "LOOK!" The press quickly shifted their cameras from Harley and focused on a snub-nosed pistol lying in a puddle of golden motor oil.

Chapter
FIFTY

Ken Perry didn't want to run with the Stevenson story. "This has nothing to do with the first attack over there," he told the small group gathered in his office. "Stevenson was into some dirty business."

"True," Canfield said. "But we can't pretend we don't have a photographer who was shot over there. Are we going to run this story as a goddamn obit? Or an international brief?"

"But he was on leave..."

"FOR CHRIST'S SAKE, KEN!"

"Okay," Perry said. "But I don't want more NAFTA-bashing. This has nothing to do with NAFTA. And I don't want any talk about Mexican corruption without bullet-proof evidence. People are using that kind of talk to attack NAFTA."

"My God, you seem to have some strong feelings about free trade all of a sudden," the city editor said, shaking his head.

"It's probably the most important issue for this community since, uh..."

"The Mexican Revolution?" Klinger piped up from his

perch next to him on the sofa.

"Bottle it, Klinger," Canfield said.

Harley just watched. Nobody gives a shit, he thought. Eddie Stevenson had turned from a person into a story in a matter of hours. And not even a strong story, the way Ken Perry was talking.

Perry wanted the focus shifted from Mexico-U.S. drug traffickers and politics to a tragic story about drug dependency, a blight that threatened every home and business in El Paso, even the *Tribune*... Perry would write a front-page editorial, mourning the paper's loss and announcing a new Ed Stevenson Memorial Fund, which would contribute to El Paso's drug rehab centers. And Klinger would put together a front-page "hearts-and-flowers" story about Eddie Stevenson's quiet call for help.

"Quiet call for help?" Klinger asked.

"This is the kind of story, Hank," Perry explained, "where you want to go into the guy's life, and you try to figure out exactly what was...exactly what were his problems, and how, in his own quiet way, he was..."

"Klinger," Canfield interrupted, "you paint a portrait of a fuck-up. We'll edit in the pathos here."

Perry grunted and started to stand up from his desk, signaling the end of the meeting.

"Wait a minute," Harley said. "Don't we have to look into the murder? Find out who killed him, and why?"

"We don't want to wash our own laundry here," Perry said, "or spend a lot of time contradicting our previous coverage. That was exemplary stuff. It put Jiménez into jail. Let's just deal with this as a tragedy. Anyway," he added, pointing to the TV, "they say the guy with the glasses already confessed. You translated it for us."

"But they torture people to give confessions," Harley said. "Give them a few minutes, they'd get a confession from you or me."

"Listen, we're not going into the politics here."

"Torture is politics?"

"It's NAFTA politics," Perry said sternly. "And anyway, we have absolutely no proof of torture."

"But it doesn't mean we have to accept their confessions at face..."

"Listen, Harley," Canfield said. "I was going to give you a day off. You've been through a lot. But if you want to solve the murder mystery, go ahead. It's all yours."

◊

Rubén showed Claudio the pictures, laying them out on the coffee table. "See, there's Stevenson's face," he said. "It's a little blurry. I was moving fast, 'cause the cops, you know..."

"My God!" Claudio said. He picked up the photo and studied it. Stevenson with his eyes half-closed, dull as the fish at Furr's. "Now tell me what you were doing over there," he said, putting the photo face down on the table.

"That's what I've been telling you! I had my suspicions."

"And Stevenson. You expected him to be there?"

"No, that wasn't planned."

"Planned?"

"I mean expected," Rubén clarified. "He told me he'd left his German camera there. He went...at the wrong time. I didn't think when I..." He shook his head.

"When you what?"

"Look," Rubén said, his head slumped over the table, staring glumly at the snap shots. "I had a key to the place, and I gave it to him. So he could pick up his camera. I thought I was doing him a favor."

Rubén looked despondent, and Claudio softened his questioning. In a gentle voice, he asked why they'd killed Stevenson. "It couldn't have been for the camera..."

Rubén shook his head, still slumping, and then smiled. "Don't you get it?" he said. "They thought they were killing Pascual, either him or Gato!"

"Okay. Sorry. It's going to take me a while to get all this straight," Claudio said.

"Listen," Rubén said. "You always said I had a good story on the ties between drugs and industry around here, but that I needed a breakthrough to tie it all together. This could be it! Maybe Onofre Crispín ordered this killing, because these two *pendejos*, Gato and Pascual, were fucking up his whole..." He searched for the word. "His whole enterprise!"

"Did you talk to the *Times* reporter about this?"

"He's already back in Houston," said Rubén, looking disgusted. "He's not interested."

"You mean he's not interested in your conspiracy theory."

"He's not even interested in the murder story. Says it's too complicated, because he had a drug addict working for him yesterday, and the editors would ask all sorts of questions. I told him about my pictures. He said to save them. Maybe he'll use them in a magazine piece someday. Just telling me to get lost." Rubén shook his head. "Guy's a *pendejo*."

"Okay," Claudio said, standing up and beginning to pace. "What evidence do you have that Crispín ordered someone to kill Stevenson?"

"To kill Pascual."

"I mean Pascual. Or Gato. But how do you know that?"

"All these cops were circling, waiting for them. They absolutely knew the two of them were headed there. Pascual arrived and I swear, ten minutes later, the place was surrounded by these big green army trucks."

"So it sounds like they wanted to arrest him, not kill him."

"The government wanted to arrest him, but Crispín wanted him dead. Don't you get it?"

"And what evidence do you have, besides this 'feeling' you talk about, that Crispín wanted him dead?"

"Man, sometimes I don't think you even want to understand! I don't know why I bother..." Rubén looked at the floor and shook his head.

Claudio tried to be more accommodating. "So you say you heard the gunshots before Pascual got there."

"Right," Rubén said. "Probably a half-hour before he got there."

"So you'd be a useful witness for your friend..."

"I guess..."

"But they'd probably ask you what you were doing hanging around there all morning," Claudio said. "That could get awkward."

Rubén considered that for a moment. "So what do I do about the story?" he asked.

Claudio picked up the photos and started flipping through them. "I'd say first things first," he said. "According to you, an innocent man is in jail charged with murder. I'd figure out who committed the murder. I'm not saying who plotted it, or who paid for it. If you find the triggerman, you might be able to draw a straighter line to the people behind it." Claudio lifted one of the photos and scrutinized it. "Is there something special about the door at the car wash?"

"You can see it's unlocked," Rubén said. "That was after the shots, but before Pascual arrived."

"And how about this one?" Claudio held up a photo of a blurry face, a man with wide eyes, black hair slicked back, and nothing but blue sky behind him.

"That was the guy who fixed the camera for me."

"Out there?"

"Uh huh." Rubén was still thinking about nailing Crispín. "I was reading somewhere that cell phones are easy to listen to. I mean, the signals are all over the place. Do you think there's a way that we could somehow, like, tap into Crispín's line?"

"Rubén, you're not going to crack this case with

technology," Claudio said, still flipping through the pictures. "You're going to do it by finding people. And, specifically, the killer." He held up another picture. "Who are these guys?"

"That's the same guy that fixed my camera, with his old man, I think. Walking down the street."

"What's he holding?" Claudio asked, squinting. "Looks like a pair of shoes."

◊

Harley had trouble getting started on the murder story. He didn't know who to call. He found himself watching Klinger, who was prowling the newsroom asking women about Eddie Stevenson and whether Stevenson's reputation as a Don Juan was justified. Was Eddie, in his quiet way, calling for help?

Most of the women resisted his personal questions, telling him to cut it out. But as Klinger's tour brought him closer to Harley's desk, Irma Tayler, a heavy-set copy editor who wore her hair in a thick, gray braid, pulled him aside and volunteered that she'd slept with Stevenson.

This surprised Klinger. "Did he... Would you say that he was looking for help in some way?"

"What kind of help?"

"I don't know. Was he lost in some way?"

"Hank." She put a wide hand on his arm and smiled. "Eddie wasn't lost. He was horny."

Klinger laughed nervously and struggled to come up with another question.

Harley called him over and asked if he'd talked to Estela.

"She's not answering the phone," Klinger said.

"I think I know where she is," Harley said. Then, against his better judgment, he directed Klinger toward the duplex on Copia Street.

Klinger hurried out, crossing paths with a smiling Canfield, who was strolling to Harley's cubicle, signaling a T for Time out.

"I got to call you off your murder investigation for a few minutes," he said. "Ever write a stock story?"

Harley nodded, though he couldn't remember any.

"I need a quick hit on the Grupo Espejo. The stock's up eight points today, to forty. Find out why, and where it's going to go. This is a local company making big waves."

"You want me to tell you when to sell?" Harley asked. "Or will you wait for the story?"

"Funny man, Harley," Canfield said, walking back to his desk.

Chapter
FIFTY-ONE

"She left the gun in the toilet," Diana told Harley. "I checked when I came back from work." She said that she'd given Estela $10 for a taxi, and that Estela had reluctantly lugged her boxes to a friend's house, somewhere in the barrio.

They avoided talking about Eddie Stevenson, for the most part. Harley had brought up the killing when he arrived and Diana said she'd heard about it at work. When he told her that he'd been there, at the scene, Diana said, "I don't want to talk about it, okay?"

What else could they talk about? Harley couldn't think of anything, and was just about to leave for the hotel when the phone rang.

Diana sighed and answered it. Then she handed it to him. "It's for you."

It was Klinger, drunk and emotional. "Thank God I found you," he said. "You and Eddie, you were tight, weren't you?"

"Well..." Harley said.

"I mean. Nobody cares, nobody gives a fucking shhhhit. If you or me get killed..."

"How'd you get the number here, Hank?"

"Claudio."

"Listen," Harley said. "Maybe we could talk later..."

But Klinger was busy describing his afternoon of reporting. Apparently, he'd pulled up at Diana's duplex just as Estela was putting her boxes into a cab. He followed the cab all the way to the barrio, to an old woman's house. Turned out she was Rubén's aunt.

"Who's Rubén?" Harley asked.

"He's my source, man!"

Diana, Harley saw, was making knowing gestures, as if this Rubén was someone he should know about.

"Your source?" he asked Klinger.

Klinger ignored him. He was going on about Rubén's aunt, who apparently mistook him for an official from the *maquiladora* industry. "She was telling me that Rubén is some kind of prize-winning journalist, a ffffucking Woodward and, you know, the other guy, rolled into one."

Things were clicking in Harley's mind. "What's this Rubén look like?" he asked.

"A scrawny little dirt bag."

"Was he shooting pictures in Juárez for the *New York Times*?"

"Nooo. He was translating."

"Jesus," Harley said.

Klinger was crying now. "You know, that story I wrote, the hearts and flowers piece. It was fucking sad."

"I'll bet it was."

"Not a bad clip though," Klinger added with a sniffle.

"Hey," Harley said. "Why do you think Rubén's aunt thought you were from the *maquilas*?"

"What do I know? She said some other guy had been looking for Rubén. A big guy."

◊

Diana came back from the kitchen and handed Harley a cold bottle of *Dos Equis*. "What do you want, fettuccine alfredo or chicken Dijon?"

"Are you kidding?"

"What?"

"TV dinners?"

"What are you, some kind of snob?"

She didn't seem terribly bothered that Stevenson was lying on a slab in a Juárez morgue, his shirt in some evidence bag, with two bullet holes in it.

Harley didn't want to think about it.

The chicken tasted like something sold at a ballpark. He washed it down with beer and tried to piece things together. The guy taking pictures was Rubén. Maybe he and Claudio were lovers, and Claudio was trying to help him out in the journalism business. That might be why Claudio mentioned, right before Pascual shot the Tlaloc statue, that his friend was hungry for headlines.

If Rubén was in Juárez the day before with Stevenson, he was worth talking to. He must have known something to show up at the *Lavarama* with that camera.

And what was Olmos up to at Rubén's house? He certainly wasn't offering him a job at an assembly plant. More likely he was tracking down Pascual and Gato. And that would explain how Crispín knew about them when he and Harley talked... Was that only two days ago?

When they'd finished eating, Diana volunteered that she'd learned some things from Estela. She agreed to talk about it, but wanted him to promise that he hadn't come over just to interview her. He promised. Then he asked her what she knew about Rubén.

"Estela talks about him constantly."

"And you knew he was at the murder scene?"

"No. When we talked, Eddie hadn't been... He was still alive. But Rubén was there when they beat him up and broke his cameras."

"Estela told you all this?"

"Sure she did. She said Rubén has had some kind of crush on her since they were kids, but she also thinks he's gay." Diana pointed to a stack of frozen entrees. "Want more?"

"No, thanks."

"So anyway," she continued, "Estela says Rubén is going to be a famous journalist someday. She says he's brilliant. But he hates Eddie." She took a deep breath. "Or hated him, I guess."

"Does she think Rubén set it all up?"

"Well, Eddie...was still...in the picture when we were talking. This was last night, after you left, and a little bit this morning."

"And those guests she had. Did she say they were Pascual and Gato?"

"Yeah. Apparently one of them was really a creep. She said she took the gun away from him. She was afraid he might use it."

"He already had, sort of." Harley drained his *Dos Equis*.

"Want another?"

"Not yet, thanks."

She put both plates in the sink and opened the refrigerator. "Dessert?" She pulled out a tin tray of Sarah Lee butterscotch brownies.

"Maybe I'll have that other beer now."

"With a brownie?"

He shook his head. "So did she say why those two guys were staying with her? Did Rubén put them up there?"

"She didn't say. Or she might have. When she talked fast I didn't understand her."

"Sounds like you understood quite a bit."

She told him about her grandparents speaking Italian and Portuguese at the dinner table in Queens. Then she mentioned someone at work, Adam Pereira, whose father was from the same Portuguese town as her grandfather.

Diana opened a beer and set it on the table, then sat down and took a bite of a brownie.

"I talked to that guy Adam today," Harley said, "about Grupo Espejo."

Diana's eyes lit up. "You're covering finance now?"

"It might be related to the drug story."

"The stock went up from $32 to $40 today," she said.

"I know. I think my city editor owns some of it."

"Everybody's wondering how long to hold onto it," she said.

Harley didn't want to talk about money. "You know something funny?" he said. "Onofre Crispín apparently sent one of his men last week over to Rubén's house. I think he was looking for Gato and Pascual."

"So you're thinking that he was looking to kill them, and got Eddie by mistake?"

Harley thought about it. "Not exactly. But that's a pretty interesting theory."

Chapter
FIFTY-TWO

Harley had another beer. It wasn't the greatest approach for investigating a murder. But it was easier drinking beer at the kitchen table than returning to the living room and confronting the issue of whether he and Diana were going to touch each other. He wanted to postpone that awkwardness.

They sat across from each other, deep in their own thoughts. Then Diana spoke. "So, it's sort of a dirty little rumor around the firm," she said, "that Onofre Crispín's a front for Mexican drug money. I never really gave it much thought until tonight."

Harley looked at the kitchen clock. 9:47. Late, but not too late to make calls while working on a murder story. "Should we ask Claudio about Rubén?" he asked.

She nodded avidly.

Harley opened the thick phone book on the counter. "What do I say if Rubén answers?" he asked, finding Claudio's number and punching in the number.

"Ask him why he was over there with a camera."

The line was busy. He tried again. Still busy. "We might

just have to go over there if he doesn't get off the phone," he said. "Who else should I call?"

"Jiménez. Didn't you say he had a cellular?"

"That's what they say. But I don't have the number."

"How about the *Times* reporter?" Diana suggested.

"Okay." Harley called information. "You don't mind the long-distance calls?"

"I'll send the bills to your paper."

The phone rang three times in Houston, and Byron Biggs answered, "Yeah," as if he expected an editor.

It occurred to Harley that Biggs was probably closing his own story on the murder, and wouldn't want to talk to a competing newspaper. But he plowed ahead, introducing himself and asking about Stevenson.

"I'm afraid I'm not going to be able to say anything about it," Biggs said apologetically. "You understand, it's a sticky situation for the newspaper, given his apparent...tie to the *Times*. Anyway, I'm not covering it. It's Mexico City's story now."

"I'm just trying to figure out who killed him," Harley said.

"Was he...a friend of yours?" Biggs asked softly.

"A colleague."

Biggs offered to talk off the record. And when Harley agreed, the *Timesman* described the reporting day in Juárez, starting with the man-in-the-street interviews Monday morning. "The photographer was pretty quiet," he said. "I picture him hanging back, looking for something to eat." After those interviews, they returned to El Paso, he said, and got stuck in a long line at the bridge. "I don't remember Stevenson talking too much. It was the other guy, the translator, who did all the talking."

Rubén, Harley thought. "What was he talking about?" he asked.

"Oh, he wanted me to write this big conspiracy story, about drugs and industry and money laundering. You name it.

He had all these ideas... A bright guy, really. You could tell. But what an imagination."

"Did any of it make sense?"

"Not for...my paper," Biggs said, tactfully avoiding comparisons.

"So that was it? A morning of immigration reporting in Juárez?"

"Yeah. For all practical purposes. We did make one more trip to Juárez in the afternoon. Big waste of time. We went and saw this *maquiladora* baron."

"Crispín?"

"That's right. He didn't have one interesting thing to say about immigration."

"But you went, because Rubén had set it up."

"Exactly. This Onofre was in the middle of his conspiracy theories."

"Let me guess," he said. "Crispín gave you tequila and ants eggs."

Biggs sounded ill. "No tequila, but it might have helped."

It was almost midnight when Harley and Diana pulled up in the Civic at the curb of the Prospect Street apartment building. They found Claudio sitting on the front porch, gazing at the lights of Juárez. "I was wondering if you'd come by," he said.

"Your phone was busy for hours," Harley said as they walked into his apartment.

"Yeah. Sorry. I had it off the hook."

Harley and Diana sat in chairs on opposite sides of the one-eyed statue. "Were you getting too many calls from Rubén?" Harley asked.

"I was going to tell you about him," Claudio said apologetically.

Sitting down, he launched into the story of his former student's whirlwind journalism career. When he got to Rubén's final exposé, he excused himself and disappeared into his bedroom. "It's a little depressing," he shouted, opening a drawer, "that even with a sexy headline, only seven people bothered to take a free newspaper in the first three hours. Attests to an illiterate student body."

He came out holding a copy of the community college newspaper, *Semana*. "I saved one, as a curiosity," he said to Diana and Harley.

He laid the paper on the coffee table. BORDER INDUSTRY LAWNDERS DRUG MONEY, read the headline. Under it was a chart with lots of names in boxes, all of them connected with arrows. Harley saw Gustavo Jiménez in one box, connected to the Cali cartel. Another arrow linked him to Grupo Espejo. And from there, a quiver of arrows pointing to General Motors, Texas Interstate Bank, and the Bush family, among others.

"If the community college ever tried to discipline me for this," Claudio was saying, "I planned to use that misspelled 'lawnders' as proof that I had nothing to do with it. It was the first time in my life that I thanked God for every misspelling."

"Take a look at that," Harley said to Diana, pointing to a Dunwoody & Briggs box on the chart.

"We would have sued in about five minutes!" Diana said, seeing that only Grupo Espejo and Gustavo Jiménez stood between her firm and the Cali Cartel.

"Truth is the ultimate defense," Claudio said, "though I doubt the college would have spent much money defending Rubén and me." He stood up and stepped toward the kitchen. "Would you like a cup of tea?"

Harley and Diana both shook their heads. "It's late," Diana said.

"I have Sleepytime."

"No thanks."

Claudio sat down again and described Rubén's visit that afternoon. "He thinks Onofre Crispín hired a hitman to kill Pascual and Gato, and he got the wrong guy. So I ask him, 'Where's your evidence?' And he says to me, 'Don't you get it?'"

"He must have known something was up, to be hanging around there with a camera," Diana said.

Claudio nodded. "So Rubén has his story and these pictures," he said, "and he can't get newspapers interested in the story. He says to me that he's going to start calling the TV news magazines. You know, *Hard Copy, Dateline*. I wouldn't be surprised if he gets one of them down here."

"I'd like to see Katie Couric sitting down with Onofre Crispín," Harley said, "maybe playing racquetball."

"It could happen," Claudio said. "Though I imagine a jailhouse interview with Gustavo Jiménez would get better ratings. That's who you should talk to, Tom."

"I don't have his number."

"I'd look hard for it," Claudio said, sounding like a professor. "I don't think your friend, the police chief, is going to spell things out for you."

◊

Harley walked out with Diana onto Prospect Street, where his car was parked. A dog barked, then another. The twinkling lights of Mexico stretched out to the Juárez Mountains.

The two of them were at that awkward point where they'd agreed, tacitly, that eventually they'd be sleeping together. But neither took the first step. It didn't seem appropriate even to be thinking about it hours after a murder.

Diana reached an arm around his waist, drew close to him, and asked what he was thinking about.

"Oh, I don't know," he said. Stevenson was lying cold

under one of those lights, he thought, and his killer was hiding somewhere near another one. The *Lavarama,* he figured, was only about a mile away.

"Come on," Diana said, pulling him toward the car.

"Wait a minute." He sat on the steps and gently pulled her down beside him. They could hear the low roar of the traffic on I-10.

Diana whispered to him, "You sometimes like to hide behind all your voices and languages, don't you?"

"That's what people say." He turned toward her. She was looking up at him, the streetlight reflected in her eyes.

"Talk to me," she whispered. He wondered if she'd whispered the same words to Eddie Stevenson.

Harley looked at her mouth, that gap between her front teeth. "Why did you pick him over me?" he asked.

She pulled back. "Eddie?" She collected herself. "He called... You didn't. He said he wanted me, the very first night I met him."

He nodded, looking into her eyes, trying to figure her out. "I do want you," he said, holding her by the arm.

She smiled, looking relieved, and started again to pull him toward the car. But he tugged back. "Come on up," he said. "I almost forgot I live here."

◊

Hours later, in the middle of the night, Harley found himself wide awake. The breeze from the overhead fan blew dust bunnies and a few scattered receipts across the bare oak floor. Out the window, the courtyard palm blocked his view of Juárez.

Diana stirred and opened her eyes. She looked surprised to see Harley, then collected herself, kissed the tip of his nose, and made her way to the bathroom. When she returned, she asked if he did Onofre Crispín's voice.

"You mean do I imitate it?"

"Right."

He performed Crispín in his Monterrey accent, talking about football: "*Lo que les falta a los Cowboys es un linebacker duro de verdad, tipo Lawrence Taylor.*"

"That's the way he talks?" She looked pleased with herself.

"More or less," he said.

"Then I have an idea for you."

Chapter
FIFTY-THREE

A few minutes later Diana slipped out, saying that the Murphy bed was killing her back. Harley tossed and turned the rest of the night, practicing the voice of Onofre Crispín and wondering what the future held for him and Diana Clements.

He was in the shower early the next morning, weighing Diana's idea. It was risky to the point of insanity. There were also ethical issues.

But threads of the story were coming together. Still dripping, Harley called Billy Sanchez, Stevenson's fellow photographer. He was already at work. "One question, Billy," he said.

"Shoot."

"When Stevenson was on that last assignment in Juárez, taking pictures of Jiménez's hotel, that was for the *Baltimore Sun*, right?"

"Right. The *Baltimore Sun*."

"And did you have to explain to the *Sun* what happened, and why there weren't any pictures?"

"I called them," Sanchez said. "But I never could find the

guy who ordered the pictures. Some kind of screw up. Like a *malentendido*, you know, Harley?"

"Uh huh..."

Had Rubén orchestrated Stevenson's photo shoot in Juárez? Harley thought about it as he made himself a pot of espresso. He felt energized for a minute or two and started to reconsider Diana's plan. Then doubts again seeped in.

The coffee boiled over. Still brooding, he poured some burnt coffee into a mug, stirred in sugar, and then walked outside to pick up his newspaper. Standing on the porch outside Claudio's apartment, he read Klinger's hearts and flowers story. *"In the end,"* Klinger wrote, *"Eddie Stevenson died as he lived most of his life: alone, surrounded by his mounting troubles, calling softly for help in a voice that no one heard."*

Give me a break, Harley thought.

He read on.

"The Tribune *photographer, 37, who was on leave from the paper to iron out his addiction troubles, was found murdered Tuesday at a notorious Juárez drug warehouse. Stevenson had cocaine in his pocket and traces of it around his nose, according to Juárez police, who later arrested a suspected drug dealer, Pascual Garza, charging him with the murder.*

"'Our hearts go out to Eddie Stevenson and his family,' said Tribune *editor Ken Perry, who added that the* Tribune *would redouble its efforts to battle drug addiction* (See Editorial, page one).*"*

Harley skimmed the rest of the story. Klinger didn't even mention the beating in Juárez until after the jump, near the end of the article. And he didn't point out that the murder and beating had both taken place at the *Lavarama*.

Perry had to be under pressure to be back-peddling so fast

on the drug story, he thought. Maybe the corporate folks in St. Louis had heard rumors of an advertising boycott, and told him to turn around on NAFTA.

Whatever the reason, Harley decided he wasn't going to lie down for them. He'd been doing that, one way or another, for ten years.

The phone rang upstairs. He raced into the building and vaulted up the steps three at a time.

"Hello?"

"Did you make the call yet?" It was Diana.

"Not yet."

"Chicken."

He told her that he'd made other calls, and that he had reason to doubt that the *Baltimore Sun* had ordered photos of the Xanadu Hotel.

"So what if the *Sun* didn't order the pictures," Diana said. "What's the big deal?"

"It means that maybe someone called, saying he was from the *Sun*, with the idea of getting Stevenson over in Juárez. I'm thinking of Rubén."

Diana chewed on that one for a while. "But even if you tie a lot of this to Rubén, it's not a big deal, is it? He's not exactly a big shot."

"Probably not. But he might be the string that ties together some big shots."

"Well then, why don't you get busy and call them."

"Where are you, at work?"

"Yep. The market opens at 7:30."

"How's Espejo doing today?"

"It's not trading yet," Diana said. "But I'm betting it'll keep going up for a while. At least until you get your story."

◊

Gato's sister didn't have a phone. But they took messages for her at a little store around the corner. Wednesday morning, a boy from the store knocked on her door, saying there was a call for her brother.

Gato pulled on a pair of his baggy shorts and hustled to the phone. He'd already heard about the Stevenson killing and Pascual's arrest. The radios in the neighborhood talked of little else. Now, he figured, Pascual was either dead or escaped.

He nodded politely to the *señora* behind the counter and reached for the phone. "*Bueno?*"

"*Hombre!*" It was Pascual.

"Where are you?"

"*El CeReSo.*" He sounded excited. "On *don* Gustavo's cellular."

"You're with him?"

"Yes. I'm sort of his assistant. He got them to bring me up here yesterday. He's got a perfect situation in here, with a cook, and a couple of women who come into his room. Last night we had *quesadillas de camaron* and chicken *mole*, with some kind of white wine from France..."

"Did you kill the photographer?" Gato asked.

"Of course not."

"Oh, I thought..."

"No. He was dead when I got there..." Pascual didn't want to elaborate. "The important thing," he said, "is that *don* Gustavo understands me very well, and he appreciates the work I—I mean we—have been doing..."

"You told him about me?"

"Of course. We're his allies. When we get out of here, probably after *la NAFTA* gets passed, you and I are going to be his lieutenants, he says."

"You're lisping."

"Oh yes, that. They broke some of my teeth yesterday. But remember how I always tell you not to take the product? Well, *don* Gustavo says that it works very well as a local anesthetic.

304

And it does! And now I'm coming up with more good ideas than ever. *Don* Gustavo says he'll bring in a dentist today, or maybe tomorrow."

"If you didn't kill him, who did?" Gato asked.

"The photographer? *Don* Gustavo says he knows. But he hasn't told me yet. We're only getting to know each other. But you know what, Gato?"

"Tell me."

"He also reads Dr. Rivapalacios! He's even read works I haven't found yet. That's why I called. I was wondering if you could buy five or six books and bring them over here."

"Go there? Me?"

"Yes, I guess I could send one of these jailers who buys the food..."

"I'm not going near there," Gato said.

"No, come! You should meet *don* Gustavo. He says you could even move in here, if you want..."

Gato borrowed a pen and a piece of paper from the woman behind the counter and wrote down the names of the books. "I'll send a boy over there to drop them off," he told Pascual.

"Very well," Pascual said, sounding disappointed. "But soon I want you to see for yourself, Gato. We've made it!"

◊

Harley drove the Civic over to the Cliff Inn to check out. En route, he worked on the Crispín voice. He listened to it in his mind and then repeated, listened, and repeated. That's how he learned voices, from the Beatles to Bill Clinton. He often added a stuffed-nose sound to his new voices. It fogged over some of the weak points.

He checked out of the hotel and drove home. He had decided to make the calls, but not from the office. Apart from any ethical issues, people were always shouting in the newsroom, which would destroy the effect.

Back in the apartment, he started to write out a script, but threw it away. It was always better to have the voice alive in the head, and to improvise.

First, he wanted to test drive his Crispín voice and see if it worked on Chief Muller. If it didn't, nothing lost. He'd just tell the chief he was having fun, and Muller would write him off as an eccentric *gringo*. He dialed the number, mumbling to himself as Crispín.

Muller's secretary answered.

"*Muuuuy buenos días. Jefe Muller, por favor,*" Harley said in the voice of Crispín with a stuffed nose.

"*Cómo no, licenciado. Un momento.*" He heard her telling the chief that *Licenciado* Onofre Crispín was on the line.

"*Buenos días, don* Onofre," Chief Muller said.

Harley froze for a second, trying to remember Muller's first name.

"Onofre?" the chief asked.

"Good morning, Chief," Harley said in Crispín's self-important Spanish. He was planning just to ask Muller for Gustavo Jiménez's cellular phone number. But at the last moment, he decided to try something far riskier. "Chief," he said gravely, "I've got a confession to make."

"What's that, *hombre*? Do you have a cold?"

"It's the change in the weather," Harley explained, even though the heat had been unrelenting.

"The change?"

Harley plowed ahead. "I don't know exactly how to tell you this, but forces under my control were responsible for the unfortunate shooting at that car wash yesterday morning."

"Are you on your cellular?"

"*Claro,*" Harley said, startled by the question.

"I have no idea why you're making this call to me now. It's highly irregular for you to use any phone, much less the cellular, for communications of any importance. If you need to talk to me, we will have to do it face to face."

Harley considered breaking into his own voice and telling the chief he was just kidding. But this was too serious.

The chief continued to scold him for using the cellular. But Harley took charge. "ENOUGH, MULLER! I SHIT ON THE MILK!" That was one of the Spanish expressions he'd heard Crispín use. "Listen," he said, lowering his voice a decibel. "I have work to do, things to arrange. I'm going to be out of touch for two days. *Incomunicado.* Do you understand?"

"*Si,* Onofre," Muller said, back on his heels.

"What I need from you now is the phone number for that *pendejo* Jiménez."

"But you call him all the time."

"I LOST THE NUMBER! I SHIT ON THE MOTHER!"

"Fine, fine," Muller said, in full retreat. He gave him a phone number and added meekly, "You're not going to say anything sensitive over the cellular, are you?"

Harley unleashed his Crispín chuckle. "Heh, heh heh. Don't you worry about it." Remembering Muller's first name, he added, "We'll be talking, Beto."

Chapter
FIFTY-FOUR

Time to call Gustavo Jiménez. Harley couldn't afford to wait, or the real Crispín might talk to Chief Muller and figure out what he was up to. Sitting in his tiny dining room with a pen and paper ready, Harley started dialing the number. Then he hung up and called Diana. He had to confer with somebody before taking this leap.

"What'd you find out?" Diana asked.

"I just talked to the chief. I haven't called the other guy yet."

"Oh."

He explained that he'd used the Crispín voice, and made the confession.

"And the chief wasn't even surprised?"

"No. He just told me not to use the cellular for sensitive calls."

Diana whispered. "That means Crispín's in on it. Right?"

"It's a pretty clear sign."

"Wow."

"What?"

"It's just...just that it could be a big story. And now you're going to call Jiménez?"

"Uh huh. Right now."

"Oh Jesus."

"Okay. We'll be talking."

Harley considered calling Claudio for advice. But he'd object to reporting with false voices. At this point, Harley didn't need any interference.

He said a few sentences to himself in Crispín-talk. Then he took a deep breath and dialed the number.

"*Buenooo?*" It was a young man's voice.

"Gustavo?"

"I'll get him right away."

Harley heard the young man asking where *don* Gustavo was, and someone else, a woman, saying he was in the bathroom. What kind of jail was this?

"He's indisposed now," the young man said. "Would you do me the favor of leaving your number, and he'll call you back."

"Onofre Crispín here," he said. "I must speak with him now."

The man relayed Crispín's name and the woman told him to carry the phone to *don* Gustavo.

"In the bathroom?" He sounded reluctant.

"*Claro,*" she said.

Next thing Harley knew, a more mature voice was saying, "*Muy buenos días, Onofre.*"

"Gustavo?"

"*A tus órdenes.*"

"Gustavo," Harley said with the simulated stuffed nose. "I have bad news for you. You'll recall that assurances were made to you about a timely release from jail. That will no longer be possible. I've spoken with authorities at the highest position, who have told me that all deals are off."

"What are you saying to me, *mano*?" Jiménez sounded

stunned.

"What's more, all financial obligations between you and me are now considered history. Done for. Eliminated."

"What the devil are you talking about, *hijo de la chingada!*" Jiménez said, coming to life.

"You've betrayed me. I'm not paying you one peso."

"*Hijo de la mierda!*"

"I SHIT ON YOUR MOTHER, THE WHORE!" Harley lifted Crispín's voice into a shout, and then hung up.

He looked at his hand. It was shaking. He paced back and forth, from the bathroom to the kitchen, replaying the conversation in his head, trying to come to terms with what he'd learned. In a while, he would have to call Jiménez again, in his own voice. But he had to wait, at least a half-hour, or *don* Gustavo might see through it.

He sat down at the phone and called Diana. She was out, the receptionist said. Did he want her voicemail?

"Out?"

"She said she'd be back in an hour."

Harley left a voice message that everything had gone as planned, or even better. Then, with the phony calls behind him, he hopped down the stairs and knocked on Claudio's door.

Claudio was on his way out, wearing his faded jeans and a black T-shirt and carrying a folder of graded papers in one hand. But when Harley told him what he was up to, he motioned him inside the apartment and shut the door.

"I'm sorry I don't have time to offer you any tea," he said.

Harley said it didn't matter. Then he told Claudio about his calls to Muller and Jiménez.

"And they both believe they talked to Crispín?" asked Claudio, wide-eyed.

Harley nodded, feeling a little proud.

"That means you've lied to them."

"Sort of."

"There's no 'sort of' about it. You've got to call them both, right now, and say that it was a prank, and apologize."

"And how about the information I've learned?"

"You've got to learn it some other way."

"But Claudio, these guys are criminals. The FBI uses all sorts of tricks and scams to catch criminals."

"True. And the FBI bugged Martin Luther King's hotel rooms." Claudio sat down on the corner of the sofa. "Journalists have a bad enough name in this country as it is. If we start calling people and lying about who we are, no one will ever trust us."

Harley considered that. It was true enough. But he couldn't see himself calling back Gustavo Jiménez and apologizing.

"So," said Claudio, breaking the silence. "You say that the police chief wasn't surprised when he heard that Crispín ordered the murder."

"Not at all."

"And Jiménez appeared to have some sort of financial dealings with Crispín?"

"Definitely." Harley wondered if it was time yet to call back the drug lord.

"That means Rubén's right," Claudio said slowly, looking dazzled. "This would be one hell of a story if you could nail it down."

"I was thinking, maybe I'll call Jiménez now. See if I can go over and see him."

"Call him in your real voice, you mean?"

"Yeah."

"Well, okay." Shaking his head, Claudio hurried off to his class, and Harley climbed the stairs to make his phone call.

◊

The news arrived from Washington that President Clinton, after vacillating for months, was finally determined to push hard for NAFTA. He would stump around the country and call in all his political chits to get the trade agreement through Congress, even if it meant a nasty fight with the unions.

Mexican stocks were rocketing on the news. And Grupo Espejo, the sexiest new stock on the market, had shot up $5, to $45. Canfield, listening to the stock news through one ear of his Walkman, was energized. He paced back and forth across the newsroom, the *Wall Street Journal* rolled up tight in one hand. "Where the fuck's Harley?" he asked Klinger.

Klinger, bent over his terminal, twisting his long blond hair around one finger, said he didn't know.

"I want a follow-up story on Espejo," Canfield said. "It's a goddamn local success story."

Klinger agreed.

"Holy shit," Canfield said, listening to the radio. "It's up to forty-seven. Hey Klinger," he said, walking back to his terminal. "Not that it's any of my business, but why don't you get a fucking haircut?"

◊

When Harley called Gustavo Jiménez, the drug dealer didn't even wait for a question. "Come over to *El CeReSo*," he said. "I want to have a talk with you."

Harley felt a wave of panic and considered hanging up. He wondered whether the drug lord had seen through his game. If so, he was a lot safer staying in El Paso.

"How about if we talk by phone?" he suggested. He was speaking with a strong *gringo* accent. "My car's not working too well..."

"I don't say anything important on the phone," Jiménez said. "Come, now, and you'll get your story. Hurry." And he hung up.

Harley considered his options. He could always bag it. That would be an ethical option, since he'd set the stage for this interview with a lie. No one had to know that he'd turned down an exclusive interview with Gustavo Jiménez. The editors wanted to bury the drug story now anyway...

The phone rang, and he answered.

"What's going on?" It was Diana.

"Not much."

"What do you mean, 'not much'?"

He corrected himself. "I mean everything's going according to the plan. Jiménez has called me over there for an interview."

"When?"

"Now." He waited for a second, then added, "You want to come with me?"

She laughed. "Can you imagine? Hi, I'm a reporter, and this here's my banker..."

Harley was far too wound up to laugh. "You don't want to come?"

"I have to work. The market's going nuts. Especially the Mexican stocks."

"So you think Jiménez has a piece of Grupo Espejo?" he asked.

"That's what it sounds like."

"And what's that worth?"

"Depends how much he has. But let's see... The stock was issued at $10, and they raised half a billion dollars, selling forty million shares. The original investors probably have ten million shares... Now, you don't know how much of that Jiménez has, if any. That's what you'll have to ask him in the interview... Maybe you can get a separate interview with his accountant. Or his banker."

"I thought you guys were his bankers."

"No. We work for Onofre Crispín."

"Oh yeah. Got them confused for a minute. So how much is that ten million shares worth now?"

Diana paused. "Maybe a half billion, or even higher by the

end of the day, the way the market's going."

"Geez, I'd sell," Harley said.

"Knowing what you know, I think a lot of people would."

Harley remembered his pending interview and felt a sense of dread. "You sure you don't want to come with me?"

"Can't. Do you think you'll run your story tomorrow?"

"Probably," he said. "For sure if he gives me the interview."

They signed off. Harley carried his miniature tape recorder and a thin reporter's pad to the car. Opening the door of the Civic, it occurred to him that he should call Canfield. The editor would never forgive him if he had a jailhouse exclusive with Gustavo Jiménez without taking along a photographer. But by going alone, Harley could turn around if he felt threatened, or just ditch the story altogether. He wanted to keep all options open.

He turned the key of the Civic and heard just a tiny click.

He saw the headlights had been on, and turned them off. The battery was drained. He had a Triple A card, but couldn't afford to wait around for a jump. He hurried upstairs and put the tape recorder, the pen, and notebook into a green knapsack. Then he rolled up his right pant leg and carried his yellow Raleigh down the stairs.

Chapter
FIFTY-FIVE

Gustavo Jiménez told Harley to stick around for lunch. The drug lord, tall and gaunt, with a deeply creased face and a missing front tooth, looked over at Pascual, who was standing by the door. "Isn't it *huachinango a la veracruzana* today?"

"*Si, don* Gustavo."

"Red snapper," Jiménez translated for Harley in surprisingly good English.

"They call it '*parguito*' in Venezuela," Harley continued in Spanish, using his hideous *gringo* accent.

Jiménez nodded. "In Colombia too." Then he smiled for the first time, turning those long creases in his face sideways. "Important detail, no, *reportero*? Reputed drug lord admits he has eaten fish with Colombians."

Fifteen minutes into the interview, and that was the first mention of drugs.

When Harley arrived at the jail, flushed from his ten-mile bike ride, and nervous, a guard greeted him by name and led him past the security apparatus, up three flights of stairs, and down a long gray corridor. He knocked on a wooden door, and

Pascual opened it. Harley was about to say that this was the wrong room, that his interview was with Gustavo Jiménez, but Pascual was smiling with his wounded mouth and saying, "*Pásale, pásale.*"

Harley walked in. The door closed behind him.

It was a big, high-ceiling room with a couple of barred windows high up. The floor was concrete, except for a faded blue rug in the middle. The only furnishings were a large rectangular table made of boards, a couple of folding chairs, a boombox in the corner with a pile of CDs, and a cellular phone lying on top of them. There was a battered green couch by the wall.

When Harley first saw him, Gustavo Jiménez was lying on the couch, hands under his head, looking at the ceiling. "*Pásale, Tomás Harley, famoso reportero del prestigioso* El Paso Tribune," he said in the chanting voice of a Mexican priest. Then he swung around slowly and sat up. Harley looked at him for the first time. He was surprised to see the wrinkles and the missing tooth, and the sparse hair. He couldn't tell which eye was glass. Jiménez wore his blue jeans too high, and when he stood up to shake hands, his tight belt dug into a stomach that was thin and flabby at the same time. He didn't look like a man with a harem.

The two men sat on folding chairs and exchanged small talk. Jiménez apologized for the furnishings. He didn't know how long he'd be staying, he said, implying that with more time, he'd dress up the room in style. He said he'd been staying with friends down near Copper Canyon, and that this arrest was inconvenient and embarrassing, but that such things happened during certain political "seasons." He mentioned that many foolish things had been written and said about him and that he hoped, with this interview, to "set the record straight."

Harley sat and listened, his knapsack on his lap. He hoped that Jiménez, at some point, would simply spill the story to him. In the meantime, it seemed improper to take out the notebook and tape recorder and start asking tough questions. They were still getting acquainted.

Following Jiménez's quip about the *huachinango*, Harley asked about Pascual. "Isn't that man over there," he said, "the one charged with the murder of Eddie Stevenson yesterday?"

Jiménez leaned forward and nodded gravely. "Yes, he is. That was a tragedy, and you and your colleagues at the *Tribune* have my most sincere sympathy." He pointed to Harley's knapsack. "Don't you want to write this down? Or do you have one of those phenomenal memories that can play back every conversation in exact detail?"

Harley dug into his knapsack and pulled out his notebook. Then he ran his hand around the bottom of the bag, looking for a pen.

"Pascual," Jiménez barked. "*Una pluma para el señor Harley.*"

Pascual hurried over to him with a Bic in hand. Harley looked up at him, trying to connect his eyes to the ones that peered through the ski mask at Claudio's window. As Pascual stood by Jiménez, waiting for another order, Harley heard him sniffing. This led him to wonder if Pascual was doing coke. Of course, the sniffling might have something to do with that ugly mouth wound he had.

He considered asking Pascual, point blank, if he was the one who took a shot at him. Maybe tell him he hit the statue of the rain god instead, right in the eye. Break the ice. Maybe even talk about *tuertos*. But Pascual walked back to the door, sniffing, and Harley left the question unasked. Better not to focus the interview on Pascual. Jiménez was the link to Crispín.

"Do you mind if I use this?" he asked the drug lord, pulling out his tiny tape recorder.

"How about if we do it the old-fashioned way: I talk, you write," Jiménez said, looking a little uneasy. His right eye seemed to spin askew for a second.

"Okay."

Harley looked over at Pascual, who was sitting in one of the chairs, reading a book.

"Pascual," Jiménez said, "put on a CD. That one by Agustin Lara. Then take a walk."

"So it seems you're not locked in here?" Harley said.

Jiménez stared at him, his eyes in concert again, and shrugged. "I'm not living in misery."

The violins started up and Agustin Lara sang about some long-ago nights in Acapulco with "*María Bonita, María del alma...*"

Pascual departed with his book, carefully shutting the door. And Harley was alone with Gustavo Jiménez. "According to my sources," he said, "you are an important primary investor in Grupo Espejo. Is that true?"

Jiménez stared straight ahead for several seconds and then nodded slowly. "Without me," he said, "Grupo Espejo wouldn't exist."

"How much money do you have in it?"

"How much did I put into it? How much do I have now? Or how much do I get out of it? You have to ask more specific questions."

"How much did you put into it?"

"Not much. About thirty million dollars, not including commissions, licenses, filing fees. Money the *gringo* bankers collect."

"You invested this money directly?"

"Through Onofre Crispín. My partner."

"So you put up $30 million, and Crispín put up the rest?"

"Don't be absurd," Jiménez said, chuckling. "Crispín is a pauper. I put up $30 million and some associates of mine put up the rest. Crispín? He might have contributed enough to pay for the postage stamps. Maybe the fax paper."

"Your associates?"

"Business associates. Men of means," Jiménez said.

"The ones who eat '*parguito*'?"

Jiménez leaned back and smiled again, showing the gap in his teeth. "Very cleverly worded, your question, *señor* Harley."

Harley waited for the answer.

"Let's assume I say yes, my associates are men who enjoy a good *parguito* for their midday meal, and they use that word to describe it. Would you write simply that the associates of Gustavo Jiménez hail from '*parguito*-eating' lands? Or would you draw a line straight to the Medellin and Cali cartels?"

"You tell me," Harley said, beginning to enjoy himself.

"I am going to say, quite simply, that my associates are a very cosmopolitan group of investors. Some of them, it's true, call it '*parguito*,' some call it '*pargón*.' Some of them probably call it '*huachinango*,' others speak with accents like yours, and call it 'red snapper.'"

Harley fought back an urge to show off his good Spanish for Jiménez. "So the total investment of your group," he asked with the same American accent, "is $100 million?"

"Half of that," Jiménez said dismissively. "Some *gringos* put up the rest."

"Which *gringos*?"

"God knows."

"And how did you make your money? How did you get to be so rich?"

"Construction," Jiménez said. "Commerce. Some well-placed investments. I have a good sense for the markets." He touched his long, angular nose. "In fact, I transferred much of my Espejo position to a business associate just last week."

The drug lord said the stock was just climbing too high, on NAFTA speculation. "I invest on solid business principles," he said. "I don't gamble on politics. It's politics, after all, that has me living in here for the time being."

"So how do you go about transferring ownership of such an investment?" Harley asked. "Do you just call a broker?"

"In a manner of speaking."

"Does he know that you have inside information?"

"Would the front page of your newspaper be inside information?"

Jiménez stood and pulled up his jeans. Harley feared for a second that he was calling the interview to a close. But the man simply retreated to the couch and lay down. "You have much to learn, *Tomás* Harley," he said, looking up at the ceiling. "There is no such thing in Mexico as inside information. There is simply good information. Everything else is the chatter of *pendejos*, if you'll excuse my expression."

Harley changed his tack. "Do you know who killed the radio journalist two months ago?"

"Not an idea in the world. Probably his lover."

"And do you know who killed Ed Stevenson?"

Jiménez pursed his lips and paused for a few seconds. "As far as I know," he said, "it was this fellow who answers my telephone."

◊

Espejo shares climbed to $52 by lunchtime. Onofre Crispín made some calls and learned that heavy buying in Guadalajara was driving up the price. Crispín ordered a lunch of smoked salmon quesadillas and guava juice and sat down in his dining room to read the Mexico City papers. Only the liberal *La Jornada* put the Stevenson murder on page one. And even there, it was only a small headline, advertising the story inside. The story itself was harmless. It tied Stevenson to the drug business and didn't even mention *maquiladoras*, much less Onofre Crispín.

Relieved, Crispín called up Chief Muller to ask about the murder investigation. "Did you find any fingerprints on the pistol?" he asked.

"Heh heh," the chief answered. "Not yet, Onofre. You're

not on your cellular, are you?"

"I never call you on the cellular."

"Good, good. That's the idea... I thought you were going to be incommunicado for a couple of days."

"What's that?"

"You said you were going to be out of touch for a while."

"That must have been somebody else," Crispín snapped. "What other evidence do you have in the investigation?"

"None to speak of, except for the confession. You're just lucky that this Garza stumbled in there at the right time, followed by the entire media," the chief added. "Otherwise there would be loads of evidence."

"What do you mean that I'm lucky?"

"That those forces under your control, you know, the ones that were there earlier... I don't have to go into this."

"What forces under my control? What the devil are you talking about!"

"You know. What you told me earlier. But listen, we don't have to go into this now. Forgive me for bringing it up." The chief changed the subject. "It sounds as though your cold is much better."

"My cold?" Crispín puzzled over that as the servant brought in a steaming plate of quesadillas arranged neatly around a puddle of guacamole with tortilla chips sticking out of it.

"Never mind," the chief said. "Often one is hoarse in the morning, and then it goes away by midday."

"But I didn't talk to you this morning."

"Good, Onofre. That's the right approach. Very good."

"But we didn't talk!"

"I agree entirely. It's done for. It never happened."

"I SHIT ON THE MOTHER, MULLER! Did you talk to someone claiming to be me this morning?"

"That's what it must have been," Muller said, playing along. "Someone claiming to be you."

"And what did he tell you?"

"We don't need to..."

"I SHIT ON THE HOST, MULLER. SPEAK!"

Muller began to sense that Crispín wasn't kidding. "You just... He claimed a bit of responsibility for the murder..."

"*Hijo de la chingada!*"

"...and you said you would be incommunicado for a while..."

"*JESUCRISTO!*"

"...and, let's see. And I gave you—I mean *him*—Gustavo Jiménez's cell phone."

Onofre Crispín lifted his lunch plate with his right hand and heaved it against the dining room wall. Its fragments tinkled to the ground as green dots of guacamole rained down on the worm-eaten convent table.

Chapter
FIFTY-SIX

Gustavo Jiménez wasn't on coke, that much was certain. For the last half-hour, he'd been lying on the couch, answering questions slowly, much of the time with his eyes closed. Harley had many more questions, but now worried that his source might fall asleep on him. He also had trouble keeping Jiménez on the subject of drugs and Grupo Espejo.

At one point, Jiménez turned toward Harley, opened both eyes and said, "Would you mind if I asked you a rude question?"

"Shoot," Harley said, relieved to see him stirring.

"You live in a city where half the population is Mexican, no?"

"*Mexicano Americano*," Harley said.

"Whatever. People from this culture. You'd think your newspaper could find reporters who--again, no offense--speak prettier Spanish than you."

"Look at it the other way," Harley said. "If a reporter wants to cover City Hall, are you going to tell him that he has to cover the border because his parents came from here?"

Jiménez shrugged. "Maybe not.... But perhaps you could get one of those *colegas* to help you with your pronunciation. You seem to know a lot of words, but it's almost like you're trying to sound bad."

Harley felt a jolt of panic. He looked at Jiménez, his sideways face on the couch. The drug lord had both eyes open and was looking at Harley with a half-smile, as if he understood everything.

Harley closed his notebook and eyed the door. But Jiménez promptly dropped his line of uncomfortable questions. Rolling onto his back, he gazed at the ceiling with his one working eye and proceeded to sketch out an apocalyptic future for Mexico.

He predicted civil war and political killings. He said that even as Mexican trade negotiators were nailing down the free trade accord, a rebel army was growing in the south. Harley found it hard to believe. "We have never had a political transition in Mexico without war and assassinations," Jiménez said, his eyes closed, his words barely a whisper. "This marriage with the United States will breed more of the same." Straining to hear him, it occurred to Harley that Jiménez might be on heroin.

The door banged open and Pascual Garza entered carrying a tray with plates of red snapper, each fish flanked by rice and quartered limes. In his other hand, he held a bottle of chilled white wine, the water beading on the glass.

That seemed to be Harley's cue. Every additional second he stuck around carried risk. "Thank you very much for the interview," he said, standing up. He shoved his reporter's notebook into his back pocket and looked for his knapsack.

Gustavo Jiménez rose from the sofa, but didn't bother shaking hands with him. Instead, he walked to the table, squeezed a bit of lime on one of the fish, and took a pinch with his fingers. "This isn't a la veracruzana," he said, tasting it. "This is al ajillo."

"*Adiós!*" Harley said, raising his voice over the music, and waving. No one seemed to be paying attention to him.

The phone rang and Pascual picked it up.

Harley wanted to leave, but he felt funny slipping out without saying goodbye to Jiménez.

Pascual handed the phone to the drug lord, who said, "*Buenoooo.*"

Harley stood by the door, feeling gangly and out of place. He heard a familiar voice shouting from the receiver. Jiménez was holding the cell phone away from his ear. He turned, and their eyes connected for one terrifying instant.

Harley reached for the doorknob and twisted. The door opened and he slipped out. He hurried down the concrete corridor, expecting any second to hear shouting voices, or to see Pascual Garza chasing him. But he heard only the echo of his own footsteps, nearly running. He found the stairwell and began to hop down the steps three at a time.

Harley had climbed down two of the floors when an alarm sounded. It was a high-pitched bell, clanging. He stopped. He opened the door from the stairwell and peeked out to the second floor. It was the same as the fourth, a neon-lit corridor, echoing with the ringing alarm. Just a few feet from the stairwell he saw an open door. It was a closet with mops, brooms and buckets, and a tower of toilet paper.

He stepped in. After a few seconds, the alarm stopped. But it kept ringing in his head. He could hear footsteps on the floor above, and more in the stairwell. He pictured Pascual chasing him, catching him and banging his head against the wall, dragging him back to the newly energized Gustavo Jiménez... But even in a Mexican jail, they wouldn't let accused murderers track down journalists, would they?

Harley recalled his time locked up in the Juárez police station. Back then, he feared he might be facing years in custody. Now, from the janitor's closet, the future looked shorter and more violent.

Maybe he could just walk out. They had no reason to arrest

him, unless the Mexicans enforced tough laws on phone pranks.

After a few minutes, he ventured out of the closet and down the final flight of steps. Everything seemed back to normal. He walked to the glass booth and returned his plastic badge that said "*visita*." He filled in the hour of his departure: 2:13 p.m. The guard smiled at him.

"What was that ringing?" he asked.

"Probably someone fooling with the fire alarm," the guard said. "It happens all the time."

Harley walked outside into the sunlight, feeling relieved. But his stomach tightened when he saw four prison guards leaning against the two cars in the visitors' section of the parking lot. He slipped in the other direction, past some bushes, to the prison sign, where his bike was locked. He unhitched it and wound the chain around the seat. He reached behind himself to adjust the knapsack, but it wasn't there. He'd left it behind. And the helmet too. He felt the notebook in his pocket. That was enough.

He started pedaling. If he rode along the sidewalk back to the driveway, the way he came, he'd pass right in front of those prison guards. The only other choice was to brave it across 200 yards of prickly, tire-popping desert to the airport highway.

He rode by the guards, giving them a wave.

"Hey!" one of them yelled. The others made some noise, but none gave chase. Looking in his rearview mirror, he saw two of them hurrying back into *El CeReSo*. The other two stood still and watched.

Now the question was whether to ride all the way home or to lock his bike somewhere and take an airport cab. He pedaled across the highway and glanced in his rearview mirror. The two guards were still looking at him. He turned left and pedaled past the airport, back toward El Paso.

He shifted into high gear, stood up on the bike and pushed

hard, passing the congested car traffic. He raced past junkyards and the dog track. Ahead he saw the Franklin Mountains. If he could get to that side of the river, he'd be safe.

Harley figured that Jiménez or Crispín had sent someone to find him. Or maybe they'd pick him up at the bridge. The stakes were too high to ignore. He calculated the numbers as he rode. If they put in $50 million, it was worth $250 million now, or a little more. They could lose a quarter of a billion dollars if they let him return to El Paso and write his story.

Harley was making his way into the city, his usual stomping ground. He passed the *Xtasia* discotheque and a row of restaurants, all of them advertising their specials in dollars. One of them sold pitchers of margaritas for $5—a deal to keep in mind, he thought, if it was ever safe to return to Juárez.

Another two miles, he figured, and he'd be at the border. He could swing left, into the *centro*, to a downtown bridge. There he'd be close enough to lock his bike and walk across, blending in with the foot traffic. But the downtown was also full of cops. He veered right, toward the Free Bridge, where most of the industrial traffic crossed.

He looked in the mirror and saw a cement truck and a Jeep. No cops. He kept riding along a rare tree-lined avenue, past a statue of Abraham Lincoln. He checked the mirror again. The Jeep was right behind him. Still no cops. Then he stole another look at the Jeep and caught his breath when he saw a familiar wide face with a prominent nose.

Olmos saw him, and he gestured for him to pull over. Harley kept pedaling flat out. Olmos revved up and pulled the Jeep even with him. He lowered one of the electric windows and yelled in Spanish. "Pull over! I just want to talk with you."

Harley pretended not to hear. Five more blocks and he'd be at the bridge, where he knew the Jeep would get hung up in a twenty-minute line. Olmos pulled the Jeep closer to him and started to angle him off the road. Harley banked right and turned, his tires skidding on gravel. This put him on a residential street, with little houses and garages and wrought-iron fences. Behind him, he heard Olmos hit the brakes.

Harley turned left onto a smaller street. He didn't know where he was, but El Paso's mountains loomed to his left. He figured he could get to the bridge by bobbing and weaving on these side streets. He came to a dead end, jogged right and then left again. He hit another dead end and took another left. He had to be about three blocks from the border now. He was pedaling toward a big, noisy avenue with lots of trucks. Beyond it, just a couple hundred yards ahead, he saw El Paso's Border Highway. Now he knew where he was. This was Juárez's own border highway, leading to the *maquiladoras*.

Harley simply had to make his way left for 150 yards, and he'd be on the bridge. But to get there he had to cross four lanes of truck traffic. He looked left and right again and again, waiting for a hole in the traffic. When the stoplight at the intersection turned red, the line of trucks heading toward the bridge would back up, and he might be able to weave his bike between them—if he could get past the line of eastbound traffic. He looked in his rearview mirror. No sign of Olmos. The light turned red and the traffic halted in the El Paso-bound lanes. Gazing to his left, he waited for four eastbound trucks to pass.

He didn't see when a Jeep, traveling against traffic on the left shoulder of the street, cut him off from the right, brushing against his front tire and spilling him to the ground.

By the time he regained his footing, Oscar Olmos had a firm grip on the handlebars. "I have to talk to you, *señor*," he said, sounding more like a servant than a henchman.

The bodyguard yanked the bike back onto the residential street. Harley followed. Olmos wore a blue Dallas Cowboys polo shirt that showed off his biceps. He guided the bike gingerly and had trouble keeping it in a straight line. Finally he picked it up and carried it. Turning around, he flashed a smile. "You were going forty-five kilometers per hour on

Avenida de la Raza, señor. On a level grade."

Trying to establish some rapport, Harley thought.

Olmos put down the bike and leaned it carefully against a thick mesquite tree. Then, like a medieval courier, he delivered a memorized message. "*Señor,*" he said, "my boss sends his greetings and he compliments you on your command of the Spanish language. He says you are an excellent journalist and he would like to meet you, at an hour of your convenience, to see if there are efforts at which the two of you can collaborate. He realizes that you are extremely busy today. He sent me to offer you preliminary terms."

Olmos paused, waiting for him to respond.

"Preliminary terms?" Harley asked.

Olmos reached into his back pocket and pulled out a thick, folded envelope. Harley accepted it before realizing what it contained. "This is a down payment," Olmos said. "As I said, *don* Onofre Crispín respects you greatly, and would like to work closely with you on a series of articles detailing the exact nature of relations between our two countries. Such a series, he says, would benefit both countries, fomenting mutual understanding at a crucial time in our history."

Harley held the envelope at arm's length.

"I have a telephone in the car," Olmos said. "And if you would like, *don* Onofre can confirm his offer to you. But he says that a face-to-face meeting is preferable, especially considering"—he coughed politely—"your recent adventures on the telephone."

"I cannot accept money from him," Harley said, still speaking in the *gringo* accent he'd used with Jiménez.

Olmos ignored him. "The down payment is fifteen thousand dollars. It is not much, *don* Onofre says, only a sign of good faith. The balance, reaching a total of one million dollars, will be paid in installments as you, working closely with *don* Onofre, successfully complete your journalistic series."

"One million dollars?" Harley was stunned. "I can't accept that."

"The balance is nine hundred eighty-five thousand dollars."

"What happens if I say no?"

Olmos stared at him blankly for a moment. "I have been instructed to make sure you say yes."

Harley dropped the envelope. It thudded on the cracked sidewalk. "No," he said.

Olmos reached down and picked it up. He dropped his ceremonial tone and spoke like a boxer. "This is your ticket out of Mexico," he said, calling him by the informal "*tu*."

"And if I don't take it?"

"You go with me back to *casa* Crispín."

"And if I take it?"

"You ride your little toy back to *Gringolandia*."

Harley took the envelope and jammed it into his pocket. Without saying another word, he mounted his bike and pedaled toward the bridge.

Chapter
FIFTY-SEVEN

Mexican Police on the phone, talking Spanish. It had to be something about Harley, Canfield thought as he handed the phone to Rudi Torres. But it turned out that Juárez Police had recovered two *Tribune* cars, Stevenson's old Dodge and Klinger's Grand-Am. Canfield walked over to Klinger's cubicle to deliver the good news.

He was stunned to see his favorite reporter with a crew cut, exposing ears that stuck straight out and a scrawny neck. "What the hell did you do to yourself?" he asked.

"You've been telling me to get a haircut for months," Klinger said.

"Yeah, but I was just getting used to it."

"I made a bet with myself," the reporter said. "By the time my hair grows out, I'll be..." He caught himself and shut up.

"Working at the *Dallas Morning News*," Canfield finished the sentence for him. "Well, you better let it grow out a little before you start your interviewing. You look like a goddamn vulture now... Oh, and by the way, Klinger, they got your car for you in Juárez. You can go pick it up now, if you want."

Klinger let loose a war whoop that echoed through the newsroom.

"You can thank Stevenson for that," Canfield told him after he quieted down. "He doesn't get himself killed, you don't get your car back. You going to the funeral Friday?"

"I thought we all had to."

"I just wanted to make sure you won't be taking a personal day, going to Dallas or someplace."

Harley's phone rang, and Canfield picked it up. A woman with a strong East-coast accent asked for Harley. "You wouldn't be Diana Clements, would you?" the city editor asked, looking at Harley's terminal. "He's already got his computer covered with messages from you... That's right. Let's assume he'll call you if he ever comes to work."

Canfield hung up and made his way back to his terminal. The Stevenson story was turning out to be a problem for him. Ken Perry, now acting like a charter member of the Chamber of Commerce, was blocking any serious coverage of drugs or official corruption in Mexico. He insisted that he didn't want to undermine the paper's previous coverage of Jiménez. "That stuff could get us a Pulitzer," he said. "But we have to end it with the jailing of the drug lord. The judges love results."

Meanwhile, the *Journal* was running hard with the story. Rick Jarvis had located a cab driver in Juárez who detailed the photographer's last night of bar crawling. Jarvis named some of the strip clubs they visited, and went so far as to describe a blond who sat on Stevenson's lap while he fondled her. Canfield, his curiosity piqued, wondered how much Juárez strippers charged for lap dances.

It irked Canfield that *Tribune* staffers seemed to have talked to Jarvis for his story. He quoted "colleagues" who recalled a smelly water pipe Stevenson kept in his apartment. They said he was "burned out" at work. They told Jarvis about his Mexican girlfriend, "Stella," and hinted that she lined him up with the drug dealer who killed him.

Canfield called up the stock market ticker on his terminal and punched in ESPO. Grupo Espejo rose to $53 and then dropped $4 at the end of the day. He kicked himself for not selling at lunchtime, when it was at 52 3/8. Then again, if Clinton twisted enough arms to get NAFTA through, the stock might shoot up to $70.

Canfield jumped when he heard Ken Perry's voice by his ear. "The stock's a real firecracker, isn't it?" the editor said, looking over Canfield's shoulder.

"I'm thinking about a follow-up story," Canfield said, trying to explain the numbers on his screen.

"Since when do you assign business stories?"

"This is more than a straight business story. It's tied into NAFTA..."

Perry smiled and patted him on the shoulder. "Come on into the office. We have to do the front-page meeting."

Just as the two of them walked into the corner office, Harley stepped out of the elevator with his bike. He was a dusty mess. His armpits had salt rings around them and his short hair, lacquered with dried sweat, stood straight up. He looked spooked.

"Lemme guess," the city editor said as Harley entered the newsroom. "You went dirt biking and saw a ghost."

"I talked to Jiménez," Harley blurted. "He confirmed that Espejo's backed by drug money. And I think Crispín had something to do with Stevenson's murder."

"Whoa, whoa, hold on a minute there, Harley," Canfield said. "Come into the office here, and we'll take it a little slower."

Harley sat on the couch next to Canfield, facing Perry at his desk, and he ran through the whole story. He told them how he'd been cultivating Crispín, how he had played racquetball with him and shared Mexican delicacies. The editors were impressed.

Harley told them about Rubén and his role as a go-between, and how he suspected that Crispín ordered a hitman to eliminate Pascual, and that the killer shot Stevenson by mistake. "We don't have enough to run with that one yet. That could take a while." Finally, without mentioning the phony calls to Chief Muller and Jiménez, he reviewed the interview with the drug lord, telling the editors how many of the points were backed up by other sources.

He added, as an afterthought, that Stevenson's accused killer was working as a jailhouse butler for Jiménez.

At the end, Perry shook his head, dumbfounded. "I'm going to be frank," he said. "I didn't know you had it in you."

"Neither did he, did you Harley?" said the city editor.

Harley smiled.

"Still, I think we should wait a day," Canfield went on. "If we're going to run this story, we want to do it right. First of all, we don't have any art, because Harley here insisted on going..."

Harley interrupted. "There's one more thing I forgot to mention." He stood up, reached into his pocket, and pulled out the thick envelope. He pushed one finger into the top of it and ripped it open. Then he dumped the pile of hundred-dollar bills on Perry's immaculate desk. "This is $15,000," he said. "At least, that's what I've been told." He explained how Olmos cut him off with the Jeep and coerced him into accepting it as a down payment on a $1 million bribe. "I had to accept this money to get back home in one piece."

Perry let loose a low whistle as Canfield rocked back on the couch, looking stunned.

"My problem," Harley said, "is that if we don't run this story right away, Crispín's going to think he has a deal."

"He's not going to think anything of the kind," Perry said, slapping his palm down on the desk and sending a couple of the bills fluttering to the floor, "because we're running the goddamn story as big as we've ever run any story since I've been at this paper." He glowered at Canfield. "And I can't believe that you would even consider holding back this story. It leads me to wonder what sort of interests you have outside this newsroom."

"We all have interests outside the newsroom," Canfield responded quietly.

"Well, Harley here just turned down a million dollars," Perry said. "I think we could learn something from his example."

"Not to quibble," Canfield said, "but Harley turned down the *promise* of a million dollars, which isn't exactly the same thing."

"You're dealing with harder assets, aren't you?" Perry asked.

"Let's not dwell on it," Canfield answered, looking depressed.

The three of them were quiet for a moment, staring at the pile of money on the desk. "Hey," Harley piped up. "How about we put down the $15,000 as Onofre Crispín's contribution to the Ed Stevenson Drug Prevention fund?"

"That's my editorial," Perry said, happy to be calling the shots.

◊

Harley was still tinkering with his lead when his phone rang. Diana, already home from work, was anxious to know if he had the story.

"Yeah, I got it," he said, rearranging his lead as they talked. "It got pretty hairy over there."

"But you're running with the story on Espejo?"

"Uh huh." He pushed down one failed lead with the cursor and started another.

"So Espejo's backed by drug money?" She sounded very excited.

"I'm not supposed to talk about it. But, yeah. That's part of it. There's the whole business about the murder, too. But that's tomorrow's story. I have to find Rubén and some other people for that..."

Diana pressed for more on his interview with Jiménez.

"He seemed like he was on heroin or something," Harley said. "I thought he was falling asleep on me." Maybe, he thought, he'd lead with the drug lord lying on his couch, waiting for his *huachinango*...

"Let's celebrate," Diana said.

"Okay." Harley typed: *"Juárez drug lord Gustavo Jiménez gives new meaning to the word 'cell phone.'"* No. Way too glib.

"You're busy, aren't you?" Diana asked.

"Wait a minute." His other line was ringing. He put Diana on hold and answered. It was Claudio.

Harley told him he had to find Rubén.

"That's what I'm calling about," Claudio said. "I got a message from him, saying he was leaving to join some kind of revolution in Chiapas."

"Chiapas?"

"And Estela's going with him."

"Funny," Harley said. "Gustavo Jiménez was just talking about the same thing."

He hung up just as the freshly shorn Klinger arrived in the newsroom, looking alarmed.

"What's the matter?" Canfield asked. "You didn't get your car back?"

"I got it back," Klinger said, raking his fingers over his scalp. "There's this shag rug glued to the dashboard, and a tiny little steering wheel, about six inches wide. The muffler's gone. Gone! And it's got these big new back tires. I feel like I'm driving a sled."

"It doesn't have a pair of big furry dice hanging from the mirror, does it?" Harley asked.

"That's the only thing that's missing."

◊

Diana poured Harley another glass of *Veuve Cliquot* and lay back on the couch. "Maybe if we had a fire burning," she said, "or a bear rug on the floor..."

Harley sipped the champagne, deep in thought. "When I called Crispín for a response," he said, "he acted...betrayed, and hurt. Made me feel like a real jerk."

"Did he ask you about the fifteen thousand?" Diana asked.

"He pretended he never offered me anything," Harley said. "The guy's not dumb. He said his driver, Olmos, was just supposed to offer me work as some sort of writer. Said the job paid well."

"So he expected you to quit the paper and work as a writer for him?"

"Oh, no. I wouldn't be worth anything to him if I quit my job at the paper."

"Oh...I see." Diana got up and put on music. Ella Fitzgerald singing "*Bewitched, Bothered and Bewildered.*"

She sat down beside Harley and tousled his hair. "What's wrong?" she asked, stroking a hand down the side of his face. "You don't feel like celebrating?"

"Claudio was telling me," he said, "that I should apologize for using those voices...I sort of apologized to Crispín. I said I was sorry about the misunderstanding. But it was closer to a lie than a misunderstanding. Know what I mean?"

"I think you're a little hard on yourself." Diana held his face in her hands. "Why don't you just relax, and celebrate?"

"Celebrate what? I'm still in the middle of this thing. There's the whole murder story that I'm not even close to nailing down yet. For all I know, Jiménez was feeding me some sort of a line. And then I have no idea how Crispín and Jiménez are going to respond to this story I've written. I might have to move back into that hotel."

"Or here." She leaned over and kissed him between the eyes.

He shrugged. "They might lose hundreds of millions of dollars tomorrow. What do you think the stock will do when the story comes out?"

Diana smiled. "We're talking free fall."

"Well. That makes my stomach crawl... Did you hear that?"

"What?"

"My stomach just went 'boiiiing.'"

"Listen," she said, "there's something I should probably tell you."

He listened.

"I told you how when Raymond left, I felt sort of trapped here, because I didn't have enough money to leave?"

"Uh huh."

"Well, that's been sort of...gnawing at me. Not that I still want to leave. But, you know, feeling sort of poor."

"I sometimes feel the same way," he said.

"And you weren't tempted to take that million dollars?"

"Not for a minute. I mean, the whole value of money is that it makes you free. But you're not free if you sell yourself to somebody like that. Plus," he added, "I doubt I would have seen any money. He just wanted to kill the story."

Diana nodded. "Anyway, I was feeling kind of poor, and I took a position in Espejo, because I heard these rumors that all this money from Guadalajara was into it, and that it was going to go way up. I bought in at $10."

"And did you sell today?"

"Uh huh. At fifty-three."

"So you made five hundred thirty percent."

"More or less. Then I ran around borrowing money. I even borrowed some from Raymond. I hadn't talked to him in months. I gave him ten percent for a two-week loan."

Harley nodded slowly, not liking what he was hearing.

"With all that, I bought options on Espejo stock, so that I'll make money with each dollar as it falls."

"Did you hear it this time?" Harley asked, looking ill.

"What?"

"My stomach just did it again."

"This all makes you nervous, doesn't it?" Diana asked, opening her brown eyes wide.

"I don't know if 'nervous' is the right word," Harley said. "If you don't mind my asking, how much money do you stand to make from all this?"

"I could clear three-quarters of a million."

"Jesus." He sipped champagne and swished it around in his mouth. "And a good chunk of that came from information you got through me, right?"

She nodded.

He took in a deep breath and exhaled. "I don't think you can take it."

"Well, I do," she said softly.

"I mean, I don't think you *should* take it. Ethically speaking."

She arched her eyebrows, signaling that she understood his qualms, but dismissed them.

Harley swirled a gulp of champagne in his mouth, thinking. He swallowed, took in a deep breath, and exhaled. "Here's what you could do. How about if you take all the profits you make from my information, and donate them to the Eddie Stevenson fund?"

Diana kissed him on the forehead and then pulled back to look in his eyes.

"You're kidding," she said. "Right?"

The End

About
ATMOSPHERE PRESS

Atmosphere Press is an independent, full-service publisher for excellent books in all genres and for all audiences. Learn more about what we do at atmospherepress.com.

We encourage you to check out some of Atmosphere's latest releases, which are available at Amazon.com and via order from your local bookstore:

Twisted Silver Spoons, a novel by Karen M. Wicks

Queen of Crows, a novel by S.L. Wilton

The Summer Festival is Murder, a novel by Jill M. Lyon

The Past We Step Into, stories by Richard Scharine

Swimming with the Angels, a novel by Colin Kersey

Island of Dead Gods, a novel by Verena Mahlow

Twins Daze, a novel by Jerry Petersen

Abaddon Illusion, a novel by Lindsey Bakken

Blackland: A Utopian Novel, by Richard A. Jones

The Jesus Nut, a novel by John Prather

The Embers of Tradition, a novel by Chukwudum Okeke

Saints and Martyrs: A Novel, by Aaron Roe

When I Am Ashes, a novel by Amber Rose

The Recoleta Stories, by Bryon Esmond Butler

About
THE AUTHOR

Stephen Baker has worked as a journalist and writer in many cities, including Paris, Mexico City, Caracas, Quito, Madrid, New York, and El Paso. His non-fiction books, including *The Numerati* and *Final Jeopardy: Man vs. Machine and the Quest to Know Everything*, explore the effects of technology on society.

His first novel, *The Boost* (Tor Books, 2014) is a near-future tale that, like *Donkey Show*, takes place along the U.S.-Mexico border. Kirkus Reviews called the book "a true delight of a techno-thriller that has deep, dark roots in the present." Before moving to the New York area, Baker was Paris-based European technology correspondent for *BusinessWeek*, where he headed up the magazine's coverage of wireless technology and the mobile Internet.

He is a graduate of Columbia University's Graduate School of Journalism and earned his B.A. at the University of Wisconsin. He lives with his wife in Montclair, NJ. They have three sons.

Made in the USA
Las Vegas, NV
07 December 2023

82284951R00204